RELUCTANT CONCUBINE

DANA MARTON

www.danamarton.com

ISBN-13: 9781940627106

Second, Revised and Updated Edition
This book was originally published in 2012 as THE THIRD SCROLL

This book is dedicated to Jenel Looney, and my new favorite fantasy author, Grace Draven.

With many thanks to all who provided encouragement and/or their special skills along the way: Diane Flindt, Susan Mallery, Adel Kiss, Linda Ingmanson, Toni Lee, Pat Cleveland, Anita Staley, my friends at SHU who gave me early feedback, and all my fabulous friends in the Dana Marton Book Club on Facebook. I appreciate you more than words can say.

To escape punishment, Tera, a maiden healer sold to barbarians must hide the truth: she has not yet come into her healing powers. Born into a much gentler world, she struggles to survive in a land of savage warlords and their cruel concubines. When ancient prophecies begin to come to pass, can the healer-slave save the realm and awaken the High Lord's heart?

"It's impressively easy to become immersed in Marton's fantasy world. Readers will find it impossible not to care what happens next..." Kirkus Review

CHAPTER ONE

(Twelve Blue Crystals)

"One eagle from the north. An omen for change," Koro said next to me in the tree top.

He hung on to the nearest branch with both hands, his sateen tunic —befitting the only son of a wealthy trader—soiled from the climb. The wind ruffled his golden hair, pushing it into his eyes, the exact mellow brown shade as the tree bark.

The endless canopy of the forest stretched in front of us, the sea— with a narrow strip of rocky beach where my father would be even now fishing—at our back. The knar eagle, rarely seen this far south, circled above.

My people, the Shahala, did not believe in omens, but Koro's father had brought Koro's mother from a distant land.

I sized up the eagle. "Change in what?"

I had passed into womanhood from childhood, but my healing powers had not arrived. I was desperate for change in *that*.

Since my mother had died, people no longer came from far away for healing. Few of the sick made the trek to our rocky beach, even from the nearby village.

We did not have rice to eat with the fish my father, Jarim, might catch. We have not had rice for a long time. We did not always have fish, either. As I sat in the swaying branches on the top of the tallest numaba tree, I prayed that we would have *something* for that night.

A nervous smile danced on Koro's face. "I talked to my father about visiting yours tonight."

I looked away. "Jarim is in a bad mood. He had nothing but the most rotten luck with fishing lately. Maybe another day."

"Tomorrow my father will leave on another trading trip."

"When he comes back, then." I turned back to Koro whose smile had disappeared.

Guilt pricked me, but at the same time despair welled inside my chest at the thought of him coming with his father to present an offering. I would never have my healing powers if I married now.

"Tera," he began in that soft voice of his that had comforted me so many times after my mother's death. "You are—"

"When your father returns from his journey," I cut him off in a rush.

A trip to the farthest Shahala villages could take a full moon crossing or more. Maybe enough time to cajole the spirits into sending my powers to me. Powers like my mother's, not like my great-grandmother's, I added silently, to make sure that no spirit who might be listening to my thoughts would misunderstand.

Koro nodded, his disappointment already clearing, his eyes holding nothing but kindness and full understanding. Truly his face was welcome in my sight, his friendship valued from the bottom of my heart, but I could not give him what he longed for, not yet, not for a while.

My stomach growled.

My resolution wavered.

I could refuse Koro, but how long could I say no to the bride price? Even if I could endure the hunger, a good daughter would not starve her father.

Koro glanced up at the lone cloud above us, the eagle gone now.

"The caravan will hurry on this trip. The traders will want to be back before the rainy season begins."

For a second I saw the sky as it would be soon, a damp gray blanket thrown on the sun, keeping it captive. I swallowed the lump in my throat, blinking the image away.

Jarim and I could not survive another rainy season like the last. Toward the end, only the occasional strand of seaweed washed up on the rocks had kept us from starving. I could still feel the dark, gnawing pain in my belly every time I thought back.

Those hunger-filled days taught me one harsh lesson: if I could not heal, I was nothing.

The breeze from the sea strengthened and moved the branches around us. Our perch swayed. Koro held on tightly, his face turning pale.

I felt as safe as a babe rocked in loving arms. "Maybe you should go. Your mother might need help with the twins."

"Of course. And you would want to perform your ceremonies."

His tone held nothing but kindness, yet I caught a flash of disappointment in his eyes, along with a faint trace of hurt. I had managed to offend him, at once implying he could not handle the height, and that I did not want him with me.

He slipped to a lower branch with care. "I will visit again in a few days, if you do not mind."

"You are always welcome to stop by." But even to my own ears, the words sounded insincere. I did care for Koro, my childhood friend, but the great shadow of marriage had come between us lately, threatening the only thing I ever wanted.

I watched him lower himself with awkward movements then disappear in the dense foliage, swallowed by a profusion of round leaves, each as big as his head. Then I turned to the task that had brought me to my perilous perch. As a healer, or almost one, I spent a fair amount of time gathering ingredients for various potions.

I said my prayers to the spirits and bowed before them. I thanked the numaba tree for sheltering the moonflowers that lived in the crook of its branches. As befitting a great gift, I thanked the flowers at length for their dew.

Then I lifted one of the large flowers, the haunting color of the twin moons, and tipped it to the phial that hung on a cord around my neck, collecting the tiny drops that nestled inside the creamy soft petals. Once the dew ran down the inside of the glass, I moved on to the next flower and the next.

The ritual of the harvest filled me with peace, but as soon as I finished, frustration nudged its way back into my heart. I loved preparing potions, but the time had come when I wanted more.

The spirits know when the healer is ready, Tera, my mother had told me a hundred times, trying in vain to quell the sea of impatience inside me.

I was so very ready. Why could the spirits not see?

I pushed to my feet on a sudden impulse, balancing on the swaying branch, and stood over the endless forest that covered our hill. Mountain of No Top stretched on the horizon, the dwelling place of the spirits.

Beyond the mountain lay the desert then the Kadar cities. For all I cared, they could all fall into the sea. Of the large Island of Dahru, I cared only about the Shahala lands of my people and my family's beach.

Careful of my center of balance, I spread my arms and tipped my head to the sky, the wind whipping my hair around my face.

I shouted my heart's desire into that salty wind. "Great spirits, I am ready!"

A wild gust rushed my words across the undulating emerald carpet of the treetops, ruffling the leaves. Birds startled into flight, a flurry of flapping winds—red, blue, yellow, green—like dazzling jewels tossed into the air.

I waited for the spirits to respond, to touch me, but I felt nothing. I could hear only my mother's soft voice in my ears, words I had heard a million times. *You cannot rush the spirits.*

I hung my head. My mother would have been dismayed by my willfulness and impatience if she were with me. The spirits would not bless a healer who demanded blessing.

Disappointment clenched my teeth as I climbed down, watching where I put my feet at every step, even though I had made the climb a thousand times before. I stepped from branch to branch, then from one thick vine to the next as they wrapped themselves around the tree's smooth bark.

My clothes stuck to my skin. Up in the treetops, I had the wind, and at our home on the beach, a constant breeze blew from the sea. But in the woods, the hot air stood still.

I wished my mother were with me, showing me wonders like the flowers and birds that lived on top of the tall trees. Maybe she had many more secrets she had not had time to share, things I would never know, could never show my own daughter someday.

I did want a family. But not before my healing powers came to me. I could cure without those powers, help others with potions and poultices, powders and teas. But true healing, my mother had warned me—the knitting of bones and binding of spirits—would be lost to me forever if I rushed the sharing of my body.

I had to make sure Jarim understood this before anyone came to offer for me. I climbed faster. In my hurry, a broken branch snagged the worn linen of my thudi, leaving a slight tear in one of the puffy legs that gathered to narrow cuffs at the ankle. The thudi's waist was fastened with a twisted length of blue shawl, as tattered as the strip of linen bound tightly around my middle up to my armpits.

I kept moving. I never thought that the snag might be a warning from the good spirits resting on top of the numaba tree. If they had whispered *Little Sister, do not rush, watch out*, I did not hear.

On the beach side of the thick trunk now, to avoid another sharp branch, I had to turn away from the tree. Jarim stood in front of our home, four men around him. I brushed the hair out of my face and pushed a leafy branch aside for a better glimpse of their strange clothing.

Foreign traders, I thought. *If only we had something to trade.*

Jarim was gesturing as if trying to convince them of something very important, his arms going up and down in a choppy motion like the wings of the small chowa bird.

What if they came for healing?

I smoothed a hand down my breastbinding. I had left my dress and my veil at home, as always when going for a climb. I could not let strange men see me like this. Yet if one of them was in pain...

I had tried to help the few unfortunates who had not heard of my mother's death and made the arduous journey, but despite the healing potions, I rarely succeeded. Jarim said I did not have the power in my hands, but I knew the truth: I did not have the power in my heart.

Something inside me was missing, and the spirits sensed it.

Sometimes, secretly, out of sheer frustration, I blamed *him*. My mother had been a Tika Shahala, a healer from the highest order. Jarim, a foreigner, weakened her Shahala blood, robbing me of my heritage.

I slipped to the next branch, and it dipped under my weight. As the leafy end shifted, I could see the visitors' ship at last, bobbing in the water some distance from the beach. Black sails. Despite the heat, I shivered.

A slaver.

I had seen a slave ship once, years before. An illness on board had brought them to seek my mother. The fame of her powers drew all manner of people to us day and night, never giving her a moment of rest. She did not seem to mind. She did everything with a smile. She had the kindest face of any woman, always comforting, making the sick believe they were already well even before she began her cure.

I only saw her sad once in all her life, the day the slave traders came to shore. She helped them, like she would anyone else, taking a boat to the ship and staying on it well into the night. When she returned, she looked empty, as if she had left her heart behind.

The Shahala did not own slaves—my people found the practice distasteful. But the Kadar did, attracting unscrupulous traders from the nearby kingdoms that dotted the sea.

The Kadar had to be the most terrible people anywhere, I had thought at the time, but it was not until months later that I truly learned to despise them. Visitors brought news that the Kadar High Lord had fallen gravely ill. My mother, with her caring spirit, wished to go and heal him.

She sailed away and never returned. Two whole moon crossings passed before word reached us from a trade ship that she had died on

Kadar land. Whatever healing their High Lord had demanded of her had killed her.

I had sworn many times that somehow I would find out exactly how she had died. I swore to the spirits that someday, when I was a true healer and had enough crystals to afford the long journey, I would find her resting place and recite the Last Blessing over her grave.

After her death, many a night I had lain on my tear-soaked pillow, wishing to be a sorceress of old, so I could curse the Kadar. But as time passed, I let such thoughts drift away with the outgoing tide, for I knew they would have saddened my mother. She could not have borne to see me with hatred in my heart.

Still, forgiveness did not come easy. The Kadar made war, brought injury and misery, while the Shahala healed and lived in peace. I used to think the good spirits that sometimes rested on top of the numaba trees must have been the spirits of the Shahala who had passed on. The bad spirits that lived in the depths of Mirror Sea, to grab after anyone who sailed it, had to be Kadar.

I was not surprised that Mirror Sea churned under the slave ship. I could almost see all those restless Kadar spirits angry because the traders no longer brought them slaves. Maybe those dark spirits were trying to pull the ship under so they would have servants once again.

When I finally slid to the ground from the lowest branch of the tree, I ran through the forest, knowing every rock, every root I had to jump over. Then I reached the edge of the woods, and bending low, I rounded some boulders, ran down the stone stairs and kept to the bushes until I reached the side entrance of our wooden house. Better to sneak in and retrieve my clothes before the men saw me. I did not want to shame Jarim or my mother's memory.

The men made loud bragging noises as they talked in the front. I frowned at the sound. Polite people talked little and pleasantly, bringing no more attention to themselves than necessary.

To talk so loud was as if one painted a sign on one's forehead: *Here I am, look at me.* Then everyone would have looked at him and seen him for a fool.

I hoped they did not come for healing, for I feared what people such as these would do when disappointed. I hoped they had come for medicinal herbs. Dried herbs I had aplenty.

I hurried to my room and pulled on my short tunic, regretting for a moment that not one piece of my worn clothing matched any other. We had better clothes when my mother had been alive. We had fine robes and food and laughter.

I put away the memories that seemed less than real, like legends from a golden age, and wrapped my veil around my head in the proper manner for a healer, then hurried toward the front. I pushed through the wind-torn curtain that covered the entrance.

"Apar," I greeted Jamir—calling him father for the last time.

The traders fell silent. Their gazes poured over me like icy water.

I could scarce keep from staring back at them. Shells and small disks of metal decorated their clothes in a dizzying array of patterns I had never seen before. The richness of the materials, the sheen of the fabric, the glitter…

Jarim caught my gaze and smoothed down his thin tunic. He wore better clothes than I, but still he could have been mistaken for a servant next to the strangers.

"Everything you say is true?" the tallest man, made taller yet by his wrapped silk headpiece, asked Jarim.

I sucked in my breath at his rudeness. To question the word of a Shahala was unthinkable. Though no Shahala blood flowed in Jarim's veins, since he'd been married to my mother, people had always extended him the same respect.

"Very good healer. Only daughter of a Tika Shahala," Jarim boasted just as rudely, as if not at all offended.

He spoke a little of most languages used around our area. I knew them as well as my own, learned from the many visitors who had come to my mother.

I wished Jarim had not said such a thing, even if he said it only because he did not want to shame me.

The leader's cold eyes narrowed. "Ten blue crystals."

I stifled a gasp. Ten blue crystals were more than we had seen in a long time, many times more than my help was worth had I been willing to give it. I tugged Jarim's sleeve.

"She is worth twice that," Jarim insisted and hushed me when I tried to speak.

I had never seen him like that before. A healer did not bargain over healing or ask payment. The sick gave gifts according to their abilities, despite reassurances that no payment was necessary.

"Twelve." The trader's impatient tone signaled the end of bargaining, and he handed Jarim a worn leather bag.

To my horror, Jarim counted the crystals. Then he nodded. Perhaps he did not feel the need to show manners in front of people who had none.

When the traders started toward the ship and motioned to me, I followed obediently, if a little dazed. I stopped after a moment when my mind cleared.

"My herbs." I turned toward our dwelling, taking mental inventory. I should probably grab a little of everything.

But the man who had bargained for my services said, "You will not need those."

Of course. They traveled many waters. They probably had their own herbs on the ship. Maybe I would even see something new and exotic. The thought cheered me a little.

I looked at Jarim, but he would not look at me.

"Come," the lead trader ordered, and I followed him.

I hoped they wanted me to heal slaves, although I was unsure whether my ministrations would be much help. But trying would have been easy, as my heart went out to the unfortunates. And I had to try now, whether master or slave languished in the sickbed—Jarim had already taken the payment.

Our shore met the sea not with a sandy beach but with boulders and rocks the waves beat against. Because of this, most ships docked in Sheharree, the nearest port, and our visitors completed the journey over land. But this time a grizzled man, wet from the spray, waited for us, holding the rope of a massive boat wedged between two scarred rocks, each as large as the boat itself.

I eased in, fear stealing into my lungs as we shoved off. The next wave could push us back and smash the boat against the rocks. But the men who handled the oars handled them well and mastered the waves.

What would they do to me if my healing failed? Would they bother to bring me back and demand their crystals? I could too easily see them tossing me overboard, into the rolling sea.

I wanted to tell them I was a fake, that I was sorry my father had taken their payment. But none of them talked, so I too remained silent. I did not want to make them angry, these people who stole others' lives to sell.

My heart beat a hurried rhythm at the unfamiliarity of the boat ride. I squeezed my eyes shut against the fury of the sea. My mother had always forbidden me from taking to the water, a habit I had kept even after her death. The boat tossed, and I grabbed its side, trying to pretend I stood atop a numaba tree, the branches swaying under me in the wind.

A welcome calm spread through my limbs at the fantasy, until the waves sprayed water in my face. I told myself I stood atop the numaba tree, and the rain began to fall. But my mind no longer believed the tale.

After an endless time, the traders shouted, and I opened my eyes. We had reached the dark vessel, the side covered with scars, the wood smelling moldy and sad, as if the sadness of the slaves had poured out into the ship.

I looked at the traders and wondered if anyone sailing on such a ship could ever be anything but unhappy, but their faces were closed and hard as a naga shell, so I could not tell which way they felt.

I climbed the rope ladder second after the leader, the rest coming up behind me. I did not mind the short climb, the ship not nearly as tall as the trees on our hillside. But I did mind when the wind snatched my veil. The length of fabric, like a dead bird falling from the sky, tossed on the waves but for a moment before it disappeared under the churning water.

The man behind me did not give me time to worry about the loss, he growled at me to hurry.

The deck stood deserted, the boards weather-beaten, the black sails frayed. Worn ropes tied down a pile of firewood to my left, two wooden buckets secured to the pile with twine. A handful of barrels were tied to the ship's railing on my other side.

The men shoved me down into the belly of the ship that swallowed me like a large fish that had not eaten for many days. I shivered even as my forehead beaded with sweat from the hot, stale air. I opened my mouth to ask how many were sick, but a rough hand in the middle of my back shoved me forward into a dark cabin. The door closed with a loud thud behind me.

"I will need a lamp," I called through the door. "Or a torch."

Nobody answered.

I turned back to the darkness and lowered my voice. "Is anyone here? Anyone sick?"

No response came, nor could I hear anyone breathing in there with me. I moved forward until I bumped into the wall, then laid my hands on a roughly-hewn wood plank and followed it.

When I reached the door, I pushed against it to no avail. I felt around for some furniture but found none. I was in an empty cabin somewhere in the middle of the ship. With nothing else to do, I sat down and waited for them to bring my patient to me.

Instead, I heard the scrape of the anchor being pulled up. Voices rang out on deck. Sails snapped somewhere above me. My heart shuddered when I finally realized there would be no sick coming.

I, Tera, daughter of Chalee, Tika Shahala, had been sold by my own father to be a slave.

CHAPTER TWO

(Onra)

The edge of a storm caught us, and the ship lurched and rolled without stop, battered by waves. Thunder clapped all around as the wind tossed us carelessly. I could think of little else but the bad spirits of the Kadar under the water, trying to pull us down into the deep.

Day stretched into miserable day. I tried to keep track of time by my meals of undercooked fish, but the men did not feed me on any regular schedule, so I could not be certain of the length of our journey.

Our long, narrow island, Dahru, was the largest of the Middle Islands, inhabited by the nine tribes of the Shahala in the south, and the warrior nation of the Kadar in the north. A desert of poisonous minerals stretched between the two countries, making sea travel necessary, which proved to be a much more dangerous endeavor than I had ever imagined.

I hated the dark, moldy room, the stale water I found to drink, the bucket in the corner and its stench. I hated being alone the most. I started to think maybe a giant fish *had* swallowed me, maybe I would never again see the sky, the twin moons, or the numaba trees on our hillside.

I thought maybe—despite my mother's reassurances—the spirits had not forgiven my family for my great-grandmother's sin, and were now punishing me for her terrible deeds.

Then as suddenly as the men had thrust me into my prison, they grabbed me from it again, dragged me roughly into the light. I squinted hard as I stumbled forward.

Even with the sun high in the sky, I shivered and wrapped my arms around me. A merciless wind whipped the strange harbor we had reached, cutting through my threadbare clothes to my trembling skin, its icy fingers reaching for my heart.

Nearly a hundred starved-looking men and women huddled on the dock, chained together in heavy iron, some holding listless children in their arms. They avoided looking at each other, as if ashamed of having given up hope.

I did not belong among them. I wanted to insist that someone had made a mistake, that I had only come to the ship to heal the sick. I looked up at the man who dragged me—the lead trader. I opened my mouth, but no words came.

Cold panic gripped me. Where was I? How would I ever find my way home again? As we moved forward, I looked away in shame, just like the others.

A tall stone wall blocked the view of the city. Poles as thick as my waist made up the gate, held together by massive strips of metal. The gate stood as tall as our ship's mast and wide enough to let four ox carts in side by side.

Kaharta Reh, I heard the traders say as we waded into the brimming stalls and shops of the port crowd. I knew that name—*a Kadar harbor*. I was still on our island. I gave thanks for that to the spirits.

Merchants offered their wares, mothers shouted at their children to keep up, shoppers argued over deals. The people were loud beyond bearing, offensively so, the city the least welcoming place I could imagine.

Sheharree, our Shahala port, had neither walls nor gate; indeed, such things would have been considered highly rude and inhospitable by my people.

As we passed into Kaharta Reh, once again I had the ominous feeling of being swallowed. I could too easily see the monstrous gates swing closed and trap me forever. I could not stop shivering.

We went to the auction house first, where the men led the other slaves into a holding pen. The leader still had my arm in his grip, and he looked at me for the first time. I trembled, thinking he would now chain me to the rest.

"I am a healer, daughter of Tika Shahala. I came on board to heal the sick. Someone must have forgotten," I said, although even I no longer believed it.

"I paid fifteen blue crystals for you." The words slithered out of his mouth with only the slightest movement of his lips.

Twelve crystals, I wanted to tell him. "I can earn more and pay you back," I said instead. I would have said anything to escape, too young to know that my fate had been decided beyond bargaining.

He dragged me on without a word, and I stumbled after him down narrow streets, passing people who hurried by on their daily business, paying little mind to us. In the biting cold, I looked at their strange clothes with envy. I would have been grateful for a flea-ridden horse blanket.

The men wore tight leather leggings with bulky fur tunics on top, the women the kind of one-piece robe the Shahala men wore over their thudrag. A man's thudrag covered the legs very much like a woman's thudi, but was not tied at the ankle. I saw neither thudrag nor thudi peeking from the women's heavy wool robes. Under all that billowing material, they walked around naked!

An evil land of backward people, where men wore women's clothes and women wore men's, where the sun shone without warmth, where a person could be bought and sold like a basket in the market.

My teeth chattered by the time we stopped in front of a hammered-iron door, bolted into the stone wall of an enormous building. The trader shouted for entry. We waited until a bent old man opened the door, holding it with gnarled fingers that were blackened at the tips.

No eyelashes shaded his small eyes, his gaze like the knar eagle's, his mouth thin.

As he looked me over, my heart banged against my ribs, wanting to run away in panic and leave the rest of my doomed body behind. Then the man shuffled back and closed the door in our faces.

He does not want me. I nearly sank to the ground with relief.

The light feeling of having escaped a fate too horrible to contemplate lasted only a moment, for I realized what would happen next. I would be taken back to the market to be sold on the block with the others. Panic plowed into me with renewed strength, and I sank to the cold stones of the street.

When the door reopened, a stunningly beautiful woman appeared, in a sky-colored gown, tight on top but widening below the waist like the graceful bell of the lulsa flower. Rich embroidery decorated the cloth so thickly that I could hardly make out the underlying material. She stood as delicate as the reeds of the bay, with large ebony eyes and skin like flower petals. A slender chain of gold encircled her slim waist, and from that hung a multitude of tiny figurines, chiming in magical harmony as she moved, small replicas of flowers, forest animals, and birds. On the woman's head, a golden veil streamed from two brooches of precious gems.

"She is the healer?" Even her voice sounded like music.

The slave trader nodded with a sly, self-satisfied look.

The beautiful woman inspected me briefly, then held out a bag of crystals without asking about the price. This time, the trader did not bargain.

I moved forward, my eyes misty with gratitude that she bought me. Her delicate, serene features reminded me of my mother. Once I told her of the misunderstanding, I knew she would return me to my people. I bent to kiss the hem of her gown, but before I could reach it, she kicked me.

Blinding pain seared through my head; then I heard the crack of my own skull as I bounced against the doorframe. I saw nothing but darkness, hearing her screech from far away as she called for her servants.

Rough hands closed around my ankles. My mind floated as if in a dream. They dragged me over the cold stone floor for hours, it seemed...

Then blessed darkness and peace.

———

I awoke on a pallet in a cavernous room that spun around me for a several nauseating moments. I closed my eyes. Opened them again. The walls settled.

Moonlight peeked in through rows of small holes high up near the ceiling—nine rows, hundreds of fist-sized holes in each, most covered in glass. Braziers stood against the wall here and there, coal glowing in them, pushing off heat. Silence filled the room, barely ruffled by the delicate sounds of shallow breathing. Dozens of girls slept on the other pallets on the floor around mine—all younger than I.

I sat up. Pain throbbed through my body, my forehead aching the most, worse than when I had fallen from a numaba tree on my first climb. I lifted my fingers to my temple, and they came away sticky with blood.

I could not see any water jars in the room, so I grabbed the hem of my tunic and used my own spit to clean the wound, then dabbed a few drops of moonflower tears into the gash.

My legs folded as I pushed to stand, so I stayed on my hands and knees. My whole body shook, but I crawled among the sleeping girls, toward the giant door that stood an eternity away.

When I reached the door at last, I pushed against it gently, then a little harder, then with all my strength. The wooden panel refused me freedom with no more apology than a soft creak.

I sank against it and thought for a long time about my mother, our hillside, and the numaba trees. Then I crawled back to my bed of rags and cried myself to sleep.

———

Morning came too fast for night to have sufficiently eased the pain. The little windows showed only a dim light outside when a smaller door on the other end of the room, one I had not seen in the dark, flew open and banged against the wall.

The woman who had bought me strolled in, dressed in an embroidered red silk gown, followed by two servants with torches. She gazed over the neat rows of girls as they stood with their heads bowed, then she walked to the middle of the room.

I rose to my knees but could not push all the way to standing. My body swayed from the effort; the light in the room seemed to dim. A small hand clamped on my arm and tugged me up, and even as I struggled to stand, the rows of girls before me parted like saplings bowing to the wind. Then that richly embroidered gown came into view, the color of fresh-spilled blood.

I lifted my gaze, finding neither recognition nor emotion in the woman's eyes, not even when my knees buckled, and I fell at her feet.

"You may take this morning to heal yourself." Her voice was cold and clipped. She turned to the girl who had helped me. "You stay with her and prepare yourself for tonight."

All the color washed out of the girl's face as she bent her head even deeper. Faint whispers rippled through the room. Without another look at me, the woman gave instructions to the others, designating a myriad of chores with practiced ease.

Once she moved away, I could no longer hear her, her voice drowned by the rushing blood in my ears that sounded like waves crashing against the shore. The room began spinning again. I closed my eyes to stop it. When I opened them, the room stood empty, except for myself and the girl on the next pallet. Her shoulders shook as she cried, but then she caught me watching, and she wiped her eyes.

"I am Onra." She swallowed the last sob. "Does your wound hurt?"

She had kind, water-colored eyes, reminding me of the sea at the inlet not far from our beach, the place where Jarim fished. Her hair, several shades lighter than mine, fell down her back in a heavy braid.

I reached to my forehead and felt the gap that still seeped. "I am Tera. Could you please tell me where I can find some clean water?"

She pushed to standing and padded to the door. I tried to follow, but she was already returning before my shaky limbs could carry me halfway across the room. I could have wept at the sight of a full bowl of water, more than I had been given on the slavers' ship the entire long trip.

"Thank you." I drank deeply before beginning to wash my wounds.

I went on to wash the ship's stench off the rest of my body, but Onra stayed my hand and removed the bowl, only to appear with clean water. She brought me yet a third bowl to wash my clothes. Still, it would have taken many more to wash away all the dirt, more than an ocean to make me feel clean again.

I wished I had something to give in return for Onra's gift. Instead, I had to ask for more help. "I need to go outside to find—" I did not know the word in her language so I said it in mine. "Ninga beetle. Little bug that lives in water."

She shook her head. "You have to stay here. New slaves get beaten worst. They say a good beating in the beginning saves lots of beatings later. You can find your bugs maybe tomorrow or after."

I knew enough about wounds to know I should not wait. "Where do you go for water?"

"The clay jars outside the door."

"How does water come into the jars?"

"The servants bring it from the creek at the end of the fields."

"I need to go there. I need the beetles for this." I pointed to the gash in my forehead.

After a moment, she rose to her feet. "I will go."

"No." I reached to pull her back. I wanted no harm to befall her because of me.

Her lips tugged into a sad smile. "I will not see the whip today. Kumra would not ruin my skin before tonight."

She hurried through the door before I could ask what she meant.

She stayed away a long time, until I worried that maybe she had been stopped and beaten despite her reassurances. But then she appeared with a rag bunched in her shaking hands. She set the cloth in front of me and stepped back quickly, grimacing as I began to unfold the small package.

Her expression, a mix of fear and revulsion, betrayed how little she cared for the beetles, so I thanked her even more for the gift.

Three big ningas, flat as if hit by stone, rolled to the floor in front of me. I pressed my lips together. "I need them alive. I should have told you. I am sorry."

Onra's eyes widened as she stared at me.

I rose on shaking legs. "I will go."

She drew a deep breath and pushed me down onto the jumble of rags that covered my pallet, then walked away again.

"I need small ones," I called after her, wincing with embarrassment that I had to issue yet another request.

She gave me a tremulous smile from the doorway.

I sat as close as I could to the nearest brazier that still had some glowing lumps of coal, shivering in my wet clothes. I soaked up the heat for a while, then brought a clean bowl of water from outside the door, careful not to let anyone see me.

Onra stayed away longer this time, before returning with a few squirming beetles, bundled tight in the rag once again. I lifted the first beetle and, watching my reflection in the mirror of the water, placed its pinchers against the edges of my wound, then squeezed its body.

The beetle sank its black pinchers into my skin, drawing the edges together. With a quick twist, I separated body from head, which would have held the pinchers firmly in place had I not pulled the body away too soon. I could not see enough in the water, my hand obstructing the view. I pulled the half-done pinchers out, wiped the blood, then started over.

Onra, who had been alternating between watching and glancing away in horror, pushed my hand down and picked up the second beetle, only to drop it again when it bit her.

"Like this." I showed her how to place her fingers farther back on the hard shiny-black wings.

She drew a deep breath, then another, until her hands stopped trembling, then, beetle by beetle, closed my wound.

She had nearly finished by the time a servant woman entered the room with a small bowl. She looked at Onra for a long time with tears in her eyes, then set the bowl down inside the door and left as abruptly as she had appeared.

"Who was that?" I asked.

Onra dropped the last headless beetle on the pile, cleaned up the mess we had made, then padded over to bring us the bowl. She set the food, some kind of grain cooked in milk, in front of me.

"My mother," she said in an emotion-filled whisper.

I thought of my mother, who had died and was buried somewhere in this land. I was closer to her than I had been for a long time. The thought comforted me a little.

I looked at the closed door. "Can you not go to her?"

"I will, after tonight." Onra scooped some grain from the bowl with her fingers and lifted it to her mouth, motioning to me to do the same.

I did, and the food tasted better than anything I had had for a long time, although not as good as my mother's cooking, which was now only a sweet memory.

"What will you do tonight?" I asked after I eased the worst of my hunger.

Onra's eyes filled with tears. "Kumra chose me for our Warrior Lord, Tahar."

"Is Kumra his lalka?" I used the word from my own language for wife as I did not know it in hers. "Mate for life."

She shook her head. "My mother's people too had that custom, but not the Kadar. Kumra is the favorite concubine."

"Are you a concubine?"

A fat tear rolled down her face.

I wished I could call my words back. "Forgive me. I do not know your ways."

She nodded, then pointed toward the room in a sweeping motion. "In Maiden Hall, all of us are slaves. When I reached womanhood, they moved me here from the Servant House for the pleasure of our Lord Tahar. A virgin's blood increases a warrior's valor, so he takes a girl often, and always before going off to war. For good luck." She swallowed hard.

I sat still. "What happens to the virgins afterward?"

"A few who please him much, he keeps as concubines. They move to Pleasure Hall and no longer have to work with the servants."

"And if you are not selected?"

"I will go to the Servant House." She looked away. "And after that, any warrior who pleases can have me when he wants."

I looked at her, stunned, thinking even death was preferable to that fate. "Maybe he will keep you."

But she shook her head. "Kumra hates me, and Tahar listens to her. Even if he picked me, and I moved to Pleasure Hall, I would be dead from some mysterious disease soon. That is Kumra's way."

My heart squeezed. "Can we not escape?"

She grabbed my hand and held it, her watery eyes intent on mine. "You must never try. Tahar's warriors are great hunters. When they catch you, you will die."

I considered whether that might not be a better fate than this.

"I am scared," Onra whispered after a moment.

"Is Tahar—"

"Not of Tahar. Of weakening. Of crying and bringing shame to our House. I am just a weak girl. Look at me. I have cried ten times today already." She dropped her hands to her sides.

I could not understand how she could worry about bringing shame to anyone when unspeakable shame was being done to her. I began to ask but thought better of it. "You will not cry tonight."

She looked at me with wet eyelashes that clumped together, her eyes begging. I did not know if I could give her what she needed, but I gave her what I could. "You might be a girl, but inside you are as brave as any warrior. Look at the battle you already won today."

She waited.

"The battle of the beetles."

The corner of her mouth tugged up as she wiped her eyes. "I will not forget you, Tera, even if I do not see you for a while."

She put her hands on my shoulders and pushed gently to turn me around, then combed through my hair with her slim fingers. "I will make your maiden's braid."

All the girls I had seen that morning had their hair in one long braid down their back. Kumra wore hers woven into the shape of a crown around her head.

Onra separated my hair into three equal parts and began to work the strands with quick fingers. "Slave girls wear their hair in two braids, one on each side. When they reach womanhood, they switch to a single braid like mine. After leaving Maiden Hall to go back to Servant House, their hair is cut short. Concubines keep their hair long to make into pretty weaves to please our lord."

She drew the leather cord from the end of her own braid to tie mine.

When she finished, she said, "You have pretty hair, like black silk. And eyes to match. Be careful of Kumra."

She grabbed a blanket from her cot and pulled four long pieces of wool yarn from it. "We should make you a charm belt."

I glanced at hers, made of simple yarn and decorated with small wood carvings, nothing like Kumra's gold and crystal.

"I do not know this custom."

Her fingers flew as she braided the belt. "Fire, earth, water, air," she named each strand. "They offer protection from bad luck. Better if you have charms. Better even if the charm is made by the soothsayer, but for that you would have to pay."

She pulled a reddish pebble from the folds of her dress, kissed it on one side, spit on the other, wrapped a piece of yarn around it, then tied it to the belt.

"Here." Onra held up the finished piece and helped me fit it around my waist. "I drew the pebble from the creek. It might be lucky for you. The creek gave you the beetles that helped you heal your wound."

I nodded, although I did not completely follow her logic. But she seemed happy to have protected me so neatly, and I did not want to ruin even that little joy in her day.

When she was finished, she stood with sudden determination. "I need to go and prepare. The goddesses protect you, Tera."

She walked to the small door that connected our room to the rest of the house and, without another word, disappeared through it.

I stared after her for a long time.

I vowed never to follow that path. For myself, for Onra, and for my mother's memory, I swore to the spirits to escape from this unbearable place and find my way back to my own people.

But first, I would find out how my mother had died in this terrible land and recite the Last Blessing over her grave.

———

The Kadar battle feast seemed the same and yet completely different from our Shahala celebrations. People joked, sang, ate like any people coming together. Except for the slaves who served the warriors and their concubines.

The servants came in a steady stream from outside, bringing heaping trays of food from the kitchen. Each tray stopped at a stone table at the head of the Great Hall. Giant swords carved from stone made up the table's legs, their tips resting on the ground. The swords' handles supported the table top, a large stone shield.

Carved symbols covered both the swords and the shield, angular and resembling slim arrowheads that pointed in every direction. But their pattern seemed orderly in a way—maybe some kind of writing. Onto this stone table the servants placed a small portion of food from each tray before serving the rest to Tahar and his people.

I sat in another room with the rest of the maidens, about fifty of us, watching the feast through veiled windows.

Darkness enveloped our room, while a multitude of oil lamps and torches lit the Great Hall; thus we could see them, but they could not see us. Nobody even glanced in our direction, even though they must have known we were there.

A stalwart man sat at the head of the table, his large upper body covered in formfitting, hardened leather. The wide panes of his weatherworn face glowed with color from the wine. He had to be Lord Tahar. All deferred to him.

Only men sat on the short-legged wooden benches around the low dining table, warriors to the last. Behind them, reclining on pillows, chatted their concubines. Tahar had the most, all beautiful women save the youngest, whose wide cheeks had a strong resemblance to his.

"Is she his daughter?" I whispered to the girl next to me, a willowy redhead with a tiny mole under her right eye.

She drew her eyebrows together in a disapproving grimace. "It is not to be spoken of."

"She should have been sent away a long time ago," the girl on my other side, younger and rounder than the first, whispered. "Sent to another Lord as a gift. Daughters of concubines do not stay in their father's Pleasure Hall beyond childhood, lest their father's eyes fall upon them in lust and their House be cursed forever."

"Kumra has no sons, just one daughter," another girl added as if unable to resist the gossip. "She uses every excuse to keep her."

A commotion at the Great Hall's door silenced us.

A beautiful young woman entered, dressed in a white flowing dress of the finest silk. Her hair, combed to a sheen, fell nearly to the backs of her knees. A garland of white flowers graced her head, her small feet bare on the stone floor. I did not recognize her until somebody whispered, "Onra," behind me.

She walked to the Lord's seat with trembling grace, then lowered herself to her knees and bowed deep before him. I held my breath as he looked her over, then took her hand and rose, bringing her up with him. He turned his back on the warriors at his table and led her through a doorway, deeper into the house, a servant quick to close the door behind them.

"I cannot believe she was chosen before me," the redhead on my right whispered furiously. "I should be the one to wear the dress and nothing else on my body to please Lord Tahar. When it is my turn, Lord Tahar *will* keep me."

I could barely breathe, but the celebration in the Great Hall continued as if nothing had happened, as if nobody at all cared about the brutal crime being committed somewhere near.

If a Shahala a man forced himself on a woman, he was cast out from our people, left to wander the hills alone until he starved.

I felt stricken by the vast difference between the Kadar and the Shahala, repulsed by the people who had bought me. How could the sun and the moons tolerate such people? How could the spirits? Why did the sea not rise up to wash away even their shameful memory?

How I wished for my mother, her wisdom, her strength. Silently, I asked her spirit to guide me, to help me be wise enough to know how to save myself, and brave enough to do it.

I waited for a long time to feel a response that she heard me, as I often had back home—a slight breeze on my face, the graceful dip of a tree branch, the playful slosh of a wave that sounded different from the others. But nothing happened there in our veiled room.

Then Tahar reappeared in the doorway, with Onra behind him, and I forgot to worry about my mother. Onra stood naked, her pale flesh glowing in the trembling light cast by the torches. She stayed where she stood, while Tahar, an arrogant smile on his face, seated himself amid loud cheers.

"Does this mean he keeps her?" I whispered.

"He would have sent her straight to Pleasure Hall, then," one of the girls answered.

My heart ached for Onra as she moved at last, moving slowly across the endless room. A woman servant threw flower petals on her and thanked her for bringing good luck to the House. The warriors banged their fists on the table, whistled, and made other rude noises.

She slowed when she walked by our window, blood smeared on her white thighs. Her head held high, she shed no tears. When she reached the outside door, her mother wrapped her in a blanket and led her into the cold night.

A young warrior stood from the end of the table.

"Tonight, she will be had by many," the redhead next to me whispered. "Straight from the Lord's bed, her virgin's blood still flowing. It is good luck for the men."

CHAPTER THREE

(Pleasure Hall)

That night, I had a dream—the last one for a long time to come.

In my dream, I searched the woods behind our house for fresh herbs when a great mist descended on the mountain. I crossed the foothills and reached the mountain with the speed of a dream. At first, I could not see anything. My heart flapped inside my chest like a caged bird. Then I heard a faint voice, my mother's, calling me up the mountain and deeper into the mist.

As I walked, the mist began to swirl around me. I recognized the good spirits of the Shahala, and I knew they had come down from the sky, not to harm but to protect me, to lead me to my mother. I ran forward as fast as I could, all the way to the top, and when I reached the highest snow-covered peak, the mist disappeared.

I looked down the mountain to search for my mother and saw a great multitude below: the Shahala, the Kadar, and all the people of all the lands from as far as the Kingdom of Orh. And they lifted their eyes to me.

I woke up in tears, wishing I had caught even a single glimpse of my mother instead of all the nations, but I did not have time to ponder the dream long, as the next moment, the door flew open and Kumra walked into our room.

I received one more day to heal, a day of anger and sorrow that I spent alone, missing Onra's company. The warriors prepared for war outside. I could not see them but heard them through the window holes.

The women cried their farewell as Tahar left with the best of his men for the harbor. They would sail to Wotwor, a nearby kingdom ravaged by rebellion. Their king had paid for Tahar's services.

The next morning, my first morning as a servant, I jumped up with the rest of the girls and listened to Kumra's orders as she made her way to me, her gown of golden silk trailing on the floor behind her. She stopped in the empty spot where Onra's pallet had been before— one of the girls had folded it and leaned it against the far wall after the feast. Kumra grabbed my chin with strong fingers and lifted my head to examine my wounds.

Her scent, the strong essence of the lorba flower, twisted my nose. She clicked her tongue, I hoped not in displeasure.

"What is your name?"

"Tera."

She let go of my chin and pointed to the two girls standing next to me. "You will take Tera and clean behind Warrior Hall today."

When they deepened their bows, so did I.

As Kumra moved on, I followed outside after the girls, across the gravel courtyard surrounded by stone buildings. I wrapped my arms around myself against the cold, but the wind bit into my skin. I hurried, the sharp gravel cutting my bare feet.

I shivered at the sight of all the stone around me, large, evenly cut boulders, hundreds and hundreds of them piled on top of each other to form the buildings' unnatural shapes. These stones had not been taken out of the fields by men who worked the land—my heart trembled at the thought—they were cut from the mountains.

I could see in my mind those scarred mountains and their angry spirits demanding retribution for their damaged sanctuaries.

Did the Kadar respect nothing? Did nothing stand beyond being used for gain? Did they not know that by chipping away the mountains, they were bleeding the strength from their own lives?

I swallowed my grief and made sure to note the square buildings, the high wall that protected them on what I knew was the street side to town, the multitude of small huts, the open fields behind the Servant House at the end of which, Onra had said, ran the creek.

The land stretched like flatbread toward the horizon, and although I could not see it, I could smell the ocean and heard the cry of its birds in the air. Dahru was a vast island, too treacherous to cross on foot. If I were to return home someday, I would have to go over the water again.

I shivered, my worn clothes hardly a match for the biting wind. Yet despite the chill that seeped deep into my bones, I slowed to see more, but the two girls entered the building on the far end of the courtyard and I dared not lag too far behind.

At least ten Maiden Halls would have fitted inside Warrior Hall, with room left over. The place stank like rotten kukuyu. I breathed short, shallow breaths. "Do all the warriors stay here?"

"Of course not," the taller of the two girls, the willowy redhead, spat the words at me, her green eyes narrowing with displeasure. "Only the young ones who have no concubines." She marched ahead to throw open the wood shutters.

Light flooded the room, revealing row upon row of pallets, larger than ours and with more space between them. Most had wooden trunks either at the foot or at the head. Weapons and various articles of clothing covered the floor, some stacked neatly, some carelessly scattered.

"I am Lenya." The younger girl, who still had the plump, chubby look of childhood, walked across the room toward the door in the back. "Do not mind Igril. She thinks we were sent here because of you. She hates servant work."

I followed her. The breeze finally thinned the foul air enough so I could fill my lungs. "Are we not servants?"

"We are slaves, but we are maidens. The rest of the slaves are servants."

"But you still work every day?"

"Of course." She reached the door and pushed it open. "But we handle nicer chores than this."

The smell of Warrior Hall was but a weak warning compared to what waited for us outside. The stench smacked my nose like a branch in the face. Behind Warrior Hall stood the warriors' latrines. Kumra had sent us to clean *those*. I could not blame Igril if she hated me forever.

A sudden gust of wind raced around the buildings and slammed into us, making us bend at the waist as we moved forward. I envied Igril's and Lenya's thick wool dresses that covered them from wrist to ankle, coveted the wide strips of leather bound around their feet.

"Count yourself lucky Kumra did not have you beaten." Igril picked up a bucket and handed me another. "She does that sometimes to new slaves right at the beginning to make sure they know what to expect if they disobey."

She probably meant the words to scare me, but I was relieved that at least she was talking to me. I did not wish to make any enemies. "Do they ever?"

She looked at me for a long moment, her face changing from annoyance to some deeper emotion. "Lord Tahar had my brother beaten to death."

I felt the blood leave my head first, then the rest of my body, until even my heart felt empty.

Lenya squeezed my arm. "That will not be your fate. I heard the servants when they first brought you in. You are a healer, too valuable. They did not even beat you." She cocked her head. "You are a healer, are you not?"

I knew I had to say yes—what would await me if anyone found out the truth—but my tongue refused to say the lie.

"Of course you are. Your forehead." She pointed. "It is already healed."

I reached up and brushed away what little of the beetles still clung to my skin. I always healed fast. My mother's blood worked strong within me.

Lenya smiled. "Kumra will gain even more favor with our Lord if she has you heal the wounded upon their return."

I had no mind to wait for Tahar's return or for Kumra to discover my lack of healing powers. She would send me to be resold on the block in a heartbeat.

I had but one thought in my troubled mind: escape.

———

Life without freedom runs on its own time. My childhood at home had flowed without effort, measured by landmarks of one happy event after the other, or the dread of waiting for things I disliked, like cleaning the foul-smelling kukuyu weeds my mother used for sprains.

At Maiden Hall where Kumra worked me hard from dawn to well into the night, things to look forward to disappeared. As had hope; I watched it flutter out an open window one night. Only dread remained, but as it was ever-present, it could not serve as marker for the passing time.

The days at Maiden Hall had neither beginning nor end, for sleep passed in the blink of an eye. I slept as soon as my worn body touched my pallet; then I heard the door bang open, and I pulled awake again as if no time had passed at all.

Little by little, I grew familiar with the other girls and the ways of the House of Tahar. I learned that only the sons of warriors could be warriors; the children of servants would always remain slaves, although the girls became maidens for a short time.

Daughters of warriors were given as concubines to other warriors either at their Lord's House or at another's. Anyone could take a servant girl, but the taking of a maiden was punishable by death, as was all disobedience. Some of the Great Houses had different laws, but Tahar kept with the old ways.

I made friends with as many of the maidens as would let me, and was glad never to be chosen for chores in Pleasure Hall, for I heard many tales about the cruelty of concubines.

The hatred of some of the maidens was enough, almost more than I could bear, for I gave them no reason to treat me so. But a few, seeing

Kumra's obvious dislike of me, sought to gain her favor by doing whatever they could to torture me. One had gone as far as dropping a small cauldron of boiling water on me to see how fast I could heal myself. I howled with the pain of the welts that covered both arms to the tip of my fingers.

The following morning, as Kumra sent us to do our chores, her gaze landed on my hands. Her lips flattened into a severe line. "What have you done?"

"An accident, my lady. I beg your pardon for it." I hoped she would allow me a day of rest so I could think of a poultice that could be made from the meager things available to me.

"You useless, clumsy murna," she yelled, and other offensive names followed. Then she suddenly calmed, which scared me more than the yelling. A cold gleam came into her eyes. "You will be assigned to the wash today. See that you make fine work of it."

I bowed, not wanting to anger her further by showing any emotion. A hard day that turned out to be. The hot water and lye like thousands of sharp talons and teeth attacked my injured flesh. I fainted twice with the pain of it, but dared not to leave any of the work undone.

These things happened and worse, and I learned to keep out of Kumra's way. I did nothing to bring myself to her attention and tried my best to do my work as well as I could to give her no excuse for punishment, not that she needed a reason.

The spirits watched over me, for no illness came to the House that would have required any true powers. The few cases of sour stomachs were righted easily with steamed borlan, and the various cuts and sores needed only cleaning and bandaging. Thus my lack of true worth remained undiscovered as winter progressed, each day colder yet than the one before.

The work remained hard, the food scarce, and my heart shivered within my body, for I could never get warm enough. I tied rags around my feet and stuffed them with dry grass for added protection. To keep the chill from the rest of my body, I folded a large rag into a triangle and wore it over my shoulders as a cape, the edges wrapped around my waist and tied in the back, but still my sunborn body shivered.

I was determined to gain my full strength back before true winter arrived. My limbs, always strong from climbing, had grown weak. So wherever I had to go, I ran instead of walking. If anything heavy needed to be lifted, I jumped first to grab it. I did my chores fast, then helped the other girls. All the time, I planned, asking the spirits to help me. And then one day they answered.

I was running through the kitchen with a bucket in each hand, on my way to the creek, when I saw a man whose familiar thudrag, the traditional wear of Shahala men, stopped me. Something in his face, in his being, called out to the kin in mine and drew me to him.

"Little sister, what is your name?" His eyes crinkled at the corners. The words flew from his lips in the language of my people, sweet and smooth like dripping honey.

"I am Tera." I bowed my head, since I was addressing an elder.

"Talmir is my name. By the spirits, I both laugh and cry at the sight of you."

I understood what he meant as I felt the same—happy to find one of my own, sad for he shared my sorry fate. I had so much to ask him, so much to tell. Two people standing together were ten times stronger than one. Hope filled my heart with warmth for the first time since I left our shores.

"Talmir—"

I fell silent as Kumra walked through the doors.

"Here." Talmir snatched a small sweetcake from the table and handed it to me behind his back. "Come back when you can."

I nodded my thanks, then ran out through the back with my buckets before Kumra could stop me.

I passed by servants singing as they worked. Two older women made a bawdy joke about men, and the rest broke out laughing. Strange they were, living in servitude like this, yet happy when their masters weren't watching.

Among my people, serenity and composure were the most valued traits. The Kadar, even their servants, seemed to live without restraint. They fought hard and laughed hard and danced hard, as if having no control at all over their emotions. At times they seemed like undisciplined children to me.

I did return to Talmir many times. I learned he had been kidnapped on the streets of Tezgin by mercenaries who did not understand that all Shahala could not heal. After they realized Talmir could not help them, they beat him and sold him to a slave trader who in turn sold him to the House of Tahar.

"My mother had come to these lands some time ago," I told him one day. "Her name was Chalee. Have you met her?"

His eyebrows rose. "Chalee of Sheharree?"

I nodded.

"I heard of her fame."

"She came to heal the High Lord, and then she died. Do you know where her body is resting?"

"The High Lord lives in the fortress city of Karamur. You would have to inquire that way."

Karamur. I tasted the name, which meant *eagles' nest* in Kadar. I had no idea how far or which way the fortress city lay. My shoulders slumped. "I would wish to recite the Last Blessing over her grave."

"Say it from afar," Talmir advised. "If ever the chance comes for you to escape, flee straight for our Shahala lands. Forget about the fortress city."

He would not escape with me, but he would help. He had a wife now—almost a wife, except for the nights when a warrior came to their shared pallet and Talmir had to wait outside under the stars. He had children, a girl and a boy.

"Avoid going inland. There are more towns like this there, all the way to the desert," he said one time as we huddled in the corner of the kitchen. "Do not go straight to the harbor, either. You will not be able to sneak onto a ship. They will look for you there."

I nodded, excitement like a chatty little creek rushing in my veins.

"Go to the hills. The rocks will hide your tracks."

The hills. My heart beat faster. I knew the plants that grew in the hills. They would feed and shelter me.

"The hills follow the coastline all the way to the next port town." He kept an eye on the door, always on guard. "As long as your hair is not shorn, you can pretend to be a free woman. That will save you on the streets, but we have to think of something for booking passage on a ship. Concubines do not travel. Maybe a merchant's wife."

"Or a traveling healer." My mother had traveled like that to the Kadar to help their High Lord. "I will need a length of cloth that could serve as the healer's veil."

"Fine cloth like that is difficult to find."

The laundry was closely guarded by those who received the chore. One small tear, one silk handkerchief lost, and the concubines took it out of the laundress's hide. I didn't think I could steal a veil there, nor would I have wanted someone else to be punished for my crime.

My shoulders slumped as I considered my only option. "Pleasure Hall."

"I cannot help you there."

No man could enter Pleasure Hall other than Lord Tahar.

I hoped I would be assigned a chore there soon, although Kumra liked to keep me working alongside the servants. I did not dare ask any of the other girls for help, not for fear of betrayal, although I knew some would, but because I did not want any of them to come to harm once I escaped.

Not knowing when Lord Tahar would return, I planned to leave soon. In his absence, only a handful of warriors guarded his House. When I ran, I did not want his whole army after me.

I liked the idea of cutting through the hills to the next port for a ship, but home would have to wait. Despite Talmir's warnings, I still wanted to find my mother's grave.

In the next few days, he saved me some food, and I selected two of the largest wool rags that covered my pallet to take with me. I snatched bits and pieces of cloth wherever I could, to stuff under the rags I planned on leaving behind.

The girls fell asleep fast after coming in each night. I just had to make a lump on my cot so when Kumra came to lock the door she would think all were inside. I would hide in the women's latrines until the whole house quieted, then run, evading the guards.

I timed it for a night when both of the moons would be waning. Darkness, like Talmir, would be my friend and speed me to freedom.

By the time the last day arrived, I had everything but a veil. I leapt to my feet the moment the door banged open in the morning, asking the spirits for help. I waited as Kumra gave instructions to all the other girls, then stopped in front of my pallet.

"You are coming with me." For the first time, she sounded tired.

I kept the sudden joy from showing on my face and shuffled after her to the small door with meek obedience, as if the key to my freedom had not just been handed to me. I wondered what she wanted me to clean now and imagined all the most disgusting tasks. I would have happily done all of them and more.

But once I stepped through the door, I forgot about the chores, even about my plans to escape. For Pleasure Hall was nothing like I had expected, not like Maiden Hall at all.

My feet sank into a carpet, soft and thick as shirl moss. Silk pictures of naked men and women in strange poses covered the walls, painted in rich colors so full of life the images seemed to be moving. I turned my head in embarrassment. Then a round pool in the middle of the round hall drew my gaze, and I stared slack-jawed at the rising steam.

I could not gawk long, as I had to keep up with Kumra, who hurried along without paying the least attention to the beauty around us. But in passing, I admired the graceful reclining benches covered in luscious fabrics, the richly carved low tables, and their bowls of fruit and sweets.

Before me spread a world so strange and beautiful it belonged in a dream, although I was not sure if even in my dreams I could have conceived of it.

Pleasure Hall did not stand deserted during the day as Maiden Hall. About twenty women and twice as many children filled the luxurious central space, and voices of more filtered in from the adjoining chambers. The soft sound of water that seemed to circulate in the pool blended together with the gentle chime of charms around the concubines' waists, creating something akin to music.

A few concubines watched our progress, while others embroidered, played with children, or simply rested. The only similarity between Pleasure Hall and Maiden Hall was the small window holes below the round ceiling, although the glass here swirled with a rainbow of colors. From the central space opened many chambers with curved archways, and I followed Kumra into one.

Some of her gowns were carelessly scattered on the floor where they lay in twisted poses, like beautiful bodies waiting for their spirit to enter them.

"Stop gawking," she ordered, and led me to a small chamber that opened from hers in the back.

A delicately carved bed of dark sabal wood stood in the corner, her daughter, Keela, lying upon the bed. I had last seen her on the night of the feast. The color had fled her face since. Her eyes stared but did not see.

Kumra did not bring me to clean. She wanted my healing.

"I am a Berangi," she said, emphasizing the last word. "Have you ever seen a Berangi funeral?"

I shook my head and bowed deep, not daring to look her in the eye.

In the barbaric Kingdom of Berang, when an important person died, the family had a servant killed and buried with the dead so they would have someone to take care of them in the afterlife. In the time of the first kings, they used to bury the servants alive.

"Pray you do not have to." Kumra turned back from the door before walking out. "I prefer the old ways, like Tahar."

CHAPTER FOUR

(Keela)

I stepped closer to the bed where Keela trembled. A double-layered blanket covered her, the outer panel made of blue damask and embroidered with yellow bell flowers, the inner panel finely woven wool. I had admired the cover when I had seen it in the wash. The petals had been done by such a fine hand that the flowers seemed to dance across the material. Now, in the dim room, they looked like blossoms heaped upon a grave.

I reached inside my tunic and clutched the phial hanging on the cord around my neck, my only reminder of my mother and freedom. But even that could not bring me comfort as my fears surrounded me.

I spoke Keela's name, but she did not respond. I checked her forehead, found it cool and damp with sweat. When I drew the cover down, her trembling increased until I had to hold her in place.

She wore only a thin sleeping robe and her charm belt. I freed her from the robe so I could fully see her pale body, but tied the charm belt back on, even though I did not believe in its powers. She believed, and that might make a difference.

I looked over her pale skin, expecting a bite mark from something poisonous, but did not find it even as I turned her over so I would not miss anything. She shook worse with each passing moment, until her body went into quick, hard convulsions.

A time comes in the progression of disease that all healers recognize, the last chance beyond which exists no return. I looked into Keela's eyes, the tiny black spots of her pupils that did not see me, and knew I was losing her fast.

I asked my mother's spirit for guidance and did everything she taught me. I tasted Keela's sweat—bitter. Her breath stank like tidewater trapped in the low places on the beach, and in it I could smell the poison. I ran out to Kumra's chamber to ask how long Keela had been suffering and what she had eaten, but Kumra had left, and I had no time to find her.

I returned to the girl, opened her mouth, and shoved my fingers down her throat as far as I could, until her stomach gave up its deadly charge. As the sour stench of vomit filled the room, I grabbed the clay jar from the corner and forced half the water down her throat, then made her give it back again. I did the same with the rest of the water, not an easy task as Keela sputtered and choked, resisting my efforts.

When I finished, I returned to Kumra's chamber and dragged over another jar of water to clean Keela and her bed. Then I brought in one of Kumra's throws to cover the girl, and her convulsions diminished to weak shivers at last.

As little as I had done, I had done all I could. At home, I could have tried a fusion of mixed herbs, but in this strange land I would not have known where to look for them, nor did I have the freedom to leave the House of Tahar and wander into the woods.

Without true powers, I did not have the ability to send my spirit into Keela's body to seek the illness and draw it out, to tell her spirit how to help me, what to do.

My mother used to say youth had its own healing powers, and to them I entrusted Keela. She was young, her body strong. I hoped strong enough—for both our sakes.

I held her hand, anchoring her body to life by the power of touch. I talked to her, for her spirit to hear and find the way back, should it wander. I told her the story of Lawana, the merchant and the beggar boy, the faithful wife, and by the time I got to the Guardians and the Forgotten City, her breathing had grown even.

"You would have liked the Forgotten City." I wiped her face with a wet cloth. "The houses and towers were beautiful beyond anything that exists now in the world. In the middle of the labyrinth of streets stood a round building of wonders, topped not by a flat roof but something that looked like a giant bowl turned upside down. They called it a dome."

She gave no indication that she heard me, but I went on with the tale.

"The outside they covered in sheets of lustrous gold. The inside of the building was one large open space, with seats enough for multitudes. They painted the ceiling blue and attached golden symbols for all the stars as they stood in the moment of the creation of the world. So exact were their measurements that scholars came from distant kingdoms to study them."

I glanced at Keela, and although she did not look in need of clarification, I explained anyway. "Scholars were magical people who studied all things and could explain even the unexplainable." I did not know anything more about their strange order than that.

"In exchange for seeing the Map of Eternity, they brought wondrous gifts, metals many times the strength of iron, and lamps that used less oil and burned ten times brighter than the ordinary ones. They even taught the people of the Forgotten City how to make water come to their houses, so nobody had to pull water from a well or go to the creek."

This had always seemed the most impressive part of the tale to me, and as a child, I had often wished the secrets of the Forgotten City were still known to us.

"These scholars gladly gave any knowledge they had for a glimpse at the Map of Eternity, for when they compared it to the position of the stars of their own times, they could tell many things that passed before in the world and even predict events that were to come."

I went on, for her sake as much as my own. I needed to think about something else than what would happen to me if I failed to restore her health.

"Other strange people came to the Forgotten City too, philosophers, the wise men of the world. They came together in the Forum—their name for the building with the dome that held the Map of Eternity—and by sharing their knowledge, they increased it a hundredfold. The three Guardians of the city asked only one thing of all these masters of knowledge—that before they left, they wrote their wisdom onto scrolls to preserve in that place. The walls of the Forum were covered in holes from floor to ceiling, like honeycomb. And these recesses held all the knowledge of the world."

I wondered what Keela would have said to such a thing could she have talked. Many of the Shahala did not believe the myth of the Forgotten City and thought of it as another of our many tales that were but entertainment for small children. My mother, however, talked about the Forum often and with such detail as if she had been there, so it lived vividly in my memory.

"I do not know what to tell you," I said to the pale-faced girl and squeezed her hand. "Each person must choose what they believe."

The breeze brought the smell of baking bread from the kitchen and the sound of servant women singing. I could see the blue sky through a small window that stood open to let in fresh air. It seemed as if all life stretched out there, shut away from me, and I was already buried in the dim chamber with the listless body that lay on the bed.

My stomach clenched at the thought, the hunger of my missed morning meal replaced with nausea. I had not seen any Kadar tombs around the House of Tahar. Maybe like the Shahala, they had sacred places to rest their dead. Did they bury the spiritless bodies in the hillside as my own people did? Or did they use caves like some foreigners? Did they burn the bodies until only the bones remained?

Everything I had ever heard about funerals in distant lands flooded my terrified mind, as my thoughts circled back to the same unimaginable horror again and again—what it would be like to be buried alive.

Keela whimpered, startling me out of my anxious wonderings. I wiped her brow, frustrated that I could not do more, and tucked

Kumra's red silk coverlet around the girl's body. I held Keela's limp hand and whispered to her about all the good things in life, the few that I knew. And in between, I prayed to the spirits, pleaded for their favor.

When Kumra returned, she found me on my knees next to the bed.

"I will clean these." I jumped to my feet and picked up the soiled linens from the corner, but she motioned for me to put them down.

"You will stay here." She moved toward the sheets and wrinkled her nose at the smell of vomit. "So the illness came from her stomach." She thought for a moment. "Is it out?"

I nodded, hoping and praying it would be so.

Kumra walked to her daughter, her dress swooshing over the stones as it swept the floor. "Will she live?"

"Yes," I said, not because I knew so but in case Keela could hear me.

Kumra glanced toward the pile in the corner. "I will send some-one." She looked less imposing now, standing by her daughter's bed in the middle of the sour-smelling room.

"May I ask for Onra?" I snapped my mouth shut with the last word, stunned by my own impudence.

Kumra narrowed her eyes, and I rushed on before she had a chance to come up with a punishment for my brazenness. "She helped me with my forehead when I first arrived. She is good with the sick, and she is strong. I might need to change the bed again."

Kumra looked at her daughter one more time and left without a word. I sagged against the wall with relief but found no time to rest. Keela began thrashing again, and it required all my strength and atten-tion to keep her from falling from the bed.

———

The time of the midday meal had passed when Onra finally came with a jar of fresh water and a bowl of cheese and bread from the kitchen. She looked thinner than I remembered and would not meet my eyes.

I set the bowl on the floor while she refilled Keela's jug. When she finished, I reached for her hand to still her, unsure whether she would want me to ask about what had happened to her.

"I wish we were still together in Maiden Hall," I said.

She looked up at last but said nothing.

"You did not cry." I wanted to put some honor into all that was dishonorable.

She shook her head, and her short hair swayed listlessly around her hollow cheeks.

"It must be nice to be back with your family." For my own sake as much as for hers, I needed to find something good in all that had happened.

"Mother says now that I am a woman, I will have a family of my own soon," she spoke finally. "Children would be good." Her lips stretched into a sad smile. "But so would be never seeing another man."

She watched Keela while I ran out to the latrines, but she left as soon as I returned, not daring to linger. Before she rushed off, I asked her for some goat milk for Keela, hoping we would get another chance to talk. But when the small jar of goat milk came, Igril delivered it with stars in her eyes as she walked through the splendor of Pleasure Hall.

Her lips pressed into a thin line as she handed me the jar without a word, clearly displeased that I should be assigned a task there while she had to work outside. She left the chamber in a huff, but I heard her respectful greetings to the concubines on her way out.

I forced some of the milk down Keela's throat, then waited.

She did not wake for another day, and then only to tell me she would have me beaten as soon as she felt well enough to watch. She remembered my fingers down her throat.

I cared for her as best I could, aware that each passing day brought closer Tahar's return, after which escape would be impossible.

In the mornings, I rose early and waited for Kumra to leave to issue the day's orders to the maidens. Keela slept a lot, oblivious to the noises of Pleasure Hall outside her chamber. She recovered a little more each day, so I had to act fast, for I did not know how much longer I would be required by her side.

I crept into Kumra's chamber, jumping at the slightest noise. She had several chests full of garments and cloth still on the bolt in every color of the rainbow.

With trembling fingers, I searched through her treasures, listening for any noise outside. Thrice footsteps chased me back to Keela's chamber, but they passed each time. At last I found a length of cloth suitable for a healer's veil and not so fancy that it would be Kumra's favorite and she would miss it too soon.

I wrapped the silk around my belly under my clothes, then tucked my tunic carefully back into place. As soon as I could leave Pleasure Hall, I would go to Talmir for food—he had also promised to find a small flask for water—and keep on going until I reached the hills.

But as the days passed, I still had to spend my nights on a blanket tossed onto the cold floor in the corner of Keela's chamber. And as she fully recovered, her mood only grew darker.

"Do you know Rugir?" she asked one day.

I shook my head, and she huffed, her round face snapping into the icy expression her mother wore so well. "He is the bravest warrior in my father's House."

I nodded, unsure what she expected me to say.

"Before they left to battle, he promised to perform an act of such bravery that my father would gift him with his first concubine. He is going to ask for me." She hesitated. "My mother forbids it." Her face crumpled into misery then, and her shoulders sagged, making her look much younger than her age.

I wondered when Keela had the occasion to talk to Rugir. None who lived in Pleasure Hall were allowed to cross the threshold of Warrior Hall. And no man other than Tahar was permitted in Pleasure Hall except the sons of the concubines, and they only until the age of eight, when they were taken for training.

Perhaps Keela and Rugir had seen each other in the Great Hall. If so, then Rugir was already in Tahar's favor. Only his captains and a handful of his favorite warriors attended the feast, the Great Hall not being large enough to seat the whole of Tahar's army. The rest of the warriors ate at Warrior Hall or in the kitchen, or in their own hut if they had merited a concubine and had a family.

Of course, even with Rugir being a worthy warrior, Kumra probably wanted a better match. Another warlord, perhaps. "Is that why you drank the poison?"

Keela's lips parted, and I could see the denial on her tongue. But then she shrugged.

"Where did you find it?"

She slipped out of bed for the first time and walked to her mother's chamber on unsteady legs to point at the ceiling.

Near the holes that let in air and light, someone had secured a clever ledge of wood. On it stood a number of pottery bowls with various plants growing in them, some known to me, others not. The invention seemed both marvelous and horrifying.

Plants, healing and otherwise, were the gift of Dahru to her children. We sought them on sacred journeys, revered the glens that grew them, removed only as much as absolutely needed for immediate use and drying. To have all that so close nearby, ready at the moment of need, fresh… But surely it could not be right. Anger rose inside me. How dare she keep the gifts of Dahru captive?

Keela leaned toward me, her face drained. I reached for her arm and helped her back to bed so she could rest, which she did. By the time her mother came to see her, Keela felt well enough, so Kumra allowed me to leave her chamber to work in Tahar's Hall with the rest of the maidens.

My feet light with the promise of freedom, I flew down the long corridor but skirted his chambers and the Great Hall, and stole out the back door at once. Warriors came and went in the courtyard—more than had been left behind on guard duty.

"Is Tahar back?" I asked the first servant I came across, my good mood darkening.

"With the first of his warriors. The rest are on their way."

I wasted no time but sought out Talmir.

"How did you like Pleasure Hall?" He laid a thick slice of meat onto the flat stone slab in front of him and rubbed it with dry herbs and spices. He might not have had the healing knowledge some Shahala did, but herbs and spices sang to him. All who ate his food praised his dishes.

My stomach growled at the sights and smells of the feast being prepared. He pointed to a small wicker basket of fresh-baked biscuits. I thanked him for his kindness and snatched one, still warm from the oven, but did not bite into it.

I looked around to make sure no one lingered close enough to over-hear us. "Tahar is back. I cannot escape now. It is too late."

"They will go again soon. War is coming, worse than before. It is coming here."

I barely heard his words, so deafened I was by my own misery. "Here?" I asked at last when his words reached my awareness.

Our corner of the world had not seen large-scale war for a hundred years and for another hundred before that. Not since the Kadar had settled the lands to the north. The Island of Dahru stood well-protected.

"The Kerghi hordes have a new khan. He allied himself with Emperor Drakhar."

I bit into the flaky biscuit at last and sighed with pleasure as the rich flavor melted on my tongue.

"The Emperor who seeks to rule the world." I took a few more greedy bites, not worried in the least. Drakhar's armies had been invading since I remembered, and his father's armies before him.

But the Shahala and Kadar lands—mostly mountains and desert with narrow strips of arable land along the coastline—lacked the things that wars were fought over. Any invader would realize that as soon as they set foot here, and leave us alone. "What do the warriors say?"

Talmir winced as he shrugged. "They are ready for the fight as always. They do not realize whom they face."

The Kadar always stood ready to fight. A nation that lived from war would welcome it.

"How soon will the Kerghi come?" The upheaval might bring an opportunity to escape.

"Bad always comes too soon." Talmir used a fist-sized stone to pound herbs into the meat and make it tender. "Remember the Tezgin mercenaries I told you about? They captured me to heal some of their men wounded in a fight against the Kerghi." His voice grew somber. "Such wounds I have never seen."

"Maybe they will never reach the Middle Islands." Dahru was the largest of the Middle Islands, in the middle of Mirror Sea. The Outer Islands surrounded the sea, holding great kingdoms. Beyond them lay the ocean, raked by hardstorms, its treacherous waves impassable by ship. The lands that spread beyond the ocean could be reached only through the Gate.

"I better hurry," Talmir said. "Lord Tahar has guests."

He slid the meat into the brick oven, and I caught a smattering of dark stains on the back of his tunic. When he turned, I saw the pain on his face for the first time, although it must have been there all along, invisible only to me through my veil of small troubles.

"What happened?" My sharp cry drew glances from the other servants, so I lowered my voice. "Are you hurt?"

"Worry not about me, little sister."

"Let me help you."

He started to say no but then sat on a low stool in front of me and pulled up his tunic. His back had been beaten raw, the bloodied skin mangled to expose his muscles.

"Tahar wastes no time, does he?" My fingers trembled with rage as I reached for the phial that hung on the cord around my neck, hidden under my tattered tunic. "He only just arrived home. What could you have possibly done?"

"Not Tahar. Kumra. For sending her daughter food that made her sick."

I bit my lip as I cleaned his back with water, then dabbed the worst of his wounds with moonflower tears. They were no use against poison, so I could not help Keela with them, but the drops worked well on wounds, fighting off both the yellow pus that brought with it fever and the deadly blackening.

I used all I had to help Talmir, then, when no one watched, I unraveled from my body the fine fabric I had taken from Kumra and wrapped the cloth around Talmir's wounds and pulled his long tunic over it.

"Keep that from the eyes of others," I said, knowing I did not have to. "I will come back for it later."

"Thank you, little sister." He drew me to him and kissed me on the forehead as a father would his daughter. "You better hurry before they miss you." He handed me a tray of cold sweetmeats to take to Tahar's Hall, but I barely reached the kitchen door when I bumped into Igril.

"I'll take that." She set an empty jar at my feet and snatched the tray from me. "You fetch some water. And be quick with it."

I did not mind. She probably wanted to hurry back to Maiden Hall to ready herself for the feast. I preferred the walk to the creek even in the biting cold. After being cooped up in Keela's chamber for so long, I needed some fresh air.

The sun had set while I had been in the kitchen, the courtyard teeming with warriors now. I hurried along the crowded path that led to the end of the fields, impatient with the slow pace of the water carriers and the warriors heading to the creek to wash the grime of battle off their bodies.

Something wet touched my face, and I looked up as a sparkling speck of white dust floated by me. I stopped and watched in wonder as more and more snowflakes came floating out of the sky.

I had seen snow before, on the top of distant mountains. I knew it was cold and wet. Some Shahala—very few indeed—had gone that far and brought back strange tales. But the snow on the mountains looked like a solid white blanket the peaks drew over their shoulders. Here the snowflakes floated around me as fragile tiny stars, the gifts of the sky. I tried to catch them on my fingertip, but they melted too fast and would not allow any length of examination.

I dared not linger as I knew Kumra must be waiting for the water, so I strode forth in the snowfall, smiling with pleasure as a few stray flakes clung to my eyelashes. For the first time, I saw the beauty in the country of the Kadar, the buildings and fields that were slowly sprinkled with diamond dust, sparkling in the moonlight. I kept out of the way of the men and walked up-creek for fresh water.

The wind, blowing from the sea and carrying its salty tang, gained strength. I turned my face from its icy fingers as I thought about my escape and wondered how long I would have to wait before I could flee.

In every direction I looked, I saw Tahar's sentries in the moonlight, more than he had ever posted before. Perhaps Talmir had heard right and the enemy *was* coming.

A bush rustled to my left. I glanced that way but saw nothing. Probably the wind. I filled the jar and stepped onto the bank to turn toward the house when rough fingers closed around my ankle.

A warrior had been behind the bush, I realized too late. He yanked my feet from under me, and I fell onto the withered grass, the jar slipping from my hands, the water spilling.

"No!"

My shout of alarm brought three more warriors from farther down the creek.

Instead of helping me, they stood around laughing. They were not Tahar's men. They must have come with our visitor.

"A fine one you caught," one said and whistled.

Another added, "Hurry on or the food will be cold by the time we all get a turn."

The one that had me flashed a terrible grin. I ignored the pain of his hands biting into my flesh, screamed as I struggled, but could not match the man's strength. He ripped my clothes open in no time, baring me to the cold night and his friends' hungry gazes.

He untied the strip of leather that held together his leggings, which were made of much finer cloth than Tahar's warriors wore. The other men were dressed just like him, very strangely, I noticed as I tried to scramble away in vain.

Their swords hung from wide leather belts decorated richly with gold rather than left plain and dyed dark green as was the custom of Tahar's men. They wore taller boots, better made. I could see well enough the fur lining—as the men stood close to me.

I screamed again, but the brute above me paid no heed, his fetid breath choking me as he pressed his mouth to mine and bruised my lips. I shoved him with all the strength I possessed, ignoring the small stones that dug into my back and the man's weight that crushed my lungs.

Dread filled me, for I could see only one outcome, and its inevitability slowly crept into my limbs to paralyze them. I forced myself to fight on, but I could do little damage. He held me tightly.

"What is this about?" The commanding voice that cut through the night had the power to still the man.

The warrior's weight lifted from me as he stood to attention with the others.

I gulped air as I grabbed the tattered remains of my clothes and held them together while I scrambled backward, falling into the creek. The frigid water burned my skin and stole my breath. I tried to climb out on the other side but slipped and fell back in. My gaze fluttered in panic to the men.

The one who rescued me stood tall, the moonlight gliding off his light hair. Not as thickly built as the other warriors, he wore magnificent garments studded with gemstones the likes of which I had never seen before. He seemed young, only a few years older than I. But young or not, he was in charge, the warriors' attention on him as they waited for his command.

He had arrived just in time, and I thanked the spirits for him.

He looked me over as I finally managed to scramble out of the creek on the other side, dripping, shivering from the freezing water. I lifted my long braid that clearly marked me as a maiden. And I knew he understood, but from his annoyed shrug, I also knew he considered it beneath him to be involved in my plight.

"All this noise over a slave woman? Keep her quiet," he said as he walked away.

CHAPTER FIVE

(The Palace Guard)

"Hear that?" The warrior who had grabbed me before was wading through the water with large strides that gobbled up the distance between us.

The others stayed on the opposite bank, probably not wanting to ruin their boots, counting on their friend to bring me back.

"You be quiet," he murmured, as if trying to calm a skittish animal. "We will not harm you, girl. But a man is due some entertainment after a hard battle."

In my head, I could hear my mother's warning: if a Shahala healer lost her maidenhead before gaining her powers, those powers would never come to her but would be lost forever.

"I am a maiden. It is forbidden," I pleaded as I leaped to run, stumbling on the uneven ground.

He reached me all too quickly.

"Nothing is forbidden to the Palace Guard." He bent my arm back roughly as he pawed my breast and crushed my lips under his foul breath once again.

The Palace Guard. The man who commanded them must have been the High Lord of the Kadar.

"A pretty one like you." The one on me grunted into my mouth. "Time you learn to please a man."

I tasted my own blood and fought hard as if for my life. I swore he would have to take my very breath before he could take the gift from me that I considered precious above everything.

He knocked me to the frozen ground and held me with one hand, pushing down his leggings with the other until I felt his naked skin against mine and his manly weapon poking hard into my thigh.

I went still with fear, which he must have taken as submission because he relaxed his hold and lifted his body to push my legs apart. But I jerked my knees up, and when he fell with a groan beside me, I broke away and ran toward Tahar's men and the sentries. At least they respected the customs of their own land, and I knew they would not harm a maiden.

Over the rush of blood in my ears, I heard a man in the distance calling the Palace Guard to service, and I glanced back, my heart racing as fast as my feet, my lungs struggling for air.

The men cursed after me but responded to the call and lumbered off toward the buildings. Still, I feared they were not finished with me yet, and decided to take great care to avoid the Palace Guard in the future, avoid everything that had to do with the cruel High Lord of the Kadar who had denied me his mercy.

I hoped his visit with us would be short and the spirits would give me the cunning to successfully evade his men. I despised the Palace Guard for thinking themselves above the laws of their own land, but despised their High Lord more for allowing it to be so. Any of the Shahala Elders would have given their lives to protect the smallest of our people.

The leaders of a nation set the example for the rest. With a High Lord such as the Kadar's, no wonder the rest of his people were brutal, thinking nothing of the pain of others. Behind the High Lord's fair face hid a dark spirit. He had shown his true heart, and I knew I would never forget it.

I ran through the night without my jar, over the trampled snow, barely noticing the falling crystal flakes that had forever lost their magic for me.

I hoped to slip into Maiden Hall unnoticed and repair my clothes before anyone saw me, but when I reached the large room, Kumra waited in the middle, ready to lead the maidens to the feast.

She charged at me as soon as I entered. "What have you done?"

"The Palace Guard—" Holding my wet clothes together as best I could, I cast my gaze to the floor, unable to finish.

She hit me hard across the face, splitting my lip further. Not long before, a blow like that would have sent me sprawling on the floor, but I had grown stronger of late. I stood my ground before her.

"How dare you even speak to the Palace Guard?" She hit me again, backhanded this time, harder, angrier.

Blood trickled down my chin.

"You will stay here. I shall decide what to do with you in the morning." She turned and led the girls from the hall, the set of her shoulders stiff and angry.

"She hates you because you are more beautiful than she is," Lenya whispered as she passed by, flashing an encouraging smile.

I looked after her, stunned. Nobody outshone Kumra in beauty. But I understood that Lenya perhaps sought to comfort me, so I did not open my mouth to deny her kind words, for it would have been like throwing a gift back into the gift giver's face.

I sat on my cot, not minding at all that I would miss the feast, only wishing I had something to eat. I rubbed my wrists where the warrior's rough grip bruised the flesh, and thanked the spirits that I had been able to escape with such minor injuries.

Hungry and shaken, I lay down, hoping for some rest before the girls returned—a smart idea, as I could find no sleep after they filed back into Maiden Hall.

They had plenty to say about the powerful stranger, disappointed that he had not chosen any of them. He was not the High Lord after all, but Lord Gilrem, the High Lord's brother, traveling with some of the Palace Guard.

Guests of the House of Tahar could freely choose from any of the slave women, but a guest of such honor would have been given a maiden for the night as befitting his status—a gift Lord Gilrem had declined. Igril seemed the most disappointed, nearly crying for the missed opportunity. She assured us a hundred times that Lord Gilrem would have asked to keep her.

"Imagine," she moaned the word, pressing her hands to her chest, "going back with the High Lord's brother to live in Karamur."

She went on and on about the High Lord's fortress city until we all wished she *had* been chosen and kept, just so she would be gone from among us and peace could return.

———

Morning arrived too soon, as always. I winced as I jumped to stand with the other girls at Kumra's entrance.

If I had thought saving her daughter would earn her favor, this morning thoroughly disabused me of that notion. She issued her orders maiden by maiden, leaving me last. I held my breath, for I knew she always reserved the worst chores for those she wished to punish.

I expected her to order me to the latrines or to the creek to wash the entrails of the animals slaughtered for the previous night's feast. The kitchen servants had saved them to be made into strings for the warriors' bows.

But Kumra issued no order. Instead she waited, and soon five slave women hurried into our hall, each old enough to be my mother.

"Lie down."

Cold filled my chest as I looked from woman to woman, but I did as Kumra ordered.

Four of the women descended on me, one holding each limb, my legs and arms spread as I struggled against them. "What are you doing to me?"

"Quiet." Kumra bent and snatched away the blanket I had

wrapped around my body for a makeshift covering, since my clothes had been torn beyond repair.

The fifth slave woman settled between my legs, and I panicked then and fought as hard as I could, but their bony hands bit into my wrists and ankles, still sore from the day before. They were stronger than me, toughened by their labors, hardened by their fear of Kumra.

The woman between my legs slapped my thigh hard to still me, but my fear grew too great to do anything but thrash against my restrainers, like a wild animal against the snare. I no longer cared for what punishment Kumra would mete out for refusing to follow her orders. I cared about nothing but escaping from my bonds and the unknown violence I sensed coming.

I felt the woman's fingers on me, then a quick jab, and she was searching my opening. I howled like a rabbit in the snare.

She withdrew almost immediately. "Untouched," she said, and the others released me.

I curled up on the floor and pulled the blanket to cover my body as humiliation washed over me. Hatred, like diseased marrow, filled my bones. I knew my mother would not approve, but still I shook with it.

Kumra stood over me for a few more moments before she turned to leave.

The women followed her out to the courtyard, but one came back a while later with clothes. I put on the worn Kadar garments, a long linen under-tunic and a straight wool dress that fell to my ankles, both roughly woven and scratchy. They were warmer than my Shahala thudi and tunic had been, so I set my dislike aside. I would need warm clothes for my escape.

I kept the torn pieces of my own ruined clothes, stuffed under my cot, grateful when the servant did not demand them. I planned to salvage enough of the thudi to wear under the Kadar clothes, as I did not think I could ever grow comfortable with their custom of being naked underneath.

The woman sent me to work in Tahar's Hall, and I hurried on, for I feared Kumra might change her mind about me and devise yet some other kind of torture.

At the Great Hall, I found Lenya transforming two old storage rooms into suitable quarters for Lord Gilrem, the High Lord's brother. He had slept in Warrior Hall with his guards the night before, but hospitality called for better accommodations for a guest of such high honor.

The smaller storeroom in the back would be his, while his guards would sleep in the larger antechamber. The servants had already cleaned both chambers and brought in suitable furniture. Lenya and I had to arrange everything and lay the pelts on the bed.

I worked as fast as I ever had, even though Lenya told me Gilrem and the Palace Guard were inspecting the harbor that day. Still, every time I heard a noise I jumped, scared that the men had returned to find us in their quarters. I prayed they would be gone from the House of Tahar soon, as far as their legs could carry them.

The spirits took pity on me and answered my prayers, not by granting my wish but by saving me in their own way as they often did. The following day, the last of Tahar's warriors arrived home from the distant battlefield: the wounded and the dead, and those who carried them home.

By Tahar's special allowance, I moved to Warrior Hall to care for the sick and stayed there for many days, sleeping what little I could between the cots for those brief moments when nobody cried out in need. The old bald-eyed steward of the house came with me to guard my honor, which he did, ever so sullenly, helping with absolutely nothing.

I did not attend the funerals but heard the wailing of the women, and Onra told me some things when she brought water.

"The dead warriors were placed into a large hole in the ground on the other side of the creek, together in battle formation, ready to fight for glory in the spirit world," she said with full approval.

"Alongside the dead, the servants buried food enough for the journey and exact copies of their weapons carved from the sacred wood of garon trees. Gifts for Rorin, the Kadar god of war, filled the grave so he would give warm welcome to the fallen."

On that day, and for many days after, I had little time to leave Warrior Hall for other than the basic necessities and knew little of the outside world save what Onra told me when she stopped in now and then. I did not mind the seclusion. Even with the steward forever at my elbow, I had more freedom than at Maiden Hall under Kumra's ever-watchful eyes.

The warriors treated me with respect and kindness. Most were young men who had not distinguished themselves in battle enough to be awarded the honor of their first concubine. They shared the hall with the boys who were still in training. The seasoned warriors who had families had their own huts along the fields.

Talk at Warrior Hall centered around young women, not a man there who did not have one picked out to ask for, should Tahar be willing. I enjoyed the free-spirited exchanges and the teasing among the men, the dares and playful competitions.

They hardly seemed the monsters I had once thought them to be. They helped me care for the sick, and I was even allowed to go as far as the foothills to gather herbs, with two warriors and the steward, who walked uneasily and hated me for the journey.

The boys would gather around me in the evenings and listen to the tales I told the injured whose spirits still lingered between the other world and ours. Sons of warriors were taken into training at the age of eight and sent into their first battle at fourteen. The youngest at Warrior Hall still missed their mothers, although none would have admitted it. They all put up a brave front for honor.

I indulged the boys with new tales night after night, recounting all the legends I knew, even the history of my people. The steward usually slept through this, his robust snoring providing the background music.

"The Shahala come from nine tribes: the Roosha, the Torno, the Shelba, the Mortir, the Zetra, the Fertig, the Lormen, the Tuzgi, and the Pirta, each named after the founding father." I recounted how they had lived on a large, faraway island inhabited by many nations.

"But some of those nations were evil and committed such atrocious acts as to anger the spirits beyond forgiveness," I said, and the boys listened.

"And the spirits brought the stars down from the sky and destroyed the island. Only the Shahala escaped, for they were closest to the island's only Gate and were favored by the spirits as they did not follow the ways of evil. Thus our people came to Dahru and vowed forever to live the one right way, and shun the ways of greed, and violence, and all immoral acts."

I did not mention that the Shahala had come to the island before the Kadar, for it was a matter of contention between our peoples. "They swore a solemn oath to help all living creatures and destroy none, and over the centuries, among them were born some legendary healers."

"Like you?" one of the boys asked. They seemed much impressed by my work with the wounded.

"Not me, but my mother. She even healed the old High Lord, the one who ruled before Batumar."

"Barmorid," said another boy. They could all name every High Lord back to the beginning of Kadar history.

I stood, but they begged me for another tale. And looking at their eager faces, I could not deny them.

"In the beginning, there was nothing." I began the story, and they immediately quieted again. "And in this nothing, the Great Mother floated. To ease her loneliness, she gave birth to the planets and the stars. They floated from her body and scattered across the universe. Tired she was from her labors and slept for the first time. And when she slept, she dreamed. She dreamed of plants and animals and people, nations and races. And when she woke, she saw that all she dreamed came into being. But as time passed, all she created did not please her, for her creations lacked spirit. So like a mighty wind, she rose and swept through all there is. And all who breathed her gained spirit, until the last of her was gone into the last of her creation."

The boys thought that a strange tale and asked for more, but I ignored their pleading and sent them off to bed. Morning training came early.

I spent most of the nights checking on my patients, sleeping little. I could always find something to be done. I sought to make up for the lack of my healing powers by doing everything else as well as I knew how.

The days passed very much the same, and long before the last wound was closed, I picked the creek empty of ninga beetles. I wished

I had some moonflower tears, but numaba trees did not grow in the colder land of the Kadar.

I cleansed the wounds thoroughly with boiled then cooled water, made sure to open the windows every day for fresh air. I asked Talmir to cook the kind of food that strengthened the blood: kiltari liver, whuchu greens, shugone nuts baked into bread.

In those cases where infection had already set in by the time the warrior reached home, I treated the wound with maggots. Talmir gifted me with strips of raw meat that I left in the sunniest corner of the courtyard for a few days. After a couple of winter flies found it, which did not take long, and the maggots grew to the right size, I picked them off with my fingernails and placed them in a small jar, then rinsed them, careful not to kill any.

I placed them into the infected wounds and bandaged over them, but not so tightly that they couldn't breathe. I looked at them daily and changed the bandage that soaked up the pink frothy fluids the maggots produced as they worked.

They ate away the pus and rotting flesh, until after several days I could finally remove them, easier to handle by then as they had grown fatter. The wound, good living flesh, I cleansed once again and treated with an herbal poultice that warded off further infection.

All through this I talked to the sick, talked day and night, about fine feasts and fine battles they would have after they recovered, the beautiful young women who waited, and the strong sons they would have with them. I talked until my stories became so familiar it was as if they had already happened.

The spirits stayed with us, and not one man died, although I cannot claim credit. The severely injured had not survived the long trip from the battlefield. But the warriors were grateful all the same and chose to think their recovery was a result of my healing.

They believed it with such ferocious certainty I could do nothing to disabuse them of the notion. Maybe they wanted to believe so much because the thought that someone had that kind of power, someone who could heal them again, made going into the next battle easier.

By the time the last of the injured healed enough for me to assume my regular duties, most of the Palace Guard had returned to their High Lord's fortress city on Lord Gilrem's order.

Lord Gilrem remained with four of his personal guards. But they must have brought some deadly malady with them from wherever they had come, because soon his men fell ill with a disease that attacked their innards and hemorrhaged their life force away. Kumra did not send me to them. She feared that their disease might spread, so she had them isolated in an unused hut at the end of the fields.

Lord Gilrem fell into a dark mood, grieving his loyal men. He stayed behind when Tahar left with a group of his warriors to inspect the borders of the territory he protected. Some of the servants whispered that Lord Gilrem had taken ill, too, and I feared Kumra would send for me to heal him. The High Lord's brother could not be simply carried out to some crumbling hut and left to die alone. But what could I do to help him? And if I couldn't... I knew Kumra would be vicious had she found any shortcomings in me.

Then Kumra did order me to Lord Gilrem's side, but not to heal the man. She had a darker purpose.

She held me back in the morning, after the other girls had left to do her bidding. I followed as she led me to Tahar's Hall. Dread wrapped around my face tighter than a healer's veil.

She led me to the larger chamber where the Palace Guard had stayed previously. Now only one cot remained.

"This will be your place."

I felt the blood drain out of my face.

"Lord Gilrem feels poorly. Not the same disease that had taken his guard, praise Rorin and the goddesses. It's but some temporary weakness. Even so, he shows favor to my daughter," Kumra said, and for the first time since I had known her, her words filled me with relief. "You will be here day and night to care for them."

She pulled two glass phials, one white, one black, from the folds of her dress. She handed me the white one. "For Keela. I want to make sure she conceives a male child."

I nodded, having heard of such potions, although the Shahala would not have dreamed of trying to influence the spirits in such a way.

She handed me the second phial, and I nearly dropped it. The cold glass seemed to burn my skin.

"For Lord Gilrem. One drop in every cup he drinks. I can do this much for them, but no more. You will do the rest."

I looked at her bewildered, for truly I did not understand what she expected of me.

"Lord Gilrem will leave when Tahar returns at the next moon crossing." Her sharp eyes narrowed. "If Keela is with child, I will ask Tahar for a favor. He has never denied me yet. I will ask for your freedom."

My heart leaped with joy. For such a price, I would have done anything. If only I understood what she wanted from me.

"But if Lord Gilrem leaves before planting his seed in my daughter, you will be chosen for Tahar at the feast. And after that, the warriors… I would not be surprised if they all had you. Especially if they thought your healer's blood made them invincible."

She said this without the slightest malice in her voice, as if she were telling me what foods she had asked Talmir to prepare for the evening meal. And then she turned on the wooden heels of her jeweled slippers and left me to think about her words.

That veil of dread returned and tightened around my face until I could scarcely breathe. Did she fathom I had powers such as to create new life in the womb? Not even the best of the Shahala healers had the ability, not even my mother.

I paced the outer chamber, not daring to disturb the couple in the smaller one as I contemplated my sorry fate.

Soon Lenya brought a tray of food but could not stay to talk under strict orders from Kumra. I decided I would have to go to Keela and Gilrem at last, for they might have been waiting for the meal. So I called Keela's name loudly, and when she bid me to enter, I carried the food in.

Since I had set up the room with Lenya, a great transformation had taken place. Soft pelts covered the floor; embroidered pictures of silk hung on the walls, showing men hunting and women bathing in enchanted pools. Satin pillows lay piled high on the bed.

Keela stood in the corner by a large chest and sorted through a pile of elaborate dresses, some of which I knew to be her mother's.

"I heard you will be helping us." She tossed the dresses aside.

I set the tray on the carved bedside table and added a drop from the white phial to Keela's cup. She came and drank it at once.

Lord Gilrem lay upon the bed, his tunic removed, wearing only his leggings. He hummed a lifeless note, himself as listless as the song, as if his strength had been drained.

"He feels poorly." Keela picked at the food without sitting. "Mother has been giving him something to help him recover, but I do not think it works. Maybe you can do better."

I stepped closer and looked into his vacant eyes. He did not seem to recognize me. I did not expect him to. He had last seen me in the dark, from some distance away.

I placed my hand in the middle of his chest to touch the rhythm of the life within. *Slower than it should be.* His body was awake, but his spirit was sleeping. I knew of only one thing that would make a person so: the juice of the lantaya.

I had seen such a man once before, brought to my mother by his family, he himself not even aware of his illness, protesting. People who drank of the lantaya were like that. No herb would cure such a person, for herbs went into the stomach to diffuse into the body. The lantaya juice did not go into a person's stomach. It went into his head and his heart and filled them up until no room for his spirit remained.

Only a very strong spirit could have fought against such a curse, but those whose hearts and minds had been so corrupted tended to lose their spirit.

My mother had talked to that man's spirit for many days and nights. The lantaya did not like what she was saying. It fought against her and against the man, nearly killing him before he recovered.

When he left, my mother gave him a mirror to look into every morning. She told him the day he no longer recognized the man in the mirror, it meant the lantaya had come back to take him again. For that was the worst thing about the lantaya—it took people in such a treacherous way, they were unaware that it had their heart. So my mother gave that man the mirror so he could see through his own eyes into his own heart and know who owned it.

But even that failed. Sometime later, we heard from a visitor that after the man had returned home, the lantaya grew strong in him again. He broke the mirror and left his family so they would not make him fight against the curse.

I prayed to the spirits for Lord Gilrem and put a drop from the black phial into his cup, then lifted it to his lips, hoping Kumra had some strong medicine.

I repeated this for many days with each meal while snow storms raged outside. At times, the wind blew so fiercely that I could not walk even to the latrines and had to bring a bucket into my chamber.

I cleaned the inner room every morning and did whatever other task Keela demanded. Mostly I listened to her talk, as she took to coming to my chamber to spend the time while Gilrem slept through most of the day.

"Can you make him better?" she would ask each time.

I begged the spirits with fervor for Lord Gilrem's recovery and the blessing of a child. My freedom depended on it.

"Let us pray for Rorin's favor," I would say. "And the blessing of the goddesses."

The Kadar disliked mention of the Shahala spirits. They believed in their god of war ferociously. The warriors prayed only to him, while the women prayed both to Rorin and to his many concubines, the goddesses.

Keela would sigh as she sat next to me on my pallet, then recite her prayers.

"At least he stopped talking about leaving. I could not live if he left without me. I love him," she said one day and flushed at the confession.

"What of Rugir?"

A moment of uncertainty crossed her face before she responded. "Mother was right. He is beneath my station. I am the favorite daughter of Tahar."

I wondered if Tahar or her mother had told her that, or if she thought so because she had not yet been sent to another Lord's house.

She glanced toward the door. "Lord Gilrem loves me too. I see it in the way he looks at me. If only he had more strength."

I nodded. If Lord Gilrem's strength returned, he might yet fight off the lantaya and break free.

"I have been thinking," Keela said and cocked her head to the side. "Maybe his illness came from the manyinga."

"An herb?"

"His beast." She rolled her eyes as if I was too stupid to know anything. "All the Kadar used to have them back in the old days." She shuddered. "They are sure death to women."

"They eat women?" I recoiled at the thought of Lord Gilrem possessing such beasts and letting them do as they pleased.

Keela laughed at me. "Of course not. They draw your life through your blood."

I must have looked stunned at this revelation, for she continued to explain. "When the Kadar came to Dahru, they brought with them many manyinga. The beasts were peaceful then. But this land did not like them, and little by little the great herd lessened. Not many remain now. They are all at Karamur, in the High Lord's service."

"You think one might have bitten Lord Gilrem?" If his troubles came from some unknown venom and not the lantaya, there could be a cure.

Keela rolled her eyes at me. "They obey their warriors who ride them to battle. Gilrem probably rode one to Kaharta Reh."

I grew even more alarmed at the thought of such a beast at the House of Tahar and wondered where it must be hidden. But as Keela went on, she allayed my fears.

"It is probably at the High Lord's stables at the port."

"How could it hurt Lord Gilrem, then?" He had not appeared sick upon his arrival.

"The manyinga can draw a man's spirit out of his body through his blood. The warriors ride the manyinga into battle, to crush the wounded enemy beneath their mighty feet and soak up their spirits from their spilled blood. Women never ride them. Should you have your womanly flow, the beasts could suck your spirit right out of your body through it. No woman would even touch a manyinga."

She rubbed between her fingers one of the many protective charms that hung from her belt.

I wondered what such fearsome beasts looked like. I had known many animals that could take away someone's life, but I had never heard of one that could take the spirit. "But would such a beast harm its own master?"

"I heard that as their numbers decrease, they grow more ill-tempered."

I tried to separate the truth from Kadar superstition, of which a good measure seeped into every story, especially tales told by Kadar women. They were wholly attached to their charms and other small rituals to ward off bad luck and ensure good fortune.

I wondered if the manyinga simply had their bad reputation because of their size and the fact that they fought in battle.

"Mother says if I am with child, Gilrem will take me with him for certain." Keela switched topic suddenly as if even talk of the beasts could bring us harm.

"He has many concubines, but none has given him a son. If I give him his first son, I will be the favorite in his Pleasure Hall, the mother of his heir, the mother of the High Lord's nephew. I do not seek it for myself, of course." She moved away as if regretting the familiarity. "It is your duty to help. My son will bring great honor to the House of Tahar."

She stayed with me and talked and talked about the glorious future and her part in it. Even when Lenya brought their evening meal, Keela kept me to listen to her instead of taking food in for Lord Gilrem. And when she finished talking, she insisted that I go to the servants and ask them to prepare a bath for her in her chamber.

Four slaves carried in the large wooden tub and worked hard to fill it. Then Keela ordered me to help her undress and wash her with the scented potions her mother had prepared. I sniffed and tested each, but they seemed to be harmless waters of vanity, scented with the essence of flowers.

My fingers turned numb by the time I freed her elaborate braids secured in place by small metal clips and held up by the grease of having gone unwashed for many days. Their creation required much effort and time, so some concubines were reluctant to undo them for the mere sake of cleanliness. I worked soaproot paste into her long tresses, then rinsed them, repeating the task many times.

At home, it had been my custom to wash every day in the creek that ran down our hillside. A healer should always have a clean spirit and a clean body, a lesson my mother had taught me well. The Shahala valued cleanliness as one person's courtesy to the other.

The Kadar paid less attention to such things, and I wondered if their cold northern land had something to do with it. Maybe they were reluctant to bare their bodies to the chill. But Keela did not have to worry about that, for a strong fire burned in the brazier and filled the room with warmth.

Half the night had passed by the time I could feed Lord Gilrem and give his medicine to him. He grabbed my wrist as I lifted the cup to his lips. I did not expect such strength from him, so I looked up, into red-rimmed eyes that seemed more awake than I had seen them in a long time.

He too smelled in need of a bath, but I did not dare risk offending him by offering. He surprised me by opening his parched lips for a whisper, his voice so hoarse with effort I barely understood him.

"Help me."

CHAPTER SIX

(Lord Gilrem)

I pried off Lord Gilrem's fingers from my wrist, sloshing some of his drink before I could pour the rest into his mouth. He choked and sputtered it all over the pillow. I wiped his chin and switched pillows to make him more comfortable.

"Will he be better soon?" Keela asked, sitting on the wooden chest in the corner, combing her hair. "I wish he would laugh and talk again like before. He sleeps so much now. Except when I lie next to him and do what Mother told me." She sighed. "You would not know about such things."

I did want to know what her mother had taught her, but I dared not ask. The matter of lying with a man had been discussed at length at Maiden Hall, but the chatter had done nothing save confuse me.

Some of the girls claimed to know more than others, but their tales grew too outrageous to be believed. My mother's explanation made the most sense, although even about that, I had some doubts.

I understood that after a girl became a woman, a man might ask her to become his wife. And if that man wanted to, he could put his manpart into that woman's secret cave, and that manpart would leave a seed.

If the spirits favored their union, they would make the seed grow into a babe. And the babe grew until it outgrew the cave, and then it crawled out.

But my mother had said nothing about the blood I had seen smeared on Onra's thighs, nor the pain in her eyes. Tahar's manpart must have done something awful in Onra's secret cave.

Yet Keela seemed happy about such things. I wished my mother still lived so she could have taught me more. I thought I might ask Onra the next time I saw her. But what happened the following morning pushed those questions from my mind.

When I brought Lord Gilrem's medicine to him, he pressed his lips together and knocked the cup from my hand.

"Poison," he whispered.

Keela had gone to the latrines as the weather had turned milder for the day. Gilrem had been using the pot under the bed in good weather and bad, sometimes with my help.

"No poison here, my lord."

He ate the same food from the same tray as Keela, and I poured his water from the same jar as I had for Keela and myself.

"The lantaya made your spirit weak," I told him. "You must drink Kumra's medicine."

He turned his head in refusal, and I let him be this once. For all the days I had been giving him Kumra's potion, he had not improved any. *Neither had he gotten worse*, I thought then, and hesitated.

What if the contents of the black phial had kept him alive? So I made a new drink, but when he refused to open his lips, I did not force him. A healer sometimes had to let the sick choose their own fate.

At the midday meal, he waited once again until Keela left the chamber, then begged me, with more force this time, to bring him only water. Same at the evening meal.

The following morning after Keela had gone outside, Lord Gilrem sidled out of bed and shuffled to the water jar, dipped in his cup and drank it empty. Surprised by his show of strength, I stared as water ran down his chin.

The spirits be praised, his malady was leaving him at last. I hurried out of the chamber to share the good news with Keela at once.

"I need your services, girl." Lord Gilrem's rusty voice stopped me at the door.

His efforts brought color to his face, and he looked better than he had for many days, although I could see the trembling in his muscles.

"What are you in need of, Lord Gilrem?" The breakfast tray had been taken, but I could run to the kitchen and bring him almost anything he wanted.

"I must break free."

"Free, my lord?" From the lantaya? Only the man's own spirit could help him with that.

"Away from here."

"But, my lord, you are free to leave any time you want. You can walk out the gate." I snapped my mouth shut as I remembered what Kumra had said would happen to me if Lord Gilrem left before Keela conceived. "But you are too weak to travel. You must stay a little longer."

He shook his head. "The longer I stay, the weaker I grow. If I do not leave now, I might never leave again." His eyes, still somewhat clouded, held much desperation but resolve as well. He stepped toward me. "Where is the medicine?"

I held out the black phial. My heart seemed to stop as he opened it and emptied it into the pot under the bed. I could do nothing to save a drop.

"Lord Gilrem—"

"Ten crystals, girl," he said, "for not telling anyone I am better. For helping me away from here."

Strange how sometimes we cannot see things simply because we do not expect to see them. Even after living among the Kadar all that time, I was still not used to looking for deceit behind their words. But at that moment, I finally understood everything.

Kumra had been giving him the lantaya, or some other herb like it, to rob him of his spirit so he would do her will.

"Twenty blue crystals." Lord Gilrem upped the price.

I could not comprehend such a sum, more than I had been sold for. A wave of cold resentment rose in my heart. The Kadar stole my life and turned me into a slave. Lord Gilrem himself could not be bothered to stay the hands of his warriors when they had been upon me. He had left me to his men at the creek.

Why should I help him?

Because he needs my help, the answer came swiftly.

But if I helped him, I would seal my own fate. When he left, Kumra would have her revenge upon me. On the other hand, if Lord Gilrem stayed and Keela birthed a son, I would be set free.

Maybe she was with child already. Being her first, she might not notice right away. I resolved to start watching her more closely.

"I order you to help me," Gilrem snapped, even as he collapsed onto the bed.

I hesitated. Maybe he was as much a prisoner as I. But he did not have to work. Nobody beat him. All he had to do was stay in his chamber and put seeds into Keela's secret cave. Was it a fate so terrible that I should die for helping him?

And I *would* die if I defied Kumra in this, of that I was sure, whether by poison or beating.

I would have died for a number of people without another thought. My people. Or Onra, even though she was a foreigner. But not for a dark-hearted Kadar lord.

"I cannot help you, my lord. Forgive me," I said, then ran away.

———

I dreamed a strange dream that night. In my dream, *my* heart and mind were filled with lantaya, not Lord Gilrem's. The juice ran dark, the same color as the phial that held it. The lantaya rose up within me like the tide and drowned the spirit my mother had breathed into me at my birthing.

I woke with a fright. I reached under my tunic to clutch the empty moonflower phial between my fingers, as I searched my clamoring heart and mind to make sure my spirit was still within me.

I did not have much time to think about my dream. Keela woke soon and needed my service in the inner chamber.

"Which one?" She wore only her under tunic of fine linen, several dresses on the floor before her.

Her belly did not seem to have grown. Nor did her breasts look swollen the least. Disappointment settled on my shoulders.

"The golden?" The color looked particularly nice on her, the tight bodice and billowing skirt especially slimming. Blue silk trimmed the fine damask, the rich cloth embroidered with pearls and enamel.

She kicked the dress away. "It makes me look pallid."

"The green, then? The color matches your eyes." Elaborate flower patterns had been woven into the light wool, the cuff and hem decorated with a thin strip of silky fur.

She thought for a short while before shaking her head. "The crimson." She pointed to the silk dress embroidered in gold. "Red is Yullin's favorite color."

I had forgotten all about the upcoming holy day of Yullin, one of the war god Rorin's many goddesses. Kadar women believed the warm wind, which would soon come to melt the snow and start the new season of planting, was the hot breath of Yullin as she sighed in pleasure in Rorin's bed.

The goddess Yullin watched over all growing things, beginnings, and fertility. Keela seemed especially eager to attend the day's sacrifices and offerings.

The outer door to my chamber creaked open—probably one of the maidens bringing the tray. It would be some kind of cooked small grain that represented plenty, and chicken or pork. Chickens scratched good luck from the dirt, while swine rooted it up. Kadar custom forbade the eating of fish or any flying bird on a holy day, as fish could swim away with someone's good fortune and the birds would fly away with it.

"Shall I bring in your morning meal?" I asked Keela as I shook the slight wrinkles from the red gown, the fine silk hissing. A faint scent of perfume rose from the material.

"Not yet. Assist me first."

I helped her dress, then restored her hair to its proper splendor, tucking in a thin braid here and there that had come undone during the night. All through this, Lord Gilrem lay motionless on the bed, his eyes fixed on the ceiling.

I brought in the tray and served Keela first as she demanded. She ate only a few bites, then left to join her mother. I carried the tray to Lord Gilrem, and he sat up to eat, consuming more food than I had ever seen him take.

Once again, he ordered me to aid his escape, offered crystals first, then threatened. Then he offered to take me with him and make me a valued concubine in his Pleasure Hall.

I left the room with the tray as soon as he finished his meal.

I ate some of the mangled leftovers while I waited for one of the maidens to fetch the tray. Kumra did not have separate meals sent for me, for Keela and Lord Gilrem left plenty each day. I was chewing on a piece of cold chicken when Onra sailed in.

"Kumra ordered that you should stay here all day to attend Lord Gilrem." She pressed her lips into a narrow line of exasperation.

I shrugged. "Yullin will not miss a Shahala woman."

"She will know you are not there, and she will withhold her favor from you for certain." Her expression darkened. "You must give me something of yours to place in the offering jar."

I looked about my person, more to please Onra than to garner favor with Yullin, but I had precious little to give. Other than my clothes, my only possession was my charm belt, five small charms hanging from it now, two given to me by Onra and Lenya each, the last one by Talmir's wife.

I untied that one, the bird symbol of my ancestors' tribe, and handed it to Onra. Maybe if I reminded the goddess that I was a Shahala, she would show mercy and send me back to my people.

Onra palmed the small carving with a nod of relief.

"I shall say many prayers for you," she promised, then rushed off so she wouldn't miss anything.

I had some peace then before Kumra stopped by after the ceremony, bringing melted snow consecrated by Yullin. She sprinkled the bed and Lord Gilrem in it. I could have told her about his plans of escape. I could have asked for more medicine and sneaked drops into his food unseen. I could have taken the water jar from the chamber so he would have been forced to drink whatever I brought him.

Those thoughts swirled in my mind as Kumra passed me with a narrow-eyed look on her way out. I said nothing. I had not promised my help to the man, but neither could I harm him.

Because I had a Shahala heart. And my mother's spirit.

I could see myself in those thoughts at last, as if in a mirror, and disliked what I saw. I had wanted, all my life, to be a daughter worthy of my mother, to become like her. Yet what would she think if she could see me now? Had I become like the self-serving Kadar I despised?

I had, I feared. I had been so sure I was ready for the spirits to bless me with true powers, yet I still behaved as a child.

A Shahala healer could not choose whom she helped. Who was I, barely a woman, to decide who was worthy? My duty was to help everyone as best I could with no questions asked. If I assisted Kumra with ensnaring Lord Gilrem, I would have gained my freedom, but I would have lost my spirit, a fate as bad as if the lantaya filled my heart and drowned it.

So I told Lord Gilrem I would help him, and poured water into the black phial, and at every meal, I dropped a drop in his cup in front of Keela. And every day he drank and pretended to be weak. But as soon as Keela left the chamber, he rose and walked around the room to stretch his limbs.

On the third day, after Keela had gone to visit the latrines and I knew Kumra would be at Maiden Hall assigning chores, I turned to Lord Gilrem. "My lord, the time is here."

At once he donned his short undertunic and doublet, wrapped his feet and pulled on his boots, then stood ready.

"The shortest way out is through the door that leads from Tahar's Hall to the street," I told him, remembering well the door through which I had walked into slavery. "The steward keeps it locked at all times, but he cannot refuse you exit."

Lord Gilrem shook his head. "We cannot waste time looking for the man."

He was right. Keela could return any moment, and the steward, one of the oldest men at the House of Tahar, oversaw many things from the spinning to the purchases that came in from the market.

"The War Gate, then." In my mind I mapped the path to the wide portal through which the warriors marched off to war and returned. "We shall have to cross the courtyard." Which would be busy this time of the day. "We will have to move fast." And pray that we would not be seen by Kumra or Keela.

"I stand ready." His eyes, almost completely clear now, glinted with determination. He was still but a shadow of the warrior prince I had first seen by the creek, but his richly embroidered golden doublet lent him stature, and the sword by his side gave an illusion of strength. The effort of getting fully dressed for the first time in a long time had put some color into his face.

I stuck my head out the door but saw only servants, so I rushed down the corridor, Lord Gilrem close behind me. I checked once again before we stepped out to the courtyard.

"We will go straight for the gate." We had to spend as little time in the open as possible.

But no sooner did the words leave my mouth than Kumra appeared at the door of Maiden Hall. We drew back and watched from the shadows as she marched to the kitchen.

I grabbed the phial hanging from my neck. Knowing this was my last chance, I whispered the question I had not dared ask before. "My mother was at Karamur some years back to heal the High Lord. Have you met her, my lord?"

"My brother is never sick. Must have been the High Lord before him." His shrug said he cared not about some foreign healer. "What now? We must be quick."

Disappointment brought a bitter taste to my tongue. "We must chance it."

We had to cross between the kitchen and Maiden Hall and pray that Kumra would not see.

Only a short distance separated the two buildings. We would be in the open the whole time, and Kumra could step from the kitchen at any moment. And Keela too could easily see us, on her way back from the latrines.

Could they stop him? They could call the guard and claim he was delirious from his illness, have him carried back to his chamber. He did look pale and weak. Kumra could force her potion on him and gain control of him again.

My gaze darted around the courtyard.

Lord Gilrem nudged me from behind.

"Keep your head down, my lord." I stepped away from the doorway.

We hurried through, paying little mind to the servants who bustled about. The air filled with their voices and the sound of hammer striking metal that came from behind Servant House, the blacksmith crafting more swords.

I could smell meat roasting in the kitchen as we neared, my heart beating faster when we came to the open door. Kumra, her back to us, threw one order after another at Talmir.

We sped our steps and came out behind the kitchen and Maiden Hall at last. I glanced briefly in the direction of the women's latrines. I did not see Keela. We hastened to the War Gate.

Lord Gilrem moved in front of me once we neared. "You best stay for now. The guards might question if I take a maiden who has not been given to me."

He strode through the gate without looking back. The guards stood at attention as he passed.

For the first time since we had stepped outside, I noticed the bite of the cold and shivered. Lord Gilrem turned toward the port and strode out of sight in a few steps. *Free.*

My throat burned with longing to be on the other side of that gate.

I *would* leave someday. *Run for the hills.*

A sudden gust of wind pushed against me. I blinked hard then hurried back to the guest quarters. By the time Keela returned, I was cleaning the inner chamber.

When she realized Lord Gilrem no longer lay among the tangled covers, her eyes widened in confusion. "Where did he go?"

I kept my head down. "He wished to leave."

A brittle, hard silence followed, the room growing cold around us. I glanced up at her face, distorted by hatred and outrage.

"You let him go?" She closed the distance between us and slapped me hard across the face, then flew out the door, wailing.

Running would have done me no good, so I stayed in place until, in a few moments, Kumra rushed in with Keela on her heels. She glanced around the room as if not believing her daughter, then grabbed me by my hair.

"You stupid murna. You will regret your disobedience." She spat the words into my face, the look of hatred that distorted her beautiful features identical to her daughter's. They had never looked more alike than at that moment.

Pain spread through my scalp. I pressed my lips together.

She did not let me go but instead dragged me outside, dragged me through the courtyard to the flogging post next to Servant House, and tied me herself.

She screamed for a warrior, but suddenly none seemed to be in sight. So she tore the whip from its peg on the side of the post and shoved it into the hands of one of the male servants who came around at the commotion.

"Whip her!"

The first strike did not hurt at once.

The pain was such a shock, a moment or two passed before my body caught up with it. But fast enough came the second and the third, and I felt my clothes rend first; then my skin split. My knees gave. Only the rope held me up, tearing my shoulders.

The whip kept coming.

Pain such as I had never felt before seared through my body. The courtyard swam before me. A few warriors gathered around, then more and more. I prayed to the spirits to allow me to faint. I thought of Igril's brother who had been beaten to death at this same post and wondered how long he had been able to bear the pain.

As my eyes rolled back in my head, I reached for the sweet oblivion of death, welcoming it.

"Stop!" Kumra's voice snapped from far away. "Cut her down. I want her conscious so she can fully appreciate the rest."

The rope suddenly gave, and I fell to the ground, scraping my face, the gravel under the thin layer of snow cutting my lip.

I did not feel cold. Flames danced on my back with unbearable heat. I could neither move nor see.

"She was found in shame, no longer a maiden," Kumra declared. "Any of you may have her as you please."

I forced my eyes open a slit. The hem of her crimson gown swept by my face, swirling in the powdery snow as she walked away, her charms jingling.

"Cut off her hair. All of it," she called back, probably to a servant woman. Then her hem disappeared.

I heard Onra's voice, pleading with the warriors. "Give her to us."

To my horror, she offered herself in exchange. I lay helpless, my lips unable to move to protest such sacrifice. But she pleaded in vain. Rough hands lifted me up, and the warriors carried me away.

CHAPTER SEVEN

(Batumar, High Lord of the Kadar)

I had no strength left to care about what would happen to me next—
the pain could scarcely grow worse. But the warriors did not hurt me.
They cared for me as if I was one of their own, as I had cared for them
in the past. They kept me safe at Warrior Hall, out of Kumra's reach.

I remained with them day after day, Talmir bringing soups from the
kitchen, made from tender kiltari liver and whuchu greens, and bread
too, baked with spicy shugone nuts. Onra stayed with me whenever
she could, and Lenya sent messages.

I healed fast, my mother's spirit working within me, and by the
next moon crossing, I stood ready.

I planned on sneaking away through the fields to the hills as soon
as the sun set, to give myself as much time as I could before they
discovered my absence in the morning. As much as the warriors liked
me, they would have to report a runaway slave or pay the heavy price
when accused of aiding my escape.

Only Onra and Talmir knew of my plan. I asked both to join me, but both chose to stay, Talmir for the sake of his wife and children, Onra for the sake of her mother.

Talmir brought me a small bundle, shoes of tough leather strips that would stand up to the rocks of the hills, a flask for water, and food. He returned the length of cloth I had given him, clean and beautiful as ever, ready to provide me with my disguise.

I could scarcely believe that Kumra had not missed it yet. A whole winter had passed since I had owned anything other than my ill-fitting Kadar dress. I could not fathom a life of such abundance that someone would not miss a possession of such beauty for so many days.

I catalogued my supplies as I catalogued my injuries—both would greatly influence the outcome of my escape. Itchy and new, the skin on my back still pulled as I moved, but I could walk without much pain. And I had to walk only as far as the next port. I could finish healing on the ship.

I would not sail home, not yet. I would journey to Karamur first to find my mother's grave and to find out how she had died exactly. As great a healer as she had been, as strong as the spirit had worked within her, I could not imagine her succumbing to a simple traveling illness. Now that I knew the Kadar better, I suspected foul play.

Onra popped in to bring me a handful of healing herbs at the last moment. I was tying them into my bundle after we had said our last tearful goodbye, when suddenly the horn sounded at the War Gate.

My whole world stilled, then restarted again with a great rush. The few warriors in the hall ran outside, and after a while I could make out some of the shouting in the courtyard, even through the sudden pounding in my ears.

"Lord Tahar returns!"

Fear locked my muscles in place until I realized that I need not worry about Lord Tahar's feast. I was no longer considered a maiden.

Warrior Hall had large windows with wooden shutters, unlike the small holes high up the wall at Maiden Hall and Pleasure Hall. I rushed to an open window so I could see the servants in the courtyard, running back and forth between the kitchen and the Great Hall as they prepared for the feast. Tahar had not sent a runner. He was arriving in a rush, wholly unexpected.

His arrival turned out not to be the only one nor the biggest surprise of the day. Soon the horn sounded for the second time. Unfamiliar warriors marched into the courtyard. Their long swords hung from wide leather belts elaborately decorated with gold.

The Palace Guard.

Had Lord Gilrem returned for vengeance? Would he remember me kindly? If he set me free…

But even as I stood in the window, I knew he would not help me. He had refused his aid when his warriors were upon me. He had not taken me with him when he had walked through the War Gate, even as he knew I would receive the punishment for his leaving. He had not given me the crystals he had promised for his freedom, not that I had expected them. To Gilrem I was a lowly slave woman, beneath his notice.

A couple of the Palace Guards headed straight for Warrior Hall, so I grabbed my bundle and slipped out the back door, held my breath as I ran behind the warriors' latrines, then kept my head down as I crossed the courtyard and hurried straight to the kitchen.

The weather had turned warmer in the past few days, the gift of Yullin, the servants said, but I was certain the favor came from the spirits. At least I would not freeze in the hills. As soon as night fell, I would slip away.

I found Talmir stuffing partridge with bits of bread and herbs, a whole row of them waiting for his attention. Steam rose from a pot nearby and filled the air with the scent of rosemary.

I pulled into a dark corner behind him. "I wish I had gone last night."

He tied the bird's legs with string and set it aside, then grabbed the next. "Wait until after the feast. There will be mead tonight enough, unmeasured, in honor of the High Lord Batumar. You can slip away while most of the warriors are asleep."

"The High Lord?" Unease settled into my limbs.

"He is preparing for the war, visiting the most important warlords of the land."

Let him visit. He had nothing to do with me. I had no time to waste on worrying about him. Instead, I asked again about the hill I had to scale, the villages, the harbor where I would have to find a ship willing to take me.

As I memorized every detail, a servant woman rushed by Talmir with a steaming pot of soup and scalded her wrist, crying out in pain. I rushed forward without thought.

Lenya stepped into the kitchen at the same time, two warriors behind her. The sad look on her face spoke to me before she ever opened her mouth. *I wish I had not found you.*

"We have been looking for you all over. The High Lord asked for you," she said aloud.

Run now! a small voice urged in my head; then I looked at the warriors. They might have ignored Kumra for my sake, but they would not disobey an order from Lord Tahar and their High Lord.

I glanced over my shoulder at the dark corner where my bundle waited, ready for the journey. *Kind spirits, do not desert me now.* I would leave this place no matter what I had to do.

Talmir nodded as if reading my thoughts.

I turned and followed Lenya, the warriors behind us, escorting us all the way to Maiden Hall's door.

Only Kumra waited for us inside, the maidens at the feast already. Her hair more elaborate than ever, she wore a gown of flowing peach silk embroidered with gold thread, cuffs and hem covered with black pearls. Yet I could no longer find beauty in her, for I knew the darkness of her heart.

Her eyes settled on my long braid, uncut despite her order. Rage simmered in her eyes as she tossed a bundle of clean clothes at me, servant's clothes but unsoiled and well-repaired. In silence, she watched me dress. Even when I turned, I felt her gaze on the skin of my back like I had felt the sting of the whip.

"You will come back to me. He will not keep you." Her voice dripped with hatred. "And if he does, know this: he has killed every woman he has ever chosen. All his concubines are dead."

A chill ran down my spine.

I followed her through the small door to Pleasure Hall and to Tahar's Great Hall from there, to Lord Tahar's table—the place I had sworn I would never stand as long as there remained breath within me.

Kumra bowed with grace, then backed away.

I kept my eyes cast to the stone floor.

"Is she the healer your warriors spoke of?" a deep, unfamiliar voice questioned.

"She is, my lord," Kumra said behind me.

"Tera." The voice called my name.

Since he had named me, I could lift my head and look upon his face.

He bore little resemblance to his fair-faced younger brother. He viewed me with a frown of displeasure, his narrowed eyes as black as obsidian, matching his heavy mane of hair. His rough-shaven face was as sharp-angled as cut rock. A hideous scar ran from the corner of his right eye to his chin, unbalancing the line of his lips.

I gaped, for among my people I had scarcely seen any with such a deformity. The best of our healers could heal even the worst wounds without a scar.

I knew I was staring, but he did not even blink. He let me look my fill.

He was the most fearsome man I had ever seen, and at last I dropped my gaze, only to have it catch on his enormous frame. His shoulders stretched wider in his plain black tunic than those of an average warrior in full battle armor. Power shimmered around him. When he spoke, the Great Hall listened, and all men within.

"A House is lucky to possess such a healer as she."

Lord Tahar replied at once. "She is yours, my lord, if you wish it."

So even the Kadar, or at least some of them, had manners. Among the Shahala, when an esteemed guest praised something, a courteous host would offer it to him. A courteous guest would thank the host and protest, indeed refuse.

But polite manners ended with Lord Tahar's offer, for the High Lord simply pointed behind him for me to sit. I stumbled forward as I reached to the cord around my neck and held tight the empty phial of moonflower tears, as a child might reach for the familiar comfort of his birthing blanket. At a feast, behind each warrior sat their concubines, but none sat behind Batumar. I sank onto one of the pillows, not too close but neither so far that I would give offense.

Kumra reclined gracefully behind Lord Tahar and shot me a look of cold fury, but I had bigger things than her to worry about. Had Tahar given me to the High Lord for the night or forever? Was I given as a healer or as a concubine?

I sat in the concubines' place. Surely not a good sign.

Resentment welled inside me, at Lord Tahar who had kept me as a slave and now gave me away like a measure of wheat, anger at the spirits who had abandoned me once more. I looked at the High Lord who would either take my body tonight or my freedom forever, or likely both, without a thought to my wishes.

I might have met him only that night, but I knew him all the same. He was a man who lived by his strength. He led his nation to war season after season. His people cared little about the ideals that were most important to mine. I had known his Palace Guard, and I had known his brother, and what I knew about them told me a lot about the High Lord. I had despised him before I ever set eyes on him, and now that he owned me, I despised him more.

The servants served the feast, tray after tray brought to the High Lord's table after the small offering on Rorin's stone altar. A servant woman stepped forth to sing, her bittersweet song of home and returning bringing tears to my eyes.

When she retreated, the oldest of Lord Tahar's captains rose from the table to entertain the High Lord with gory battle tales. He spent much time on bragging about the number of enemy killed and the fierceness of the Kadar.

His eyes sparkled with excitement, his arms waving at times to demonstrate a crucial bit of swordplay. He moved with the agility of a seasoned warrior, his body fit and trim, although he was probably a grandfather, his hair already graying. He sat amid applause when the story ended, then rose again after some cajoling to tell another.

He straightened his doublet and looked at the expectant faces around him. "At the beginning of time, the god Rorin fought a battle with some of the lesser gods who connived against him. The sparks that flew from his sword in the fight became the stars in the sky. And thus was the world created."

He drew a long swallow of mead before he went on, his voice ringing across the hushed hall. "After the fight, Rorin, for he was not without mercy, took the daughters of his enemies as his concubines. As he claimed them one after the other, their virgin blood dripped down onto the land, and from this were born the first people of the Kadar."

I shuddered at the thought of a nation born of blood. No wonder they thirsted for it still.

"No greater warriors lived than they. Their fame spread in the world, far from their homeland. So blessed were they with skill and courage that kings from distant nations came to ask for their help in battle. In the whole world, there were none their equal."

The men around the table all nodded in agreement. Some even stomped their feet.

"But one day, their legendary exploits came to the attention of Noona, the dark sorceress."

Faces around the table turned somber at the mention of the name. Charms jingled as the concubines grabbed for them.

"She worked with her minions to thrust into servitude the people of Torzab. She thought to make them her slaves and use their children in her sacrifices, but although many of them fell, others resisted her magic. And so she came to the Kadar High Lord, Brathar, to ask for his help in taking the land by force."

I held my breath as I listened to this new tale I had not heard before, and I saw the people around the table holding theirs with me, for the captain told his story well, his voice rising and falling as the events required.

"But Brathar, wary of the sorceress, refused to help her and thus invoked her wrath. She called upon the darkness and brought forth great magic, and with it she stole the High Lord's heart, and, as it was in his heart, his courage. She cursed the House of Brathar, and from that day on one great ill after the other befell it, until most of his battles were lost, his sons killed, his concubines sick with a mysterious disease."

Charms jingled anew as the concubines offered quick prayers to the goddesses.

"But Lukeeh, a powerful soothsayer, appealed to Rorin. After much fasting and many sacrifices, the god told him that Noona had cursed the ground upon which the Kadar walked, so they drew the curse into themselves through the soles of their feet. Their afflictions would continue from generation to generation until they all perished.

"Lukeeh reported this to the High Lord and offered a solution. The Kadar must leave the land if they were to live."

He paused again for another swallow of mead, then wiped his drooping mustache on his sleeve. "But if they all left, Noona would feel the breaking of the curse and follow them. So Lukeeh offered to stay behind."

A couple of warriors around the table nodded in appreciation of such self-sacrifice and courage.

"And thus came our people to Dahru, a deserted island, through the Gate, and rebuilt our nation. And so we grew in wealth and fame to be greater than ever before."

He sat down amid the men's cheers.

I ignored that last bit about the "deserted island." Everyone knew the Shahala came to Dahru first and the Kadar after us.

Although my body did not wish for it, I both ate and drank at the feast, still hoping I might get a chance to return to the kitchen for my small bundle and run away that night. Those thoughts so preoccupied my mind that I barely noticed the time passing, the High Lord standing to leave. I looked up only when his guards were suddenly around me.

I followed them to the same quarters Lord Gilrem had occupied before. The High Lord strode into the inner chamber while his guards settled into the outer room.

They were not the same men who had been here with Lord Gilrem, but I stayed as far away from them as I could, not trusting any. When High Lord Batumar motioned to me to enter his chamber, I did so, hoping he would ask me to heal some old injury, then send me on my way.

Kumra's finery still decorated the chamber. The servants had cleaned the place for the High Lord and left trays of more food and drink, and a bowl of water to wash. He did look at the basin, then tugged off his tunic.

Old scars and new covered his skin, but he did not ask me to take the pain of any. In silence, he threw water into his face, his hair, onto his chest. I looked away, my mouth dry, my heart beating wildly in my chest, my glass phial clutched tightly in my fist. With every drop of blood within me, I feared him. I stood by the door, as far from him as possible.

When he finished, he sat upon the bed and kicked off his boots. The furrows on his forehead deepened, exhaustion bracketing his crooked mouth. Even his scar seemed more pronounced.

He blinked his eyes closed briefly, looking like a battle-worn warrior and not at all like the most powerful lord of the land. He lay back on the covers, his great mane of hair spread upon his pillow.

I froze, but he did not even look at me.

"Serving me means no disloyalty to your Lord Tahar," he said after a long moment.

"My loyalty is to the Shahala."

He did turn to me then, his eyes darkening. "So you refuse a new master and pledge to stay loyal only to your own people?"

"I have no power to refuse a new master, as you well know, my lord," I answered him, then lifted my chin. "But I shall stay loyal to my people until my dying breath."

He watched me for several heartbeats before he turned away again. "You will not come to harm at my hands today," he said and went to sleep.

My knees shook with sudden relief, but I did not waste time by waiting for them to stop. I turned to the door and opened it as quietly as I could. The guard outside shook his head, pushed me back inside, and closed the door behind me.

Defeat constricted my throat as I slid to the floor.

If the High Lord had come the next day, I would have been gone. I could feel the soft shirl moss of the hillside under my feet, the breeze rushing through the woods, could almost hear the chowa birds and their song of freedom.

The spirits had seemed to desert me completely. Maybe they *had* decided to visit punishment on me for my great-grandmother's sin. Maybe they could not forgive that the woman whose blood ran in my veins had tried to become a sorceress.

I knew but one thing: I still had my own spirit, the one my mother had breathed into me at my birthing. And I would not let the Kadar steal that spirit. Not the Kadar, and not their High Lord, Batumar.

You will not come to harm at my hands today. He had spoken the words without effort, straight like truth. I believed him, though the promise seemed strange. Not at his hands, he had said, but he did not promise not from anyone else in his command. And not today, but he did not pledge not ever. His words stood as much a warning as a promise. *You have nothing to fear*, he had said, *as long as you do not go against my people or my will.*

Yet his will included taking me to his far-off Pleasure Hall in Karamur and keeping me there as his slave. So, against that will I had to match my own.

I had left behind childhood when I had stepped on the slave ship. And I had changed more at the House of Tahar, had gained some strength of body and spirit. I hoped it would be enough for what awaited me.

CHAPTER EIGHT

(The Road to Karamur)

The weather had been growing milder for some time, but the day of our departure brought blustery northern winds.

After a morning meal of cold meats, boiled eggs, cheese, and bread served in the bedchamber, Batumar's great procession assembled and flowed to the near-deserted harbor of Kaharta Reh. Trade and other travel had slowed for the coldest season and was only now starting up again.

The winter storms had blown away the stench of the harbor. I could smell only the salty water in the air, untainted by the stink of rotting fish and masses of unwashed men arriving from long voyages.

The waves whipped high enough to wash over the quays that reached into the sea like giant wooden fingers. A handful of ships bobbed in the harbor, and I shuddered at the thought of another voyage in a dank cabin.

To my relief, we did not go to the water's edge, but to a sprawling building. And from this building the warriors led forth the most monstrous animals I had ever seen. I stood frozen to the ground, as I knew what they were—manyinga beasts.

Many times the size of the largest warrior, shaggy brown fur covered the beasts everywhere but their eyes and the end of their agile trunks, on either side of which enormous tusks curved toward the sky. They moved with lumbering steps but obeyed their masters.

The men made the beasts kneel before them with nothing but a pat to the animals' knees. The warriors strapped some kind of a fur-covered box on the back of each animal, then helped Tahar's frightened servants secure large bundles of traveling supplies behind the strange boxes. When the servants scurried back to the House of Tahar, the warriors climbed the beasts. And then their manyinga stood.

My throat went dry at the sight.

Many Shahala farmers used lornis, horses the Kadar called them, for working the fields and carrying the crops to town. Sometimes they used lornis to travel, as the largest of them could easily carry the weight of a man. But when sitting on a lorni, a man's feet nearly touched the ground. On top of a manyinga, Batumar and his warriors sat high up indeed, and I shuddered at the thought of one of their animals bolting.

Only one beast remained on its knees, waiting for its rider. With startled dismay, I realized it must be waiting for me.

My leg bones turned soft suddenly. I did not think I could go a step closer to the monstrous thing, let alone touch it or climb on. I remembered well what Keela had told me about the manyinga, how they could draw a person's spirit right out of the body. Especially a woman's.

At the time, her words had seemed silly superstition. Not now, however, that I had seen the beasts.

Then I caught the High Lord's gaze on me.

A test? If so, why? Kadar women did not ride.

But I was not Kadar.

I drew a slow breath. If they were testing me, I would show them the courage of a Shahala. The Kadar knew only the courage of facing one's enemy in battle and fighting to the death. I would show them the courage of facing one's fears.

I gathered up every bit of strength within me, pulling all from the deepest secret places of my soul, from my mother's memory, from the love of my people. I willed my knees to bend and put one foot before the other. I did not look at the Kadar, but straight at the manyinga. Its brown eyes, nearly as big as my head, looked back at me.

Eager for its prey?

My steps faltered, but I pressed on. The animal neither growled nor did it bare its teeth, which had to be enormous, of that I was certain.

I reached the beast at last and did not allow myself any hesitation but pushed my hands into its long fur and grabbed hold as I had seen the warriors do, aware that every eye fastened upon me.

The manyinga's fur felt coarse and dirty under my fingers. And very real. Not at all like some magical beast.

I filled my lungs with cold sea air. My heartbeat slowed its mad race.

I planted my foot on the animal's bent knee. It remained still as I climbed to the seat and sat upon the furs, then drew around me the cloak I had been given by one of the warriors at the High Lord's command earlier. The wind coming off the sea seemed colder up that high.

I grabbed the seat and held tight with both hands, then braced myself for the swaying as the animal stood, but it remained on the ground. A minute passed before I realized the manyinga was waiting for a signal.

As I slid forward in my seat to pat its head, my knees touched the back of the animal's ears. And with a low sound not unlike the groan of an old man, the beast rose to his feet.

I allowed a small smile of relief.

Contact with the manyinga had not brought instant death as Keela had led me to believe, and now that I sat atop the great monster, neither the height nor the slight swaying bothered me—no worse than the top of the numaba trees. I had climbed much higher in search of moonflowers, had hung on to branches shaking much more violently in the wind.

I finally dared to look around into a sea of astonished faces around me. Then from the corner of my eye, I caught sight of a warrior striding from the stables, pulling a wooden contraption behind him, a strange cart, larger than I had ever seen.

He stopped in his tracks to stare at me. Laughter from a couple of warriors broke the silence, and his face grew red, and so did mine for at that moment I understood. I had been meant to travel in the cart. *He* was supposed to ride the beast.

I would have gladly dismounted had I known how to make the manyinga kneel again. I could not reach its knee to pat it from all the way up where I sat, so I waited for help. But Batumar pointed the man to another warrior and his manyinga.

The man bowed to the High Lord and secured the cart behind that beast, transferred the bundles from the manyinga's back to the cart, then climbed up behind the first warrior to share the ride.

We were ready to leave.

———

The manyinga did not move fast, but they could carry a fearsome load. Many of the warriors held obvious affection for their animals. Some even called their beasts by name and talked to them as to old friends. We traveled inland, north, farther and farther away from my people with each step.

I had many questions about the manyinga, but I stayed away from the guards, although the men riding with us did not behave like the ones who had come to the House of Tahar with Lord Gilrem. Still, I stayed as close as I could to the High Lord, despite knowing that his promise of the night before did not carry to the present day.

Riding behind Batumar had its advantages. His beast, the largest of them all, blocked some of the wind. No one spoke to me, but I could make out from what I overheard that we would visit only one more warlord before the High Lord returned to Karamur. We were on our way to the House of Joreb, a day's ride away.

We did not stop to eat nor to take a break of any other kind. When a warrior had the need, he would stop his beast, do what he had to, then catch up with us. But every time I tried to hold my beast back to stay behind—I noticed by accident that it did that if I placed my hand on its back behind my seat—one of the warriors fell behind with me.

Soon I was so full of water it could have floated a ship. Thank the spirits, Batumar must have felt the same at last, as he brought his animal to a halt, and when he did, all his guards stopped, for the first time that day.

I did not think he stopped on my account, I did not think he even remembered by that time that I traveled with them, but I felt grateful to him just the same. He slid to the ground with ease, then, before he walked into the woods, he ordered a man to help me off my mount.

The warrior patted my beast's knee, and I could finally escape. I did my best not to show how tired I felt or how sore. On legs numb from all that sitting, I hobbled in the opposite direction from Batumar.

The Shahala forests were always loud with the cries of colorful birds and cheerful with a multitude of flowers. But here I barely saw a bird or two, small and drab in feathers of brown and gray, nervously flitting from one branch to the next.

Soon I came to a stand of bushes in a hidden spot where nobody could see me from the road. Then I finally gave my body the relief it so badly needed. For several moments, I did not even think of running away. But once I did, the urge to bolt came swiftly, the uncontrollable instinct of a wild animal.

With a pounding heart, I flew through the woods, silent like the night birds. Then I saw the guards and froze, unsure what to expect. An arrow? Or at the least to be apprehended at once and bound while I awaited punishment. One man stood among the trees ahead of me to the right, the other to the left. They watched me in silence as I stood there frozen, my heart hammering even harder.

When neither arrow nor an order to drop to my knees came, I backed away from them and sulked back to the road to my beast, grabbed the long, coarse hair behind his ears, and put my foot on his bent foreleg to pull myself up to my seat.

Not a day had passed since my arrival to the Kadar that I did not think about running away. I was greatly disheartened at how easily my first true attempt had been defeated.

I wanted to go to Karamur to find my mother's grave and the truth about her death, but I would have rather traveled on my own. If I reached the city with Batumar, I might be summarily locked up in his Servant Hall or Maiden Hall. Either way, I would be *his*.

I would never again have the freedom to do as I pleased.

As I mulled how to best escape the next time I received an opportunity, the High Lord returned and strode to his beast without sparing a glance for me. If his guards had told him what I had tried to do in the woods, he showed no sign.

We rode on until we reached the House of Joreb.

Lord Joreb, of course, held a feast in the High Lord's honor. His Great Hall looked much the same as Tahar's. Servants bustled about, their eyes never meeting ours as they saw to our needs in silence.

Once again, I sat in the concubines' place behind Batumar. I held my breath when he was offered a slender maiden, but he politely declined.

I felt relief for the maiden's sake, but only doom for myself. I could eat no more, just sat on my silk pillow, praying to the spirits until the feast ended.

The Palace Guard led me to the High Lord's chamber. Could I be as lucky once again as I had been the previous night? At least I did not have much time to work myself into a true panic. He strode in but a few moments later.

He reclined on the pelts that covered his bed and watched me as I sat on the floor in the corner by the hearth, my arms around my knees.

"Tahar's warriors claim you to be a healer of much skill."

A moment passed before I gathered the courage to respond, rising to show respect. "I know the uses of herbs."

"You are a Shahala. What else are you?" His obsidian eyes narrowed until I squirmed on the stone.

"I do not understand, my lord, I am but a slave."

He looked at my hair. "Why are you still a maiden?"

I grew embarrassed at his words, for I knew what he meant. I was older than the girls at Maiden Hall. Even among the Shahala, young women my age had long had their rija feast and were called wives and mothers.

He did not move his attention from me. "Why were you not with the other maidens? They had to search for you for some time."

I had not thought the High Lord had paid any mind to me at all, but now I began to think maybe little escaped his attention. Yet I could not answer his question, for that would have been a long tale, one that stretched all the way to his brother.

Did he know how Lord Gilrem had fared at Kumra's hands? Since he did not mention his brother, neither would I. Maybe the High Lord did not wish to be reminded that his brother had fallen victim to the scheming of women.

I trusted not that he would reward me for my part in Lord Gilrem's escape. As far as I had seen, gratitude or acknowledging a debt of any kind was not something practiced among the Kadar. Neither would a High Lord want to be indebted to a slave.

So I put the tale of Lord Gilrem out of my mind and said instead, "I was under punishment, my lord."

He nodded, the punishment of servants common in his lands, no doubt. "I would hear the story of how you came to the House of Tahar."

I found talking a preferable task to whatever else he could have required, so I began with our Shahala land and told him a thing or two about how civilized people behaved.

Cautiously I started, but grew bolder little by little, less and less afraid of offending him. I had survived deadly flogging at the House of Tahar. If truth brought punishment, so be it. I would not cower in fear for the rest of my life like a child.

I recounted the day Jarim had sold me. I told Batumar about the traders, leaving nothing out, neither the scum of the ship nor the hunger, nor the despair of those herded to the auction house. I told him about Kumra too, and the flesh stripped from my back, only I did not tell him why. But I wanted him to hear the whole horrible unfair truth, so he could never say he knew not the cruelty in his lands. So if he let it happen, he would know what he gave his approval to, so he could not lie to his own twisted soul in the night.

The more I talked, the darker his face turned, but I pushed on to the end, even while knowing he might break me like the lantaya man had broken the mirror my mother had given him, not liking what it showed him.

Never had Batumar's face looked friendly with that scar, but his expression turned truly frightening as he listened. I stood my ground, cringing back only when he shoved to his feet.

"You will not come to harm at my hands today," he said; then he strode out of the chamber.

The words did not sound like a threat now. They sounded careful. As if he wished not to promise more than he could keep. But any man that careful with his words had to be an honest man, didn't he?

Yet, as eager as I was to believe such fancy, I could not. Still, his quick forgiveness of my frank words did surprise me. Had I said as much at the House of Tahar, I would have been beaten half to death.

A jumble of emotions fought each other in my heart as I snatched a blanket from the back of a chair, dragged it back to the corner to bundle up in, then drifted off to sleep.

When I woke in the morning, the High Lord was dressing by the bed, one of his guards waiting in the open door.

I scrambled to my feet and straightened my dress. At the House of Tahar, servants always rose before their lord. At Maiden Hall, all maidens stood ready for the day as soon as the door opened to allow Kumra through. Had she found anyone sleeping, I imagined the punishment would have been severe. I wondered how bad a beating this day would bring me and vowed not to walk to the whipping post meekly as I had before.

"Joreb has a prisoner," Batumar said. "An enemy spy too ill to talk." He strode to the door. "I would have you see if you can heal him."

I looked at him, confused, for I had expected scolding. Then my thoughts flew to the unfortunate who needed my help, and I hoped I could give him at least some measure of relief. I followed behind Batumar, wary at his lack of visible anger. I had learned since having lost my freedom that those who hid their fury the best were sometimes the most cruel.

And suddenly I had more than sleeping late to worry about. What would the High Lord do when he found out I was no true healer? Would he send me to be sold on the auction block, would he keep me as a household slave, or would he toss me out and let me go?

Since he was Kadar, I could not conceive any possibility of that last option. Then another thought occurred to me. Would he be embarrassed by my lack of skills in front of one of his warlords? Would he think his servant shamed him? Would he have me flogged? I followed Batumar to Joreb's Great Hall with a heavy heart and a determination to face my fate with courage.

The servants had already cleared away the remnants of the feast from the night before. The double doors that led to the courtyard stood thrown wide, allowing in enough sunlight so we had no need for torches.

Two warriors held up the limp body of a burly man in front of Joreb. The man's head, with its matted long hair, hung onto his naked chest, his scars telling tales of many battles. Fresh bruises and blood covered his body from his last fight.

Batumar watched for what I would do.

For the time, the man was mine. So I said, "Would you set him down?"

The warriors looked at their lord, who nodded.

I knelt next to the man and saw at once the bloody hole below the last rib where his spirit was slipping away. Even if I still had some of the moonflower's tears left... He needed so much more. The sickness went too deep inside him.

My mother would have sent her spirit to talk to his, to tell it to stay. She would have showed him how to push out the bad blood, the rotten bits, the pus. She would have called on the good spirits to strengthen him for the fight. And for her, the good spirits would have listened. Under her fingers, blood vessels would have flexed, and the severed would have joined back together as whole.

I knew what needed to be done, only I could not accomplish it. My spirit had never been the wandering kind. No matter how many times I had tried to send it into a sick person, it never so much as budged in anyone's direction.

I craved true power in that moment more fiercely than I ever had before, so fiercely that it scared me. Was this gnawing, all-consuming need what my great-grandmother had felt? Her powers had come late too. But then they had grown to eclipse all others until she had forgotten her vows and wished to use her powers to rule over our people. She had broken the sacred trust, and for this her family had been cast out, living on a secluded beach, even though by the time I was born my mother's own faithful service had redeemed our name.

I had no great power like my great-grandmother or even my mother, but I could not leave the injured man without trying to help, not with the pain etched onto his face, pain so fierce I could feel it in my own bones. So I asked the warriors to bring me a blade and a pan of hot coals, and water first boiled, then cooled.

I blocked out everything but the man before me, noticing all that healers use for guidance: the pallid tone of his skin, the shallowness of his breath, his half-hooded eyes that barely seemed to see, the slight trembling of limbs, and lack of sweat despite the heat of his forehead. I barely noted when Batumar moved on with Joreb to continue their talks from the night before.

I washed the man's face and his wounds the best I could, removed as much dead skin and flesh as possible. Then I seared the wound closed with the hot blade. He screamed, losing awareness for some moments before he regained his mind and began moaning.

I put my hand on his forehead, telling my arm to tell my hand to tell my palm to tell the skin to feel cool upon him. Then I sent another message, this time to dull the pain. I had gained some skill while healing Tahar's warriors over the long winter. My senses had sharpened; my fingers had grown more knowing.

Had I been even more skilled, I would have been able to pull the pain completely, but the best I could do was to send some numbness into the man's mind so although the pain still roared in his body, it could not fully reach him.

He began to speak at once, feverish words of nonsense, and at this, one of the warriors ran off to fetch Batumar and Joreb. A boy of about eight summers came with them, Joreb's son from the looks of him. He had that stiff-lipped look of boys recently taken to war practice who missed the warmth and softness of their mother but would die rather than show it.

The two warlords listened closed-faced to the man's gibberish. More warriors were called in, but none knew the man's language.

"No use to us, then," Joreb said. "Leave him to die."

The man spoke again, and this time I caught one word that seemed familiar. It sounded like the tongue of the Kingdom of Orh, only distorted like an echo. I closed my eyes to concentrate on that distortion, and more and more words began to make sense—like looking at yourself in a pool of water, strange but recognizable.

He begged me to let him die.

I hesitated, not knowing whether I should plead for his life with Batumar and Joreb. If the man recovered, they might torture him to death again just to find out what they wanted. How did I know he was a spy? The word of a Kadar. He could have been a slave like myself, caught in escape.

Sometimes a healer did the best service by allowing a man to die. I put my hand on his forehead again and blocked his pain as well as I was able. The rest I would leave to the spirits to decide.

They lifted him roughly and dragged him away at once, his boots scraping over the stone floor, disappearing from sight just as more guards burst in, dragging a scared youth of maybe twenty summers. By the looks of his sackcloth shirt and pants, he must have been a peasant from one of the villages.

At Lord Joreb's questioning glance, his guard reported. "Caught him skulking outside the gate, my lords."

"What is your business here?" Batumar demanded from the captured man at once.

For a moment, the battered youth looked defiant, but then he folded, suddenly tearful. "I must bring a map of Kadar fortresses to the Kerghi. If I don't, they will kill my mother, my lord."

"Your mother is already dead, boy," the High Lord said without emotion. "Will you join my army?"

The youth sobbed, tears and snot running down his face. "I will, my lord. Just spare my life, and I will serve you to my dying day."

Batumar nodded to the guards to release him. They did and

stepped back. And the High Lord drew his sword and cut the spy down where he stood.

I gasped as he fell, his blood gushing onto the stone floor. Tremors racked my body at such cold-blooded murder.

The guards dragged the body out without the slightest show of emotion. Joreb's boy, having taken a quick step closer to his father, now stared wide-eyed at the bloodstain.

"Do you know why I had to cut this spy down?" the High Lord addressed him.

Startled by the great honor, the boy hesitated.

"Once a turncoat, always a turncoat, my lord," he said at last, as Batumar wiped his blade. "He betrayed his people to the enemy for his mother, then betrayed his new lords and pledged to join our armies to keep his own life. He would have betrayed us too."

Batumar nodded. "Well said."

Joreb did not exactly smile, but his gaze softened.

I reeled from the hideous, merciless violence but refused to let my knees tremble. I would not have any murderous Kadar see me weak.

I was about to ask the High Lord for leave when one of the Palace Guard strode in to report that a horseman had ridden ahead to Karamur to carry news of our approach.

Batumar dismissed him, then turned to me. "You may go and prepare for our journey."

So I hurried away, out of the room, away from the ruthless men in it.

Later that day, as we rode on for the High Lord's seat, Batumar slowed his beast until it walked next to mine. "Where did the first prisoner come from?"

For a moment I thought to feign ignorance to avoid punishment, but I had just that day decided that I would no longer cower in fear in front of any Kadar, even if the price be my life. "The Kingdom of Orh or somewhere near."

"What did he tell you?"

I flinched. I knew nothing escaped Batumar's attention. I should have expected the question. "He begged to die, my lord."

"But you healed him."

"I tried."

"Will he live?"

"If the spirits will it."

A moment of silence passed before he said, "If I see you practice deceit again, you will not live to regret it."

I knew him to be a man who meant the words he spoke. "But I will not come to harm from you today?" I asked, trusting that if he said so, I would be yet safe to see another morning.

He shook his head. Some resemblance of a smile played at his crooked lips, the expression so unlike him, I found it more frightening than friendly.

———

We rode hard, stopping briefly at midday. I picked some stinky kukuyu weeds from the side of the road where they grew freely and prepared a poultice for the leg of a manyinga that had begun to limp. I had to crawl between the beast's legs, each double the thickness of my waist, to apply the medicine.

I asked the manyinga to stay still, told him I understood his pain and was trying to help. With a single step, the beast could have broken more bones in my body than a person could break and still live, but the manyinga stood still as I worked. I caught a couple of warriors watching me, although they turned every time I glanced their way.

Once I helped the beast, I strode into the woods to relieve myself. I did not try to run away this time—I tried to sneak away. But once again, I could not sneak past Batumar's guards. His men worked together in a way I had not seen among Lord Tahar's warriors or among the Shahala. He scarcely gave orders. They simply knew his will and did it.

Before I could find a solution to this problem, we mounted and rode on.

I watched the injured manyinga, and it seemed the poultice took some of the pain as he did not favor his leg as much as before.

When the sun slipped low in the sky, we stopped and dismounted, and the guards went about setting up the tents.

Some warriors spread out to collect firewood for the night, and I did the same, aware that no other servant traveled with the small group but I, surprised that they did not expect me to do all the work. None were assigned to guard me, but every time I walked any distance, one would move so he could keep me in sight.

I grew so accustomed to constantly having their eyes on me that I didn't sense another kind of watchful gaze.

I was collecting dry twigs at the edge of a clearing where it met the thick woods. When I heard the rustling behind me in the bushes, I thought it another warrior. The sudden rumbling growl had me swirling around in a hurry.

And then I saw the tiger.

CHAPTER NINE

(The Fortress City)

Warriors moved in slowly, gliding silently over the ground.

They would not reach me in time. The tiger growled again, louder, a yellow expanse of fur flashing behind the branches, way too close to me.

I stood rooted to the spot and stared at the giant cat, double the size of the ones that roamed the Shahala forests.

She watched, her muscles tensing for the jump.

I could see her better now. Her belly hung low. She had recently eaten—I hoped enough. She was also swollen with milk, although I could not see her cubs. She growled again. I slipped back a step. Her litter had to be nearby. Maybe she was just warning me off.

I slipped back another slow step and hummed the spirit song my mother had taught me. She had sung it when once a snake twisted around my ankle on top of a numaba tree. The song had no words. I hummed the melody while sending its meaning to the tiger in the way of the spirits.

Oh great mother, I told her, *I mean no harm to you or your children. Oh great sister*, I said, *we are both children of the earth and the sky.*

I hummed and backed away step by step.

She let me go but did not relax her muscles. Her fierce gaze moved to something behind me. Keeping one eye on her, I glanced back in time to see one of the warriors nocking his arrow.

I yelled for him to stop, but warriors took no orders from slaves or from women. He let the arrow loose at the same time as the tiger lunged, her powerful hind legs propelling her over my head as she flew at the man.

He missed the tiger, but the arrows of the other warriors dug deep into her side before she pounced on her target and brought the guard down in a crash that shook the ground. The man yanked his dagger, not much protection against claws and teeth.

I drew back in horror as grunts mixed with rumbling growls.

Then, just as suddenly as it began, the burst of violence ended, and the two opponents lay listlessly on the blood-soaked ground. The warrior had been badly mangled. The dozen arrows hanging from the tiger's side bled her strength.

The rest of the guards closed in to finish off the great animal, but I ran to her side without thought.

"Stop," I begged, and the men did, not because of my plea but because the High Lord burst into the clearing, his sword drawn.

The warriors parted before him, awaiting his command. He sheathed his weapon, shoved the injured tiger off the man, and lowered himself onto one knee beside his guard.

He turned his sharp gaze upon me. "Will Zordak live?"

Skin and muscle hung from the man's shoulder in strips, revealing the bone beneath.

"If the spirits will it." I stepped another step closer to the tiger and stretched out my arms to protect her. All I could think of was that her innocent cubs would starve to death in the woods without her.

Batumar's dark eyes narrowed. "For the life of my man, I would give you the life of the tiger."

He did not understand the way of healers. I would have tried everything in my power to heal the fallen man without promise of reward. And I would have done everything to save the tiger even under threat of punishment.

"I will help Zordak as best I can. But the spirits hold his life, not I."

Batumar gave a curt nod as he stood, and the warriors lifted Zordak to return him to his tent with haste. I followed close behind.

As soon as we reached our camp site, I began to boil and cool water to cleanse the wounds. I had some herbs to prepare a potion against infection, although not enough, and no moonflower tears.

I numbed the man's mind against pain and told his body to heal, not knowing whether it would listen. I called to the spirits, in case they had not completely abandoned me.

When I had done all I could, I returned to the clearing where two guards stood a good distance from the tiger, their arrows nocked and ready. I stepped right in front of those arrows.

The tiger gave a weak growl.

I hummed. *I came to help, great mother.*

She understood. She stayed still as I pulled the arrows and smeared disinfectant paste on the wounds that were not as deep as I had feared. She still wore her thick winter coat, a veritable armor. She bled, but I did not think the arrows hit anything vital deep in her body.

I had sinew and a bone needle but did not close any of her wounds. Should infection set in, they needed a way to drain. She might, in any case, tear out the stitches.

At least, the disinfectant paste drew the edges together tightly enough for the bleeding to nearly stop. As the herbs I used had a bitter taste, I had hope that she would not lick off the paste.

Her cubs mewed faintly in the thicket as I worked. From time to time, she lifted her massive head to look that way. Silently I sang to her about her pain lifting with the vapor of her breath, of strength returning into her as she drew in the crisp air of the woods.

The guards never lowered their arrows as long moments passed. Then at last, the tiger stood on shaking legs. I stayed on the ground, perfectly still.

She limped toward the thicket on paws as big as my head, stopping only once to lick blood from her fur and look back. And maybe she had her own spirit song, because for a moment a perfect peace descended on me, right there in the middle of the Kadar forest.

The guards ended that, urging me to return to their injured brother. So I hurried back to our clearing and the man's tent. I found the High Lord inside when I entered.

He turned to me from inspecting the warrior's wounds. "Can you do something for the fever?"

I stepped closer to feel the man's forehead, the heat a shock against my palms. I pulled off his blanket, leaving his body exposed to the cold air. But he needed more, so I wet some rags and covered as much of his near-naked body as I could.

I checked the infusion of feverfew in his cup. I had prepared the medicine before I had left to see to the tiger. The color looked right, so I soaked the end of a clean rag in the liquid, then squeezed and dripped as much as I could between the man's cracked lips.

I wished I had more resources than the healing plants I had received from Onra and the ones I had gathered during our journey. Accumulating herbs anytime I passed through woods or fields was as habitual as breathing, my gaze constantly searching for familiar shapes and colors, but the forest was just awakening from its winter sleep, my pickings slim.

The High Lord watched my ministrations closely. Did he look to find fault in me? Did he understand that no healer could change the will of the spirits? My hand jumped, and I dribbled some of the infusion onto my patient's neck. I quickly wiped it off with my sleeve.

"Zordak wanted only to protect you," Batumar said.

"The tiger wanted only to protect her young." The guard had moved to attack first. Until then, the tiger had been willing to let us go with a warning.

Batumar watched me for a moment but said nothing as he left us. I breathed a sigh of relief and stayed until Zordak rested peacefully at last.

The aroma of cooking food scented the night air as I stepped from the tent, so I walked toward the small fire in the middle of our encampment. One of the warriors handed me a bowl. I sat on the cold ground away from the men and ate my evening meal, nearly dizzy with exhaustion, barely tasting the thin stew.

When I finished, I rinsed the bowl and left it with the rest. I walked back toward Zordak to stay the night with the injured warrior, but one of the Palace Guards strode out of the darkness and led me to the High Lord's tent that stood in the middle of our encampment.

I went without protest. Zordak would not be alone. Unlike their High Lord, the warriors slept four to a tent. If he turned for the worse, one of the others could come and fetch me.

I stepped inside Batumar's empty tent, grateful for the small heat of the torch stuck in the ground in the middle. Although the tent had a small smoke hole, no one had lit a fire. I wondered how cold the weather would have to turn for the High Lord to consider one necessary.

A water jar stood to my left, Batumar's trunk and cot taking up most of the space, the latter covered in furs. I grabbed a handful of pelts, then settled down in the corner.

The furs and my cloak kept me warm but did little to soften the hard ground. Still, I thanked the spirits to be sleeping under cover and not out in the open. I doubted slaves on the road were accustomed to such luxury as I was afforded.

I dozed, barely waking when Batumar ducked in. The wind picked up and howled outside. I burrowed deeper into my coverings.

The tent in front of our Shahala house where my mother used to receive the sick was made of cool linen, letting the breeze through to provide everyone with fresh air. The Kadar made tents from animal hides, the panels sewn together tightly, the wisdom of which I was beginning to appreciate.

Batumar stood over me. "My men say you healed the tiger."

"A mother should not be taken from her cubs."

He stood in silence for a while. "She did not harm you. Tugren says you sang to her. Must have been some song." A brief silence passed before he went on. "I know a man like that, Lord Karnagh, a warlord of great power from Regnor. His people talk to tigers, even bring them to battle."

I thought about the tiger in the clearing. I did not want the High

Lord to think that I would or could talk the tiger into following the warriors into a fight. "Those must be wondrous people indeed. This one allowed me to heal her, but she could have just as easily turned against me."

Another moment of silence passed as he considered my words. "Stay on your manyinga during the day; even tigers will not attack the beasts. At the midday break and in the evenings, stay close to the tents and the warriors."

To do otherwise would have been foolish, so I agreed. This once I had been lucky.

I had to accept the fact that traveling through these woods alone would be too dangerous. On my way home from Karamur, I would have to find another way.

War approached; everyone said so. When the High Lord and his warriors left the fortress city, I would sneak away and seek a caravan heading south. Maybe they would be willing to take a healer along even if I could not pay the fee.

And I would find my mother's grave in the meanwhile and find out how she had died. I would say the Last Blessing over her grave. The more I thought about that, the more certain I became that it was for that very reason the spirits brought me all this way.

"Sing me the tiger song."

Without the tiger, I had some trouble finding the words in my heart. *Oh Great Mother—*

How could I call the High Lord my mother and sister? But then new words sprang to life, and I hummed the song, talking to him in the language of spirits.

Oh Great Lord, I said without words. *Hear the plight of your people. Hear the cry of your slaves. Oh great man, set me free.*

He listened for a while. "That stayed the tiger? You said nothing, just made noises?"

Not words that could be mistaken for a compliment. "The tiger spared me because she had a full belly."

I did not think Batumar understood my spirit song. Maybe there could never be such a connection between a Shahala and a Kadar. They did not respect the spirits and worshipped only their god of war.

"Will she attack us in the night?" he demanded then.

I sighed. Animals were nobler than men, knowing nothing of revenge, I wanted to say, but then I realized the true meaning of his question. He was asking whether I had told to tiger to attack so that I could escape.

"No, my lord."

"I do not want you to talk to any beasts. I would not have you put fear into my warriors' hearts."

He had nothing to worry about, for truly I could not talk to animals; I merely sang songs in my heart. Perhaps they sensed my spirit's songs, or perhaps they were calmed by the humming. I could certainly not claim that I had ever made an animal do as I pleased.

"I shall not talk to any beasts," I promised.

"Then you may rest, for you will not come to harm at my hands today."

Batumar turned and grabbed the torch, stuck it in the ground upside down, and plunged the tent into darkness. His cot creaked as he lay down upon it.

———

We traveled north, farther and farther from my people, for seven days and nights through the wild forests. Although the trees broke the wind and it snowed only once, cold seeped inside me until my very heart shivered. I kept my cloak drawn tight and dug my legs into the manyinga's shaggy fur to soak up the warmth of his body.

Zordak, the injured man, rode in the cart, and the warrior whose manyinga I rode took the man's beast. Our days passed very much the same. We could have ridden on the main road that snaked along the towns of the large plains below, but the journey would have taken many more days, and Batumar wanted to hurry.

On the seventh day, a warrior ran forth to announce our imminent arrival and carry the High Lord's instructions. On the morning of the eighth, we broke out of the forest, and before us spread Karamur in all its majesty, flying a myriad of gold and red banners, the High Lord's colors. By then, Zordak had recovered enough to ride his own beast once again.

The silver dust of frost covered the fields and huts that dotted the road leading to the fortress, the rising sun adding gold speckles as it glinted off the white rocks of the city.

My new prison.

And yet I could not deny that the fortress city held some foreign beauty. My mother had been here once and seen these walls. The thought softened my heart a little.

The High Lord's seat had been built into the side of the mountain. The back of the palace—the largest building—was carved from the mountain rock itself, with the front walls and towers built on.

I felt as if the Forgotten City itself had risen up from the myths, and would not have been surprised to see the Guardians coming to greet us. But no round dome of the Forum rose in the midst of the houses. And I did not think the Forgotten City had ever been this closely guarded. That city had been a gathering place of wise men and not armies.

The moment we pushed into the open, the horns sounded on the walls, and people ran down the road to welcome their High Lord. Warriors, women, and men of all walks of life from merchants to servants, children by the hordes, cheered us along. I understood at last from whence Batumar's power came. His people loved him.

Lord Tahar was respected by his warriors. His men, concubines, and slaves obeyed him without question. But he had never been greeted upon return as Batumar was now, with smiles on every face.

Yet I could not rejoice at the thought that my new master seemed to be a better man than the previous had been. I wished to belong to no one but my own self. And Batumar would not be the only one under whose authority I now belonged. I scarcely dared think of Batumar's favorite concubine.

Instead, I watched the people, some of whom brought out instruments and played feast songs while others broke into dancing right in the street. Yet others had tears of happiness in their eyes. A Shahala elder would have thought they had all lost their minds to so abandon all decorum.

I understood them a little better now. People who lived from war appreciated the good moments of life more perhaps. They knew the next battle might be lost, their loved ones might never return. They lived in the now, while my people revered times gone so much, I think given a chance, they would have preferred to live in the past.

We rode up the road to a tunnel-like opening in the outermost stone wall of the fortress itself. Workmen toiled at the foot of the wall, strengthening it with rocks and mortar, but even they stopped as we arrived.

I looked up at the guards cheering on the walls above us, and saw the strangest of devices suspended above our heads. Metal bars sharpened to points formed a gate that hung from iron chains. I shuddered as we passed under. How could I hope to escape from such a place once they lowered the gate?

Small, evenly cut holes dotted the ceiling of the stone corridor through which we entered. I could see the wall guard through the gaps. I did not draw a breath until we came out the other side into the town square, where more people surrounded us at once.

Stone towers dotted with narrow windows rose to the sky in the back, smaller buildings at their feet, the purpose of some of which I recognized, while others I did not. Stables lined the far side of the square. From a small building next to them came the familiar clanging of a smithy.

Merchant shops lined the streets, offering all manner of food and clothing. More people rushed forth from them to join the crowd that followed us to our destination, the High Lord's palace.

At the palace gates, servants led our manyinga away, and the warriors dispersed. Only two guards remained with us. They walked behind me as I followed Batumar through the winding hallways, grateful to be out of the cold and walking on my own two feet.

At Kaharta Reh, the weather had at last begun to warm up after the long season of snowstorms, but the chill of northern winds still ruled at Karamur. I hoped Yullin would warm these lands too with her breath, by the time I found a way to leave.

I pushed my fur-trimmed hood back to better see where we headed. I scarcely knew what to look at, so strange the palace seemed with its large chambers that opened into each other, each with a roaring fire, and hangings covering all the walls. But unlike the silk hangings of Tahar's Pleasure Hall, Karamur's pictures were made of dyed and woven wool, showing battle scenes.

A servant woman ran to follow us two steps behind, ready to offer service should we need it.

Then at last we reached the Great Hall, lined with many tables, servants rushing to and from every direction in their hurry to finish preparations for the feast. Bowls and plates clanged against tankards; great hounds growled in protest against being shooed out of the way.

The pleasant scents of burning fruitwood and cooking food filled the air, but I wished for nothing save a pile of blankets to rest on, as close to a fireplace as possible. Before we passed through the main hall, however, Lord Gilrem strode through a doorway and bowed to his lord brother. He wore simpler clothes than when I had seen him at the House of Tahar. Now he dressed much like one of the warriors, as was Batumar.

"Your people welcome your return, brother, and none more than I. I hope your journey was swift and successful." His gaze slid over me, hesitating only for a moment. If he recognized me, he gave no sign.

"Thank you, Gilrem. The warlords are ready. And how have you fared?"

"Forgive me, brother, for I fell ill and had to return to Karamur. But once I recovered here, I saw to it that the warriors trained often and hard. They stand ready. Skilled men are strengthening your fortress."

"Then you have served me fine well and have my gratitude." Batumar clapped him on the shoulders.

He stood half a head taller, heavier built, darker in the color of his hair and eyes, while Gilrem was fair of face and hair, handsome as ever a man was, and as quick on his feet as he was to smile. Batumar reminded me of the silent, dark rock of the hills, Gilrem the creek that ran around it.

"Let us talk together." The High Lord strode to a great carved chair near the fire and sank onto it as Gilrem joined him.

The servant woman who had been shadowing us until now escorted me away.

"My name is Leena, my lady. I am at your service."

She had a strong, honest face, still beautiful despite her age. Her eyes were the shiny black hue of ninga beetles, her hair dark as well, with but a few strands of gray mixed in.

I followed her uncertainly. I never before had anyone at my service, even temporarily. I expected her to take me to the High Lord's Maiden Hall—as befitting a woman still untouched—and already dreaded the whip of the favorite concubine. When we reached an enormous door that reached to the height of two men, just the thought of what awaited me behind those doors made me flinch.

Carved images of flowers and frolicking women decorated the light wood. Around the edges, carefully burned into the wood, stood a row of sacred Kadar symbols, probably for protection. Leena pushed the door open, and before me spread a large round hall, lined by chambers too many to count.

Dust covered everything, the air stale and cold, as if the fires that burned brightly had been only recently lit. In the middle of the hall, a pond-sized hole gaped in the ground. Servants bustled about, cleaning and lining the benches with furs and silks, but still so abandoned and forgotten the place seemed that I had taken several steps inside by the time I recognized my surroundings.

Not Maiden Hall, but the High Lord's Pleasure Hall was this.

CHAPTER TEN

(The Summons)

My gaze darted around, but I could not see a single concubine.

Kumra's words—which at the time I had thought born out of meanness—came back to me in a rush. *He has killed every woman he had ever chosen. His concubines are all dead.*

My heart trembled with foreboding. I took a quick step back. "I am still a maiden. I do not belong here."

"The High Lord's orders, my lady."

Leena respectfully gestured me forward and led me to a chamber larger than Kumra's. This, unlike the rest of the hall, had been thoroughly cleaned.

A sprawling bed covered with pelts and satin dominated the room. I had to step over silk pillows that littered the floor and saw more piled high on the giant wooden chest at the end of the bed. Flames danced in the small fireplace. Spending the night by its warmth seemed an unimaginable luxury.

When I spotted a small alcove with a tub of steaming water, my entire body thrilled, all my worries fading momentarily. I knew I would pay for all this, pay dearly and probably with more than I was willing to give, but for a moment, a shameless joy stole into me at the sight of all that heat.

I shed the cloak that had protected me from the worst of the long journey and untied my charm belt, careful with the few bunches of herbs that hung from it—my only friends in a strange place.

The two servant girls who entered after us eyed my treasure with mistrust and even agitation, although I could not fathom why. I fear little of me met with their approval as they looked over my common clothes, soiled from many days of hard travel.

I undressed myself, to the women's great consternation, and without assistance stepped into the tub. My eyes closed as my tired body sank into bliss.

At home, we washed ourselves in the rapid little creek that wound its way down our hill. At the House of Tahar, the maidens rubbed their bodies clean with a wet cloth, using the water left in the jars at the end of the day.

I had seen a tub before at Tahar's house, had even assisted Keela with her bath, but never had I dreamed that one day I would be allowed such luxury.

I sank to my chin and stayed until Leena fussed about the water growing cold. Then at last, to appease her, I let the girls wash my hair, then bundle me in a supple cloth large enough for a cape. They sat me on a silk pillow in front of the fire while they dried my hair. And still they were not finished.

Soon another woman came in with a dress fit for Kumra. Red and gold glistened in the light of the fire, the High Lord's colors.

"If you would hold up your arms, my lady."

Leena pulled a long under-tunic of linen as soft as a dream over my head, until the hem tickled my ankles. Then the cloud of crimson satin floated over me and spilled down my body, sweeping the floor as I stepped back.

Oh, how strange that felt. Enough fabric had gone into the gown to dress ten maidens, at least. The low bodice, drawn tight by braided ribbons in the back, pushed my breasts up until I feared they would spill out of their confines at any moment.

I tried to tug up the neckline in vain. "If I might have a shawl..."

The women respectfully shook their heads.

I had to sit again; then Leena held my dress out of the way while the girls rolled upon my legs a pair of slim silk stockings that ended at mid-thigh. I had seen such things at the House of Tahar when doing the wash for the concubines, although never anything this beautiful.

I stared at my legs as if they belonged to someone else, my mind scrambling to catch up with all that was happening.

When the women finished with the stockings, Leena pulled matching satin slippers on my feet, decorated with golden beads. They sparkled like jewels and were daintier than anything I had ever seen.

"If you would step on this stool, my lady."

I was too stunned to do anything but obey.

The seamstress checked the dress and for the last time adjusted the fit.

By the time they finished, every gaze that beheld me turned approving. And I did enjoy those few moments of splendor and attention, until I realized for what I was being readied.

My stomach clenched under the layers of luxurious fabric.

Upon his return home, Lord Tahar always called for a concubine. And as no others occupied the High Lord's strange Pleasure Hall, I had little doubt upon whom the honor should fall tonight. The women anticipated his actions, it seemed, as they arranged my hair into elaborate coils despite my protests.

I worked myself into such a state that when Leena escorted me from my chamber, my knees nearly gave out beneath me as I walked, my legs like saplings rattled by wind. But I held my head high, determined not to show any of that fear, to bear all I had to bear with dignity.

She led me into the palace's Great Hall, however, instead of the High Lord's bedchamber. I had forgotten about the feast!

Relief flooded me so thoroughly at this reprieve, that I did not balk when she led me straight to the High Lord's table and seated me on the bench next to him. The *only* place to sit, it seemed, as no concubine pillows covered the ground behind him.

An equally fierce-looking warrior picked at a roasted fowl on my other side, but I had eyes only for the man on whom my fate depended.

"I hope the evening finds you well, my lady." Batumar greeted me as one would a favored concubine.

"Fine well, my lord." I clamped my hands together on my lap.

A low murmur spread through the crowded room, but I was barely aware of anything save the High Lord's obsidian gaze as it traveled the length of my dress. When his gaze at last reached mine, I looked away, unable to bear the scrutiny.

I could not look up again until he turned his attention to his brother on his other side. Lord Gilrem paid me no mind, but the man behind him examined me openly.

His face was as lined as the cracked ground at the end of the summer drought. The braided beard that hung to his waist shone with oils in the light of the hundred torches that burned brightly in their sconces. His protruding eyes did not seem to be connected and moved independently of each other.

When his hand fisted on the table, my breath disappeared suddenly, as if his gnarled fingers were closing around my throat.

I tore my gaze away, and I could breathe again. After that, I kept my attention on the hall and the people who had gathered there for the feast.

Warriors sat at the tables with their concubines and ate together. Husbands and wives always sat together among my people, and their children with them, one as families. I did not realize it could be so among the Kadar.

Although Batumar paid little mind to me, I could enjoy neither the meal nor the talk at the table, my mind drowning with the anxiety of the approaching night. *Pain and blood before morning came*, I believed. I had seen Onra with Tahar. Morning would see forever erased the hope that I would one day become a healer such as my mother had been.

To distract my anguished mind, I glanced at the man who sat on my other side, a fearsome warrior but not a Kadar, judging from the exotic lion mane of his hair—locks varying from the color of straw to a brown so dark as to be almost black—and his strange clothes that resembled battle armor.

He bowed at once and introduced himself as Karnagh, from a distant country the name of which I did not catch in the clamor of the feast.

A handsome figure he cut, all brawn and thick hair that fell in twisted locks below his waist. And friendly too, not for a moment without a smile upon his face. I tried to remember where I had heard his name before but could not recall.

An empty seat gaped on his other side, and so he had no one else to talk to but me. He sampled every tray the servants brought around, and praised the food.

"Do you mind?" He pointed to the bone of the pheasant thigh I had just finished.

He had been throwing his leavings under the table from time to time, and I assumed he had his hound at his feet. Until I felt a heavy tail fall across my slippers. The tail began to beat the floor restlessly, and I heard a low rumbling growl as Karnagh tossed the bone under the tapestry that covered the table.

And then I remembered where I had heard his name before. He was the warlord Batumar had told me about on the road to Karamur— Karnagh, whose people talked to tigers and took them to battle. *He would not…*

I paled at the thought. And even as I tried to convince myself I could not possibly be right, something massive rubbed against my legs under the table.

"Tigran," Karnagh murmured under his breath, and the beast moved away from me. The man gave me a conspiratorial wink and pulled the tablecloth up enough to allow a glimpse of the largest tiger that lived in all the lands.

I froze in my seat. The beast looked at me as if bored. Lord Karnagh dropped the cloth back. I understood at once why no one sat on his other side.

"Batumar said you would not mind. Everyone knows he is harmless unless he is hunting or we are in battle. I do not know why the womenfolk around these parts always squeal if he comes near. It is fair heartening to find one brave lady in the castle," he said with a wide smile.

I steeled my spine, not wanting to tremble and disappoint the man. "He does as you bid him?"

Lord Karnagh's smile stretched wider as he started into the story of their last fight.

He most certainly managed to distract me from my fears of the upcoming night. So preoccupied was I with the beast under the table that could at any moment decide to sample me for dessert, I did not think of Batumar until he rose to leave.

I dared not breathe or move until I was certain he had left the hall, for fear I would draw attention to myself. He did not call my name.

A short reprieve, then, I thought, and as others rose, I took my leave of Lord Karnagh to return to my chamber, wishing to be alone for as long as I could before the High Lord sent for me. I knew I had but a moment's delay. To take my body was his right; indeed, I was his possession. And the Kadar liked to take.

I could have never found my way back, but as soon as I stood, Leena appeared by my side.

I barely recognized Pleasure Hall. Steaming water filled the great hole in the middle of the floor, heated through some magical mechanism from below. Silk pictures, finer than any at the House of Tahar, hung on the walls. I turned from the images and prayed that Batumar would never want to do any of that to my poor body.

But why else would he have ordered the pictures to be hung if not to educate me before I went to him? I wished the High Lord's Pleasure Hall had other concubines so I might ask how such things were conducted. I seemed alone in the great space, however, save the servants. I did not take that as a good sign.

I remembered the tales I had heard at Lord Tahar's Maiden Hall about concubines who brought shame to their lord or displeased him. They were put to the sword, their bodies hung from the whipping post for days for all to see. I heard whispers of Lord Tahar's father, who had one concubine sewn into a burlap sack with a selection of snakes and tossed into the harbor. Her lover had been castrated, then burned alive.

I thought of the endless row of empty chambers in the High Lord's Pleasure Hall. It seemed impossible that this many women could have displeased Batumar.

Would *I*?

I was too distraught to appreciate the gossamer night rail that lay upon my bed. But then I took a closer look. *Sweet spirits.* I could see the embroidered flower petals of the coverlet clearly through the thin fabric that shimmered in the light of fire.

Leena moved to unlace my gown, but I sent her away. I would have been too embarrassed to wear such a garment in front of her, let alone Batumar. I smoothed down the thick brocade of the gown—the more barriers between me and the High Lord, the better. I wondered whether it would have been untowardly if I put on my traveling cape.

I sank onto the padded stool to wait in front of the fire, but as time passed and my back ached, I lay upon the bed, snuggled against the small mountain of pillows.

———

I awoke to the morning light filtering in through the small windows high on the wall, and to noises made by a servant woman stoking the fire in the hearth. She had a bent back and hair of silver, one of her eyes milky white and almost certainly blind.

"My name is Tilia, my lady. I am at your service," she said with a bow as soon as she saw me come awake. She brought my morning meal and apologized for the lack of fresh mosan juice.

"The mist is upon us. May the goddesses save us." Her aged hands trembled. "It came on early before anyone could go to market. No market now and not anything else either," she mumbled on as she served me.

"A snowstorm?" I had hoped the season of snow was behind us. Escape would be easier in fair weather.

"Nay, not snow. Not bad weather it is, but great evil, my lady."

The honest fear in her voice sent a chill down my spine.

"It will pass by tomorrow, but the streets will be empty until then. Not a soul would walk into the mist, not one. Thick it is like goat milk and foul. Many unwary fools have disappeared into it never to be seen again. They say invisible beasts live in the mist and feast on human flesh."

She held on to a clump of charms that hung from her belt. I ate my boiled eggs and cheese in silence as her words darted around in my mind like frightened mice.

She took the tray when I finished my victuals, and other servants came to attend other chores. All had charm belts around their waists now, although I had not seen that custom followed at Karamur the previous night.

By the time they combed and arranged my hair, the dressmaker stood in the door again. She worked with me that entire day with but a few breaks. She did not leave until the servant women came for me in time for the evening meal. It seemed the High Lord's household ate together every evening when the High Lord resided at Karamur, and not only on special feast days as did the House of Tahar.

"I hope the evening finds you well. Have you yet recovered from our journey?" Batumar asked, once I took my seat, careful of the tiger.

His plain white shirt stretched over wide shoulders, his dark hair spilling down his back. He wore no symbols of his station, yet he looked as regal as a king. Were he dressed as the last beggar, he would have still looked a warrior. His fearsome sword rested on the bench on his other side, ready in its scabbard.

"Yes, my lord."

He watched me for a moment; then his gaze moved to the man on my other side. "Lord Karnagh, have you given more thought to our discussions?"

I felt awkward for being in the way of their conversation, although neither seemed to mind.

"An alliance will be easy enough to forge," Lord Karnagh said after some time. "But bringing armies together would be almost impossible."

Batumar nodded. "No one will leave their homes undefended. Our armies stand scattered on a host of islands to be trampled one by one, while if we stood together with one force and met Woldrom's hordes as such…"

The men's faces reflected their frustration.

"If we could know for certain where Woldrom will attack next," Lord Karnagh suggested.

"A good spy would be useful. Rorin knows, Woldrom has spies everywhere. Best would be to stop him before he comes this far. Can any of his captains be turned against him? Has any the power to bring him down?"

Lord Karnagh shook his head. "He lets no one close enough to harm him. Gives no one power enough to replace him. He does not even have a second in command."

"He is isolated, then. We will use that to our advantage."

As the two lords talked, I looked around. The lizard-eyed old man next to Lord Gilrem watched me just as closely as he had the day before.

When the High Lord turned to his brother, I dared ask Lord Karnagh, "My lord, would you tell me who sits by Lord Gilrem?"

"Shartor, Karamur's soothsayer," Lord Karnagh said without much enthusiasm.

I spent the meal talking with him once again, my feet tucked carefully beneath my seat.

Little laughter rang out over the Great Hall, unlike the night before. Dark tension thickened the air, the torches flickering as if preparing to fail at any moment. A chill touched me that I had not felt the previous night. More than one servant mentioned the mist in passing.

Batumar rose to leave early, without bidding me to follow him, and as soon as he left, the Great Hall was fast deserted, all who had dined within eager to return to their chambers.

I was just as eager to reach mine. Having escaped the High Lord for the second day, I grew hopeful that he only wanted me as a healer. Maybe he only housed me in Pleasure Hall because it stood empty, available. I held on to that thought.

He had required nothing but healing of me all this time. I needed to start readying for more of that at once, before my services were called upon and he caught me unprepared.

"I shall need an escort to the forest tomorrow," I told Tilia, who was once again feeding the fire in my chamber.

Alarm flooded her lined face. "Lady Tera, the High Lord's concubines never left the palace, except at his request and in his company." She bowed deep.

So he *had* concubines in the past. I filed that ominous thought away.

"I am a healer. I will need a good supply of herbs. Perhaps if I told you what to look for, you could bring them to me."

True horror flooded her face then as she shook her head and threw herself to the floor, crying and protesting that I should not ask her to do such a terrible thing.

As I could not understand her anguish and wished to cause no more, I sent her away.

When Leena came, I sat patiently while she unlaced my dress. I had learned that a tight bodice was most uncomfortable for sleeping, and also I knew what hard work went into the servants restoring a dress from a wrinkled state. I would relent and wear the night rail.

I feared that bringing up herb collecting might distress Leena as it had Tilia, so I decided to find out why the servants had such an aversion to herbs before I brought up that subject again. Instead, I asked a question that had formed in my mind during the evening meal.

"Lord Karnagh seems an esteemed guest. How is it that he is not offered a maiden? Does he not take offense?"

"Such is not practiced at Karamur, my lady. No Maiden Hall here. The High Lord does not keep with many of the old traditions. And Lord Karnagh would have enough women ready to warm his bed would he only ask."

"He does not?"

"A Selorm he is."

"A priest?" I heard about such practices in faraway countries, men dedicating themselves to their gods and forswearing all women.

"Nay, my lady. Selorm are his people. Different from us they are. But one woman for every man, and one man for every woman for as long as they live."

"It is such among my own," I told her, beginning to like the man even more.

"Gets stranger, the tale." Her fingers never stopped moving as she talked. "It is said that sometime after Selorm males reach manhood, they are beset by a powerful urge to mate. They cannot until then, you see. And they do not choose their mates in the common way, either. They 'call' from deep within. Some strange vibration it is. And only their one true mate can hear it, and she will hurry to her man's side. They can call across endless distances."

I thought of Lord Karnagh and wondered whether he had yet called himself a mate.

Leena said, "Their sacred tradition it is and taken most seriously. I've heard tell the worth of a man is measured by how fast his mate responds to the call, and from how far he was able to call her. The wait, if long, can be most painful."

I could scarcely imagine such, and would have asked more questions, but a young woman at the door interrupted us.

"The High Lord sends his summons, my lady."

CHAPTER ELEVEN

(Leena)

I had to press my palm against my chest to calm my clamoring heart as Leena brought a white, fur-trimmed cape. Not as thick as a traveling cape, the chamois had been delicately worked and fell in soft folds around me. I slipped my feet into matching fur-trimmed slippers, too nervous to enjoy all the finery.

I followed the young woman down twisting hallways with increasing dread. She left me at a simple wooden door, and for a moment I thought of bolting. Then I straightened my spine and held my head high. "My lord?"

No response came. Yet I knew I was meant to go in, so I pushed the door open.

A spacious antechamber spread before me, lit by a multitude of oil lamps. The two men inside looked up at my entrance. I could not puzzle out the High Lord's thoughts from his gaze, but the other man, whom I had not seen before, watched me with open suspicion.

He wore odd garments, a tunic too long, woven with a jumble of colors most unpleasing to the eye. Slightly built and shorter than Batumar, he stood with his chest puffed out and chin held high, as if trying to give the appearance of a strong presence. But the lines on his face betrayed his worries. He grew more restless as he watched me, while Batumar grew more relaxed.

"We have an emissary from the Kingdom of Orh," the High Lord said. "One of the Palace Guards could translate most of his message, but I would know all of it."

I could have flown to the ceiling, I felt so light with relief.

"How many warriors does your king need?" Batumar asked, and I translated.

"As many as the High Lord can spare, for the enemy is fierce." The emissary shifted on his feet.

"Has your king sent emissaries to others?"

"To all that are famous for fight." The man's gaze darted between Batumar and me.

"Tell me what you know of the Kerghi," Batumar ordered.

"The number of their warriors has grown a hundredfold, so they fight to settle new lands. They need the ore of the mountains for armor and the wheat of the fields to feed their armies."

The man rushed on, "When they take a kingdom, they kill all the women past childbearing age and all the males over the age of twelve, unless there is a slave market close enough to drive them there. The younger women they use for labor and to breed future warriors; the boys they carry off for military training."

The spirits save us from the Kerghi hordes, I thought as I translated.

"The enemy has already taken the palace," the man said in a grim tone. "My king is even now hiding in the mountains. He pledges to you all the crystals of his treasure chamber if you come to his aid."

"I do not like leaving my own people unprotected," said Batumar, and the man's shoulders sagged in defeat.

"But Woldrom must be stopped," Batumar went on. "I will take as many warriors as I can spare and help your king."

The man fell on his knees in front of him. "You shall be known as the savior of our people."

"He might be lying," Batumar said to me in Kadar, and I knew he had noticed the man's odd gestures as I had. "It could be a trap."

I could feel the fear and desperation in the emissary's heart. They did need the help. I did not doubt their survival depended on it. "Perhaps he fears you will say no, and his king will punish him for bringing an unfavorable answer."

The man spoke again, listing the treasures his king promised, reaching up several times to rub his chin. I translated all to Batumar.

"It is as if the lies he speaks drip down his chin and burn his skin," I added, still in Kadar, at the end. "But only when he speaks of payment."

Batumar nodded, and I went on, emboldened. "If the enemy already has the palace, they probably have the king's treasure." They might have even taken it out of the kingdom already.

Batumar questioned the emissary on this at once and did not rest until the man finally admitted the truth.

I translated back and forth for near half the night.

When the High Lord finished with his inquiry, he sent me away, but from then on, instead of spending my days at Pleasure Hall, I was assigned to his personal service.

He spoke many languages but asked me to translate when needed, and from time to time, he would ask my opinion on the worth of the man before him.

I served him like that until the day he marched off with his warriors to help the King of Orh at the next mooncrossing. Not for the treasure, which he had little hope of seeing, but because he wanted to stop the Khergi hordes before they reached our island.

Lord Karnagh joined him with the small troop of warriors he had in Karamur. They added quite a splash of the exotic to Batumar's army.

Offerings were heaped high on Rorin's altar at the feast the night before the army's departure, all the right foods served to ensure a favorable outcome for the battle.

When a servant summoned me to Batumar's chambers after the feast, I expected to be once again required only to translate. But when I walked through the outer door, the High Lord's antechamber stood empty, the door to his bedchamber ajar.

"Tera." He spoke the single word softly.

My heart trembled.

Yet I had no choice but to go to him.

His bedchamber was smaller than I had expected, holding nothing more but a large bed covered in black pelts that shone like silk in the light of the fire of a giant hearth. A small table and a single trunk stood to the side.

Batumar sat on the bed's edge, his elbows resting on his knees, exhaustion etched on his forehead. He had been everywhere at once since he had returned to the city: training with his warriors, meeting with dignitaries, guiding the work to strengthen the fortress.

He wore a plain linen shirt and worn leather leggings, scuffed black boots on his feet, the same as all his warriors. Yet something about him, even when worn out by work, always remained regal. Awareness shimmered under the surface even when he was resting. I had no doubt that, if the occasion called for it, he could and would take charge of any situation at a moment's notice.

"We leave for battle tomorrow," he said, his large frame illuminated by the flames.

I feared I understood too well for what purpose he had summoned me. "I did not think you kept with the old customs. Your army is strong, my lord. You do not need the luck," I rushed to say.

His lips twisted into a rueful smile. "I might not follow the old ways, but all men need luck. And even the strongest need some comfort now and again."

I reached for my phial, but it no longer hung from my neck these days, so I ended up clenching my hands together in front of me.

He noticed. "Do you not feel honored to serve your High Lord and your people?"

I pulled forth all my courage. "My people, the Shahala," I emphasized the last word, "would find distasteful such sacrifice. As for honor —what honor could be found in forcing a slave?"

Even as I spoke, I knew my brazen words had rushed forth far too recklessly.

His face darkened. "You are not a slave." His words came out clipped. "You are no longer a slave," he repeated, as if for some reason he found that important.

I challenged him, knowing I risked my life. "May I then return to my people?"

His gaze did not move from my face. "Do you despise me?"

In truth, I despised all Kadar.

Nothing but the crackling fire broke the silence.

At long last, he did look away. "Come, then, and serve me the way you are willing."

He pulled his shirt over his head and twisted his bare back toward me. "See what you can do to silence my old injuries before I add new ones to the list."

He caught me with that. I could not abide to see anyone suffer. I moved forward, wary of a trap, but he sat still.

Firelight played on his wide shoulders, glinted off twisting cords of muscles. He was built for war. I was only too aware that he could snap me in half like a young boy snaps a twig.

Yet I sensed no danger from him.

As soon as I laid my hands on his warm skin, a river of pain coursed through me as if my own. I had always been able to feel the pain of others, but never this strongly before, never this deep inside me. That he would suffer this without asking me sooner to heal him troubled me greatly.

The pain in his shoulder, and now suddenly in mine, proved to be a bone that had been broken and badly healed. He lived in constant pain, yet for as long as I had known him, he had never shown sign of it.

"If you would lie down, my lord," I said, and he did so, facing his pillow, the High Lord obeying the slave.

I slid my palm over his scarred skin until I found the spot where the pain pulsed the strongest. I nearly wept with the hurt of it.

One hand on his shoulder, with the other I grabbed my own, which felt just as ill-broken. As pain threatened to swallow me, I fought against the waves of agony. I nearly forgot the man and my hand upon him as I called on my mother's spirit to heal me, to take away my pain.

In my mind's eye, the bones under both hands were one and the same. And as the healing spirit rose up within me to ease the pain, I felt the muscles in Batumar's back relax, and at the same time my own breath came easier. I felt the bone in his shoulder soften as if melting, then harden back again, following the pattern of my own good bones resting under my other hand.

I had never been able to do healing such as this before. I did not know how I had deserved the sudden gift from the spirits, but as my limbs trembled, I knew they did exact some price for it.

When Batumar reached out to draw me to the bed with him, I was too drained to resist. I could only pray that he would not take advantage of my weakness.

I looked up and found his gaze intent on my face, his expression unreadable. With what little strength I had left, I moved to leave.

He held me in place. "Rest now, Tera of the Shahala." He said my name as a free woman's. "You will not come to harm at my hands this day."

———

I woke alone. The light of day illuminated the thick glass window that looked to a courtyard. Someone had already fed the fire. I stretched under the silky soft pelts, enjoying the warmth of the hearth.

A master must have carved the white stone of the fireplace, decorated with battle scenes. In the middle, smoke and flames had turned the white gray, giving those battles a more sinister feel.

I enjoyed my cozy nest for another moment, then slipped from the bed and straightened my dress, regretting the wrinkled mess I had made of it. I smoothed out the material with my palms as best I could, and nearly ran into Leena as I stepped from the High Lord's outer chamber.

She bowed immediately. "Does the morn find my lady well?"

She had been most kind to me since my arrival, showing not only the deference and respect that was expected of servants, but also a genuine caring for my wellbeing.

"Fine well." I had been fully warm for the first time, and had the best night's sleep since I had left my Shahala home.

I was sunborn, through and through. My body had grown to tolerate cold at Lord Tahar's House, and my clothes had thickened with added layers, but it seemed the chill always found a way to my skin. And the stone castle of Karamur, on the northernmost tip of the island, was colder yet than Kaharta Reh.

The fire never stopped burning in the hearth in my chamber, but the flames across the room provided not half the heat that had Batumar in the bed all through the night.

"The High Lord ordered that you should have your own servant to assist your person. I have asked him for the honor, my lady. He left the decision up to you."

Two servant girls and a number of women stopped by Pleasure Hall regularly to see to my every need. I hardly required help beyond that. At the House of Tahar, not even Kumra had a personal servant. "Thank you, but I already receive sufficient assistance."

The smile slid off Leena's face, and she bowed deeper. "Forgive my brazenness, my lady."

I had not meant to hurt her with my rejection. I drew a deep breath. "I shall be happy to have you attend me."

She looked up then and smiled, the sun coming out on her face and erasing her age for a moment. "I shall do my best to serve you well."

As we walked to Pleasure Hall, I looked back at her and considered our new bond. Since she did seem to care for me, maybe she would not betray me if I asked her some questions.

"Have you served long at the palace?"

"For some time."

"Have you met a Shahala healer, Chalee? She came to heal Barmorid."

Her lips stretched wide enough to reveal that, despite her age, she still had all her teeth. "A blessed soul she was, my lady, although, before my time in service here."

Hope leaped. "Do you know where she is buried?"

"A strange affair that turned out to be." Leena's face clouded. "The High Lord Barmorid her laid out as if she were a prized warrior or favored concubine. But the body disappeared before the funeral. The palace help gossiped that she was taken back to the Shahala lands by her own kind."

This I knew not to be true. Heaviness filled my heart. How would I ever find my mother's grave now? Other questions joined that first in my bewildered mind. Who had stolen her body and why?

"Do you know how she died?"

"A sudden illness, my lady."

This I did not believe.

"Did you know the Lady Chalee?" Leena asked, but I did not reply.

Instead, I asked a question of my own to distract both of us from the topic. "Tell me, Leena, do you have a family?"

We turned down another long hallway, Leena a step behind me. I glanced over my shoulder when no immediate response came.

She shook her head, her expression clouding once again.

Maybe when they had taken her as a slave, her family had been left behind. Did she look as I did, every day for a way to escape? If so, could we not succeed together? Batumar had left and taken many of his warriors with him.

But I did not yet trust her enough to share my thoughts, so I asked another question instead. "Will you move to Pleasure Hall?"

I did not know what rules governed personal servants and hoped she might help ease my solitude. Also, I hoped to grow to know her well enough to decide whether I could involve her in my escape.

"It is not our custom for the servants to live with the concubines." She wrung her hands. "Forgive me, my lady."

"I am the only concubine," I said as we reached the carved double-doors, and I pushed them open. I looked down the row of empty chambers. "If I knew what the others did to displease the High Lord, maybe I could avoid their fate."

Horror flooded her face. "Do not say such a thing, I beg you, my lady. What happened here will never happen again."

I slowed my steps. "You know, then?"

She looked ready to flee, so I took her hand and sat on a pillow-smothered bench in our path, determined to hear the tale.

"I heard talk when I came into the High Lord's service," she said with great reluctance.

"Will you tell me?"

I could have ordered her but did not. Truly, the role of concubine was as uncomfortable for me as the role of maiden and slave. Tera I was, a Shahala, daughter of Chalee, all I had ever wished to be.

Leena's glance skittered to the side. "We should not speak of it. I wish not to scare you, nor… Some say it is a curse, but truly it is not," she rushed to say.

A curse. Invisible cold fingers danced down the middle of my back. I released her hand. "What kind of curse?"

The fine lines deepened into furrows on her forehead. "Lady Tera, you must pay no mind to such gossip."

"If you do not tell me, I will but imagine worse things than what happened." Already the most gruesome images filled my mind.

She bit her lips, drew a deep breath, opened her mouth, then closed it again.

"Leena, please."

"At one time, High Lord Batumar had many concubines," she began finally, wringing her hands, her voice barely audible. "Not as many as Barmorid, the High Lord before him. Batumar was still young. But Barmorid honored him with a number of maidens before he died, and once the rest of the warlords had elevated Batumar to sit upon the high seat, many of them gave him their daughters to strengthen their alliance."

I could almost see Pleasure Hall filled with the laughter of young women and children. "What happened?"

"The fairest among them, Nolla, was his first concubine and his favorite. In time, she gave Batumar three little sons, the joy of his eyes." Leena's voice broke for a second. "But as it is in many Pleasure Halls, jealousy…" Her shoulders sagged. "Some say a concubine faces as many dangers on her silk pillows as any warrior in battle."

I remembered Kumra and nodded.

"Elrid was the oldest of the women and the most used to power, for her father had allowed her much in her youth. When she finally bore a son, she thought if only Nolla and her children did not stand in her way, Batumar would come to care for her more." Leena pressed her lips together as if afraid to let the rest escape.

"What did she do?"

"She poisoned…"

I gasped at her words but did not doubt them. Kumra too had grown poisonous plants under her windows. "She killed the mother with her babes?"

Leena swayed, rubbing her hands over her face. "And to make everyone think they were taken by some strange disease, Elrid poisoned some others too, those she thought the High Lord most favored."

"Did no one suspect?"

"Batumar fought at war. The soothsayer said the concubines had done something to offend the goddesses. He bade them to purify themselves and make offerings."

"What happened to Elrid?" I wondered if even now she was somewhere in the palace's dungeons.

"She thought to take one more woman, Loren. Loren grew suspicious, you see. So Elrid poisoned her water jar, then retired to her chamber, claiming to be too tired to even stand. But that night as the servants brought the evening meal, one of them dropped the mosan juice the concubines liked so well and spilled it. She was slow to return with a new jar, so Loren brought her own water jar to fill everyone's cup."

I held my breath as I waited to hear the rest of the dark tale.

"All died but a few of the children, a boy and four girls who fell asleep before the evening meal and were not woken for it. When Elrid found out what happened, she knew Batumar would see the truth. She did not want to wait for the Palace Guard to come for her, so she bound her babe to her breast and climbed to the top of the highest tower of Karamur."

"Did she jump?"

Leena closed her eyes. "As Batumar was crossing the gate."

Neither of us spoke for a while, the picture conjured too terrible to bear.

I understood at last why the servants had been so wary every time I had asked for herbs. They had likely thought me another poison-wielding concubine.

"Where are the children who survived?" I asked after some time.

"Grown up and gone. The last of the girls had gone to Lord Remlan not long ago, a warlord on the eastern borders. Such impatience you have never seen, my lady." Leena's lips stretched into a thin smile. "She had seen him when he came to petition the High Lord, and she would not leave her father a moment of peace after that."

Longing filled her voice. Maybe she missed the girl.

"And the boy?"

"He became a brave young warrior." Leena's voice turned somber once again, a tear glistening in the corner of her eye. "This past spring, he died in battle."

I thought of Batumar then, High Lord of the Kadar, the most powerful man on Dahru, and I thought about the hidden sorrows of his heart. Wounds of the flesh could be grievous indeed, but not hopeless if a healer had the skill. Injuries to a man's spirit were far more complicated.

Leena dabbed her eyes with her sleeve. "War is a dangerous game, my lady."

Her words brought me a new batch of troubling thoughts. "When a warlord dies, what happens to his concubines?"

"The older ones might go to live at the House of a grown son. The young ones and their babes go to his brother's Pleasure Hall."

I thought of Lord Gilrem, and silently implored the spirits to keep Batumar safe in battle.

CHAPTER TWELVE

(Shartor)

In Batumar's absence, I had plenty of time to roam the palace and plan my escape. Karamur did not hold my mother's grave. As soon as I found out how she had died, I would leave.

I had to hurry. I did not know how long the High Lord would be away. Unfortunately, unlike at the House of Tahar, Batumar's guards watched the palace as tightly in the High Lord's absence as when he resided within the gates, the number of his warriors great indeed.

Although I was the favorite concubine—the servants much insisted on this—I had none of Kumra's responsibilities, having neither maidens to direct nor other concubines to watch over. Batumar's stewards looked after his palace and its affairs. Lord Gilrem performed his brother's day-to-day functions, so I saw more of him and his guards than before and was careful to keep out of their way.

To Leena's consternation, I spent a lot of time in the kitchen, liking the activity and the variety of people who passed through all day long.

I hoped I might overhear some gossip about my mother or something that might aid my escape.

I stayed out of the way as much as I could, as my presence made the servants uncomfortable. For the first few days, they asked my permission for each little task they were about to do. But once I reassured them that I merely wanted to learn the ways of the palace, and enough time passed so that my actions gave support to my words, they slowly began to relax and their easier ways of talk and jesting, which I had so enjoyed at Tahar's kitchen, returned.

I even taught the cook, managing as best we could with the lack of some ingredients, a few dishes of my own people. These he eagerly made to the high praise of all, although I could not be sure if the compliments spoke to the merit of the dish or their fear of my position. Still, after some time, the servants grew easier in my presence.

In truth, other than the lack of freedom, I had little to complain about during those days. Leena pampered me as a mother would, and I grew most attached to her company. To make up for my isolation, she entertained me with tales of the Kadar, legends of the High Lords of the past, and stories of Batumar.

"Back in the beginning," she told me one day, "the Kadar had no High Lord. The warlords of our people ruled their Houses as kings and often warred with each other."

We were enjoying the steaming pool in the middle of Pleasure Hall. Not long before, I had at last found a way to coax Leena into the water, which she had eyed with longing since the pool had been filled.

As a servant, such was not allowed to her, and even when I had assured her I would not the least mind, she could not bring herself to break the rules. So I feigned an ache in my shoulders and asked her to attend me in the water to massage the sore muscles in the rising steam. An order for the benefit of her lady she could not refuse.

"Then a strong and wise warlord arose," she said. "Coulron saw how sparring weakened his people against their enemies. Some warlords would even fight on the side of outsiders against other Kadar." She rubbed my shoulders with hands strong from labor yet gentle with care.

Such kindness she showed me day after day that in my dreams her face and my mother's began to look more and more alike. And as the days passed without the High Lord returning, Leena became more like a mother than a servant to me. I trusted her in all things except with my plan of escape.

"And Coulron," she went on, "called the First Council of the warlords, and to them he brought those matters. He gave his word to forgive all trespasses of the others, to avenge neither the loss of land, nor the loss of man, nor the loss of livestock that had gone before. And he spoke of a future in which Kadar warriors would be like brothers, and they would stand firm against even the most fearsome enemy, and the borders of their nation would expand, their fame traveling to distant lands."

She rinsed my shoulders, then continued her kneading. "His words like dripping honey, his countenance as handsome as Rorin's own, his dark locks fell upon shoulders as wide as—" She paused. "For truth, I believe he looked a lot like our High Lord, my lady."

I glanced over my shoulder. A great champion of Batumar was she, blessing his name for one thing or the other near every day.

"Coulron's strength drew the other warlords. They trusted his words and honor. And so the First Council decided that from among them they should choose a High Lord who would act like the head of the body, keeping the parts working together. And thus they chose Coulron over them. And he did all he promised and more, and the Kadar grew in strength and number."

She started into another tale, only to be interrupted by Tilia, who came in to add wood to the fire.

"One of the servant girls ran off from the kitchen," she told us amid much head shaking. "Fell in love with a merchant, she did. Wants to go home with him when his caravan leaves at the next moon crossing."

Everything within me stilled. "To which port are they headed?"

"Some southern port, my lady. I cannot recall the name." She ducked her head in apology.

Southern port. That meant a Shahala town, most likely.

My heart thrilled. I could barely sit still as Tilia left and Leena finished her story. I barely heard a word of it. Like an obsessed weaver I wove my plans of escape, hope grabbing hold of me with fervor.

First thing the next day, I headed to the kitchen to see if I could find out more. I had not yet reached the door when the high-pitched scream of a child tore the morning's silence. I rushed forward.

An ashen-faced woman was pulling a little girl from a puddle of steaming soup on the floor. She had likely tipped the boiling pot on herself. The servants crowded in as the crying mother cradled the girl's head on her lap.

The child's father rushed from the pantry, pale with anguish, the first to notice me. He stopped in his tracks, bowed, and apologized for the ruined meal.

It happened so quickly my head spun. My spirit poured forth into the child before I ever touched her, her pain so sharp on my skin that I staggered. My lips opened, but I could not hear myself talking. Still, I must have, as servants moved to do my bidding.

The father lifted the child and placed her on a cleared table where her mother began to peel off the still-steaming clothes. Two strong women had to hold me up so I could walk to them.

I touched the girl's forehead and drew the pain until she breathed easier. But all that pain filled *me* now, and I could barely stand up under the weight. How had my mother drawn such pain and worse without ever showing sign of the strain?

My spirit moved through the child and cradled hers, even as it prepared to flee from her body. I cajoled that spirit, held its flickering light, whispered into it the will to live.

Servants returned with my scant store of herbs, although I could not remember asking them. They made healing teas for which I could not recall giving instruction. I dripped a strong tincture between the girl's lips, measuring carefully.

I cooled her skin with water, over and over, then made a new potion, poked a hole in a clean leather bag, filled it, then pumped it with a rapid squeezing motion to mist the contents over the child's injuries.

An eternity passed before the tide seemed to turn at last, and the girl's eyes fluttered. The power of the plants that had grown from the power of the earth, mother of all of us, worked from the outside, and my spirit and hers worked from within.

At long last, the pain inside me ebbed, and none too soon. My spirit returned, and I could see again the girl's face and not just the inner workings of her injury. The angry red welts on her face had disappeared, the skin near healed with no sign of infection, only a small scar remaining under her chin. I reached out to heal that too, but I collapsed summarily.

I saw through a haze as the child sat up, hugged by the mother with more tears in her eyes, and saw the women reach for me to carry me to my chamber, as male servants could not touch a concubine. I saw the tall doors of Pleasure Hall open, but I saw nothing beyond that. Darkness enveloped me.

I slept through the rest of the day and that whole night, not awakening until the noon meal of the following day, with Leena weeping at the foot of my bed.

From then on, no servant would pass me without a smile. Gifts began to show up in my chamber, little bunches of herbs, as many healing plants as they knew, until I had a fair store, although not nearly as complete as had been my mother's.

I had asked for those plants many times before and had always been evaded, had meant to plead with Batumar but had always been too distraught and distracted when in his presence. But now at last I had my medicines, and a good thing too, for the sick began to come, fearful at first, then more confident, in a never-ending trickle.

So often did a servant woman come to beg for my help, I began to spend more and more time in the kitchen where I could be approached by those in need, male and female alike.

The kitchen had an endless supply of boiling water, which I often needed. I liked the warmth of the cooking fires and the back door to the street—for the vendors who brought fresh goods to the palace each day—which could be open for fresh air as needed.

And so the power of healing finally awakened within me. And as the days passed, I learned that like the power of the muscles that moved my body, the more I did one day, the more I could do the next and easier. I instructed the seamstress to prepare a proper healer's veil and wore the thin linen around my shoulders like a shawl at all times to keep it at hand, so often did I have to don it.

I often asked the servants who came to me whether they had served under the previous High Lord, Barmorid. If they had, I asked them about another Shahala healer, Chalee. Some remembered her and blessed her name. They claimed she died of a sudden illness, but none knew where she was buried.

I wondered whether I might have more luck with the caravan. They might be the very people who had spirited away her body from the fortress city.

I had my mind on that when Leena came for me one morning. "Lord Gilrem summons you, my lady."

From the servants' whispers, I had learned he had his own House within the fortress, fit for a prince, with a Pleasure Hall of legendary proportions. He did, however, despite such comforts, spend a lot of his time at the palace, especially in Batumar's absence. The High Lord trusted him with much responsibility.

I thought maybe he needed my healing.

Leena escorted me to him.

Most of the time, she went about her affairs arranging my meals and the cleaning and renovation of Pleasure Hall, but from time to time, she attached herself to me and would not let me out of her sight.

We walked through the door of the Great Hall, where Lord Gilrem and Shartor waited. I moved forward. Lena remained by the threshold, at a respectable distance.

"I hope the morn finds you well, my lords." Neither man seemed ill.

"Fine well, my lady," Lord Gilrem said without warmth.

Shartor cut a tall figure in his gray robe, his braided and oiled beard reaching nearly to his thin waist. But of all his features, his eyes stood out as the most unusual, moving independently of each other. He looked like a giant lizard, ready to dash his fearsome tongue out and swallow me whole.

I shook off the fanciful notion and bowed to Lord Gilrem first, then to Shartor, and hoped I did not miss the order and give offense.

"Your fame grows throughout the palace," Lord Gilrem said.

He wore rich garments as he had at the House of Tahar. When with

Batumar, he dressed more simply, similar to the warriors, as the High
Lord himself did.

"And yet I wonder," he added. "What other powers do you have?"

As I tasted Lord Gilrem's question, my shoulders tensed.

Shahala healers indeed had powers known to few others, but to say
so would have been unpardonably rude, a crass bragging. "No
powers, my lord, but some measure of skill to ease certain pains when
the spirits will it."

Shartor sucked in his breath at my last words, and too late I remembered that some Kadar took mention of the spirits as a slight to Rorin.

"You are modest." Lord Gilrem examined me closely. "I do not trust
that in a man or a woman. It is our nature to make the most of our abilities and make others believe we have even more."

"I have no great powers, my lord," I answered truthfully. What I
could do was nothing compared to my mother's deeds.

"You have the power to break the chains of evil women." He hinted
for the first time of remembering Kumra and her daughter and all that
had happened to him at the House of Tahar. "And you have the
wisdom to know I do not want to speak of it. You have not come to me
for payment. Perhaps you think you hold me in debt and like the
thought?"

I said nothing, for I felt none too comfortable in his presence. Like a
volatile flame he seemed, and at any moment I expected the scorch of
his blaze. Although I could not understand why, my instincts said
Shartor was the fuel behind the fire.

Lord Gilrem stepped closer.

"You did not seek the favor of the High Lord by telling him how
you saved his brother. If you had done so, I would have denied it and
you would have been punished swiftly for the lie. And yet, you did
find favor with Batumar. Karamur is filled with the talk of you." He
watched me, his gaze thick with suspicion, his voice tinged with barely
controlled anger.

My mother had once told me that strong anger in a man with a
weak spirit was a dangerous thing. I felt that danger all around me.

"You see too much, Tera of the Shahala," he said. "And you have
power far too much for my liking, no matter how you deny it."

He turned to the soothsayer in a sudden move. "What say you, Shartor? Is she a sorceress?"

I heard Leena's faint gasp behind me in the silence.

Shartor's left eye focused on me, while the right one seemed to examine the smoke-stained ceiling. "She knows no respect for Rorin. Gives all her thanks to the spirits."

The burning torches cast dark shadows on the walls around us.

"As is our Shahala custom, my lord," I said respectfully. "I intended no slight to Rorin."

Shartor waved my words away like one would swat at bothersome summer flies. "Think of the evil, my lord, that befell you at the House of Tahar. Did she not administer the poison herself? She brought on the illness, then cured it, hoping her reward might be to return with you to Karamur as your new concubine. And when my lord proved too wise for her wiles, she worked her magic on the High Lord Batumar."

I glanced from one man to the other, my throat tightening, cold spreading in my chest. "My lords, I have no magic."

Lord Gilrem drew his body taller. "Sorcery is a most serious charge."

Shartor ran his knobby fingers over his beard. "I would not speak it lightly, but we must consider the welfare of our nation and that of your brother. Did he not swear he would not take another concubine?"

Lord Gilrem nodded. "He swore."

"And here she is, holding the will of our High Lord and of the palace servants too, having enthralled them already."

My throat was so tight I could barely push the words out. "My lords, I am innocent of these charges."

"She rode the manyinga. All of Karamur saw her." Shartor pronounced the words like a death sentence. And then a sudden dark light brightened his predatory eyes. He opened his mouth to say something else to Gilrem but seemed to change his mind and turned to me, instead. "Leave us now."

I did so with great relief and some curiosity about what he would say once I left.

Leena followed close behind as I walked down the hall. "You made a bad enemy, my lady."

"Better to have a known enemy than an unknown one." I surprised myself by repeating words I had heard from Batumar.

"You must take care to keep out of his way."

I planned on following that advice. "Does he spend much time at the palace? I have only seen him at the feasts before."

"He lurks at the House of Gilrem these days, my lady. When Batumar became High Lord, Shartor sought to be his chief advisor. But Batumar listens to his warlords and keeps not counsel with sooth-sayers as Barmorid did before him."

So Shartor had lost much power under Batumar.

For the first time, I felt relief when the tall doors of Pleasure Hall closed behind me.

"Lord Gilrem puts much stock in his advice," Leena said as we entered my chamber. "He is these days Shartor's biggest supporter."

I thought of Lord Gilrem, who would forever live in Batumar's shadow. The High Lord cast a wide shadow indeed. To be always an afterthought, the second in command, would have grated even on the most loving of brothers. And Shartor stood ready to whisper the unjustness of it all. Shartor, trying to build back his lost empire.

"Why would Shartor be bothered by someone as unimportant as I?"

For the true inquisitor had been Shartor and not Lord Gilrem. Lord Gilrem might have been weak and callous, but nothing I had seen of him showed a truly evil heart. Shartor's influence on him showed, brought on a layer of darkness that sent a chill down my spine.

"You are the favorite concubine, my lady."

Was I even a concubine? I had only served Batumar with my healing so far.

In his absence, Lord Gilrem ruled as lord of the castle. If Shartor managed to convince him that in me they had a true sorceress…

I shivered and pulled closer to the fire.

———

Three days remained until the departure of the caravan, days I had to survive and use for gathering what I needed. I could have saved food from the trays brought to my chamber every meal time, but Tilia always stayed until I finished, in case I had need of something else. And I had to eat those meals anyway. I could not weaken my body by starving it, for the journey would be long and arduous.

My traveling supplies would have to come from the kitchen.

I spent enough time there so the servants barely noted my presence. My elaborate gowns had room enough to hide some food, but not yet. I would collect what I needed only the day before my departure. The bread would grow stale enough on the long journey.

Other than food, I also needed a disguise. I could not travel dressed as a concubine. The thought of that vexed me greatly, until talking with Leena about Shartor brought me the perfect solution.

"What is the punishment for sorcery?" I asked her, regretting that I would have to leave her behind. I would miss her. Once, I had considered the two of us running away together, but by now I knew her loyalty to Batumar was steadfast.

"A truly powerful sorceress cannot be caught, they say. But she might be tricked by a truly powerful soothsayer." She would not meet my eyes.

"And then?"

She paled, wringing her hands. "The only way to kill a sorceress is to boil her in tar."

Cold crept into my heart. The thought of dying among the Kadar and lying in my grave without the Last Blessing like my mother made me shudder. But then it made me think of a way to gain clothes for my disguise.

"Would you summon the seamstress?" I asked with great calm. "If I am to die, I would be buried in the clothing of my own people. As my only wish, surely it would not be denied."

Tears filled her eyes. "The High Lord will be home soon, my lady. Then you will be safe and Shartor's power once again reduced."

"I pray to the spirits that you are right, but the clothes would give me comfort in the meanwhile."

If I were to convince the caravan to take me on as a Shahala healer, I had to look like one. I needed a proper Shahala thudi and tunic.

I would have loved to travel with the caravan all the way south, but our ways would have to part outside Karamur's gate. Once my absence at the palace was discovered, the Palace Guard would be scouring the city and the road, looking for me.

When the caravan reached the end of the open fields, I planned on disappearing into the woods. I had less to fear of wild beasts than of men and prayed the spirits would keep the tigers away. I would follow the caravan from afar, so as not to lose my way.

Some distance from Karamur, I might even be able to rejoin them again.

"You need not prepare for death, my lady," Leena protested tearfully and, as if she herself became soothsayer, predicted a long and happy life with Batumar. "You will have sons, my lady, you will see. They will be strong warriors."

But at long last, I convinced her to go, and soon she did return with the seamstress, still wringing her hands and bidding me not to despair.

All I required was ready by the next day and, oh, how my heart thrilled just trying on the garments. Light I felt—so light as if I could fly—in the simple thudi and the short tunic, both made from thick, sturdy wool as I had instructed. Considering the cold spring, I would also take my fur-lined Kadar traveling cape.

I spent the next day planning my escape, wandering the hallways —always keeping an eye out for Gilrem and Shartor—noting the position of every guard, the time of their comings and goings. I could find my way around the palace well and knew many alternate routes so I could go around any obstacles, but I feared what would happen once I left the sprawling building.

I did not know the streets or the alleys of the covered marketplace. I had only crossed the city once, upon my arrival, but I had been exhausted from the journey and now had only a dim memory.

I had no way of solving that problem and thought it best not to worry about it. I had plenty of other challenges, such as how to leave the palace in the first place, without the Palace Guard seeing me.

I spent a whole day examining every door and window, with care not to cause suspicion, always ready with an excuse should I be caught and questioned. In the end, I decided to exit the palace in a flour jar, of which many were brought to the kitchen every day in a narrow wagon.

The miller exchanged freshly ground flour for his empty jars in the morning. I hoped in the cavalcade of the busy kitchen, I could find a moment to slip into one of the jars unseen.

I begged the spirits for an opportunity, the wisdom to recognize it, and the courage to make the most of it. They answered me, taking me from Karamur, but in their own way. Instead of finding freedom on the road back home, I found it on death's doorstep.

CHAPTER THIRTEEN

(Into the Mist)

The last day of waiting I spent in nervous agony. I gathered food first thing in the morning—cheese, cured meat, flatbread, and apples. I hid them under my bed, along with a rolled-up blanket. My hands trembled by the time I finished.

My anxieties only increased as the morning progressed, and I suddenly thought of a great many things that could go wrong with my escape. Better to spend the rest of the day in my chamber, lest I gave myself away.

By the time an unfamiliar servant woman asked to see me after the noon meal, I was grateful for the distraction, guessing she had come for healing.

Leena followed on the woman's heels, her face in a displeased frown. She reached out to tug the stranger back. "I told you, my lady is not accepting visitors."

But the portly woman fell to her knees and bowed until her forehead touched the pelt-covered stones.

"Lady Tera, I beg your forgiveness for disturbing you. I plead for a mother's life." Her voice shook, as did her hands that clutched her worn shawl.

"I will gladly help if I can. Tell your master to bring her to the kitchen. I shall wait for her there."

Her master was probably one of the merchants who regularly visited the palace and had heard of my healings. He must have sent the servant because he had a sick concubine.

"My lady cannot be moved. She is near death in childbirth." The woman sobbed with the last couple of words. "She lost two babes in these past years, and now the third might take her. A boy this time, the soothsayer is sure."

Leena tugged her up, appearing not the least touched by the sad tale, despite the soft heart I knew she possessed. "I am sorry for your troubles, but my lady cannot leave the palace. The High Lord is away. We cannot ask him to give her leave."

I stared at the pair, dismay flooding me.

Something deep inside me railed against Leena's words. She had called me her lady, but for all my beautiful clothes and my spacious chamber, I had little more freedom than a slave.

"I beg you to send your powers to my lord's house." The woman tore away from Leena to fall at my feet. She looked at me with a tear-streaked face, brackets of despair around her mouth.

"I wish I had powers as such." Tales of my healings had grown so exaggerated, people were willing to believe anything. "But I cannot tell what ails her until I see her, and I cannot heal her unless I know what ails her."

She sobbed then in earnest, still prostrate before me, her body racked with grief.

Never had I hated not having my own free will more. And from that frustration, resolve was born the next moment.

I was a healer. No High Lord and no threat of punishment could ever change that.

I lifted my veil from the end of the bed and wrapped it around my head, even as Leena's eyes widened with alarm.

"Lead me, then," I said to the woman.

If by some misfortune I could not escape before Batumar returned, let him flog me if it pleased him. Shartor had already accused me of sorcery; what worse charge could they construct against me?

Leena threw herself across the doorway, barring my way, bolder than I had ever seen her. "I beg you, my lady."

I could not be angry at her disobedience. She had my best interests at heart.

"Ask her who her lord is," she insisted.

I did not care. I cared only about the birthing mother in pain.

"She is from the House of Gilrem," Leena said at last, her voice hardening.

Her words stilled me for a moment. Would my healing bring further charges of sorcery upon my head? Was it a trap? If I failed... And even if I succeeded...

Fresh tears washed the servant's face.

"Did Lord Gilrem send you?" I demanded.

"No, my lady."

"He probably forbade them to come." Leena's accusing gaze shot to the woman.

She did not respond, just hung her head.

"You must not go, my lady," Leena begged with renewed force then. "The High Lord will be greatly displeased, and if something should happen to Lord Gilrem's concubine..."

She did not have to finish. Lord Gilrem's punishment would be swift and deadly, of that I was certain. And still, I could not refuse to help, not even at the price of my own life. I had time enough before the departure of the caravan.

I walked forth, and the women followed, Lord Gilrem's servant with a hopeful face, Leena weeping now. Such a fuss she made, servants poked their heads into the hallway to see us pass.

I walked to the nearest side door of the palace.

Only six guards faced us here, all startled to see me intent upon leaving. They asked respectfully that I would return to my chamber. Before I could fully explain why I could not, the Captain of the Guard was sent for and rushed to us with more warriors yet.

Old scars crisscrossed his face, his breastplate scratched and dented. He drew his thick eyebrows together. "My lady, you cannot leave."

I could not push through them. They stood like the mighty trees of the forest and I a slight sapling before them. And yet the woman's pain called me from the distance. Then a simple thought unfurled among the frustrated swirls of my mind, a whisper of the spirits perhaps.

How could they stop me without being allowed to touch me?

I stepped forward. The guards exchanged glances but stood their ground, barring the way.

I took another step. Then another. "I mean to leave."

I stood but a breath from them now. With the next step, we would collide. I moved ahead; they stepped back. I drew a deep breath, then strode forward with purpose, and they could do naught but part before me.

They followed behind, forming a half-angry, half-stunned escort.

"For your protection, my lady." The captain ground out the words, his scowl making clear that he strongly disapproved of my actions.

I pleaded not to be sent with such force, until he agreed to leave all save his three strongest men behind, but he himself insisted on coming.

I hurried down the streets behind Lord Gilrem's servant, careful to note every detail that might aid me in the morning. The city bustled with life, many curious glances directed at us as we progressed. I marked in my mind the street that led to the market, the narrow alleys where I could move unseen. I learned a lot by the time we arrived at the House of Gilrem, a grand house built into the rock wall, its stone columns nearly as majestic as those of the palace.

The servant woman led us not through the bronze-strengthened front door but through the kitchen, a shorter path, I suspected. We hurried through, straight to Pleasure Hall's carved doors, where my guard had to stay behind.

Inside, concubines huddled around in groups, anxiety etched on every face as they clutched their charms. Small children clung to their mothers, all girls. According to Leena, Lord Gilrem had had but four sons. All had been taken by the spotted fever that had swept through the city some years ago and had hit Lord Gilrem's House especially hard.

In a chamber in the back, a woman lay in bed, writhing with pain, unaware of those who came and went around her.

"You will live," I said at once in a strong voice, in case her spirit was listening.

I placed my hands upon her belly and felt the child, nearly dead, his weak life force ebbing away. His mother's spirit prepared to follow.

At first I could not see the illness. The child, indeed a boy, had no deformities; the cord had not twisted around his neck as sometimes happened. I looked harder, deeper, and gasped aloud when I finally understood what ailed him.

The babe's blood ran thick with poison. But not the mother's. How could such a curious thing be accomplished? Had the mother deliberately consumed some evil plant that would harm only the child? I had heard such a thing whispered among the lowest of Kadar serving women but had never believed it to be real.

I looked more carefully, and I saw that the poison came not from what the mother had eaten. Her blood attacked the child, thinking it her body's enemy. This I remembered from one of my mother's lessons but had never seen before.

Although the concubine had shared her spirit with Lord Gilrem and they conceived this child of mixed spirits, their blood could not flow together in the new life they created. Nor could it ever, each child they made being attacked by his own mother's body worse than the one before.

The child's life force weakened with every passing moment. He would have another few pulses of the poisoned blood and no more. I knew not how to help him, although I could feel the pain of his small body as my own, I could feel the pain of his mother and the anguish of her spirit.

I drew all that pain into me as I had done with others before, and with it I tried to draw the poison.

My blood burned as a terrible weakness filled me. I fought against it as I sent my spirit into the child and gave strength to his.

Once his heartbeat steadied, I sent my spirit to strengthen the mother's—slow work and hard, since the poison weakened me. On top of the weakness, agony raked me as the woman labored, her pain my own.

By the time the babe pushed into the world and gave his first mewing cry, I had not the strength to stand or to open my eyes to see him.

I called for my spirit to return as I folded to the floor, but my body brimmed so full of poison no room remained for anything else. Since I could not see with the eyes of my body, I watched with the eyes of my spirit that lingered above as Leena cried over me.

She ordered the servants to bring in a cot, then helped the women to place my body upon it and carry it out to the door where the captain and the Palace Guard awaited.

The men grew ashen-faced at the sight.

The captain stepped forward. "Back to the palace. Hurry."

They rushed through the house to the kitchen but stopped when the outside door creaked open.

Fear widened their eyes as they looked into a thick mist that had descended from the mountain while we had been inside.

Leena sobbed, holding my hand. "We cannot leave."

"We must," said the captain, the set of his face determined.

One of Lord Gilrem's guards looked at the captain as if he had lost his mind. "Nobody walks in the mist."

"We will surely perish, taken by the evil spirits," Leena whispered to my listless body as if hoping that I still listened.

I did, but I could not influence the men. I sensed the fear that coursed through them, gripping their hearts and freezing their limbs, but I did not understand it.

The mist swirled, so thick they probably saw not a hand-width in front of their eyes, but my spirit eyes felt through the mist and found no evil in it. No life, either. The streets stood deserted.

The captain said, "We will take her where her servants can attend her. If she dies, she will do so in her own bed with the cries of her people to honor her. For the Lady Tera and for our High Lord, we must make it so."

He stepped out the door, and after a moment of hesitation, the guards followed.

The captain walked with one hand on the wall. Behind him, a guard held the left corner of the cot with one hand, the other on the captain's shoulder. A second guard held the cot's right corner. The third guard carried the back of the cot. Leena walked by my side, holding my hand. Thus we were all connected.

I could see them with my spirit's eyes as I hovered above. They could not see each other or the wall, walking by feel, their hearts trembling, even the captain's.

No guards stood outside the gate of the palace, but when the captain banged on the door, it opened, revealing a wary group of warriors who had not expected anyone at such a time. They quickly barred the door behind us.

The men carried my body to Pleasure Hall's door, where they handed the cot over to the servant women who hurried me to my chamber to be laid upon my bed.

The chamber filled quickly with servants who wept on their knees. I wished to console them, but could do nothing. Their cries filled Pleasure Hall, until Leena sent them to Rorin's altar to pray to him and the goddesses.

"Will she die?" the last servant girl whispered on her way out.

"She will not," Leena snapped, but I knew she did not believe her own words, for when all had left, she changed me into my Shahala clothes.

With tears in her eyes, she prayed to both the goddesses and the spirits, falling asleep at last while holding my hand and waiting for my shallow breathing to cease. My body grew weaker with every passing moment, the poison too strong to fight.

I did not mind the dying; I only wished I could die on our hillside among the numaba trees. I pushed hard against my body with my spirit, trying to get in.

Leena slept, the servants busy praying in the Great Hall. If my spirit would return to my body for just a short time, I could go to the kitchen and hide in an empty flour jar. If I could hang on to life until morning and get through the gates with the caravan, if I could live long enough to walk away from them into the woods, at least I would die as a free woman.

I forced my spirit into the limp body on the bed. And in my limbs, I felt a quickening, and after some time, I could open my body's eyes. No real improvement was this, for I knew that people about to die often regained some strength and appeared to feel better just before death claimed them.

I had often thought the short reprieve a gift of the spirits, allowing the dying to say their last farewells and prayers. I could feel strange coldness in my bones—death coming.

I gathered the strength to sit, and my hand slipped from Leena's. She stirred but did not wake. I stood, none too steady, and little by little shuffled from the chamber.

The corridors stood empty; I did not have to be so careful there. The farther I walked, the more hopeful I became. I dragged myself to the kitchen, my legs shaking all the way.

I prayed to the spirits that I would find the kitchen empty, and in their mercy, they answered my prayers. The room stood in darkness, only a few embers glowing in the hearth in the middle of the night.

I moved to the empty flour jars on the small wagon and leaned against one. Then nearly cried. As weakly as my heart beat, I knew I would not survive to climb out in the morning.

Yet I craved freedom with a desperation that gave me a last little boost of strength. I cast my gaze upon the door that led to the street, secured only with a lock. No guard now, not when the mist covered the city. They knew nobody would be moving outside. I lifted a fork from a sideboard and shuffled to the door, pried the lock open and walked out into the mist.

Weak and confused, I saw little now that I was looking with my body's eyes. I kept shuffling forward, stopping often, a few times nearly collapsing. Then I walked into a stone wall. I somehow ended up behind the palace at the sheer cliff from which the back of the building had been carved.

I had been aiming for the city gate, in the opposite direction.

I leaned against the rock and squeezed my eyes shut, not having enough strength to cry. But as my hand slid down the rock, my fingers caught on a small crevice.

A crevice that could be a foothold.

My mind had gone beyond reasonable thought. I thought of the numaba trees and began to climb.

Many times I had to stop to rest; many times I nearly slipped. But my body remembered climbing, and my limbs moved of their own accord, working from memory, each muscle knowing what it needed to do.

Sharp edges cut my hands and bruised my knees, but I barely noticed. I lost sense of time. I thought I might have somehow crossed over to the afterlife. But at last I ran out of rock and reached the top of the cliff. I pulled up with the last of my strength and collapsed on the ground, tears spilling from my eyes.

I was once again a free woman.

The mist swirled thinner up here, and I could see before me the edge of a vast woods, with tall trees and good earth upon which to die. I had to reach just that; then I could leave my body behind and let my spirit go to find my mother's.

A long moment passed before I realized I wasn't alone.

Something moved in the mist.

CHAPTER FOURTEEN

(The Forgotten City)

Shadows separated from the swaying landscape that swam before my eyes. As I tried to blink away my confusion, the three monoliths drew closer.

No, not rocks were they, but...*men*.

The bitter taste of disappointment filled my mouth. I had no more strength to run, could do nothing but watch as they approached. They walked in a solemn procession, their long, white beards cascading over brown robes that remained unmoved by the breeze.

They surrounded me, standing at the points of a perfect triangle, with me in the middle. I could make no sound. And even if I could, I would not have begged for my life. I was happy to part with it and the pain.

They spoke, not with their lips, but with their spirits straight to mine. Their three spirits mingled and twisted together and entered my body with a great strength. They talked to me of healing as they fought the poison. They told my spirit to gain strength and soothed my mind.

———

I woke in a long cave, lying on a pile of pelts, the rock wall reflecting the dancing flames of the fire. The three old men sat around me cross-legged on the stone, one on each side and the third at my feet.

The one on my left spoke, if the gurgling, bubbling sounds coming forth from his mouth, like water pouring from a narrow-necked bottle, could be called speech. He stopped when he realized I was listening.

"The Guardians welcome you, Tera of the Shahala," the one to my right said in the language of the Kadar. His beard spread over his round middle.

I sat up slowly, surprised that I had the strength, and drew back.

His lips stretched into a grandfatherly smile. "Do not be alarmed, child. I am the Guardian of the Sacred Cave."

I gaped.

"I am the Guardian of the Sacred Scrolls," the one at the foot of my furs said, moonlight reflecting off his bald head. The wrinkles on his face were etched into a permanent scowl, making him look the oldest of the three, although they all seemed as old as time itself.

"I am the Guardian of the Sacred Gate," said the third, a great carved stick lying across his lap, then added, "We have been waiting for you for a long time."

So I had died. I wanted to ask to see my mother. Then I moved and pain sliced through my body, strong enough to convince me that I had life inside.

But if I lived, how could I be among Guardians? Their kind had been gone for hundreds of years.

The Guardian of the Cave stood and strode to the dark opening, indicating with a hand that I should follow. I rose, the dizziness brought on by the movement passing quickly, and walked to him, gasping at the sight.

Below the cave spread a valley, a small jewel of a city in the middle, illuminated by the double moons. Ancient houses lined the twisting streets, the buildings huddled together. Some of the roofs were pointed, some round, painted in a myriad of colors. Despite the cool northern spring, the trees bore leaves, and bushes too, making the place seem out of time even more.

The building that drew my eyes and stole my breath stood tall and proud in the middle of the city, its round golden dome glowing in the moonlight.

The Forum.

"The Forgotten City." The words stumbled from my stunned lips.

The Guardian of the Cave nodded as he turned back into the cave. "Let us eat. You must regain your full strength."

My stomach growled. I had missed my evening meal at the palace.

I followed him to the fire where the others now gathered, and sat on the ground among them. I waited for them to take from the cheese and dried fruit before I reached for any, as was our Shahala custom when eating with one's elders.

We did not speak as we ate and drank. I wondered if the Guardians always ate this late, then remembered that one of them had said they had been waiting for me. Had I kept them from their dinner?

"How did you know I was coming?" I did not think anyone could have seen me in the thick mist to forewarn them.

"From our fathers," the Guardian of the Gate said. "And they were told by their fathers before them. We have waited for hundreds of years."

Blood rushed to my head, and I closed my eyes for a moment against the sudden dizziness.

"You are overwhelming her. She only just awakened," the Guardian of the Scrolls barked at the other two and yanked his gnarled beard out of the way when it nearly dangled into the fire.

"I would rather know." I struggled to catch my breath.

The portly Guardian of the Cave nodded. "We will let the Guardian of the Scrolls tell you. He knew your mother the best. You could take a walk, if you feel sufficiently recovered."

A full-grown manyinga could not have held me back.

The Guardian of the Scrolls grumbled something about old achy bones but stood and grabbed a large fur from one of the sleeping places to wrap around his shoulders. When he handed me another, I did the same and followed him out of the cave without trouble. The food had returned some of my strength.

The Guardian limped ahead of me on the path, moonlight glinting off his bald head.

"Grandfather," I said, talking with the utmost respect, "may I try to ease your pain?"

He stopped to look at me, anger on his face and impatience. "Fresh from death's door. Have you not learned anything?" He snorted with derision. "Do you not think I could take my own pain if I cared to bother? Young people. They think everything that could be fixed ought to be. Maybe sometimes an old man just wants to be left to die."

He continued down the narrow steps cut into the rock, mumbling as he went.

I caught only a word here and there, missing most of what he was saying, only catching that he wished I had not come until he had died and his son had taken over, and that he surely hoped at least he would die before the rest of the trouble arrived. Then he fell silent as we reached the bottom of the steps and walked the starlit road toward the city in the valley.

Soon we passed by a strange flowering bush covered in round flowers. The petals reminded me of the purest alabaster, white to the point of translucence and silky by the looks of them, although I did not dare to reach out and touch a thing of such beauty. The flowers' sweet, spicy scent filled me with a giddy pleasure.

"Is it magic?"

The Guardian stopped and turned back, mumbled something under his breath. "A rose. Hot springs crisscross the valley under the surface." He moved on without giving the flower a second look.

I kept turning back, until I stumbled over some rocks. After that I kept my attention forward and on the path. *Hot springs.* That explained the lush green of the valley, how a flower that looked liked it belonged to a much more southern climate could bloom this high up the mountain.

He shuffled on, lost in his own thoughts, looking neither left nor right but walking straight toward the strange city in the hollow of the valley. Even as we reached the first houses, he said nothing.

"Grandfather, did you truly know my mother?" I asked after some time, thinking he had forgotten about me.

He walked awhile before he spoke, his voice somewhat softened. "There was one worth the bother."

Hope leaped. "Do you know where I can find her grave?"

He turned toward a round clearing among the houses, the ground covered in grass, a silver tree in the middle. He strode to the tree, and I followed, then stopped when he halted at a crystal rock that reached to my knees. The rock sparkled in the moonlight, the exact color of the petals of the moonflower that grew in our Shahala hills.

I could scarcely breathe.

I fell to my knees and hugged that rock, not sure if I could ever let go. *Mother. I am here.*

Some time passed before my tears dried. I blinked a few times. Sniffed. "Did she have the Last Blessing?"

The Guardian looked at me as if I was a senseless child. "She certainly did."

A small, empty corner of my heart filled with peace.

I sat back on my heels and noticed a faint inscription on the rock. *Spirit, be strong. Heart, be brave.*

I ran my fingers over the letters. Strong and brave were Kadar values.

"It should say *Spirit, be kind. Heart, be true,*" I whispered. *That* had been my mother.

But the Guardian shook his head. "Her last words they were."

I looked at the inscription for some time, trying to make sense of it. Maybe she had so encouraged herself at the end because she knew she was dying.

"Did you meet her when she healed the High Lord Barmorid?"

The Guardian lowered himself next to me, his joints creaking. He crossed his legs and rested his hands on his knees. "I first met her long before that. When she injured him."

"Had she come to Karamur twice?" I only remembered the one journey.

He drew a labored breath, as if preparing for the effort of speaking. "When your mother, Chalee, first came into her healing powers, they were so extraordinary that her fame spread far and wide on the island."

This I knew. I waited for more in the silence. The streets slept, no other human being in sight but the two of us. Unlike Karamur, the Forgotten City had no night guard.

"Barmorid, a young warrior still," the Guardian continued, "had suffered a grave injury in battle, and when your grandfather heard, he came to help, bringing Chalee with him. Your people and the Kadar were closer back then, the old favors each had done the other not so well forgotten."

I knew how the Kadar kept us safe and how without them we could not have our precious peace to hone our healing skills genera-tion after generation. My mother had reminded me of that often enough, so I sought to head off the lecture I felt coming. "Did my mother give back Barmorid his health?"

"She did." The Guardian nodded. "But took something a lot more precious."

"My mother would never take something not freely given and refused payment half the time," I retorted, quick to defend her.

"Given or not, she took a piece of the High Lord's heart when she left. And something else."

"Barmorid fell in love with her?" I had never known of any man in my mother's life but Jarim.

The Guardian nodded again. "And she with him."

"What else did she take?" I asked, still stunned by the first revelation.

"Can you not guess?"

I could, from the way he looked at me now, but so shocked was I, I could not speak for some time.

"Why did Barmorid never claim me?" I asked finally, when I could form coherent thoughts once again. I was half Kadar? Oh, it could not be. It simply could not!

"He never knew. No matter how much I tried to convince her, Chalee would not hear of telling him. She wanted to return to her people, even if in disgrace, preferring that to the prison of the High Lord's Pleasure Hall, for she knew he would never let her leave."

I stared, but not without some understanding. I had run away from Pleasure Hall's gilded prison even with my last breath.

The Guardian said, "Your grandfather knew, of course. A great healer like he could feel the new life within her. Perhaps that is what killed him so suddenly—a broken heart. He knew the rest, you realize, the things *to come*."

He fell silent for a long time before speaking again, his voice tired and faint, so I could barely make out his words. "Destinies are made to be fulfilled. Some roads may seem to lead in other directions, but at the end, they all loop back to where they must."

My whole world had changed in the space of a few heartbeats. I had no patience for a philosophical discussion. "What happened after that?"

"Your mother returned alone to your Shahala shore, but someone waited for her."

"Jarim?"

The Guardian nodded.

"He fell in love with her too?"

"Not at first, not for a long time, although your mother tried. I asked the Seer to search her out from time to time and tell me how she fared. I had grown rather attached to her, I suppose, never having a daughter of my own, only the one son."

"Did she forget Barmorid so soon?" I disliked the idea of my mother having a fickle heart.

"Not until her dying day."

"Then why did she become lalka to Jarim?"

The Guardian looked at me, and I saw the depth of the sadness in his eyes for the first time. "I will tell you if you wish, but it will be a hard tale to hear."

"No tale of my mother could be so hard that I would not wish to hear it."

He nodded. "The Kerghi are not our only enemy, nor are they the worst," he began. "A bigger power stands behind them and pushes them forward. The Emperor Drakhar..." His face darkened as he uttered the words. "He has been coming a long time, and before he ever started on his cursed path, he was watching. He knows the prophecies as well as you or I."

Maybe better than I, for I could think of no prophecy that could have anything to do with this.

"The Emperor knew about you," the Guardian went on, "long before you were born, and so he sent Jarim to kill you."

I inched closer to the rock crystal. All I had known as truth, my entire childhood, fell away. My father was the High Lord of the warrior race I despised, while the man who raised me had been a hired murderer.

"Your mother knew the prophecies, of course, but still she would not stay here where Barmorid could have protected her and you, no matter how your grandfather and I scolded her." The old anger and worry still rang in his voice as he spoke.

"She returned to her home alone, with child, determined to birth you in freedom, willing to face the world for it. She hoped, I think, to change your destiny. She was very young still."

He waved the old regret away with a listless gesture, then continued his story. "She had more than enough knowledge of herbs to poison Jarim, but she could not bring herself to do it, not even to save your life."

"How did she change Jarim's mind?" For I knew she must have managed that feat somehow, as I was still alive.

"Each day while he was waiting for you to be born, she fought with love every bit of hatred he had, until he came to care for her. Still, though, he planned to kill you when you were born, but not her, never harm her. He planned to make new babes with her to console her once his dark charge was finished."

"But her power of good was the stronger," I half said, half asked.

The Guardian looked straight ahead without seeing me. "Every time a man and a woman come together, not only their bodies join but so do their spirits. And every time your mother's spirit joined with Jarim's, she left a little bit of her goodness behind. Little by little, she changed the man."

"At the cost of her own spirit?" At once I understood why she had been too weak to withstand the strain of healing Barmorid for the second time.

I cried at the thought and told the Guardian how I wished my mother had not sacrificed so much for me. I did not feel worthy of such a gift.

"Your mother followed the path of her own choosing to the end, always doing what she thought right, even at the cost of her own life, even when it was forbidden."

The Guardian sighed. "When she came back to Karamur for the second time, the High Lord was ill with fever, the kind that settles deep into the blood. She had given away so much of her spirit to Jarim by then that she did not have enough power to heal Barmorid, not even with all the love in her heart. She gave her spirit to him to strengthen his so he could win the fight on his own."

I wept openly.

The Guardian stood. "The rest is in the Sacred Scrolls. You will see those soon enough. Now, let this old man go. I performed this first task; as little as I wished it, for do not think the thought of her does not pain me still. One more task awaits the Guardian of the Scrolls, and I hope I shall be dead by the time it is called for, and you will be served by my son, for he is more ready than I."

I hugged the rock one more time before I pushed to my feet and turned to the Guardian. "I thank you for what you told me. But forgive me, I cannot wish for your death, not even to bring you the relief you seek."

He nodded, weariness drawing his face into a thousand wrinkles. His shoulders sloped as if crushed by a great weight.

"Do not think of death as a sad end for me, child. I have lived a long life. I have seen winds of change and each new wind bring a worse fate for the world than the one before. I have seen men fight against evil, and time and time again lose their battle. I fought too in my own way, and I am now too tired to carry on the fight. If I found any favor with the spirits, I ask only this: that I be taken before this war comes and brings true darkness with it."

I had many questions but sensed that this was not the time to ask more.

We walked back toward the cave in silence, each deep in our own thoughts. The night itself quieted around us; even the wind stopped whistling. Confusion, sadness, and anger filled me, my mind a jumble of emotions.

Until now, even in the uncertainty of my fate, at least I knew who I was. To balance the twisting unknown paths of my future, stood solidly my past. And now I had lost even that.

We passed a round hut I had not noticed before. It had no windows at all. Grain storage?

The Guardian caught my gaze. "Selaila's hut. She is our Seer."

I wanted to ask more, but his shoulders slumped with exhaustion. As we left the Seer's hut behind us, my thoughts returned to our earlier talk. Plenty there to ponder for a hundred days.

My mother had as many secrets as a stranger. Everything I thought I knew of my beginnings was false. And still some mysterious destiny awaited me, one the Guardian of the Scrolls had only hinted at. Maybe the other Guardians would tell me the rest.

I looked up toward the cave and saw one of them approach in a rush. He waved at us to hurry.

CHAPTER FIFTEEN

(The Road to Freedom)

"The Guardian of the Gate had to leave. I shall walk you back to the cliff. You must take care not to slip," the Guardian of the Cave said, breathing hard from the rush down the slope.

"Must I leave?" I felt as if I had fallen into a beautiful dream at last after many hard and dark days. The call to waken came too soon. I wanted to see more, learn more. I wanted the tranquil peace of the Forgotten City that at its heart held my mother's grave.

"You must." He turned onto the path that led to the top off the cliffs above Karamur. "But every time the mist descends, you may come to us to learn more."

He gestured with his hand, and I hurried after him. *When the mist descends?* I had been in Karamur already for the full double cycle of the moons, and I had seen the mist but once before this.

"We shall call the mist for you. Do not worry," said the Guardian of the Cave as if reading my mind.

Such wonder stood so far beyond my comprehension I could not even question it. "What will I tell them about where I have been? The servants must have noticed my absence by now; the guards must have been alerted."

I glanced back. The Guardian of the Scrolls had not followed us but began his slow, limping climb up to the cave. He stopped to look at me. I bowed deep. He dipped his head in a small nod of farewell before turning back to his path.

I rushed after the Guardian of the Cave.

"You must make excuses for your absence. The palace is large. A foreigner such as you could easily wander off and become lost. And for next time..." He pulled a handful of thin sticks from his robe and waved them in front of my nose.

I ran my finger along a pungent stick the length of my forearm. "What are these?"

"Place one in a tankard in your room and light the end with a candle. Anyone who enters will fall asleep and stay so until the stick is doused and fresh air wakes them from their dreams. Once you light it, cover your face and leave the room," he added.

I pulled my hand back. "Is it sorcery?"

He flashed me an impatient look. "A harmless herb." He gave a name I never heard and could not pronounce. "The smoke will not harm anyone," he promised. "Our people, the Seela, use the sleeping sticks to allow rest to those in great pain."

I tucked the small bundle inside my tunic as we reached the top of the cliff. Below, I could barely see Karamur, still steeped in thick mist.

"Thank you, Grandfather." I bowed, then handed him the fur I had borrowed from the cave. I missed its warmth, but I could not hang on to it while climbing. "I hope I shall see you soon."

He smiled at me fondly. "One more word before you leave. Did your mother teach you the use of your powers?"

Sadness crept into my heart. "She died before they came to me."

He nodded as if he had expected my answer. "You must be more careful with them, Tera. Your healing spirit is sacred but not without an end. You must use your skills and your herbs, but your spirit only as last resort, only if you must, and even then..." His expression turned somber. "You cannot help anyone if you give your spirit away and give your body unto death."

His blunt words made me think of my mother's fate. He spoke the truth. I could not give argument.

"If you had not come to us, and we had not been able to help you in time, your body would not have survived," he said. "A greater purpose awaits you. You must be more careful for all of our sakes."

Like a chided youth, I hung my head and promised, wondering of what greater purpose he spoke. "The Guardian of the Sacred Scrolls mentioned a prophecy—"

"You must hurry. Dawn is upon us." His lips flattened in consternation for a moment. "Has your mother never told you, then?"

I shook my head.

"Maybe it is better that way. It is not always good for one to know all there is to come. Much of the courage comes from knowing not, I think. Be patient. You will learn soon enough," he said, then left me to disappear into the woods.

I looked after him for a long time, until a bird gave cry and took to the air from a treetop, jarring me from my reverie. I heard the flap of its wings but could not see it when I looked up. The cry sounded again, coming from farther now. The bird was flying south.

Toward Shahala lands.

The call of freedom sounded like a thousand trumpets in the air. It made me forget the Guardians and Batumar. All that had happened to me in the inhospitable land of the Kadar floated away into the dawn like a strange dream. I turned into the direction of my true home, and my eyes filled with tears, as it seemed the spirits had answered my prayers.

I was free.

I ran the first few steps, too giddy to worry about tripping over stones or roots. Had the Palace Guards realized yet that I had gone missing? They would be searching the palace first, but when the mist rose, they would spill out into the city, then outside the gate.

Enough of them served Batumar so that the captain could send some in every direction. But even that thought could not slow me down. *Home.*

Then my feet faltered suddenly. *What home?* I could not go home to Jarim.

I could go to Sheharree, I thought and ran on. My mother had friends in the port city, and even had I been a stranger, I would have been welcomed. Even if I had nothing to give in return, the Elders of the city would have made sure I was looked after. But I had something —the healing powers of my spirit.

I could be happy in Sheharree. The Kerghi hordes might never come. And if they did, why would they come to the Shahala? Our people did not fight. The Kerghi could hardly consider us their enemy.

I reached a rocky slope and slowed to pick my steps with more care, worried that at any minute the guards would be upon me. I hoped none of them would be punished because I had run away. Nor Leena. Would Batumar blame her for my escape?

She would probably look for me herself and be worried. If any sick came to the back of the kitchen, she would have to tell them I had gone. I regretted that, leaving the people who had come to depend on me. Sheharree had many healers, but Karamur had only me.

I fought against the sudden pang of guilt.

I told myself that Karamur's sick would learn to go on without my help and be no worse off than before I had arrived. And once the mist came again, and I did not go to the Forgotten City, the Guardians too would know that I had gone. Maybe I was not the one they had waited for all this time. If I had this great destiny they spoke of, would I not have known? Would I not have felt it?

I made my way down the slope, grateful for my Shahala thudi and short tunic. I rubbed my hands over my arms against the chill, hurrying the dawn, the sunshine and warmth.

At least, I did not have to fear freezing at night without a tent as long as I found enough dry leaves to gather around me. Spring was turning warmer and warmer.

Free.

I smiled at the fading stars. My plans of sneaking out of the city with the caravan had come to naught, and yet here I was. The spirits rarely gave me the exact help I had asked for, but in all important things, they had always helped me in their own way.

I filled my lungs with the crisp air, the familiar scent of the forest—the scent of freedom. I could not ask for more. I had neither food nor water, but I trusted the spirits to watch over me on the journey. I would look for edible leaves and fruit and roots. Eggs and nuts would be my nourishment, morning dew my drink.

I did not slow nor did I look back. My mother had fled from Kara-mur; the Guardian of the Scrolls had said so. The Guardians could not blame me for doing the same. How good running free felt in my legs....

And yet...something deep in my heart, a whisper so low I could not fully hear...it called me back.

I refused, even as I knew the heart, like the spirit, did not bear refusal.

A person cannot refuse his heart without losing it, my mother's voice whispered into my ear from a long ago conversation we had at the top of a numaba tree.

My feet faltered, then halted.

The Guardians had waited for me for a long time. Since when did a Shahala run away from a request for help? Maybe I could stay a little longer. Just until they called the mist the next time. Until I learned what said the prophecies.

I looked at the woods around me, at the needle-covered Kadar trees that had once seemed strange but became familiar to me during my long journey to Karamur. A few drab little birds of the north, lacking in so many things compared to the colorful beauties of my home, watched me from their branches.

What made them stay here through the season of snow, the heavy storms, and the punishing winds? Why did they not fly south? Many of them did not survive the hard freezes, of that I was sure. They had strength, these small creatures, strength and courage—two things much valued by the Kadar. The Shahala prized humility and self-sacrifice.

I stood there for some time before I turned around.

The sky grew lighter. I hurried back the way I had come, then climbed down the face of the cliff, an easier task now that I had full command of my body and my strength back again.

Once I reached the ramparts, the climb became easier yet, the mist clearing enough so I could find my way to the palace without trouble. I entered through the kitchen door I had left unlocked when I had escaped. The kitchen stood empty, although somebody had already fed the fire. I hurried through, paying little mind to the orange flames.

Luck favored me, as I did not see anyone on my way to Pleasure Hall. Leena had not raised the alarm. I thanked the spirits for that and soon found the reason.

She still lay at the foot of my bed where she had fallen asleep, worn out by the events of the previous evening.

I hid my bundle of sleeping sticks quietly in a small jar I kept for herbs in the corner.

But as I sat upon the bed, her eyes popped open. "Thank the goddesses, your health has returned," she stammered, her eyes suddenly glistening.

She pushed to her feet at once to fuss over me. She bade me to rest, which I did but for only a short while, as I had not found my return down the cliff and across the fortress all that exhausting. A strange energy hummed through my body, likely an after-effect of being healed by the Guardians or the excitement of all that I had learned in the Forgotten City.

———

For the next few days, Leena refused to leave my side.

All day long, she ordered the servants around, chiding them for bothering me, pushing them out the door as they brought choice sweets and other small treats from the kitchen until I thought I would burst. They fulfilled my smallest wish and provided me with comforts before I ever asked for anything. I had little to occupy my time, as no sick came to me. I wondered if the mist the Guardians had sent might have had some healing in it.

Finally, on the fourth day, I could not languish in Pleasure Hall any longer and decided to walk to the kitchen to thank the cook for yet another wonderful creation of mosan-berry pie. I did so, distracted by the aroma of baking apples. The cook noticed and insisted on serving me a dish immediately.

I had sat enough in the past few days, so I walked with my plate, and soon a couple of strange fish, swimming in the tub in the back, distracted me. Their scales glistened in the colors of the sunset with stripes of midnight. Pretty they would have been if not for their enormous teeth, thin as fishbone but the length of my little finger.

I stared at the fearsome creatures, wondering if they might yet eat each other, when the sudden yelp of pain behind me made me jump.

I turned. "Who is hurt?"

Nobody would look at me as I glanced from face to uneasy face. The cook had her hand behind her back.

"What is it?" I stepped closer.

"Nothing but a small cut, Lady Tera." Still she would not show me. Blood dripped to the stones behind her.

"I would see just the same."

She pulled her hand forth with great reluctance, holding the nearly severed thumb in place with her other hand. "Just a scratch. It will quickly heal." She forced a painful smile and moved to hide the hand again.

What nonsense was this? I set the plate aside and reached for her. "Let me see."

The woman fell on her knees, tears filling her eyes. "I beg you, Lady Tera. You will make yourself ill again."

"That was but once and had nothing to do with this." I took the pain and closed the wound fast, leaving not even a scar. A sudden rush of fatigue cut through me, taking away the glow of the past few days, but I felt no other ill effects.

I looked around the kitchen then and knew why I had not seen anyone sick. They thought to hide their ailments from me.

I owed them the truth. "I have been foolish with my own strength. I shall not do that again, but I would not have anyone suffer as long as I can help."

They bowed, some looking hopeful, others unconvinced.

"They need not worry so," I told Leena on the way back to Pleasure Hall.

"We worry because we care for you, my lady. Our High Lord is much loved by his people. You are his only concubine."

I understood the words she spoke as well as the ones she had left unsaid. *The House of Batumar does not have an heir.*

I swallowed my unease, for I had not realized how much his people had put their hopes in me. But as much as I wished for everyone's dreams to come true, I planned to be gone from Karamur as soon as I had found out more about my mother's last days from the Guardians, and about the prophecies, the secrets which drew me to the Forgotten City.

Then something else occurred to me, something so terrible and distasteful to the spirits I barely dared to utter the words, and yet they had to be said.

"Is Batumar Barmorid's son?" I held my breath for the answer. Was Batumar my half brother? If so, my presence in his Pleasure Hall was nothing less than an abomination.

Leena looked at my sudden agitation with concern. "Of course not."

I exhaled.

"In the old days, after the first High Lord was chosen by the warlords, his title passed down to his descendants, but soon our people learned what a bad governance that made. For hundreds of years now, at the death of each High Lord or when he decides he is too old for battle and takes the advisor's seat, the warlords choose a new High Lord from among their own number. The strongest man with the most courage and wisdom enough to rule."

She gave me a curious glance. "Batumar is such. He is respected and much loved."

Truly, sometimes I wondered if despite their difference in age, Leena was not a little in love with the High Lord. I nodded in agreement to her words, not wanting to offend her obvious worship.

We reached Pleasure Hall, and I sank onto a bench by the pool. I missed that glowing sense of well-being, the gift of the Guardians. I wished I had been able to keep it a little longer. And then, too late, I remembered the warning of the Guardian of the Cave.

I had spared little thought for sending someone for my herbs when

I had looked at the cut on the cook's hand back in the kitchen. Why should I have, when my powers were so much quicker?

Then I remembered the scores of plants my mother had collected and used. In truth, she had brought forth her powers only in the direst circumstances, but since those healings were the most spectacular, I remembered them the best.

The Guardian had been right. Like a child with a powerful tool, I was using my gift badly, wasting it, perhaps. I looked at Leena's kind face, now pinched with worry. She mistook my pensive silence and thought something was amiss.

"I promise to be more careful with the healing," I told her.

A motherly smile spread on her face as she nodded with relief.

My mind returned to Batumar. "When a new High Lord comes to the High Seat, does he give up his House to come to rule at the palace at Karamur?"

"Our High Lord still has his House, run by his stewards, not too far south of here. He visits when he can, although not much of late. He will return there once he leaves Karamur for the advisor's seat."

She must have read my confusion because she went on. "If the High Lord is not killed in fight, he steps down once he passes into old age. As the leader of the combined Kadar troops, our High Lord must be fit for battle."

I thought about that and had to admit, as strange as the Kadar customs were, some held a grain of logic.

"Will you not lie down, my lady?" Leena gestured toward my chamber, apparently still worried.

"Maybe for a little while," I agreed, mostly to appease her.

She followed me into my chamber and covered me once I lay down, but did not leave. "I saw one of Lord Gilrem's servants in the kitchen today," she said with hesitation. "He said Shartor no longer visits their House."

I sat up at the news. "Did the soothsayer leave the city?"

"I do not think so, my lady. His following has grown strong of late. The coming war worries people. They take reassurance where they can find it."

"But Lord Gilrem no longer follows him?"

"Maybe not, my lady. If we are to believe gossip… Shartor forbade the servants to seek you when Lord Gilrem's concubine and son were dying. He told them you would kill both and curse the House of Gilrem for good measure."

No wonder they had looked at me with much anxiety when I had arrived.

"Do you think Lord Gilrem sent Shartor away?"

"I would not know, my lady."

"How fares the babe and mother?"

"Fair well, my lady. Lord Gilrem shows both much favor as I hear."

Had Lord Gilrem shaken off Shartor's influence? I hoped so for Lord Gilrem's sake as much as my own.

———

As the summer wore on, little by little the sick returned to seek me once again. They came from the palace and from the city outside, some even from beyond the fortress walls. With my herbs and the skills I had learned from my mother, I healed—mindful of the Guardian's warning—and waited for the mist to descend.

It came soon enough as a low cloud on the mountaintop that grew as it made its way down to us. I hurried to Pleasure Hall to prepare, but in the corridor, I met Lord Gilrem.

"I hope the day finds you well, my lord."

"Lady Tera."

Since he stopped, I could not press on, either.

"I see you are fully recovered," he said.

"I had but a temporary weakness, my lord."

He raised an eyebrow. "I saw the servants preparing your funeral wreath in the Great Hall."

Nobody had told me about that. Yet I wasn't surprised. The servants had seen enough death to know the look of it, and without the Guardians, I would have most certainly died.

He strode to Rorin's altar. I thought he looked pale, although I could not be sure whether it was only a trick of the flickering torches.

"My son is growing stronger with every passing day," he said. "A miracle, my servants insist. Shartor foretold, in confidence, that the child would not be born alive."

"What says the soothsayer now?" Maybe I could find out more about the man.

"I have not seen him these past days." He watched me closely, his gaze sharpening. "Have you practiced sorcery upon mine in my House?"

The blood chilled in my veins. "No, my lord. My only gift is healing."

Silence filled the space between us.

"Perhaps you speak the truth," he said at long last. "I have heard of sorcerers taking lives, but never heard of any risking their own life for another, sapping their own strength and power."

He reached to the brooch at his neck. Gold bands held in place an emerald nearly the size of a grape in the middle. He unclipped this brooch from his doublet and handed it to me.

"My lord…" My gaze flew to his as I tried to give back his stunning gift.

But he turned on his heels without a word and left me standing in the hallway, my mouth agape.

I gathered myself at last, after another moment, and flew to my chamber, for the mist was upon us fully, and I was ready to learn my destiny.

CHAPTER SIXTEEN

(The High Lord's Return)

I hid the brooch once I reached my chamber. Never had I owned anything as beautiful and valuable. It would buy my passage with the caravan, I thought with a sudden thrill.

Tilia brought food, charms jingling on her belt with every step. Tension sat on her forehead. Nobody liked the mist, but out of everyone at the palace, the oldest servant women liked it the least.

"Thank you, Tilia." I made a show of stifling a yawn. "I should not require more of your kind help today. I think I shall retire."

She bowed, relief evident on her lined face. But no sooner did she leave than Leena came in.

I made another show of yawning. "I am retiring for the day. I shall not need anything until morning. You may seek your own bed."

Although I had given Leena leave to use an empty chamber in Pleasure Hall, she would not hear of it and continued to live among the servants.

When the mist descended on the city, the servants preferred to keep to their own quarters. Leena had told me some even barred their doors, the most superstitious among them painting the wood with symbols of protection.

She laid my sleeping gown out on the bed and assisted with unlacing the maroon dress I had worn all day. "I will stay and make sure the fire burns warm, my lady."

The mist did bring a certain grayness and chill, but I opened my mouth to protest. Then closed it. I had not yet once succeeded in talking Leena out of doing things she considered her duty.

While she shook the wrinkles out of my gown and folded it over the back of a chair, I sidled to the jar in the corner for a sleeping stick. I held the end of the stick into the flame of the candle burning by my bed, then set it into an empty tankard. The stick did not burn with a flame but rather smoldered, letting off a thin, snaking plume of smoke.

I held my breath as I inched forward.

Leena suddenly sagged against the bed, than sank to the floor little by little, her eyes closing. She blinked a few times; then her eyes stayed closed as she gave in to what must have been overwhelming sleepiness.

I grabbed my Shahala clothes from the wooden chest and ran for the door, my lungs burning. I did not dare take a breath until I was outside my chamber.

I donned the thudi and tunic, then cut through the empty Pleasure Hall and peeked out into the corridor that stretched on the other side of the great carved doors. I could not see a soul, but some indistinct voices reached me from behind the turn in the hallway. I drew back and waited until the servants passed, then a few moments later checked again. All quiet.

I hurried to the kitchen, hoping to exit the same way as I had before, but this time, I could hear people talking as I approached, two servant girls gossiping about the blacksmith's son. I did not have time to wait until they grew tired of the topic and retired to their quarters.

After a moment of hesitation, I sneaked to the stairway, then down a flight, into the storeroom where great piles of firewood towered to the ceiling. A narrow chute connected the room with the street. Up into this filthy chute I squeezed myself, my hands and feet slipping on sawdust and dirt.

I conquered the climb and, reaching the top in short order, crawled out. Nobody walked the streets but me. Even if the mist caught some unfortunate soul out there in the middle of running some errand, he would not have seen me unless we bumped into each other.

I placed a hand onto the palace wall and walked, not breaking the connection, toward the cliff. Once I reached the rock wall, I felt for a foothold, then a handhold, and began the climb.

I found my way to the Guardians without trouble. The Guardian of the Cave and the Gate greeted me warmly and offered food; the Guardian of the Scrolls nodded from the back where he sat bundled in his robe, even his bald head covered, his face in a frown.

"He looks tired," I thought, and did not realize that worry pushed those words from my mouth, until the Guardian of the Cave beside me nodded.

"And complains of it enough to drive us mad," the Guardian of the Gate grumbled sitting by the fire, his carved stick lying next to him. "Had you any trouble getting away?"

"No one walks the streets. They think man-eater beasts roam the mist."

"Oh, for all that is sacred," the Guardian of the Scrolls grumbled loudly in the back.

The Guardian of the Cave chuckled. "Not one of us has been down there for at least a hundred years."

"My grandfather used to visit. He told me many tales," the Guardian of the Gate said. "Man-eater beasts…" He snorted.

"They say people sometimes disappear into the mist." I repeated what I had heard from the servants.

"Two!" the Guardian of the Cave exclaimed. "Two, in how many centuries?" He shook his head, then continued in a calmer tone. "One of the old Guardians, a wanderer, saw more than the others. Twice he brought a slave from Karamur. Both were badly abused by their masters."

I stared at him, beginning to understand.

"The slaves had been flogged harshly enough so that everyone knew they could not have moved on their own. Their masters had left them tied to the whipping post at the market place, a warning to the others. When those battered slaves disappeared, rumors must have started among the Kadar," the Guardian of the Cave explained.

I shared their meal, barley soup and meat cured into strips as tough as leather. I chewed; they gnawed. They did not have many teeth. A comfortable silence surrounded us, interrupted only by the crackling of the fire. I had many questions, but I waited respectfully for them to speak to me.

"The scrolls are calling," their guardian said suddenly in the back, his voice sour, as if that made him exceedingly unhappy.

I turned to him. "What do they say?"

He shot me a dark look.

I tried another approach. "Grandfather, would you tell me what is written upon the scrolls?"

He looked at me as if he had never heard a question with less merit. But after a lengthy silence, he deigned to speak. "No one knows, of course."

He pushed to his feet painfully and shuffled forward to sit by us. "We believe they will tell us how to defeat the coming enemy."

"Mayhap reading them could prove useful," I suggested in a tone as respectful as I could manage.

He looked at me with disdain.

The Guardian of the Cave replied in his place. "He cannot. His duty, as was his father's before him and will be his son's after him if he joins the spirits before the battle begins, is to guard the scrolls for the time when the one who can read them appears."

"And when will the reader come?"

Hope and sorrow mixed in the old man's gaze. "You, Tera of the Shahala, are the one for whom the scrolls await."

I blinked hard. My heart missed a beat. "Maybe you are mistaken, just this once," I suggested while bowing politely. "I have no special powers." I did not want great powers. Indeed, I feared the thought, having learned well the lesson of my great-grandmother.

They said nothing. They were perhaps the three oldest and wisest men in the world. They probably did not make many mistakes.

You, Tera of the Shahala, are the one for whom the scrolls await.

I forgot to breathe.

Jarim flashed into my mind unexpectedly. Jarim, whose evil spirit my mother had softened with her own until he could not kill me, not even when the war neared. He had sold me into slavery that brought me to Karamur. And all that time, the scrolls had waited.

If this was my destiny, Jarim had done nothing but help me fulfill it. Had he had a choice? Had my mother? Could I do anything else but follow the path before me?

I tried to find answers to those questions in my heart, but I searched in vain.

"And you guard the cave?" I asked the Guardian to my left, determined to at least learn as much as could be learned from the three of them.

He nodded with pride. "The Sacred Cave that holds the Sacred Scrolls. And my father before me. And his father before him, going back all through history."

I glanced around, looking for some sign of the extraordinary. "Is this the Sacred Cave?"

"You will enter the Sacred Cave when the time arrives."

Impatience welled in me to know more, but pushing for more answers would have been impolite, so I turned to the Guardian on my other side.

"I have not seen any gates." The Forgotten City had no gates, nor did it need one, for the mountains and the power of the Guardians provided sufficient protection.

The old man smiled at me with indulgence, as a father might smile at his young child. "I guard *the* Gate."

The Guardian of the Scrolls glared at him. The Guardian of the Cave cleared his throat.

"She is The One. She should know," the Guardian of the Gate told them, his hands coming up in a defensive gesture.

And then I finally understood. "The Gate of the World?" I swallowed. "Is it here?"

He smiled again. "On the other side of the mountain."

"Will you tell me more about it, Grandfather?" I asked, expecting him to say "when your time is here," so when he began the tale, my heart thrilled.

"At the beginning of time lived the First People." He leaned back to grab a chunk of wood to throw on the fire, but the wood must have been wet because smoke rose between us.

The Guardian of the Scrolls mumbled something about fools, but the Guardian of the Gate paid him no mind, just cleared his throat to continue.

"As the only people in the world, they lived in peace. They had land aplenty, and it provided all they needed, never a fight among their men. And these First People multiplied and filled many islands. On each island, their customs and ways changed a little to fit the land, but they still remained brothers and called themselves one nation. The First People respected the spirits of their ancestors, and those ancient spirits helped them, some say even walked among them."

I barely noticed the acrid smell of smoke as I leaned forward so I would not miss a single word.

"And the wisdom of these First People stretched without end. They commanded the first metals out of stone and shaped rocks and fitted them together to create cities."

"They built the Forgotten City too," the Guardian of the Cave interjected, then fell silent again and nodded to the other man to continue.

"They could build many things, the way of which is now lost to us. They built the first ships and sailed them even over the ocean."

"The wild ocean?" I gasped.

"All the water was not so wild back then. Like Mirror Sea, the waves stretched in peace and could be sailed. But as centuries passed, the hardstorms grew more and more frequent and soon made the wild ocean impassable. So the First People built Gates to connect their nation from island to island, land to land. In their time, all the islands and lands had many Gates, but as the people of each land grew more and more different, the time came when they forgot they were all brothers."

He gave a sad, resigned sigh before he went on. "Rugar was the leader of a far distant island, his heart filled with darkness. The hardstorms spilled over his land and brought famine to his people. When they cried out in need, he looked with envy upon a neighboring land. He trained the first warriors and traveled through the Gate and killed his brothers."

The Guardian of the Cave nodded gravely. The Guardian of the Scrolls huddled under his robe and stared into the flames.

"Thus the first war began, and the unjustness of this great killing rose to the spirits and made all mankind distasteful to them so they no longer walked among men. And when they so abandoned the people, more famine came, and more war and diseases with it. And the number of those First People waned like the moons. Many of the Gates were destroyed in those times. On all the islands of Mirror Sea, only one remained."

Which was all right, since our Mirror Sea was one of the few waters where hardstorms rarely reached, so our waters could still be sailed.

I had heard of the Gates before, from travelers who had come to seek my mother from distant lands. But back then, the stories seemed like children's tales to me, and only now did I understand the full wonder of such a creation.

"Ages after that, new people arrived from faraway kingdoms and repopulated the islands, but they knew little of the First People or their extraordinary ways," the Guardian of the Gate said.

"In places, the few First People who remained were hunted and tortured for their knowledge. They were enslaved and abused until the last of them died. Their brothers, hearing of this on other islands, hid and never passed on any of their wisdom. When the last of them disappeared, so did their secrets. Some of those distant islands still have Gates, but no one knows now how to open them, so the people who live there are trapped."

I drew closer to the fire to keep warm as I listened to the Guardian.

"On Dahru, our people the Seela showed great respect for the First People, and thus they shared their knowledge with us. They knew, I think, that their race was coming to an end. A new world emerged, with new ways that left little room for theirs."

"It is said the blood of the First People mixed with that of the ancient Seela, and we carry it on still," the Guardian of the Cave interjected.

The Guardian of the Gate nodded. "So say the legends."

He poked the fire before he went back to his tale. "Those lands that have Gates use them if they can and guard them, for they are true treasures the likes of which can no longer be made. Those who settled on lands without Gates or lost the knowledge to use their Gates are cut off. They no longer remember where they came from and forgot the rest of us. There are many islands and lands like that and many people. We call them 'Sorlan'—Beyond."

He shifted on the hard stone of the cave floor. "Some of the islands of Sorlan are thick with magic, they say, and ruled by sorcerers." He fell silent.

I had heard some of this before, as parts of the story were familiar to my people, but not the whole history. I knew little about the First People, and I had never before heard of the people of "Beyond." The Shahala stories spoke mostly about our kind, how they came from afar and settled on Dahru where they found sanctuary. And how the Kadar came after that. My people thought the ancient race of Guardians long extinct.

The Kadar warriors protected the island, and when their numbers grew greater, they went away to fight foreign enemies in faraway places, never giving those enemies a chance to reach our shores. The Shahala lived in peace, and the power of healing in them grew even stronger, and they repaid the Kadar by healing them from the wounds of war when their services were called upon.

I told the Guardians as much, and they nodded, for they knew that tale as well. And the Guardian of the Cave knew even more—the names of all the great healers of our people and the names of all the great High Lords of the Kadar, from Coulron all the way to Batumar.

At the end, my thoughts circled back to the Gate. "I never knew our Dahru held the Gate of the World."

"Not many people do." The Guardian of the Scrolls glared at the Guardian of the Gate again. "We do our best to keep the Gate's true power concealed, lest it become a prize fought for by evil men."

"Most Gates can open only to a handful of other Gates, their range limited. The Gate of the World can reach all the other Gates," the Guardian of the Gate said with pride.

"As long as it has a true Guardian," the Guardian of the Cave added.

"Why do you stay hidden?" I asked them the question burning in my mind. "If you have the powers of the First People, you could do such good in the world."

"We have little of the power of the First People, but even for that little, our ancestors were hunted without mercy," said the Guardian of the Scrolls. "Other nations came to Dahru before the Kadar and Shahala settled here. Some of those nations used the island as a resting place on their way to other destinations; some sought to conquer our people the Seela and stay here." He fell silent for a moment, and I knew he had more tales of those dark times, tales he did not care to share.

His frail body shuddered as if wanting to shake off his grim inter-loping thoughts the way furry land animals shake off water. He rubbed his knee and went on with the tale. "The wind of centuries blew away the conquerors. They died of wars and diseases, hunger and treachery. We feared that soon the Seela too would perish, so we hid ourselves in the mountains and swore to protect the last of our people so we could go on preserving our ancient knowledge."

We talked about the past for some time, mostly about the First People, until the Guardian of the Gate pushed himself to his feet with effort. "The High Lord is returning. We should not hold the mist much longer."

I had wanted to see my mother's grave again, so I stood with some disappointment but said farewell, even to the Guardian of the Scrolls, who did not seem to notice I was leaving. I hurried back to the palace after a brief glance at the path that led south through the mountains. Freedom still awaited there, but many warriors would be coming home from battle who would need my help with their injuries. I found I could not desert them.

I reached the palace unnoticed, just as the light of morning broke through the disappearing mist. Walking into my bedchamber, I left the door open behind me to allow in clean air and held my breath as I dipped the glowing tip of the sleeping stick in water. I changed into my gossamer nightrail, lay upon the bed, and pulled the cover over me.

Leena's eyes fluttered open after a short while. I closed mine and listened to her move about the room, readying my clothes for the day.

I must have fallen asleep, for I woke to the sound of the horns proclaiming Batumar's return. Leena barely had the time to help me dress and arrange my hair before the High Lord sent his summons.

She fed me a few bites; then we rushed down the corridors, Leena clinging to the single charm hanging from the belt she wore only when Batumar was out of the palace.

My stomach clenched as her anxiety spread to me. Had he been injured? If so, I prayed to the spirits the injury would not be beyond my abilities.

I pushed open the door of the High Lord's antechamber, leaving Leena outside. I did not need escort when I was with Batumar. I breathed a sigh of relief when I saw him and closed the door slowly, allowing Leena a glimpse.

He sat on one of the ornately carved chairs in his antechamber while one of his stewards stood before him with a scroll in hand, giving his report. Batumar's gaze cut to me when I entered, but he did not interrupt the steward. I bowed, startled by his appearance. Like a stranger was he, in clothes stained and soiled beyond recognition, most of his face covered by a generous growth of beard, except the jagged line of his scar.

His obsidian eyes shone with intensity, his large frame, even slumped in the chair as he sat now, radiated true strength. His dark hair, longer than when he had left, hung in the thick braid some Kadar preferred for battle. He looked as if a warrior of old had come to us from the legends.

The steward droned on about supplies stored for the eventuality of siege, while the voices of servant women filtered from the sleeping chamber. I skirted around the men and walked in there, not wanting to disturb the report.

Two servant women poured water into a wooden tub, the largest I had ever seen. They bowed as I entered. They were palace servants, assigned to someplace other than Pleasure Hall, so I did not know their names. I helped them lift the heavy pails despite their protests. They were older than Leena, and besides, I always welcomed exercise. A healer had to have enough strength to lift or turn her patients if needed.

At home, I had roamed the woods and climbed numaba trees all day long. At the House of Tahar, I worked alongside the servants. But since I had come to Karamur, I had barely done more than walk from Pleasure Hall to the kitchen. Climbing the cliff made me realize how soft I had grown. The effort strained me more than it should have.

When I finished with the last pail, I moved out of the women's way and caught sight of Batumar watching me from the doorway. A good fire roared in the hearth, its heat touching me as if I stood right next to the flames.

The scent of freshly split wood filled the air, coming from the armload that must have been carried in recently. The servants noticed the High Lord too, at last, and fell silent, bowing to him as he strode into the chamber.

I had forgotten how tall he stood, how imposing, how mismatched we were in strength. I swallowed and glanced away. Perhaps I should have run while I had had the chance, while I had the advantage of his absence. Had I doomed myself by remaining?

The bed groaned under his weight as he sat and stretched his feet toward the fire. The women immediately set to undo his boots and strip off his clothes. His armor of leather, worked nearly to the hardness of metal, already lay in the corner.

One of the women removed his doublet, and I caught my breath at the sight of fresh blood on his tunic. I had hoped the blood stains on his outer garments were the blood of the enemy. I watched his face to see if the movement of any limbs caused him pain, and searched from afar for the site of the injury.

I found it as soon as they pulled the tunic over his head—a gash in his side where he had caught the tip of a sword. I could not see how deep the cut went, as dried blood covered most of the wound. I searched his body for other injuries but did not find any, although the women had tugged off the last of his clothes, and he stood before me naked.

Even tired, dirty, and wounded, his body looked more powerful than any warrior's I had seen, and I had healed many. He did not have that lean look of youth—he had daughters probably not much younger than I—but instead he was built with solid muscle, his skin covered in scars. Decades of battles had shaped the man, his body having been sculpted by fighting, honed by sword work.

He stepped to the tub and sank into the steaming water, closing his eyes the moment his head came to rest on the edge. As the women washed him, I picked up his discarded clothes to set outside the door. Then, having nothing else to do, I waited for him to be ready for my healing.

The women washed him without gentling their touch as they scrubbed around the cut. *Oh, for the spirits' sake…* Had their eyesight weakened with age and they mistook the wound for grime? I stepped forward. The water had turned red too fast. Too hot, I guessed, making Batumar's blood flow faster.

I walked out to the antechamber, moving to the corridor where Leena waited should I have need of her.

"If you could bring clean cloth for bandaging, and lavender for cleaning, chamomile and hyssop for infection, and ruhni powder too, I think. I have a small bundle of shlunn hulls. Please bring all of it. He is not injured badly," I added as she wrung her hands, her eyes clouding with worry.

Then I went back and sent the servant women away with instructions for more water. "Warm, not hot. Comfortable to the touch."

I disliked the look of that soiled water. I wanted him out so I could clean and close his wound. The women had done a fair job of washing him, so I had not much left to do.

"Your hair, my lord."

He sat up without sparing a glance back. Water ran in rivulets down the hills and valleys of his muscles.

I swallowed as I reached for his thick braid that needed to be loosened first. Then I combed the tangled strands with my fingers as they fell over his shoulder to the middle of his back. He dipped under the surface to wet his hair, then sat up again. Steam rose from the water, the fire burning hot behind me. As my skin tingled with heat, I wished

I had on a lighter gown. Better move to the other side of the tub, away from the fireplace…

But the women were returning with water, and soon their buckets were lined up there, so I stayed where I was, resolving instead to hurry with my task.

Leena followed the women, bringing strips of white linen and my herbs. I set those aside, not ready for them yet, and reached instead for the small jar of powdered soaproot on the floor next to the tub. I lathered a handful of the powder into Batumar's hair.

He closed his eyes and kept them closed, even as he dismissed all the servants.

The fire crackled in the hearth, the only other sound in the room the soft, oddly intimate squishing noises as I worked the suds into his hair and beard. His hair was roughly textured, almost like the manyinga's fur, but I liked something about the way the thick strands slipped between my fingers.

I stepped back. "Ready to rinse, my lord."

He stood and reached for one of the pails by the tub, then poured water over his head, then another pail and another. I busied myself with carrying out the empty pails as he finished rinsing and walked to the bed.

I had seen and healed many naked men, but now a sudden desire to run from the chamber grabbed hold of me.

"Come."

I turned, filled my lungs, then went to him as he had commanded. He did need my healing.

He tugged on a clean pair of leggings and sat on the bed with his arm out to the side to give me a better view of the gash.

Even with his gaze intent on my face, I forgot about my misgivings at once, my full attention on the injury, on the blood still seeping down his skin. The cut went deeper than I had thought, its edges dead, the severed muscles underneath infected and swollen.

I kneeled next to him, then ran my fingers around in a circle on his hot skin and drew the pain. I grabbed for the edge of the bed as it slammed into me and throbbed through my veins.

He caught me by the arm. "No."

I closed my eyes and focused on the pain, letting my spirit fight it, extinguish it little by little like raindrops cool a fire. A hard battle—the infection was the worst kind, and it had gone deep.

"Enough." He let go of me and stood, the movement pushing fresh blood from the wound. "It is true, then. Healing does not simply tire you. You give your own life strength to others when you heal." He stood over me, thunder on his face, his voice roughened as he said, "I will not allow it."

"It is my duty—"

"You speak of duty?" He paced the chamber. "You have left my Pleasure Hall and my palace."

I hung my head. How could he already know? He had only just arrived. But gossip spread on birdwings in the palace. I had done what was forbidden. He had it within his rights to kill me.

"You entered the House of another." His voice tightened. "His Pleasure Hall, even."

Oh, that. "Lord Gilrem was away, my lord. I went under protection of your guard."

He stopped and turned to me. "You should not be so ever-willing to exchange your life for others."

"I am a healer, my lord."

"You are—" he began in a voice filled with frustration but did not finish.

At last I lifted my gaze to his. Dark fires burned in his eyes. Blood seeped from his side. There was a wildness to him that both scared me and made it difficult to look away.

Again, part of me wanted to flee. The healer in me held me in place. I reached for my herbs. "These, at least, my lord. If you would allow me."

I had planned to use the herbs, having given my promise to the Guardians to be more careful with my healing spirit, but once I had touched Batumar and felt his pain, everything else had flown from my mind. I was yet slow to learn.

After a long moment, he sat down and lifted his arm for me again.

I cleaned the wound thoroughly, then prepared and applied the paste for infection, wishing as I often did for moonflower tears. The ruhni powder reduced some of the swelling almost instantly and also drew the edges of the wound together but not enough. The gash gaped too wide and jagged for ninga beetles, so sending for them would not be of any use, either. The shlunn hulls were all I had.

Batumar touched his finger to some of the ruhni powder that dusted his side and lifted the finger to his nose. "Do you know poisons as well as you know healing potions?"

"Yes." Not to use, not ever, but that I would recognize the signs if anyone had taken them by accident or will, so I could give the proper cure.

"You could kill me." His voice carried neither fear nor accusation.

"I could not." I stepped away in haste as if he had slapped me. "It is true I have the knowledge, but I do not have the spirit to accomplish such a deed." Not for freedom, not for any other purpose, not ever, no matter what he might do to me yet.

He nodded.

I pulled my small roll of dried shlunn hulls and selected five, each the width of a finger and about the length of one as well. Days before, I had dried the flat leaflike hulls to a rich color of yellow, and now I dipped them into clean water, one after the other.

A sticky paste formed on the underside, and I pressed the strips across the wound. They would hold it together as the water dried and the strips shrank and stuck to the skin. I rolled some bandage over on top of them to make sure they stayed in place and did not get brushed off too early.

I watched Batumar's face, for I knew the pain must be returning by now. Drawing pain gave but temporary relief if the injury was not healed completely. As I had used herbs instead of my healing powers, the infection would need time to abate, the cut would take days, if not longer, to grow together.

"I have weathered worse," he said as if sensing my dismay.

"Yes, my lord." I moved away, skirting the tub that took up most of the room. "I will have the water removed." Leena would call the servants back for me.

"Another moment." He stood and drew a small blade from the

table, then stepped to the tub where he shaved off his still-wet beard. The hair fell like clumps of fur and floated on the top of the water.

I held back a groan. Had he told me he was going to cut it, I would not have wasted time washing the mangy thing.

"Would you have denied me even that small pleasure?" he asked softly as he finished and turned to me.

I flushed, flustered that he should read my thoughts so easily.

He put away his blade before he walked to the bed and lay down on top of the covers. I did call for the servants then and waited until the women emptied the tub pail by pail; then two men came to carry it away. I walked behind them on their way out, but Batumar's words stopped me at the door.

"I would have you stay."

My body jerked as if lightning had cut through me. *Help me now, blessed spirits.* I turned slowly.

He slid to the middle of the great bed, looking as if he very much expected me to join him.

I clamped my hands together. *Spirit, be strong.* I had not thought he would want more of me than to heal his injury. He *had* to be too exhausted and hurt to want to... I bit my lower lip to keep it from trembling as I walked with great reluctance to lie beside him.

Heart, be brave. I chided myself for being such a coward. Whatever pain he would cause to my body, I could heal it as fast as it began. And now that I had my full healing powers, I could never lose them. I had no need to fear the loss of my maidenhead. And I was already Batumar's concubine. I would not be given over to others like Onra had been. All these thoughts and more rushed through my mind in a jumble.

I hesitated next to the bed until he reached for my hand and pulled me to him, my back against the hot skin of his chest as I lay down. His chin rested on the top of my head. I held my body rigid in his arms, expecting him to take me at once, and braced myself for the pain.

I had grown up in many ways since I had been taken from my home, had grown in spirit and strength, but at that moment, I felt like a young girl on the brink of her womanhood, years younger than my true age.

Batumar placed a warm hand on the hollow of my waist, his touch sending a tingling sensation across my skin, despite the barrier of my bodice.

"Do you fear me, Tera?" He pronounced my name with a deep rumbling R, differently from the Shahala. The sound resonated inside my chest.

"Nay, my lord," I said after a moment, surprising myself.

He was the most powerful man on Dahru. He could do with me as he pleased, even take my life. He was a Kadar, and that alone should have given me reason for concern. And yet as I lay there, a new emotion surged within me, one that sped my heartbeat just as fear would have, but this was something else.

CHAPTER SEVENTEEN

(The Sacred Scrolls)

"Do you fear my touch?" Batumar asked in a rough whisper, his breath fanning my scalp.

I thought of the blood on Onra's thighs. Then I thought of the pain of the warrior's grip upon my flesh as he had pressed me into the frozen ground on that creek bank at the House of Tahar. I nodded, unable to speak the words, hating to be such a coward.

Batumar's grip on my waist tightened for a moment, then relaxed. He remained silent for a long time. His chest rose with each breath, pressing against my back.

"Fear not, then," he said, "For you will not come to harm at my hands." And after an eternity, I heard his breathing even. The High Lord of the Kadar slept.

I sagged against him, my muscles going lax. I could feel his heart-beat through the fabric of my dress as his body heated mine. Even as summer warmed the air outside, the stone walls of the castle held the chill inside. Yet I did not feel any of that cold now. In all of the great castle, Batumar's bed had to be the warmest place. Soon the anxiety seeped out of my bones, and I fell asleep in his arms.

A servant woke us sometime later, announcing from outside the door that the feast waited. Batumar rose to his elbow to look at me, blinking sleep from his dark eyes. He did not seem so fierce then, but still my heart began its race as always when he was near. In my sleep I had turned to rest on my back next to him, his hand still on my waist.

I could do naught but stare into his obsidian gaze.

"Shall we go to the feast, my Lady Tera?"

His sleep-heavy voice felt like a caress on my skin. My breath caught when he leaned closer as if not wanting to miss a word of my response.

"Your people await you, my lord," I said in a rush and scrambled out of his arms and off the bed.

I escaped to the antechamber, and when I saw he would not be coming after me or ordering me back, I relaxed enough to think of fixing my hair, which had gotten mussed from sleep. I did this in the small mirror on the wall, watching from the corner of my eye through the open door as he dressed in a blue tunic and matching gold-stitched doublet worthy of a king. When he finished, he strode after me, offered me his arm, and led me to the feast.

I sat next to him at the table, only half listening to the tales of battles his men recounted and applauded. But still the words found their way into my ears, and I understood that although the small army of Kerghi warriors Batumar had fought had been pushed back, their khan, Woldrom, was far from defeated. Indeed, it seemed the Kerghi hordes were growing in number as they rolled like a wave across the world toward us.

The chatty concubine of one the captains sat on the bench on my other side and talked of silks and fashion until I wished for Lord Karnagh and his tiger. When I inquired after him, a servant told me he had left for his home straight from the Kingdom of Orh after the last battle, with a strong agreement between he and Batumar to come to each other's aid when the need arose.

Many people smiled at me from the long tables and inclined their heads in greeting—not only warriors but advisors and the most influential free masters of the city. No feasts were held in the High Lord's absence and no gathering in the Great Hall, but I had met many as I roamed the palace, and some had come to me for healing. Everyone seemed to breathe easier and smile wider now that Batumar had returned to the fortress city.

His gaze strayed to me often during the meal, so after the feast when he asked me to return to his chamber with him, I was not surprised. I wondered if he had reached the end of his patience with my reluctance, or if the pain of his injury had returned and he simply wished for my healing.

He sent the servants away as soon as we entered his chambers.

"Does your wound pain you still?" I asked once the door closed behind us.

When he turned to me, his face was lighter than I had ever seen it. Even his scar did not seem so fierce.

"Well worth was the injury to feel your hands upon me," he said with a wry smile as he pulled his tunic off and prepared for bed. "Mayhap I shall seek danger for more of it."

"You must not, my—" I stopped, embarrassed when I realized he merely jested. I stared. I had not before seen much humor in him. It made him look younger.

"Will you stay the night?" he asked, his casual tone betrayed by the intensity of his dark gaze.

My heart in my throat, I bowed. "If you wish."

He stepped closer. "Do you wish it?"

How could I refuse the High Lord? The palace dungeon probably held people even now for lesser offenses. I was his concubine, sharing his bed my duty. Still, I could not make myself say the words.

"Let us rest together," he said after a while.

I nodded in relief.

He drew me to the bed, then removed his clothes, save his leggings. I removed nothing. But I lay next to him and closed my eyes, willing sleep to come. After a while, when I was certain Batumar slept, I peeked from under my eyelashes and found him watching me in the light of the flames.

"I find I cannot sleep," he said.

I could but whisper, unnerved by his gaze. "Will you watch me all night?"

Sadness shadowed his scarred face. "If you saw what I have seen in this last battle, you too would wish to look upon something beautiful to make you forget all the hideous acts of men."

I wished I could comfort his spirit, for indeed it seemed weary within him. Only I did not know how such a feat could be accomplished. I could have comforted his body, had I been brave and brazen enough to offer mine, but I was neither. And then I remembered what he had said about liking the touch of my hands upon his skin. I could at least give him that small pleasure.

I did not dare touch his face, but I reached out a finger to trace a faded scar on his chest and felt a shock of heat as if I had reached into invisible flames.

I watched the path my fingers took over the hills and valleys of muscles, between the coarse hair, across ragged scars. The heat at my fingertips and the vibrations that ran up my arm did not fade but instead increased in intensity the longer I touched him. On its own, my palm flattened against his chest and soaked up his strong and steady heartbeat.

He made a low sound, not much more than a grunt, but it awakened me as if from a dream, and I snatched my hand away. I looked at him, flushing, sure I had displeased him, if not with the inexperienced caress, then with its withdrawal. And found his gaze on my lips.

My mouth felt parched, my throat as dry as the endless desert that bordered the Shahala lands.

He wants to kiss me—the realization, like a rockslide, buried every other thought in my mind. I pressed my lips together tightly in a thin line, then grew embarrassed at my cowardice and puckered them, unsure how to proceed further, although I had seen servants do such things in the shadowed corners of the pantry.

He lifted his gaze and must have seen my bewilderment, as his lips twisted into a lopsided smile. "Not tonight, Tera. I could not stop there if I started. Even a High Lord is only human underneath all his armor."

He pulled me close and wrapped his arms around me.

He did not touch me in any other way during the night, although he did brush a kiss over my brow when he quietly slipped from the bed at dawn.

———

In the days that followed, he did not send for me again, nor did I expect him to, as delegates arrived from distant lands, one after the other, and Batumar held audiences late into the night.

I did not see much of him during the days, either, as those injured in the battles for the Kingdom of Orh began to arrive and kept me busy from sunup to sundown, keeping me from even the nightly feasts. I eased their pain and healed their injuries, using my herbs and healing skills, careful with my spirit.

Such horrible wounds I had never seen: jagged gashes inflicted by some terrible weapon the likes of which I could only imagine, crushed limbs, torn flesh. The men looked as if they had fought wild animals. I shuddered each time I thought of the Khergie hordes, that terrible enemy reaching closer and closer to our island.

When Batumar was not giving audience, he was planning the next battle with Lord Gilrem and a handful of warlords who had arrived. Each day passed very much like the one before, until once again the mist descended and swallowed Karamur, and I could go to the Forgotten City.

I did not see the Guardian of the Gate when I reached the top of the cliffs, but the other two waited for me on the path.

"He is on the other side of the mountain," the Guardian of the Cave told me after a heartfelt welcome, brushing some crumbs from his round belly. "Many people are coming and going these days."

We walked together toward the city. The Guardian of the Scrolls seemed ever glum, bent lower than before, as if the weight of his duty had shrunk him since our last meeting. I wondered if he still spent most of his day wishing for death.

"Today," he pronounced out of the blue when we reached the point where the path branched off into two. Displeasure doubled the wrinkles on his lined face. He limped off toward the cave without explanation.

"What if I fail?" I asked the Guardian of the Cave, doubts like fist-size rocks sitting in my stomach.

"We all of us have been called to a purpose by the spirits, Tera. When you follow that true calling, you can accomplish the impossible if only you dare accept your true power."

But all I had ever wanted to be was an ordinary healer. "What is the purpose of that rose bush, then?" I pointed far ahead down the road. "All alone on the path, battered by the winds?"

"To cheer those who pass by it. The rose gifts us with its scent and beauty." He looked at me with grandfatherly affection. "But a flower cannot reach its true purpose if it stays tight in a bud."

I thought about that as we walked.

The Guardian of the Scrolls had already lit an oil lamp by the time we caught up with him inside the cave. He looked at me sharply, then moved to the back of the cave into the darkness where the late-day sunlight could not reach. The lamp illuminated only a small circle around him, making him look like a floating ancient spirit.

He gestured to me with impatience, so I followed, unsure what he wanted me to see on the uneven rock wall.

The Guardian of the Cave shuffled after us. He stepped up to the rock and placed his hands upon its rough surface. Under his palm appeared a slight crack. Or had it been there before? I could have sworn it grew straight from his touch. The line expanded until it reached from the floor to the top of the cave; then it widened as if pulled apart by invisible hands.

The Guardian of the Scrolls entered without hesitation.

I held back, glancing at the Guardian of the Cave. "Will you not join us?"

"I must hold open the entry."

I blinked. What would happen if his attention wandered or he fell asleep? Would we be sealed within? Not a question I could ask without appearing cowardly, so I stepped forward. If this was my destiny, I could not run from it.

The Guardian of the Scrolls lifted his lamp to light the naturally formed corridor that appeared in front of us, and muttered something about self-important old fools.

I followed him in the narrow passageway, barely seeing anything, for he held the lamp in front of him, and his body blocked the light. I had hated dark enclosures since my days in the belly of the Kadar slaver, so I stumbled after the Guardian with unease.

At least the narrow passageway did not have the dank stench of the moldy cabin. Incense wafted in the air, its sweet scent as soothing as a dream.

Soon our path widened, and we came to another cavern with many openings. Some of the tunnels were so narrow only a child would fit through, some wide enough for two people to walk side by side. Some seemed to go up, others sloped down. The Guardian held out the lamp and walked into one of the passageways without hesitation. Here, white walls reflected the light, so I could see better than before.

I gasped as I realized the lines on the rock were no random formations or play of the shadows but richly carved images of people, all manner of beasts, and strange things I did not recognize.

"Are these the First People?"

He did not seem to hear me. He hurried forward, and the light from the lamp slid from picture to picture, revealing just enough so I wanted to see more.

I kept up. If I strayed, I might be lost in the stone labyrinth forever. Solemn silence filled the endless space, the only sound the echoes of our footsteps, the rhythm of their clatter matching the beating of my heart.

Another passageway, this one sloping down, crossed ours, and the Guardian turned left. More carvings here, people running and dying. A shiver ran up my spine, for the pain on the faces seemed eerily real, the dance of the flames making their lips appear to be moving with silent screams.

I gladly left that passageway behind when the Guardian turned into yet another sloping corridor carved from the rock. We descended. These walls depicted a barren land, a few stick figures hiding deep in caves. Forests overran the cities; wild animals prowled the streets.

We passed several passageways before the Guardian turned again into a new one, so low that I had to bend to keep from hitting my head on the ceiling.

As we weaved in and out of these tunnels, I recognized some of the stories on the walls from my mother's tales of our people. Others I did not know. They might have been the stories of the Kadar and the Seela.

When the Guardian suddenly stopped in front of me, I nearly ran into him.

He turned, and more light flooded the walls. "How fare you with the Kadar?"

I blinked at him, wondering if he had only now thought of the fact that I had been brought to Karamur against my will.

"I have come to no harm since I have been in the palace." My glance swept a large carving of a battle scene, warriors clashing swords with the enemy in the foreground, while others in the background strung captives together with ropes.

"Uncivilized brigands." The Guardian's voice held loathing. "Murderers to the last of them. I would care not if the Kerghi came and swept the whole bloodthirsty lot away. And yet we must protect the Kadar, since they protect the island."

His sudden outburst surprised me. "Some of them—" I began to say, then stopped, hardly able to believe that I was about to defend the Kadar. "They follow the path of their ancestors as we follow ours."

"I find their customs distasteful." He swung the lamp back, leaving me in semidarkness once again as he shuffled forward in the corridor. "Their superstitions know no bound."

"But things are changing slowly in Karamur."

Leena had told me some things during one of her exultations of Batumar. How he had ended the practice of slavery at the palace—she and all others served of their own free will. He encouraged the citizens of Karamur to do the same. Many followed his example, if not happily, then to gain the favor of the High Lord.

He was a warlord, chosen to lead his people in war. He did not rule over the Kadar as a king over his kingdom. He did not make the laws, although he had a role in enforcing them if needed, Leena had said.

We had argued, or rather I had argued with her, as she would not openly contradict me. I had told her I considered the keeping of concubines the same as slavery, for was I not kept captive in Pleasure Hall? She had wept in distress that I could not understand such honor.

For the moment, I was free of Pleasure Hall but not much happier for the freedom. The weight of the future pressed heavily upon my mind.

We forged ahead in silence until we arrived at another widening that led to a large chamber, the ceiling so high the light from our lamp did not reach to the roof. Here the Guardian of the Scrolls stopped at last.

In the back of the chamber a ledge protruded from the rock, and on this ledge lay three scrolls, each as thick around as my arm, bound with leather cords in an intricate pattern of knots.

The scrolls looked ancient and fragile, and I feared they would turn to dust if I even touched them. Yet I had been called to read them, according to the Guardians.

Spirit, be strong. Heart, be brave. I had come so far, I would not hesitate now. I stepped forward, then looked back at the Guardian. "May I?"

His shoulders up, his back as straight as he could manage, he looked younger, as if the presence of the scrolls invigorated him. He nodded.

I turned back to the three scrolls. "Which one should I read first?"

"Listen to their call."

I listened in vain.

At last I drew a deep breath, then picked up the scroll closest to me with much care. How light it felt upon my palm, and right and comforting in a way that touched my heart, like holding my mother's hand when I had been a child. For a fleeting moment, I felt her spirit once again, and tears filled my eyes. Then the moment passed, and I blinked away the tears.

I stared at the scroll, trying to make sense of the knots. Gentle tugging accomplished nothing, as the leather had dried and would not loosen. I could not simply slip the scroll from its binding; the leather strip was woven around the ends as well. I tugged this way and that; then, after all my attempts failed, I set the scroll aside and chose another.

I had no luck with that one, either. Worried now, I picked up the third. The leather binding looked just as old and dry, just as impossible to loosen, but as I tugged, the knots slipped undone with ease, some, it seemed, before I even touched them.

I breathed a sigh of relief and heard the soft hiss of the Guardian's released breath behind me.

Then the long cord finally fell to the ground, and in my trembling hands lay the unbound scroll, holding the destiny of three nations—the Shahala, the Kadar, and the Seela—if not the destiny of the whole world.

The scroll seemed to be made of some kind of pressed plant fiber I could not name, thin and smooth, obviously manufactured with great skill. I rolled the fragile material out a hand-width and looked at the strange letters, squiggly and mysterious like snake tracks in the sand. I rolled some more, but the same writing followed. The cold taste of failure filled my mouth.

"I cannot read this, Grandfather." I hung my head as I whispered the words.

The Guardian stepped closer and peered at the writing. A look of disbelief came over his face, soon replaced by the grim mask of defeat. "You must. All depends on it."

I scrolled another hand-width and another and stared at the flowing rows of nonsense letters, mostly black, but here and there a more ornate grouping in red.

"The writing is of the First People." Heavy regret laced the Guardian's words. "I know the sound of the letters, but the meaning of their words has been lost to us for generations."

I sank to the stone floor, careful with the scroll. The Guardian set the lamp down and sat next to me, pointing at the beginning. "Eptah lorriem, fahl dan metrem, kalmata norga."

"This is an account of the vision of the Prophet Eptah," I said as the words he spoke gained meaning in my mind, like hopeful buds pushing through the snow in the spring.

He looked up, the deep lines of his face relaxing. "You understand, then?"

"My mother used to talk to me like this when I was a child. Ancient tales and nursery rhymes and— She spoke the language of many people. I have heard these words, but never have I seen them in writing."

"A Elhar redala tarni..." He read on for me.

And I listened.

The light of morning follows the night, and it is darkness the light turns into at the end of the day. Such is the fate of every man and every people. For as there are darkness and light, so there are evil and good, as there have been from the beginning of time. When one triumphs, the other is exiled, but in its time, the exiled shall return. I, Eptah, the last prophet of my people have seen the coming darkness and set forth here a true account of it.

I did not translate the words for the Guardian; he did not stop for me to do so but went on with Eptah's prophecy.

Once we were a great people who ruled the lands. We were a good people, the keepers of life, but our time is now coming to an end. Many people will come after us and will build their cities on the ruins of ours and will forget us. And among these many nations will be some good and some bad, but never all good or all bad within any nation. And after a time, there will come a nation that will grow faster than any other, for its ruler will have a hungry heart that is never satisfied. It will feed on goodness and draw many men with dark hearts from far away. And the evil will increase until it gains much power, but it will want more still.

And there will come a time when the darkness spreads out over the land until it dims but the last of the light, and it will fight against the people who hold that light in their hearts. And if the darkness succeeds, it will rule for a hundred generations, and cruelty and misery with it.

But on Dahru, a child will be born, well-favored by the spirits, for she will have all three spirits of the people of Dahru and even the spirit of our forgotten people. And she will know all people, for she will have been all people. And they will raise their eyes to her with hope so that as she had cast out their pain, so she might cast out the darkness also.

I have seen this and spoken of it, and set it down as a true account for those to come, by my own hands, Eptah, the last prophet of my people.

Silence filled the cave when the Guardian finished reading.

I drew a deep breath, then told him all I had learned.

He flashed a puzzled look. "The scroll says nothing more?"

"No, grandfather."

His shoulders sagged, a troubled expression settling on his lined face. "All that we already knew."

I had not, but the scroll did not fully satisfy me, either. I had expected some kind of instruction, *do this, do that*. Some plan we could follow. What use were Eptah and his empty platitudes? A great enemy was coming indeed. Well, we had known that. We searched the scrolls for solutions, not to be told that which was already obvious.

"Eptah's prophecy was handed down from generation to generation among our people, spoken around every fire. I expected more to be on the scrolls, not less," the Guardian murmured.

"Less?"

"Mayhap our storytellers embellished the prophecy as they passed it down. Or maybe Eptah told more of the vision to his followers than what he wrote. The scroll did not mention anything about you walking out of the mist at the top of the cliff."

"But you knew?"

"Everybody did. We called the mist every time the stars were favorable. Only we did not know you would come that day or even in our lifetime. We waited every time the stars aligned the right way. Our fathers did the same before us, and our sons are already trained to continue on after."

"It is not me you waited for, I think," I said with some relief.

"You are. We sensed it in your mother. She too knew the truth of this."

Yet she had given her spirit to Barmorid and died and left me to face my fate alone. For the first time, I felt a rush of anger and disappointment when I thought of her. But those emotions quickly disappeared, and then I just missed her again.

"Maybe the other scrolls." I reached for them and tried to loosen the strips again, to no avail. I placed them back on the stone ledge with dismay.

"They will open when the time is here." The Guardian picked up the lamp and groaned as he stood. I could feel the ache in his bones.

I rolled up the open scroll. "May I take this with me?"

He thought for some time, then nodded.

The way out seemed much faster than the way in, maybe because I had much to occupy my mind. The Guardian of the Cave waited for us at the opening, his face painted with questions. But he looked at our dejected expressions and did not ask any.

I wished I could help them. Part of me wished I had the power to save nations. Yet I feared great power with all my being, knowing my great-grandmother had it and she had been thoroughly corrupted by it.

The Guardian of the Cave sealed the gap in the rock behind us. "The Guardian of the Gate has not yet returned. He will be sorry he missed you. We do enjoy your company."

They would have enjoyed results even more, no doubt, but he was too polite to say this.

"Come." He gestured. "Warm yourself by the fire before you leave."

I settled in, then gasped as my gaze fell on the leather sack next to him. He smiled at me and drew a blue crystal the size of my head from the half-open pouch. Such a crystal had value beyond measure and perhaps even the power to turn away storms.

"Is that—" I began to ask, breathless suddenly.

He nodded. "A city father brought it as a gift. It was found in an old cellar." He held the crystal over the flames, and the light of the fire shone through the great rock, revealing a myriad of fissures within.

The guardian tapped his treasure slightly against one of the stones that outlined the fire pit, and as I gave a startled cry, the great crystal disintegrated into shards.

"What a terrible waste," I moaned.

He was not as perturbed as I. "Nothing is to be cried over. Everything is to be learned from."

A lesson? I could barely think.

"She should go. She can learn another day." The Guardian of the Scrolls, who had been picking through the messy pile next to his sleeping place, now straightened at last and brought me a small length of rough cloth.

I had brought the leather cord from the inner cave with me. He helped me wrap the scroll, then watched with approval as I tied it to my waist with care. The way down the cliff face was not overly diffi-cult, but we both wished to see the scroll safe.

Outside the cave, dawn lightened the mist. I bade them farewell and hurried to the cliff, thinking all the way about the great crystal. Power with a flaw. I thought about my great-grandmother once again. I pondered her fate as I climbed, but had to set those thoughts aside once I reached the bottom of the cliff.

The mist lifted just as my feet touched down. Soon people filled the streets. I could not go to the front gate, so I thought to try my luck at the kitchen and turned into the narrow side street that led to the door. But Shartor strode my way from the opposite direction, a fair crowd following him.

His eyes narrowed as he spotted me and pointed with a knobby finger. "I say she is a sorceress. Look at her clothes. Unnatural. I say at night she roams the streets to find the weak points of the fortress city. I say she roams the mist."

The crowd, mostly men, rumbled.

I turned tail and ran.

Their boots slapped on stone as they pursued me.

I broke out onto the main street and grabbed a rag from the back of a cart, wrapping it around my head. My concubine weaves covered, with my small stature, I hoped I looked like some street urchin hurrying about his business.

I ran past the Palace Guard at the front gate, looking away from them so they would not see my face. I rounded the palace, dashing through a cluster of alleys, reached the wood chute, and slipped in, then closed its metal door behind me.

I reached for the scroll and found my precious charge unharmed, but still my heart did not stop clamoring until I was halfway to Plea-sure Hall, hurrying down a deserted hallway. Then I pushed the door open, and my heart lurched into a mad race again. I nearly fell over two servant women who lay on the floor inside, both asleep. The slight forest scent of the sleeping stick permeated the air. I held my breath and left the door wide open behind me.

More people slept farther in, servants stretched out on the floor. I picked my way across the hall, careful not to step on anyone. The sight that greeted me in my chamber paralyzed my limbs. Leena slept curled in a ball in the corner, and on my bed snored gently Batumar, his sword hanging from his side.

Quickly I extinguished the sleeping stick and fanned the door to remove its drug from the air. I could not hold my breath through all this. My eyes grew heavy as I breathed some of the perfumed smoke.

With movements too slow, I hid the scroll in the trunk at the foot of the bed, then stripped out of my thudi and donned the nearest dress as best I could. I had to twist like a water willow to lace it up in the back and only managed halfway before Batumar opened his eyes.

My arms at my sides, I made sure not to present my back to the High Lord. I plastered a smile on my face.

Leena woke with a gasp. Voices filtered in, others awakening.

Batumar's gaze darkened as he glanced around, his brows drawing tight with anger. He stood and strode to the door on unsteady feet, his heavy boots scraping the stone. He roared at the servants as loud as any manyinga beast. "Be gone!"

I stared. I had never known him to abuse anyone under his command. Leena cast me a worried look, ready to defy the High Lord's order for my sake, but I nodded to her to leave. Whatever trouble I had earned, I did not want her harmed.

Batumar spun to me as the last of the servants scuttled out of Pleasure Hall.

"I will *not* have sorcery practiced upon me, upon my people, in my very palace. If that is where your healing comes from, I want to see no more of it." He tempered his voice to a low tone, but it scared me no less than his shouting.

His face looked like the night sky erupting in thunder, flashes of anger thrown from his obsidian eyes. Like an enraged beast was he, defending his own from an unexpected enemy.

"I—"

He advanced toward me. "The war is upon us. And the mist comes more often than ever. People lock themselves in their houses in fear. And now this—" He stopped. "I sent a servant for you. She did not return. I sent another. Then another. And when I came looking, I found them asleep on the floor and you gone."

His anger filled the room, the air vibrating as after thunder. I had thought him fearsome when I had first seen him at the House of Tahar, but during the time I had spent at Karamur, I had grown more comfortable in his presence. All that disappeared in a heartbeat. A fearsome warrior he was indeed, confronting his enemy.

"Where have you been?" His sharp words flew at me like daggers.

"In the kitchen—"

"Do not lie to me!" he roared then and stalked closer. "Did you talk to the enemy? To the spy you healed at the House of Joreb? He escaped later, but you must already know this. Is he in Karamur?"

He grabbed me by the shoulders, his merciless gaze searching to read my soul. I trembled under his hands.

When he spoke again, his voice was tinged with disappointment. "Have I been a fool, then, and Shartor right? Should I have put you to death the day I found you?"

I could not utter a single word.

"Are you Noona the dark sorceress come to find us through time and endless distance to destroy our people once and for all?"

I recoiled from his words and sank to my knees at his feet. I bowed deeply. "I would bring you and your people no harm. I swear upon my life."

A cold silence followed; then he lifted me up to look into my face. "I know you wished this union not. But I thought with time... Do you seek to disgrace my House by lying with another man?" His voice was measured, and hard enough to be broken against.

He had seen the back of my dress unfastened.

I shook my head, unable to speak.

"I will know the truth of it, Tera, if you are no longer a maiden, if you freely give to another what you withhold from me." He reached out and tore the dress from neck to hem, then tossed me onto the bed without effort.

And for an instant, behind the rage I saw a fierce hunger flood his eyes.

I had never thought anything could feel worse than Kumra's flogging, but Batumar's accusations cut through my skin more effectively than the whip. Yet I would not beg and scamper. I would be brave, as

Onra had been. So I fought him not but lay still on the silk pillows and closed my eyes.

"Do with me then as you wish, my lord." My voice might not have been as strong as I wanted, but it rang clear and did not betray my fears.

I heard his labored breathing.

Time passed enough for at least two mooncrossings.

Then his boots scuffed the floor as he stepped away from the bed.

When I opened my eyes, I found his gaze burning into mine.

"You belong to me, Tera of the Shahala. To me and no other."

He turned away to stare into the fire. Suddenly, it seemed as if a great weight sat upon his shoulders. Something inside me pushed to comfort him, yet I dared not. I pulled my gown together in front.

"Has something happened, my lord?"

He did not answer for some time, and when he did, he did so without turning. "The Kingdom of Orh fell. Their king is slain. The Kerghi retreat was a ploy. They returned as soon as we left."

He watched the flames a while longer before he looked back at me. "Tell me where you went."

There had been a tenuous connection between us of late, some sort of a truce, the beginnings of trust, maybe some understanding. All that had disappeared. We were once again as strangers.

I sat up. "I cannot."

"You can. You will."

"There are many things still that even I do not fully understand, my lord. My tale, if told, would be impossible to believe."

He looked at me with much doubt on his face.

"I beg you to allow me more time, my lord. There is a place—" I bit my lip.

He waited. Then his eyes widened as he stared. Long moments passed as he watched me, a myriad of emotions crossing his face. "You found the Forgotten City."

My stunned expression must have been all the answer he needed, for he went on. "Impossible. It could not be anywhere near. For hundreds of years, Kadar warriors searched for it."

My mind was a jumbled mess of half-coherent thoughts. "You know of the prophecy?"

"I make certain to know everything that has a bearing on my people. I am the High Lord." He shook his head. *"When the enemy cometh, a Kadar slave, a Shahala healer who crossed the waves, shall rise up to fight the great darkness. She will find the Forgotten City and help the Kadar to victory."* He sank onto the end of the bed. "I know the myth, but I never believed it."

So many things made sense all at once. My face flooded with heat. "But you believed it enough so that you asked for me when you came to the House of Tahar?"

He scowled. "Swords win wars, not obscure legends. But some of my people are superstitious. I could not let some healer cause a distraction while I am conducting a war. I had word of a slave ship that delivered a Shahala healer to the House of Tahar. At first, I was content to leave you there, but as the war neared, it seemed wise to keep you closer. I expected a young girl dazed by her *calling*," he mused. "And easily controlled."

I felt my ire rising as he continued.

"Slaves are not often taken from the Shahala. They are our allies. A warlord might receive one as spoils of war from a faraway place now and then." He shrugged. "Then I heard the stories of miraculous healings at the House of Tahar. Servants tend to gossip in the marketplace; caravans carry such news."

"You knew a Shahala healer had been taken as a slave, and you did nothing to right that wrong?" I was too angry to consider that questioning and accusing the High Lord this way was probably an offense punishable by death. Truthfully, I had lived with such a threat for so long, I no longer cared.

"The matter of a single slave is hardly a concern for the High Lord of the Kadar."

"A true leader cares about the smallest of his people. Every one of the Shahala Elders would have given his life to save mine had they had the opportunity."

His shoulders grew rigid. "I'm protecting you now," he said. "Tell me the way to the Forgotten City."

CHAPTER EIGHTEEN

(Escape from Karamur)

"I cannot."

Batumar scowled and began to say something, but Leena appeared at the door, begging his forgiveness for the interruption. One of his stewards waited in the Great Hall, wanting to report a matter that needed immediate attention.

"We will settle this when I return," he said before he left me, his tone carrying ample warning.

Leena rushed to me, paling at the sight of my ruined dress. She brought me another one at once. "Did he harm you, my lady?"

I hesitated a moment, for Batumar had known I had been stolen from my people. He had done nothing to right that wrong, and in that he had harmed me greatly. But in the end, he brought me to Karamur and to my destiny. Could I blame him for walking the path the spirits had set out before him? Perhaps he had a choice, and perhaps he had one not. And perhaps the same stood true for me.

At my silence, Leena began to weep, and I rose to comfort her.

"Truly, it is no crying matter. He is much angered, for I refuse to tell him all he wants to know."

Leena wiped her eyes and nodded. "Forgive me, my lady."

"You ask because you care. I never regarded you as a servant. I wish we could be friends."

She looked so horrified at my words, I had to laugh. "Oh, fine well, then. Even if you will not accept my friendship, you are a comfort to me and a treasure."

Tears flooded her eyes. "And you, my lady, are like the daughter I never—" She caught herself and bowed deeply. "Forgive me if I offended you. I am but a foolish old servant."

"Have you no children?" I felt selfish and guilty for never having asked before. Had I grown so accustomed to the ways of the Kadar that I had treated her like a servant and did not even know it?

She waited a long time before she answered and spoke each word with great reluctance and visible pain. "I had a son once."

"What happened to him?"

"When he was born, the soothsayer said on the day my son called me mother, he would die."

My heart lurched at such a cruel prediction. "Did he?"

Leena shook her head. "I left him before he learned to talk."

Tears rolled down her face, and I moved to hug her. And this once, she did not draw away. *Every heart has a sorrow*, as the Shahala said.

She was the same height as I, although I had not realized it until I embraced her. I had always thought her smaller, probably because she was forever bowing before me. But now, the realization led to an idea, even as she pulled away, glancing at the floor as if embarrassed for having shown weakness and behaving so familiarly toward me.

"I would like to borrow your dress," I said.

Her gaze snapped to me. "My lady—"

"I must leave the palace without anyone knowing." I could not wait for Batumar's return. I could not let him force me to reveal the Forgotten City, which he would surely do. And if I stood strong and refused… He had looked as if he would be quite content to lock me in my chamber until I was older than the Guardians.

"You must stay, Lady Tera. The High Lord will not harm you. You

RELUCTANT CONCUBINE   213

are safe in the palace. You do not know the dangers of being alone, a woman as beautiful as you."

Horror filled her voice, and I wondered what had happened to her once she had left her child and run away to start another life. I thought of Shartor and his mob. If I ran away into the city and Batumar washed his hands of me, I would not fare well, for certain. But I meant to go to the Guardians, and there I knew I would be safe.

"I will leave with or without your help. If you care for me, do not try to stop me."

At that, she sobbed aloud but pulled her simple brown dress over her head. I thanked her and donned her servant clothes quickly.

I offered her my thudi and Shahala tunic in exchange, for I knew she would not take anything finer.

"You must stay here as long as you can," I said, and she nodded. "I do not wish you to come to harm. When they find out that I left, tell them I ordered you. Tell them I gave you herbs."

I drew a deep breath, assuring myself that as long as I had known him, I had never seen Batumar mistreat anyone under his command.

I slipped the scroll from its hiding place and tucked it under Leena's dress, then picked up an armload of clothes, hoping to use them to cover my face.

"Your hair, my lady," Leena called after me as I hurried for the door.

I dropped the clothes and reached up to yank down the elaborate coils that marked me as a concubine. If she had not called me back— "Have you something sharp?"

Lena paled. "My lady…"

I remembered the emerald brooch and dug through the trunk at the foot of my bed until I found the heavy jewel.

So Lord Gilrem, after all this time, would aid my escape yet from the Kadar. I sharpened the edge of the brooch on the rough stone of the wall, then chopped my dark hair as short as I could. An uneven cut for certain, as this once, Leena refused to help and would only wring her hands and watch me tearfully.

I tossed the fallen locks into the fire, then picked up my bundle again and lifted it high in front of my face. I stooped my shoulders and shuffled out the door. Pleasure Hall stood empty, but two guards guarded the door outside. I shuffled right past them.

When I passed out of sight, I hurried toward the servants' quarters and blended in without trouble among the men and women who bustled about, too busy to pay attention to anything else but their tasks at hand. I kept my head down and made no eye contact but hurried on like the rest.

I left the clothes by the washroom, grabbed a pinch of cold wood ash, and rubbed it into my face, then watched my complexion turn pallid in the reflective surface of a giant copper pot. I glanced around, and when no one watched, I rubbed another pinch of ash into my hair until it turned dull and streaked with gray.

I shuffled from the washroom to the kitchen, more careful here since the kitchen servants knew me best. Keeping my head bent and my gaze down, I joined a group of women carrying baskets for the market. In but a few steps, we were outside.

So fast! No time for second thoughts, and no time for panic either.

Two hand wagons stood abandoned nearby, a small flock of hens picking at the ground around the wheels. Three empty milk pails sat on each wagon. A little farther down the street loitered several guards talking. I sucked in my breath. We would have to pass by them.

Their jesting and laughter carried to my ear, their carefree mood in stark contrast to my own alarmed state. I worked my way into the middle of the group as we neared them, praying to the spirits to shield me from their eyes. To my chagrin, instead of passing by them quickly, one of the younger women tarried to talk to a warrior. The rest stopped to wait for her.

I stood cringing in the middle, the guards but a few steps away as they joked with the young and pretty women. I kept my head down and my back bent, hefting the large basket from one hip to the other— it weighed a fair load even empty. Would an aged servant so easily carry such a thing? I slid the basket to the ground at my feet.

"Old woman," a guard called out, and my heart lurched. "You should leave this heavy work to others. Have you no daughters to go to the market for you?" He strode toward me.

I shook my head but would not look up. I had met many of Batumar's guards as I walked through the palace every day and had even healed some of them in the back of the kitchen.

I sucked in my breath as the warrior, young to be in the Palace Guard, bent over me. I thought he had grown suspicious and meant to look at my face, and I nearly panicked, looking for a way to run, but he picked up my basket instead and started down the street.

"I will carry this for you," he called back. "And when the market is over, I will find you and carry your purchases back to the palace."

The spirits be praised, the group of women followed him.

The fortress city of Karamur always bustled with people, but their numbers grew twofold on market days, according to the servants. I had no trouble blending in and disappearing among them once the guard left me. I set my basket next to a merchant's busy table and walked away.

A cacophony of noises surrounded me, loud bargaining, laughter, mothers calling for their children. I pushed through the shoppers, careful not to draw attention to myself, not daring to linger and marvel at the colorful crowd or their exotic wares.

Without the mist, I could not hope to scale the cliff, for I would be seen. I waited in an alley until the market ended; then I slipped among the traders and farmers streaming out the city gates.

The walls had been reinforced since I had last seen them, and more guards stood on duty everywhere I looked. With every step, I expected the call to ring out to seal the gate. I remembered well the strange contraption of giant bars that hung from iron chains. I scarcely dared breathe until we walked through the tunnel-like passageway into the open.

In front of me spread peasant huts too numerous to count, interspersed with fields and small groves. The great forest stretched like a dark green wall on the horizon. We were at summer's end, the weather still warm, even here, half-way up the mountain.

I walked among the chattering traders until we reached the forest and were out of sight from the walls of Karamur, then I slipped into the woods as if to relieve myself. I watched from the shelter of a dense bush but, as I belonged to no one, no one stopped to wait for me.

Crouching low, I backed away until the undergrowth became thick enough so I could be sure I would not be seen when standing.

Massive emerald giants reached to the sky and waved their smaller branches as if welcoming me. The sky was but a splatter of pale blue above. I drew a shuddering breath of freedom, then turned my attention to the ground and soon found an animal trail that led up the mountain.

I followed the trail up and up, then turned east and, under the cover of the majestic trees, made my way toward where I thought the Forgotten City lay, still walking an upward path.

Other than birds, I saw no animals, not even a stray deer. Perhaps the noise of my approach had scared them away. I had lived too long among the Kadar and forgotten the way of the woods. I walked as a visitor, not as one who belonged here.

I kept my eyes open for any sign of danger and prayed to the spirits to keep me from the path of predators. I hoped not to see a tiger and, more importantly, not to be seen by one. I fortified my spirit by convincing myself that the great beasts would not wander so close to the city. And if they did, I hoped the Guardians had placed upon the mountain some protection.

Evening approached, my stomach grumbling with hunger, by the time I considered I might be lost. I looked for anything edible and found a low-growing vine that I knew had starchy, bitter roots, suitable for eating. I kneeled and with a stick dug into the soft earth around the base of the vine, not wanting half the root to break off in the ground as I pulled.

A branch snapped somewhere to my right.

My hands froze.

The snapping of a dry branch was not unusual in any forest, but this was followed by a series of softer sounds. Something moved through the woods. Toward me.

I dared not move, for the slightest noise would betray my location. If the animal had not caught my scent yet, I still had some chance of escaping its attention, huddled low by the bushes, close to the ground.

A flash of brown moved among the trees. *A tiger.* Terror gripped my heart. A giant beast it looked to be, as tall as a man, from what little I could see.

And then it finally stalked near enough to—

The Guardian of the Scrolls stepped into plain sight, looking mightily unhappy.

I slumped with relief.

"There you are," he groused, squinting. "Darkness falls fast in the tall woods."

I jumped up and ran to him, and would have hugged him if the scowl on his face did not hold me back. "How good it is to see you, grandfather. Did you know I was coming?"

He glanced at my hair and clothes but did not comment on them. "I felt the scroll."

I pulled it from under my dress and handed it to him. "Would you read the prophecy to me again?"

He nodded and turned back the way he had come. "When we are warm by the fire."

"Batumar knows," I said as I walked behind him. "About the prophecy and me. He wants to see the Forgotten City."

The Guardian shrugged. As we came out at the edge of the woods, he pointed to a gorge below us. "If he comes, this is what he will see."

The dim light of dusk revealed a steep slope, covered with jagged rocks, a puff of cloud resting on the bottom. I saw no path as he walked down into the gorge, and yet somehow he found foothold where there had been none, and stepping in his steps, I was able to follow.

We arrived at the bottom much faster than I had expected, and once we broke through the cover of mist, the Forgotten City spread before us. The soft glow of the Forum's golden dome shone in the middle like a great jewel. We were but a short distance from the Guardians' cave.

"Why are the Sacred Scrolls not with the rest in the Forum?" I asked, remembering my mother's tale about how the honeycombed walls held all the knowledge of the world. I very much wished to see that. Maybe those other scrolls, not the ones in the Sacred Cave, contained the answers to our questions.

"The Forum stood empty since before my ancestors came here, the scrolls hidden by the First People during the long decades of ancient wars. Many things they did not pass on to the Seela," the Guardian said.

Like a blow felt his words. The thought of such a treasury of knowledge lost forever ripped through my flesh. I still struggled to comprehend that tragedy as we reached the cave.

The other two Guardians welcomed me with joy and shared their simple meal of soup and bread. The Guardian of the Cave gifted me with a hooded brown robe similar to his own. Its hem swept the floor of the cave as I walked.

It made me feel, if not renewed, then different. Not Tera, daughter of Chalee, not Tera the slave or Tera the concubine, but someone I did not yet know, someone I more and more wished to become.

When I told them what had happened at the palace, they prepared for me a sleeping place in the far corner of the cave and and left me in peace to think.

But before he retired for the night, the Guardian of the Cave came to me. He pulled an apple from his robe and set it on the stone by my side.

"What do you see?" he asked gently.

"A green apple."

He gave the apple a quarter turn.

"A red apple," I said. That side must have been toward the sun.

Another quarter turn.

I stared at the dark opening of a hole in the middle of a rotten brown spot. "A wormy apple."

He offered a kind smile, then walked away.

I thought long and hard on what he meant to teach me. To see better, I thought, to see more thoroughly. *To see every side.* Of what? My destiny? The war? Batumar?

Eyes are the organs of distraction, my mother used to tell me. *They notice the smallest things, crowd everything full of useless detail, and steal attention from where the focus should be.* Many times she had bidden me to see with my heart.

I lay down. The uneven rock bed dug into my side even through the furs, so I moved around to find a more comfortable spot. Too fast I had grown used to my feather bed at the palace and the comforts of Pleasure Hall.

Although neither my hair nor my clothes needed Leena's ministrations, I missed her and hoped she was not punished for my escape. But as I lay on my pile of furs in the corner of the cave, I refused to miss Batumar. Still, I could not stop my thoughts from going to him as I looked out into the darkness and watched the stars through the mouth of the cave. I half expected to see him appear there, having come after me.

———

I spent the next three days and nights with the Guardians, most of it in the Sacred Cave of the Scrolls. I also spent some time at my mother's grave, where I felt closest to her spirit. On the fourth day, after the Guardians of the Gate and the Cave had left for the Forgotten City in the morning, I rolled out once again the first scroll, still the only one to open.

I was determined to make more sense of the prophecy, to unlock some secret meaning. The enemy neared with every passing day.

The Guardian of the Scrolls watched me from the corner of his eye but looked away when, after a while, I once again rolled up the scroll and set it aside, frustrated to the brink of tears.

"I went to visit the Seer last night," he said.

Since he brought up the topic, I did not think it would be terribly impolite to inquire further. "What did you wish her to see for you?"

"I wanted to know how your Leena fares, but—" He held up his hands as if to stop my hopes from springing too high. "Selaila was on another search."

That seemed to be her way. Her body forever in her hut, her spirit unreachable. Twice the Guardians had thought to introduce her to me, but we were sent away by her mother each time with prostrate apologies. So instead, they had shown me the Forgotten City, its curious buildings and solemn people, even the empty Forum, the sight of which greatly saddened my heart.

"Thank you for trying." I smiled my gratitude.

"You have been worried," he said gruffly and turned away.

I had spoken of Leena and Batumar a lot in the past few days, I supposed. We passed the evenings trading tales.The Guardians told me about the Seela and their past, and I talked about Karamur. They had a great curiosity for the fortress city, a place that stood so close to them yet remained mostly unknown to their people.

Still, that the Guardian of the Scrolls would go as far as seeking the Seer surprised me. Of the three Guardians, he had shown the least interest in my tales, although I had caught his gaze on me time and time again as I had relayed the happenings of the palace.

Maybe he was softening toward the Kadar. Or perhaps he was softening toward me. He had finally, the day before, allowed me to prepare for him an herbal tea, and was now moving around more easily. His complaints had decreased by half, for which the other Guardians had privately thanked me.

"Grandfather," I addressed him with utmost respect, then pointed to a short passage on the scroll, bringing up once again the thought that had been nagging in the back of my mind. *...well-favored by the spirits, for she will have all three spirits of the people of Dahru and even the spirit of our forgotten people.* I looked at him. "How could that be me?"

"You have the spirit of the Shahala from your mother," he said. "And the Kadar from your father."

"But the others? How could I have the spirit of the Seela? And how could I have the spirit of the First People when they have been gone for centuries?"

"The Seela are said to have in them some of the First People's blood and with it their spirit, from whence come our gifts."

So between the two of us, we had all four spirits. But that was not what the prophecy called for. I mentioned this to the Guardian, but he shrugged, looking not the least concerned.

"Then how about—" I read on, *"She will know all people, for she will have been all people."*

"You have been the child of a powerful mother, and then an orphan. You have been a slave. And now you are the sole concubine of the most powerful warlord of the land," he said. "Most of us start out our lives and the path before us never changes. At birth, I was a

Guardian, and I will die a Guardian. But you have walked the path of many."

"But I have not been *all* people. I have not been a merchant, I have not been a mother, I have not been a warrior—"

"You have been enough. And the next passage says: ...*they will raise their eyes to her with hope so that as she had cast out their pain, so she might cast out the darkness also.* You cannot deny that is true. You are a healer and have cast out the pain of many." He fell silent then, and we sat like that for some time, each absorbed in our own thoughts.

"You can read the scroll now," he said after a while.

I nodded. He had read the prophecy for me until I knew the words by heart and began to grow familiar with the strange letters that created them. I already knew the language, so I only had to connect letters with the sounds.

"Then you no longer need me." His voice sounded tired and listless again as it had when I first met him. "My work is finished."

"But I do need you and so does everyone else."

"I am but a useless old man. A coward at that—" His face darkened. "For I fear what is to come and look only for a way to avoid having to live through it."

I thought for a moment. "The Shahala have a saying: There is no greater courage than to accept one's destiny."

He looked up at that.

"You dedicated your whole life to guarding the scrolls, and when I came, you taught me. You sacrificed much, and there is honor in it. I question my fate with each breath of the day. You completed yours."

"I did what I had to."

"And gave up much along the way for your people and strangers you will never know."

"I would have liked to have had a family." He admitted the first personal detail since I had known him.

"You have a son."

He remained silent for some time, and when he spoke, the words fell heavy from his lips. "At the time deemed right by the Seer, a young woman was selected from the maidens of the city. She walked up to this cave and conceived our son, then walked back down, and I never talked to her again. When my son was the right age, he came to me for training. A few days before you appeared out of the mist, he ascended the mountain to purify his mind and body and to wait for my death so he can descend and take over his duty."

"And the other Guardians?"

"The son of the Guardian of the Gate is on a journey through the Gates to learn them better. The son of the Guardian of the Cave…" Disapproval filled his eyes. "A restless one, that one, and undisciplined. He decided to go on a quest, searching for other sacred caves in the mountains."

"There are other sacred caves?"

"So the legends say. One holds the great sword of Bergan. Another hides a thousand virgins frozen in sleep by a sorceress of old. And there might be more that our story tellers forgot about over the centuries."

I sat up straighter. "Could not the great sword of Bergan help Batumar win the war better than I?"

"The sword is prophesized to unite the world after a thousand years."

"A thousand years from now?" That much war I could scarcely comprehend.

"A thousand years from when the prophecy was made." He hung his head, his lips in a grim line. "Unfortunately, no two Guardians have ever been able to agree on that date. But we do not think the time is near."

All fairy tales, I thought. Especially the thousand virgins. If a cave such as that existed, the Kadar warlords would have been looking for it day and night to claim the virgins for their Maiden Halls.

The Guardian said, "In any case, those other prophesies have not been entrusted to the three of us. Our duty was to await you." The lines on his forehead eased somewhat. "Which we did with honor. And should we pass before you fulfill your fate, our sons stand ready to assist you."

My throat tightened at his words. For legends and vague prophecies, generations of young men had been forced to sacrifice their lives.

"The Shahala value families above all. No office asks its holder to forgo that. Why is it so among your people?"

"The first Guardians believed the Great War of the prophecies would come soon and their services would be urgently needed. They thought the prophecy would be fulfilled in their own lifetimes and feared a family would distract them from their duties. They forswore it for this reason. The example of the first Guardians was followed until it had become unbreakable law among my people."

I thought of those generations of Guardians, their entire lives spent waiting for me to walk out of the mist. I could scarcely comprehend such devotion.

"Sometimes our worst bonds are of our own making," he said, his tone glum.

"But it is not too late. You can still find your son's mother."

He shook his head. "Too late for me." But then he added, "Maybe not so for my son."

Before I could respond, I caught sight of the Guardian of the Cave and the Guardian of the Gate hurrying up the path together. "Kadar warriors are all over the mountain," the Guardian of the Gate said once they were close enough. "Shall we show ourselves? With the Khergi hordes so close to our island, is our time here?"

The Guardian of the Scrolls shook his head. "I do not want warriors in our city. First, let us speak to their High Lord. We have been isolated too long. Go now, Tera, and tell Batumar we are coming."

I nodded, knowing that the High Lord's anger would be fierce when I faced him. But if the spirits *had* given me a role in saving our people, I *would* do what was required of me. "When should he expect you?"

"For the evening meal," said the Guardian of the Gate, patting his belly in an absent gesture.

I rolled up the scroll carefully and left it in their keeping, then said farewell to the Guardians and went to face Batumar, hoping to find mercy in his sight.

CHAPTER NINETEEN

(The Sacred Gate)

No sooner did I walk out of the valley than I saw Lord Gilrem, his men fanned out behind him in the woods. They looked as if they had been searching the past four full days, tired and rumpled from sleeping on the ground.

"Lord Gilrem," I said calmly as if I had gone only for a stroll.

"Lady Tera." He rushed to my side, then stared at my short hair. He held up his hand to signal his men to stay back. "How do you fare?"

"Fine well. And you, my lord?"

"My son grows and strengthens."

"And his mother?"

He nodded, then asked in a voice low enough so none but I would hear. "Will you return with me to the palace?"

I searched his face to make sure I did not misunderstand him, but his intent was clear. Now that I had accepted my destiny and the fact that I could never return to the life I had once known, the choice was finally offered to me.

The spirits were not without a sense of humor after all.

I swallowed the lump in my throat. "I shall return to Karamur with you, Lord Gilrem."

He smiled his relief, then sent some of his men to the other search parties to call them off. "We have been looking for you since your absence was discovered."

"I am sorry to have caused so much trouble." Sorry for the warriors who were about to go to battle and were deprived even of these few days to spend with their families. "I expect the High Lord is angry." I winced at the thought of an enraged Batumar.

"I shall remain by your side, if you wish, my lady."

An offer of protection. A long path we had traveled since we had first met. I had learned much in that time. It should have surprised me not that the High Lord's young brother had changed as well.

"I thank you, my lord, but I must face the High Lord alone in this matter."

Lord Gilrem would not let me climb the cliff, so we returned to Karamur the long way, his men falling into place behind us. The ones who had caught me on the creek bank were not among his guard now. I did not know whether Lord Gilrem had remembered and ordered it so or if by coincidence. I trusted his offer of protection, and I did not feel afraid in their midst.

He asked me where I had gone but did not insist on an answer when I remained silent. I asked him about the war effort.

The city walls now stood finished, he said, and the city gate fully fortified, but all other work had been set aside as Batumar had sent every available man to search for me.

I asked Gilrem about Leena. He assured me that no servants had been punished for my escape, but the Palace Guard had been disciplined as they had been found derelict in their duty.

The sun had passed its zenith by the time we reached the palace. Batumar waited for us in his Great Hall, his jaw clenched as he looked me over. His clothes were rumpled as if he had just returned from training with his men. An icy expression sat upon his face, while his dark eyes swirled with fire.

"The Lady Tera and I have matters to discuss in private." He grabbed my arm and dragged me after him down the corridor, through his antechamber into his bedchamber, and slammed the door hard enough to shake the torches in their sconces.

My heart clamored like a small chowa bird trapped in a net. *Spirit, be strong. Heart, be brave.* I tried to step back, but he would not let me. His hand was an iron band around my arm, although his fingers did not dig into my flesh, and I suffered no pain.

I took heart from that. Even in his great anger, he would not hurt me.

He looked me over once more, his gaze settling on my shorn hair, his eyes narrowing with a cold flare of fury.

"Who did this to you?" Murder rang clear in his voice.

"None other but I." I somehow kept my voice from trembling.

"Why do you test me so?" His voice roughened. "You have not been harmed?"

I shook my head.

He let me go at last. "When I found you gone…" His great chest rose as he breathed. "I thought…"

I found I could not step away from him. Something in his gaze wouldn't let me. I swallowed. "I won't leave like that again."

He reached for me once more, taking my hand, then drew me closer and pressed his lips to mine.

He did not stop there.

So it happened that when most women my age already had children to occupy their time, I was finally kissed, by no other than the Kadar High Lord, Batumar.

His lips were warm and seeking, not nearly as unyielding as the rest of his body. His mouth caressed mine until my entire body tingled.

I am not sure how long the kiss lasted; my sense of time left me along with sense of anything but his lips and arms. I had, of course, thought about how it would be, like any young girl, but I had been long since a woman. And Batumar made me feel like one. When his hand wandered up my arm, I shivered as if with fever.

Then, at long last, he drew his lips away and touched his forehead to mine. His chest rose and fell heavily.

"Shall we go to the evening feast?" he asked in a raspy voice, speaking with effort. *Or shall we stay*, I guessed the unspoken second part of his question.

Stay, I wanted to say, not ready for the heady feeling to end, but I suddenly remembered the Guardians and jumped back. "You have visitors coming, my lord." Then I told him in a rush about my days at the Forgotten City.

"I should go and change, my lord," I added once I finished my tale.

He frowned, but he granted me leave.

Leena waited for me in front of his door and threw herself at my feet in tears of joy as I stepped out of the chamber. I pulled her up into my arms, and for once she forgot herself and freely returned my embrace. We hurried to Pleasure Hall while Batumar strode straight to the feast, bidding me in passing to hasten after him.

Once in my chamber, Leena, beaming with relief, pinned my hair back and attached a gossamer arrangement of veil in such a way as to cover my shorn locks.

She spread out a golden cloud of a gown, as soft as a dream, but I shook my head. I had never been a true concubine of the High Lord's Pleasure Hall, and I felt less so now than ever before. I dressed in my thudi and Shahala tunic, and pulled the brown robe of the Guardians over that.

I looked around the room and on the top of the wooden chest saw the soft glint of the emerald brooch. I had not worn it since I had received it. But now I fastened the jewel to the brown fabric cascading from my shoulders to better hold the folds together.

Leena fussed. "We best hurry, my lady."

By the time I reached the Great Hall, the feast was underway. Every eye turned upon me as I walked to sit in the empty seat between Gilrem and Batumar. Neither of them commented on my garments as they greeted me.

As the feast proceeded and the foreign emissary on Batumar's other side claimed his attention, at last I told Lord Gilrem about the Forgotten City. I think he only half believed me until one of the Palace Guards announced the visitors.

Batumar nodded, and the guard pushed the door open to allow the Guardians to enter. How odd they looked in this place, more ancient than the walls of the palace, solemn like the forgotten gods of the myths. Their brown robes swept the floor and seemed to glow in the flickering light of the torches. Gasps sounded from all around the room as the very air felt suddenly thin.

"Greetings to the High Lord and his esteemed brother and the Lady Tera. Good tidings from the Seela of the Forgotten City," the Guardian of the Cave said ceremoniously. The Guardian of the Gate held his great carved stick. Even the Guardian of the Scrolls stood tree-straight, and without frowning.

I knew them to be curious of Karamur and the palace, but they did not gawk like children at the marketplace. They behaved with solemn dignity even as Lord Gilrem gaped at them next to me.

The murmur of a hundred people filled the Great Hall.

"Greetings, esteemed Guardians." Batumar bade them to sit, and warriors moved at once to make room at the high table.

The feast quickly fell into disarray as people would not eat, too intent on guessing what the Guardians' appearance meant. They had been but mythical creatures of legends before this moment, our men's and women's astonishment as great as if the three-headed talking warthog of Morandor appeared among them, straight from the fairy-tales. The noise level in the room only rose.

In the interest of a more productive meeting, Batumar invited the visitors to his private chambers, requesting Lord Gilrem and me to follow.

"The Lady Tera tells me you are here to discuss the war. Have you any news of Khan Woldrom and his Khergi hordes? Or the Emperor Drakhar who sends them to our destruction?" the High Lord asked once we were all seated in his antechamber.

The Guardian of the Cave shook his head. "Only what is in the prophecies."

Batumar leaned back in his chair. "They are near. Within a day or two, I shall have to leave again. Emissaries come daily to ask for our help."

"Take the Lady Tera with you, High Lord," said the Guardian of the Cave. "For the prophecies are clear. With her stands our only hope of victory."

Batumar gave him a sharp look, his voice even but hard as he said, "I do not need a woman to fight my wars for me."

"But it is written—"

The High Lord lifted his hand. "She will stay here in safety."

The Guardian of the Cave would not give up. "My lord, if you would consider…"

Batumar measured up the three men for some time before he turned to me. "As you give health and life, my lady, can you also take it away?"

"I do not understand, my lord." Although I had a feeling he did not mean giving the wrong herb by mistake.

"If you stood in the battlefield, could you take people's lives without touching them? From a distance?" His gaze searched my face.

My breath caught. "I would rather die than ever try such a thing."

He nodded as if he had expected that answer.

"Lady Tera, if it is your destiny—" the Guardian of the Cave began to say, then fell silent as the Guardian of the Scrolls cast him a dark look.

My destiny.. For war

My throat tightened. It could not be true.

I looked from man to man. A swift panic rose to swallow me as the mist sometimes swallowed Karamur. All my trepidations returned.

"I have no such great power as to save nations."

The Guardian of the Cave, who sat by my side, covered my hand with his on the table as he turned to me and spoke to me in a low voice no other would hear. "Perhaps you fear not the lack of powers, my Lady Tera, but that you might be indeed powerful beyond all that you have thus far imagined."

A strangled sound of distress escaped my throat. How little, after all this time, he knew me. "I have no great power but the gift of some healing."

"Does the thought of power worry you? Do you think it might corrupt you as it corrupted your great-grandmother?"

I did not want to answer, but then I recalled the flawed crystal that had shattered into sharp, dangerous shards, and I nodded, moisture filling my eyes. *Power with a flaw.*

I wanted no great powers. I had too many flaws. What if I shattered, and the shards cut the very people who were most important to me?

"For some, their endless potential can be more frightening than their shortcomings," he said with understanding. "You have not been called to be a simple healer, Tera."

I had been trying to accept that. Had read the first scroll, even if I felt unworthy. And I planned on reading the others as they opened. I would do whatever they required of me. But as I looked around, I realized that all those around me believed I would save them through war.

How could I take lives instead of preserving them as was my sacred duty? Even for the sake of multitudes, I could not.

I stood with determination, feeling the weight of the men's gazes upon me. "I will not aid in killing." My voice rang strong and clear. "I refuse my destiny."

Silence met my declaration. A hard tension crackled through the room.

"The prophecy says you are our only hope of defeating the enemy," the Guardian of the Gate reminded me.

A stunned expression came over Lord Gilrem's face as he looked at me, then at his brother. "Who is she?"

"The One Foretold," Batumar said with a frown, as if not the least pleased.

"The One Foretold?" Lord Gilrem paled.

"I refuse my destiny," I repeated, standing firm.

More silence followed my words.

"But then how will she lead the Kadar to victory?" Lord Gilrem asked once he recovered.

"Through peace," I said, suddenly inspired, and felt the horrible weight lift.

The Guardians exchanged glances. My heart filled with hope. They were considering my suggestion.

Batumar shook his head. "There can be no peace with this enemy."

"How do we know?" I forged on. "I shall go as an ambassador and plead a treaty."

"No," the men around the table said as one, truly exasperating in their stubbornness.

"Empires rise and fall, for such is the way of the world," I said. "Dahru is precious to us, but it must be of small value to this giant enemy. It is better to have a treaty and live than to fight and perish. The First People fought, and they are no more. The Seela are fewer and fewer with every coming year. They might not last through a long war. The Shahala do not know how to fight, many would die. The Kadar are strong but outnumbered—"

"I will not crawl to the enemy as a coward." Batumar's voice held thunder.

"Then you put your pride before the life of your people, my lord." I could think of nothing else but those wounded warriors I had treated, the pain in their bodies and the death in their eyes, and the cry of the widows whose men had not returned.

Batumar looked at me, his gaze sharp as a sword. "A treaty would not work. The Kerghi are hungry for blood."

"But they conquered many lands. Their army must be stretched far and wide. What if we offered tribute? What harm can it do to try? If the spirits meant to save us through war, why would they choose me?" I looked around at the men who had grown up with and believed the prophecy. But did they believe strongly enough to accept what I had to say?

Silence enveloped the room, my words left hanging in the air.

"If she *is* The One Foretold..." Lord Gilrem rose. "I shall go. The Khergi khan, Woldrom, is said to be in the city of Mernor, his latest conquest. I shall leave tomorrow."

The Guardian of the Scrolls stood as well, and to my surprise, he said, "And so shall I."

"With a large contingency of guards," Batumar added, the lines on his forehead turning into deep furrows, his mouth drawn tight.

The Guardian of the Scrolls shook his head. "If Woldrom is open to peace, we should not need more men."

"And if he is not"—Lord Gilrem smiled with bravado—"a unit of guards will not mean much."

They both looked at Batumar, and after a while, he reluctantly nodded. "But the Lady Tera stays."

This I fought, but he would not budge, no matter what I told him.

———

The Guardian of the Gate and the Guardian of the Cave returned to the Forgotten City, while the Guardian of the Scrolls stayed at the palace. I stayed up late into the night talking with him. In the morning, Batumar assembled his warriors and their supplies so we could begin our journey to Dahru's Gate on the other side of the mountain.

Two long days we traveled on the backs of the manyinga before we reached the high plateau and I saw the Gate of the World.

The strange structure resembled not a gate at all but rather a ruin, the columns of a Great Hall that had fallen down long ago. Tall stone pillars reached to the sky in pairs, forming a circle, more pillars resting on top of them. Each such formation did resemble a gate of some sort, I suppose, but they led nowhere, only a circle of moss between them.

The Guardian of the Gate waited by the stones, but I hardly recognized him. He wore the clothes of a servant and moved slowly, his back bent with age, his hood covering his face. When he looked at me, he gave no sign of recognition.

"Why is he like that?" I asked Lord Gilrem who rode his manyinga next to mine.

"Who?" he asked and looked around as if the old man was invisible to him.

"The Guardian." I pointed as the Guardian of the Gate turned from us and leaned heavily on his staff.

"The old man? He is the groundskeeper, a position passed down in his family. Easy work, I suppose." He shrugged. "He cannot have much to do around here."

All around us, warriors covered the side of the mountain.

"The number of men guarding the Gate was recently doubled," Lord Gilrem informed me as he slid off his manyinga and helped me off mine.

The Guardian of the Scrolls was already waiting.

"Are you certain you wish to go, grandfather?" I asked him.

"Like you, I wish for peace."

A few steps behind us, Lord Gilrem called out to the Guardian of the Gate. "Which gateway would be best, you think, for Mernor?" And then he walked up to me, saying, "The caretaker has an uncanny ability to find the smoothest journey to the exact place you want to go."

The Guardian of the Gate shuffled over to us, bowed, and touched his stick to the boulder next to him. Lord Gilrem and the Guardian of the Scrolls walked through the gate side by side, an old man and a young warrior in his prime.

Lord Gilrem turned, his gaze fixed on Batumar who had stepped up next to me. "I have not always served you well, brother. This time—"

They shimmered for a moment before they disappeared.

I gasped in wonder. Now *this* was ancient magic.

"If we still had the knowledge of the First People," Batumar said after a long moment of silence, "it would aid us greatly in the war."

I turned to glare at him, wishing he could focus on peace for once.

He did not seem to notice my displeasure and soon strode to his warriors who were setting up camp. I stayed by the circle of stones, even ate my meal there, and retired to Batumar's empty tent only when the two moons rose high in the sky, their night's journey half completed.

I fell asleep before he came in to rest, and woke later to the heat of his body next to mine.

"Did they come back?" I mumbled, still infused with sleep as I turned in his arms, feeling content and safe. He had taken off his doublet, and his skin was gloriously warm.

"Not yet."

He had put out the lamp before coming to bed, and the smoke hole let in precious little moonlight, but I could see his head move closer.

"Go back to sleep," he whispered and briefly touched his lips to mine before pulling away.

Without thinking, I lifted my head and placed my mouth back against his. A low sound escaped his throat. Did he want to say something? I opened my mouth to ask, but he claimed me then fully, and thought of any conversation flew from my mind.

I felt as if falling, then floating weightless in the air. I had to hold on to his broad shoulders for support. When he moved his hand to the hem of my short Shahala tunic and pulled it up until his large hand covered my stomach, I did not protest. I soaked up his warmth.

He caressed my skin with tender fingers that moved up my rib cage. I gasped when his palm cupped my breast. I had not expected it to feel so pleasant, a sweet tingle that spread across my skin.

He lifted his mouth to pull the tunic over my head, but once I was freed, his lips did not return to mine. He kissed my neck instead, moving down in a straight line between my breasts, which ached for something unknown, something more.

His searching lips found my nipples, one after the other, and gifted them with the pleasure they sought. His hands moved lower to caress my belly once again and then the hollow of my hips as he tugged my thudi lower. As if in a dream, I felt him remove my last piece of clothing, then his, while I floated toward some mysterious delight.

When he moved over me and brought his lips back to mine at last, I clung to him with need and glided my hands over his well-muscled back. But then I felt his manpart hot and hard between my thighs, and my mind filled with images of the guard by the creek at the House of Tahar, the way he had thrown me to the ground and tore my clothes, how his rough fingers had dug into my flesh as he forced my knees apart, his foul breath on my face, his friends cheering him on, impatient for their turn.

The memory stole the air from my lungs, and the need to escape came upon me with such strength, I shoved against Batumar and scampered off the cot, to the farthest end of the tent. I sat on the furs that covered the ground, my arms folded around my knees, my heart racing as I stared into the night, its cold touch sprinkling my naked skin with goose bumps.

I waited for Batumar to shout at me or worse. Tahar would have had any woman who refused to do her duty beaten to death.

"Has any man hurt you before I found you?" Batumar's voice, soft and gentle, whispered through the darkness.

I swallowed, tears welling in my eyes suddenly. "Nay, my lord. The spirits saved me from the worst. But the memory is a weakness within me."

I was with Batumar. He would not harm me. I felt foolish for the way I had behaved, but before I could say anything, he rose from the cot.

If he came to me, I would not have flinched away again. But instead, I heard the rustle of clothes as he dressed. He went to the opening of the tent.

"Go back to bed, Tera. I need to check the sentries."

———

Since Batumar had not returned by the time I woke in the morning, I donned my thick robe over my clothes, then hurried to the Gate. I tried not to think of Gilrem and the Guardian appearing somber with rejection but pictured them joyous with good news.

I spent the morning waiting, catching a glimpse of Batumar now and then as he walked among his warriors and talked with them. Although he looked in my direction many times, he did not come over to see me. And I did not go to him, ashamed of my cowardice the night before.

I was eating my midday meal by the Gate, drawn by its strange stark beauty, when the Guardian of the Gate rose from the rock upon which he had been sitting. He scratched three swirling symbols in the dirt with his staff. Soon the air within the circle began to shimmer, and I saw the dim outlines of the two men before the detail filled in. All wrong—they were lying down. Bloodied.

I rushed to them, several warriors behind me. They lifted Lord Gilrem and the Guardian of the Scrolls and carried them into one of the larger tents, laid them on cots, then parted so I could work my healing.

Lord Gilrem lay still, his clothing torn in many places, his face and hands covered with wounds of torture. I set my hands upon him, searching for the pulse of life in his blood. I found nothing. I laid my ear on his chest, hoping to hear at least a faint heartbeat. Not there. I cried out in anguish then, for I knew his spirit had already departed.

A low sound from Batumar as he entered the tent drew my gaze. He fell to his knees next to his brother, his face dark as death itself.

The Guardian of the Scrolls groaned, and I moved quickly to him, happy for that small sign of life. But as I sent my spirit into him to heal his wounds, I found little of his life force left, and even that resisted.

"Grandfather," I pleaded. "We need you. Stay with us."

He opened his eyes and reached for my hand. He said nothing, but from the way he looked at me, I knew he had already made up his mind. Suddenly, his life force welled up and poured into me as his hand fell away from mine.

The rush of blood in my ears made me deaf, and soon I could no longer see the tent or anyone in it. A great white light—blinding as grief—and then nothing.

———

I woke alone in Batumar's tent in the middle of the night, my head still buzzing, my soul aching with grief. I squeezed my eyes shut as I thought of the Guardian and Lord Gilrem. I waited, but the great pain in my heart would not abate, so I rose from the cot and gathered my robe around me.

I walked outside and found the tent where the bodies had been laid. And there I found many of Lord Gilrem's men and the Guardian of the Gate. He sat on a stool in front of the body of the Guardian of the Scrolls, his face buried in his wrinkled hands.

"I am sorry," I said, my voice breaking. "If I had known—"

But he lifted his head and shook it, then whispered under his breath. "He wished to go. He died in the service of peace. None can wish for a more noble death than that."

We bowed our heads and offered our prayers to the spirits.

Some time passed before I broke the silence again. "Where is the High Lord?"

I was surprised not to see him by his brother's side.

"Preparing to go to Mernor," the Guardian told me. "As Lord

Gilrem did not die in battle but was murdered, his body cannot be laid to rest until his death is avenged. Such is the way of the Kadar."

I stared at him, disbelieving. How could any people think that the pain of one death could be healed by more murder? And what of Batumar? Did he value his own life so little that he would risk it so? Did he not know he was going to his own demise?

I stumbled out of the tent and wandered around in search of him. No stars shone above and no moons, the sky covered with dark clouds. I felt lost in the city of tents, tripping on roots, supplies, weapons. My bones filled with cold by the time I returned to the High Lord's tent.

Batumar stood alone in the middle of the darkness. "I was about to come look for you."

The clouds must have been moving, as moonlight shone through the smoke hole suddenly, and I could at last see his face. His features were riddled with guilt. I knew the feeling well, for it squeezed my chest with every breath. Did he blame himself for the death of his brother and the Guardian?

If so, then no more than I. And I had better reason for it. "I wanted the treaty. I should have gone. I am the one who should have died."

"No," he said roughly and stepped toward me.

"You must not leave," I whispered.

"It is a question of honor."

"You are needed here to lead your men in the war."

"I lead only by the confidence the warlords place in me. Should they think that I am too weak to avenge my own blood brother and not honorable enough to do so, their confidence would be quickly withdrawn."

Frustration clenched my jaw. Of all the foolish ways of men!

He took my hand. "If I go, a chance exists that I might return and stand ready to lead our army when the enemy reaches us. If I remain and the warlords withdraw their alliance, our warriors will stand without a leader. A new High Lord cannot be selected so quickly. The warlords might return each to protect his own territory."

"And fail separately," I said as dismay filled me.

"We must stand together." His gaze roamed my face, his voice soft, as if he was already saying farewell *forever*.

And I found I could not accept that. I pushed the robe off my shoulders and watched as his gaze followed its path to the ground. I grabbed the bottom of my short Shahala tunic and pulled it over my head.

My skin glowed in the semidarkness like a moonflower. I heard his sharp intake of breath, every other sound drowned out by the loud rush of blood in my ears.

"Have you come to offer your virginity for good luck?" His voice was as thick as mosan-berry syrup. And then after an eternity, he half turned from me. "We had enough sacrifices already."

I swallowed and forced myself to speak before I lost my courage. "I came to offer my heart."

He turned back slowly. "Tera." He whispered my name, then gathered me into his strong arms. And then he kissed me.

I kissed him back.

With a soft growl, he carried me to his cot and lowered me onto the pelts. He warmed my body with kisses and caresses, and after he removed his clothes, I returned the favor.

"Tera?" His whisper was low and urgent.

"Yes."

Then he touched me as he had not touched me before.

A-hh.

I touched him too—until I knew his body fully, and he fully knew mine, the two of us becoming one.

Afterwards, with our bodies and sprits blended, he held me in his arms with such great gentleness that it brought tears to my eyes. He held me like that all night.

CHAPTER TWENTY

(Sorceress)

Batumar had left for Mernor by the time I awoke. The morning was silent, despite the great number of men on the plateau. I walked into the forest and fell upon the soft shirl moss. I wept for the Guardian of the Scrolls, for Lord Gilrem, but most of all for Batumar. I missed his presence in every way, his warmth, his voice, his rare smiles and the gentleness he showed me when we were alone in the night.

The Guardian of the Gate found me, and from him I learned that ten of Batumar's guards had gone after him, despite the direct order that none should do so, knowing that disobeying the High Lord brought with it a punishment of death. Many more would have gone, but they determined that a large group would bring undue attention and be more hindrance than help. The ten had to be chosen by drawing lots in the end, so eager were his men to die for him.

I left for Karamur under the protection of the Palace Guard that same day, for thus had ordered the High Lord before he left. The two-day journey seemed to last two years. I spent most of it looking back, watching for a herald to catch up with us to let us know that Batumar had returned. But no news came.

I hoped then that maybe a herald had been sent to the palace and was already there ahead of us, having traveled faster alone through the vast forest, but we were the first to arrive. We had to deliver the sad news of Lord Gilrem's death, and of Batumar's journey through the Gate to avenge his brother.

A dignitary awaited him from the Kingdom of Chebbar, a minor kingdom to the east, sent by Queen Manala to plead for assistance. The invading hordes pushed against their borders. I learned this and more from Leena who, upon hearing of our return, rushed to greet me at the palace gate and would not budge from my side until we were in my chamber in Pleasure Hall. And even then, she left me only to order the other servants around to ensure my comfort.

She welcomed me with joy, but every time she stepped out, she returned with eyes reddened, so I knew that in private she wept for Batumar. She made certain I ate, bringing all my favorites and a steaming mosan-berry pie, but although she and the other servant women did their best to cheer me, my heart was heavy with grief.

Days passed without news. Rumors started in the city, servants whispering that the High Lord too had been killed. Lord Gilrem had always ruled in his stead when he had been gone before, and without Lord Gilrem, things were falling into disarray, despite the best efforts of the captain of the Palace Guard.

One morning, when Leena came to my chamber with breakfast, she brought a servant girl, her arms much bruised, her eyes teary as she curtsied.

"What is your name?"

"Mora, my lady."

"What happened to you, Mora?"

She flushed red and would not raise her gaze from her feet.

Leena nudged her.

"Men attacked me in the marketplace, my lady," the girl whispered.

I reached for my herbs and began mixing up a poultice for her bruises. "Why?"

Karamur might have been in upheaval, but it was not yet a lawless place.

"Tell our lady what you told me," Leena encouraged her.

Still, the girl would not speak, so Leena had to speak for her. "People were talking against you in the marketplace, my lady. Shartor's followers. Mora spoke up in your defense, and they turned on her."

I gave Mora the poultice with instructions, thanking her for my defense and urging her not to risk herself again in such a manner; then Leena sent her away.

"I know you walk outside the palace, my lady. I beg you not to do so again until the High Lord returns," Leena said when we were alone. "Shartor has gained much power of late. In the absence of a stronger leader, fools listen to him."

"The guards will protect us. Shartor holds no power here."

As it turned out, however, whatever Shartor's powers were and wherever they lay, I had greatly underestimated his cunning.

———

The following day began with a great uproar. The most valuable tapestry in the palace, one that depicted the Kadar's arrival to our island, had disappeared from the Great Hall. The Palace Guard searched the entire building and interrogated the servants, thoroughly occupying their time.

I sat alone in my chamber, praying to the spirits for Batumar, when an unfamiliar servant girl rushed in and begged me to follow her to the kitchen, where some accident had happened and my healing was urgently needed.

Leena had gone to the washroom for my Shahala clothes, and I had been sitting by the fire wrapped in a blanket. I would need more thudis and tunics prepared, I thought, and dressed once more as a concubine. The girl quickly helped me into a golden gown, the topmost dress in my trunk.

"Was someone burned?" Burns and cuts were the most frequent injuries in the kitchen.

"Yes, my lady." She laced the back with trembling fingers, running for the door as soon as she finished.

I grabbed my veil and herbs and rushed after her. "How badly?"

"You must hurry, my lady."

I slowed. "I might need jalik for a bad burn." I turned back toward my chamber. I had some jalik leaves drying on the mantel, not completely ready yet, but better than anything else I had.

She grabbed my hand and tugged. "Poison, my lady, you must hurry."

"Which is it then, poison or burning?"

"Both," she stuttered, so agitated as to be nearly incoherent.

Healers gained a great calm in a crisis, but those untrained in the healing arts often panicked. I did not think she would be able to give me much detail. Best to see it for myself, I thought, and followed her.

But when we reached the kitchen, we found the kitchen staff missing and only two strange men within.

The girl closed and barred the door behind us, then covered her face with her hands. The men grabbed me at once.

"What is the meaning of this?" I demanded.

Instead of responding, they pulled a sack over my head; then they stuffed me into an empty flour jar. They fastened the lid on tight.

The outer door creaked open, then I heard the noise of the street. The jar jostled as they carried it. In the narrow space, I could not lift my arms to free my head from the sack. I called for help, but the burlap and the jar muffled my cries.

My lungs burned for air. I banged my fists against the fire-hardened clay, fearing that if they did not release me soon, I would suffocate.

Thank the spirits, at long last they set the jar down and opened the lid, then dragged me forth into the light. I blinked against the sun as I gasped for air. The smell of tar twisted my nose and made me cough.

"Sorceress!" The single word cut through the air.

True fear filled me as I turned toward Shartor's voice. We stood in an alley somewhere behind the palace, the narrow space filled with his followers. The men and women looked upon me with hate, scowls on every face.

"Lord Gilrem is dead because of her," Shartor pronounced, his strange eyes bloodshot and wild. "And so is Lord Batumar. She is the friend of our enemies. I swear to you, it is she who called the war."

Cold spread through my veins. "Lord Shartor, I—"

The crowd began to chant and drowned out my protest. "Sorceress! Sorceress!"

They ceased only when Shartor held up his hands. "What is the punishment for sorcery?"

The crowd roared, "Death!"

"And what is the only way to kill a dark sorceress?"

The crowd parted, revealing a great steaming cauldron over a burning fire. "Boil her in tar!"

The two men who had kidnapped me grabbed me and dragged me forward. I protested, but the crowd would not hear my words. They closed their hearts to my pleas and were more interested in blood than reason.

Spirits, help me now.

The bubbling cauldron waited but a dozen steps away. My heart beat against my ribs in a wild, panicked rhythm.

"No! Wait!" I fought, straining my arms and scraping my ankle on the rough stone.

Then the sun dimmed suddenly. And within another step, the alley grew dark.

"The mist," women whispered, charms jingling.

And indeed, the mist descended upon us rapidly and thickened. In another few steps, I could no longer see the cauldron.

"The sorceress calls the mist. Do not weaken. The mist will lift when she is dead," Shartor shouted from somewhere in the deep fog.

I heard footsteps on stone. Moving away.

The men's hold on my arms tightened at first, then loosened. "Lord Shartor?"

"Boil her in tar," came the order, but this time, no chanting from the crowd.

A dog howled in the distance, the eerie sound echoing off the walls around us, the mist distorting the howl into something otherworldly.

The man on my right let me go first. His boots slapped against the stone as he hurried away. The man on my left was close behind him.

"Sorceress!" Shartor roared in the mist.

I ran in the opposite direction from his voice, my soft leather slippers soundless.

I could only guess the way back to the palace and prayed to the spirits the whole time to lead me. I did take some wrong turns, but at long last, I reached the cliff and began to climb. My heart clamored. I knew that the mist was the Guardians' way of calling me to them. *Has something happened?*

The Guardian of the Cave waited for me at the top of the cliff. He stepped forward, then back, unable to hold still. "You must come at once." Worry lined his face. "Selaila the Seer calls for you."

With my heart in my throat, I followed him.

A most severe man about my own age waited for us at the fork in the path. His robe hung ill-fitting on his lanky figure, the sharp lines of his face inscrutable. He bowed to me, but when he spoke, his voice held no warmth.

"I am the new Guardian of the Scrolls. The Seer awaits you, my lady." He joined us as we hurried on, keeping his gaze on the city ahead, avoiding looking at me altogether.

He had the right to blame me for his father's death. I wanted to ask for his forgiveness, but that was something not best done in a rush. I would talk to him after talking to the Seer.

We reached the city and hurried toward Selaila's hut. The streets were never crowded, for the people who lived here saw their numbers much reduced over the centuries, and those who remained were shy around strangers. We passed but a handful of men and women who peered at me with curiosity but kept their distance.

At our destination, the Guardian of the Cave called out a greeting before he entered. I followed him, the young Guardian of the Scrolls stepping inside behind me. The hut had but one chamber, round, with no furniture but some old pelts scattered on the floor. Swirling, painted images decorated the wall, mesmerizing my eyes. I had to turn from them to keep from growing dizzy.

"Lady Tera." The girl in the middle of the chamber, not yet a woman, bowed and took my hand. Her hair fell to her ankles and was completely white, as were her eyes, without irises.

"Have you seen him?" I blurted, inexcusably impolite but too anguished to stop myself.

Nothing but kindness sat on her face, even if her tone was somber. "Since the High Lord of the Kadar left through the Gate, I have gone to him each day to follow his fate, but now I can no longer see. It is all darkness, my lady."

Dread weighed down my limbs and my heart, and a thick fear clogged my lungs.

The Seer led me to stand under a round metal medallion fixed to the ceiling, then moved it aside, revealing a hole in the roof that looked straight to the sky.

"If I take you there, you might be able to find him, for your spirit is connected to his."

"I am ready."

She lifted her face into the beam of light. "Close your eyes."

I did as she asked. I would have done anything to find Batumar.

She hummed an ancient spirit song I could not understand, but my mind floated along with the melody. The sunlight shone through my eyelids, strengthening into a blinding white. And then I saw stars over a city like Karamur, only some of this city lay in ruins.

A great black tower rose to the sky in the middle. On the city wall hung ten black flags. *No, not flags,* I saw as I reached closer. Ten men hung from ropes by their necks, all dead—Batumar's guard.

I cried out and stopped, but a presence behind me pushed me forward until I stood inside the city gates. Some of the houses burned, but no one bothered to put out the fires. Destruction everywhere, the bodies of men, women, and children piled high along the streets. Soldiers fought over the belongings of the dead, snarling like animals. They did not see me.

I moved toward the palace and its broken gate, the building cold and dark inside like a giant grave. I floated forward and suddenly felt alone. The presence that had been all this time behind me could no longer follow.

I moved through hall after hall, chamber after chamber, staring in horror at the beast-like warriors who passed me unseeing. Soon I felt something pull me forward, and I descended under the halls of the palace to the dungeons. I found Batumar there, covered in wounds, barely hanging on to life.

I screamed, and the force of the sound ripped from my throat brought me back to Selaila's hut. Tears streamed down my face, but I wiped them off, thanked the girl, and hurried outside.

"I must go to Mernor. The prophecies foretold that *I* would stop the war. I should have gone to Mernor in the first place, and no other."

Perhaps the two Guardians sensed my resolve, because they did not question me. We returned to the cave for enough food for the journey and started out for the Gate.

"They seek you," the Guardian of the Cave said suddenly. "Your woman servant and the Palace Guard. They are here in the valley. Do you wish to see them, or should I direct them back from whence they came?"

I thought of my trip through the Gate, a journey that might yet prove a journey into death. Leena was like a mother to me. I wished to embrace her one more time, wished to make sure she would not blame herself if something happened to me. "I would see them for a moment."

The Guardian nodded, and as we cut through the deep woods toward the Gate, we soon met Leena and a small group of warriors, along with the Captain of the Guard, on the path. I told them what I had learned from the Seer. Of course, they insisted upon escorting me to the Gate. Leena held my hand the whole way, tears washing her face.

We traveled faster than Batumar's army had before, for we carried few provisions and were on foot, able to cut over the ridge. For once, I barely noticed the biting cold of the high mountain. I leaned into the cutting wind when we walked and huddled with Leena for warmth under our thick robes when we rested.

When we arrived at the Gate, we wasted no time. I said farewell to the Guardians and then embraced Leena. I prayed to the spirits that I would live to see her again in this life. "I thank you for all your kindness toward me."

She drew herself straight suddenly. "I shall go with you, Lady Tera."

Tears flooded my eyes at this display of loyalty. "You cannot."

I walked toward the pillars the Guardian of the Gate had selected for me.

"We will guard the Lady Tera well," the captain assured the Guardians and Leena.

I turned to face him. "I go alone." I had no plan, only the hope that having brought me this far, the spirits would not desert me now.

"Lady Tera, you shouldn't," the captain protested.

"I must. Your armor and colors would be instantly recognized." I thought of the Kadar guards hanging from Mernor's walls. "You would only get us all killed."

The captain thought on that for a moment but shook his head.

"The Lady Tera is right." The Guardian of the Cave intervened on my behalf. "This is no longer a matter of force but of destinies."

A longer silence followed his words.

The captain nodded gravely at last. "We shall wait here."

Leena stepped in front of me to speak in a whisper not to be heard by the others. "I abandoned my son once so as to save his life. I cannot abandon him again. I offended Rorin and his goddesses by trying to outsmart my fate. He is dying anyway."

I gasped. Her great love for Batumar made sense suddenly. "Is he your son? The one you left behind as a babe?"

She nodded rapidly, tears washing her face.

I took her hand, part of me stunned yet another part not so surprised, and we stepped into the circle together. I saw the archways around us, but when I looked through them, I saw not the mountain and Batumar's men but wondrous places of faraway. Only one opening stood dark as if a black fog had swallowed up everything behind it. And through this opening we leaped.

The journey passed in a bright flash of light and a moment of dizziness, a smell similar to that of lavender, and air so thin I gasped. But one gasp was all. We came out on the other side, and even in the starless night, I could see that we were in the middle of a river, on an island no larger than Batumar's palace, surrounded by dark waters.

Warriors guarded the gate, their campfires like giant fireflies dotting the island. The next moment, we were noticed. The moment after that, we were seized.

CHAPTER TWENTY-ONE

(Journey through a Forsaken Land)

The soldiers stank of sweat, mead, and dried blood that caked their armor. Their hands were rough upon us, and they had bloodlust in their eyes and filthy words dripping from their leering lips. They began with confiscating our traveling supplies. They spoke the language of the Kerghi—harsh growling sounds—and so I addressed them in that same tongue.

I looked above their heads and said in a clear voice, "I am Queen Manala of Chebbar, coming to surrender to Khan Woldrom to save my people. Take me to him at once." I could think of nothing else that could purchase us time enough to escape. I had not come this far only to be raped and killed.

They stepped back, snarling in anger and disappointment at being robbed of a night of entertainment, but more than they wanted to abuse us, they feared their khan, so two of the men took us to the tent of their captain.

The burly giant said nothing as he listened to the report of our arrival. His gaze swept my golden gown, very much the worse for wear. Not unreasonable for a queen in the time of war and on a great journey.

"You travel without your guard?" he asked after some time.

"If the khan favors my plea, I have nothing to fear of his warriors. If he does not, my guards cannot protect me."

I stood tall and would not flinch under the captain's inspection, hoping my short hair would not give me away. With luck, the Chebbar customs were not like those of the Kadar, and hair had less significance. And even if that was not the case, I wondered if a Kerghi captain would know much about the customs of the Chebbar.

"Queen Manala." He glanced at Leena, then back at me. "You will go to Mernor in the morning under escort. Rest here for what remains of the night."

"Thank you, Captain." I nodded gratefully, and after he strode out, I sank onto a wooden chest, relief suddenly turning my knees weak.

Leena looked at me with open admiration. "Well done, my lady."

Maybe. But how to proceed?

Even though the captain had promised to send us to Mernor, I had no wish to travel with his men. I did not know how long the journey to the city would last. Chebbar might fall before we arrived, and our ruse would be discovered. I did not want to be close to so many swords when the truth came out.

"It would be best if we traveled on our own."

Leena moved to the front of the tent and listened. "Two guards outside."

I slipped to the ground and lifted the edge of the tent in the back. "None here."

We were not prisoners and were on an island besides. The guards at front were probably more for our protection than for fear that we would escape. We had come of our own free will, after all.

We waited as the night wore on and the camp grew quieter around us. When I was afraid to wait any longer—we needed the cover of darkness for as long as we could have it—we crawled out the back.

Most of the men slept in their tents, some snoring the stars out of the sky. We crept in the cover of bushes toward the water, to the boats that lay like great dead fish on the shore. But when we reached closer, we found the boats well-guarded and the men watching them alert.

While on Dahru, summer was barely turning into fall, we were now much farther north, the weather much colder here. Shivering, we crept back in the other direction and down to the water's edge until we found a large log wedged into the mud. I waded into the river, Leena close behind me. My feet went numb in the icy water long before we managed to push the log into the water.

We did not let go of it but went along, submerging our trembling bodies. With our heads hidden behind the log, we floated down the river to find Mernor, and in it, Batumar. Or die in the trying.

My wet gown pulled me down, but I hung on with all my strength. I did not dare even to whisper to Leena, as the water would have carried my voice well and far.

I could barely feel my limbs by the time we floated out of sight of the island. I tried to angle us toward the bank, but we floated down-river for some time, as the current was strong and the log not easily directed.

The first light of morning dawned on the horizon by the time we finally reached land. We pushed the log back into the water, then sought refuge in the thick forest ahead. Shivering, we lay on the cold ground, holding on to each other for warmth, too exhausted to rise.

But we did not dare to stay long or to start a fire. When we were able, we stumbled deeper into the woods, feeding on the succulent leaves of lenil bushes we passed. What we did not eat, we saved, as we did not know when we might have food again.

The wind picked up and swayed the giant trees above, but low to the ground the bushes protected us. Still, even the fraction of the full wind proved enough to chill us further. My sunborn body shivered without stop; my skin stung with pain. Leena carried on better, being snowborn. She had lived through a lifetime of frigid winters.

We saw many strange plants and birds and tracks of other smaller animals. A lot of the trees and bushes had thorns, some I suspected poisonous, so we forged ahead with great care.

In a valley, we came upon an abandoned tar pit, the smell turning my stomach.

Boil her in tar. I heard the cries again for a moment as I remembered the boiling cauldron in the alley. As we walked, I told Leena about Shartor and his mob. She prayed loudly to the goddesses to burn off his braided beard and other parts that stuck out from his body.

To turn our talk more pleasant, I shared with Leena some stories about my childhood and my mother. In turn, she told me how she had been a powerful warlord's favorite concubine but gave up all the luxuries of his Pleasure Hall and became a servant to save her son's life. My heart ached for her and all that she had suffered.

Soon we reached the end of the woods and, guided by the smell of smoke, came upon some overgrown fields and the ruins of a small village.

The handful of wattle-and-daub huts were scorched, and we saw the remains of many others that had been burned to the ground. Weeds grew tall around the huts, and I knew they had no grazing animals or enough people to trample down the grass. The forest was slowly reclaiming the village.

Foreboding settled on me. Would this be the fate of my people once our lands had been conquered by the Kerghi?

We walked into the dying community, hoping for food and shelter, the warmth of their fires, but they seemed in worse shape than we were. No men, only women and children—little girls, not a boy among them. They looked at us with such hunger in their eyes, had we any lenil leaves we would have given it to them, but we had eaten them all.

They spoke a language I barely understood, similar to Tinfa, and some time passed before I could explain we were looking for the way to Mernor.

"We do not know, mistress," said one, her gaze roaming my gown. She wore thin strips of animal hide, her ribs visible under her bruised skin. "But there is one among us who might. She is hunting. You must wait for her return."

Behind her stood two little girls, thin and dirty, their eyes fearful and wild at the same time, almost like small forest animals. None of the children talked or ran around—as we would have seen had we walked into a Shahala village—they hid behind their mothers.

The air was silent, missing the voices of little ones at play and the noises of household beasts, the sounds of work—clanging of metal, and axe falling onto wood—sounds that made up the music of other villages.

The huts must have been empty, all the people outside to greet us. I looked at their wounds: bones that had been broken and had not healed well, infected cuts on arms and legs, and other small injuries that while not threating a person's life, gave pain enough to make it miserable.

We could wait awhile for the one who knew the way the Mernor. I could do some healing in the meanwhile.

Before I could offer my help, another woman stepped forward, her lips covered in festering sores so I could barely understand her when she said, "Come rest in our hut, mistress. The fire burns warmer inside."

I looked at the low flames of the cooking fire between two huts. Nothing cooked today, but they had food at one time, for I saw blackened bones stick out from the ashes.

Most had been cracked for their marrow and were hard to recognize, but some smaller ones stuck together still, held by charred sinew. A narrow paw of some sort drew my eyes. It had five fingers, half of one missing.

No, not missing, just shorter than the rest. And when I looked closer, my stomach rolled. *A human hand.*

"Thank you," I said to the women, who watched sharply as they moved into a half circle around us. "We will share your hut, but let us go into the woods and gather some food first. I am a healer and know many plants that would help your wounds and others that are good to eat."

I stepped back, and Leena followed, although I could tell she did not understand why we were leaving when we were cold and we had not seen anything edible for a long time before reaching the village.

The women hesitated.

"I will come with you," said the one with the sore-infested lips. "So after you leave, we might find those plants ourselves."

And for the first time, I noticed the blade hanging from her rope belt, half-hidden among the animal skins that covered her. I could do nothing else but nod.

I led the way in the opposite direction Leena and I had come from but found all edible plants already harvested. I collected a few healing herbs along the way, explaining their use to the woman. She kept looking back as we went.

Were others following us at a distance?

They probably were, although she could have killed the both of us alone, for she had the sinuous strength of those who worked hard to keep on living. Leena was old and tired from our journey, and although I was younger, I had no knowledge of fighting. And too the woman had a knife.

The spirits stayed with us, for they led us to a garon tree.

I rolled up my dress and tied it with a piece of vine, then began to climb until I reached the spot from where the branches spread. In that bend, in a handful of dirt blown there by the winds, I found what I was looking for, the woodsy stalks of the caringo, full of yellow berries. I tugged the whole plant away from the tree and climbed down.

"We should take this back to share with the others. Not much, but it tastes sweet." I handed the berry-filled branches to the woman.

I knew the caringo from my mother, for she had given tea steeped from the berries for pain of certain illnesses. One or two berries worked wonders; any more than that put a person to sleep. I hoped the woman was hungry enough that she could not resist, but dared not offer it to her myself as I feared it might raise her suspicion, and she would demand that Leena and I eat of the berries.

We walked on, and I did not look back at her once, not wanting her to think I was watching for something. But soon her footsteps faded behind us, and then I could no longer hear them at all.

"Let us keep on walking," I said to Leena, and we did not go back to see what had become of the woman. I did not heal her lips as I could have, for it seemed they might have been cursed by the spirits for her feasting on human flesh, and I dared not interfere with their judgment.

I did not condemn her, though, not her or her people. They lived in a stark despair I had never known. Would Dahru fall, my own people could find themselves devastated. A stark image of sacked Shahala villages flashed into my mind. I prayed to the spirits to keep us from such a fate, and doubled my resolve to do what I could to defeat the Kerghi.

We walked without stopping to rest as I told Leena about the bones in the cooking fire and my suspicions about what the women were planning to do with us. She shuddered at my words and praised me for my wisdom. We moved through the forest as fast as we could, careful not to leave tracks behind.

As the day wore on, the woods became denser, giant trees blocking most of the light. Leafy vines wove intricate patterns on the tree trunks as they snaked upward, spreading out to connect tree to tree. We kept west by the sun, what little we could see of it, not because we knew that to be the right direction but because we thought going straight whichever way would at least keep us from wandering around in circles.

We had not had any water since we had left the river, save what dew we were able to lick off leaves here and there, so when we heard a creek beckon from the distance, we hastened our steps.

Not much later, we came upon a faint path. We followed it carefully, not knowing whether it had been made by animals or humans, not knowing, indeed, which to fear more. But we reached the water without coming to harm and slaked our thirst. Water had never tasted as sweet.

The creek also held another blessing. In the wet mud of its banks grew many plants I recognized. Soon we were on our knees digging for bulbs and rhizomes to sate our hunger. We dug up all we could find before we left, carrying our treasure tied into a small bundle I made from a piece of my dress.

We took off our shoes and lifted our dresses to cross the creek, following the path that continued on the other side.

Leena, having gained some strength from the food and drink, walked ahead of me, while I lagged a few steps behind as I scanned every green thing. More food to carry with us would have been most welcome and any healing herbs too, for we'd both lost some strength since our arrival.

I saw the patch of leaves on the path in front of us, not much different than the rest that littered the ground, and yet my gaze snapped back to the spot.

I slowed. Unmindful, Leena walked on, almost at the edge of the patch now. In that one spot, the leaves seemed not as faded, not as trampled as the rest. The skin prickled at the back of my neck.

"Leena, stop!"

Too late. With a shrill cry like a bird taking to the sky, she flew high up into the air to swing among the branches.

For the briefest of moments, I thought it the magic of the ancient days or the trickery of bad spirits, but then I could see the net that kept her above my reach.

"Run, my lady," she implored. "They who caught me will catch you as well if you stay."

A length of twisted vine held the net, and I traced the vine to a tree half-covered by the dense brush. I tore at the knots with my fingers to no avail. I wished for a blade, my gaze falling on the moss-covered stones at my feet. They had no sharp edges, but I crouched and smashed two together until a chunk broke off. Then I attacked the vine rope with my makeshift weapon.

Even with the sharp edge of the stone, the sawing required time, and my knuckles bloodied from scraping against the rough bark of the tree. But finally I thinned the vine to its last fibers and yanked it hard while holding on tight. I did not want to drop Leena from such a height.

"Brace," I called up, keeping my voice as low as I could, for we did not know how close the hunters who set the trap waited.

CHAPTER TWENTY-TWO

(Mernor)

I lowered Leena to the ground and freed her, then we hurried off the path and into the woods. We moved silently and did not stop until she seemed ready to collapse.

"My foot tangled in the net as it pulled me up," she told me at last, sliding to the ground.

The woods were quiet around us and peaceful. I thought we might be safe for the moment. I sat next to her to look at her ankle.

I probed the swollen purple flesh but could feel nothing broken. "Bruised." I put my hand upon the injury, but Leena pulled back.

"No," she said. "You will weaken yourself."

"I can help." I reached again.

"The High Lord forbade it." She grabbed my hand, her gaze determined. "I forbid it," she said, issuing an order for the first time since I had known her.

She *was* the High Lord's mother. She would have had a seat at the high table at the feasts and a powerful position in the palace if she had revealed her identity. Her station was equal to that of the favorite concubine.

"As you wish, Lady Leena." The Shahala did not heal against a person's will. The choice, even between life and death, stayed always with the sick.

"Your herbs?" She eyed my belt.

I glanced at the few stalks that hung from the rough belt I had braided from some tall grasses as we had walked. "We need kukuyu pulp bound around your ankle with cold wet cloth. We have neither. Shall we stay awhile?"

She shook her head as she struggled to stand. "If I slow you down, you must leave me. You have to reach him in time."

I helped her to her feet, determined not to leave her behind in this dark place, neither her nor Batumar.

She limped forward. "Night will fall soon. We should not stay this close to the trap. We could be still in the hunters' territory."

I nodded. Whoever had set that net might decide to track his escaped prey. We moved on, not as silent as before but grateful for still being able to move.

"A large and strong net," Leena said after a while as she limped alongside me.

"Probably for deer."

"Or else," she said, "it could have been set by the same kind we met before."

I cringed at the thought of the women we had escaped earlier that day, and offered a silent prayer to the spirits asking them to deliver us safely from the woods.

As the night darkened around us, we found a suitable tree—one with branches that started low to the ground and a good cross-branch higher up—and I made a shelter of twigs and leaves for the night. Leena needed much help to climb, but she would not give up easily and reached our nest. We ate half of the bitter rhizomes we had, not nearly enough, and saved the rest.

Despite our exhaustion, we slept little, for at night, the forest came alive. Strange, unseen birds cried out, startling us from time to time; footsteps on the dried leaves below us made us cringe.

Growls we heard, first nearing, then moving away, while eyes glowed green and narrow in the darkness. We barely dared breathe for fear of drawing the attention of the invisible beasts that roamed the night.

I must have dozed toward dawn at last, as I woke to Leena's strong grip on my arm. She spoke only with her eyes, wide and alarmed. A small noise came from below us. I turned my head slowly, then let out a sigh of relief. The doe looked up at me, then went back to licking dew from the moss-covered trunk.

I sat up so Leena could also see. I had blocked her view when I was sleeping, and she had not dared to move to look around me.

"Can you climb down?" I checked her ankle, still bruised but less swollen. The night's rest had been most beneficial.

She nodded with a thin smile. "If I manage to fall instead, I will arrive at the same place." Then her expression turned sober. "Is it safe?"

I looked but saw nothing other than trees and bushes. The deer, perhaps startled by our voices, had fled.

"The spirits will keep us." The night predators, I hoped, had already returned to their lairs.

We decided to forgo our morning meal, saving our meager provisions for later in the day, and started out. Soon we reached another path, wider than the one we had found the day before and, by the looks of it, more frequently used. As Leena could barely walk on the uneven forest floor, tripping over gnarled roots with every other step, we took the path and prayed to the spirits and the goddesses to keep us safe.

We kept our eyes open for anything strange, the slightest thing out of order so that we might escape another trap. We did not talk but listened for any noise of people coming up from behind or lying in wait in the distance ahead.

And so we heard long before we saw the small family of a man, woman, and child coming up the path behind us. The man carried his daughter in his arms, the mother bowed under a heavy bundle.

They did not look like they belonged to the tribe of starving women —different clothes, different features—nor did they look like hunters.

They seemed as tired and as wary of the woods as we were, for I saw the man's gaze search the forest from time to time.

The child he carried was no longer a babe but still too young to keep up with the adults on her own. A badly infected cut disfigured her face where her flesh had been split from forehead to chin by something sharp. Considering the times, probably a sword.

We halted to wait for them, but they stopped at a fair distance from us. The father shifted the child to his hip and drew a dagger from the folds of his long tunic.

"I am a healer," I said in the merchant tongue that was spoken, in one form or the other, in most of the world. "We are looking for the road to Mernor."

The mother grabbed for the child to free both of the man's hands for fight. He inspected us at length, his gaze hesitating on the herbs that hung from my belt. He did not lower his weapon. Silence stretched between us, tense and full of mistrust.

"Can you help my daughter?" he asked at last.

The woman said something, too fast for me to understand, her face twisted with fear and worry. He motioned her forward, but she would not budge. He said something then in a low voice, and she took one hesitant step. I moved toward them too, even though he had probably just promised her to gut me at the first sign of trouble.

Leena threw me a look of disapproval but held her silence. I glanced at my herbs, though I already knew I had nothing suitable. But I could not pass the girl by. The infection would kill her before long. Already, she glowed with fever.

I reached for the child, and the mother shook her head.

The father shoved her forward gently. "Please, mistress, help her if you can."

I placed one hand, palm down, onto the child's forehead where the scar began, the other to the top of her chin where it ended. The best of healers did not need to touch the sick to heal them, but I was far from the best, and weak from lack of food and insufficient sleep.

I closed my eyes and thought of nothing but the raised edges of the wound, the sticky wet feel of pus that oozed from my gentle pressure, and the heat that burned against my skin. I could feel her pain, but she neither cried nor squirmed under my touch.

I drew the pain then and gained a better sense of the injury. The infection had gone deep. Slowly, I moved my hands toward each other, focusing my spirit on closing the wound. When my thumbs touched, I sent up a silent prayer before I removed my hands.

She was whole. My arms were trembling.

The mother cried and would not look at anything but her child. The father thanked us and told us the way to the road we sought. To reach it, we had to cut through the forest.

"But there are none there to heal who are worth the healing," he said. "Khan Woldrom put many to the sword the day the Khergi broke through the city gate. The last who defended Mernor fled to the tower, but the Kerghi caught up with them. To the last man, their throats were cut, their bodies hurled from the height."

I shuddered, the picture of the black tower I had seen in my vision still clear in my mind, the blood of its defenders staining the stone walls. My empty stomach rose, but I fought it back.

"We have not much, but I would pay you, mistress, for you have done us a great favor." The man reached into the bundle on his wife's back and offered us some bread.

This we refused as we still had a few roots, and their supply seemed hardly enough for the three of them. Then he held out a flask of water, and that we accepted with gratitude.

We went our separate ways, they on the path, Leena and I back to the forest, the shortest way to the road that led to Mernor, according to the man. No longer did I have to hold back to match Leena's slow limp. I barely had the strength to keep up with her.

We found the road by midday, wide and well trampled by wagons, beasts, and men.

We stayed behind a clump of dense bushes and ate what little food we had left, then drank the rest of our water while we watched mercenaries and warriors pass. Going among them did not seem wise, so we walked in the woods some distance from the road, far enough not to be heard or seen.

This became our luck at the end, as in a small clearing, guided by the pungent smell, I found a few plants that appeared much like the kukuyu weed. I wasted no time to prepare a poultice for Leena's ankle.

Soon our good fortune increased still further. After we left the clearing, we came upon a nut tree. We had food once again. We lacked only water, our canteen long empty by then. I prayed to the spirits while Leena beseeched the goddesses to lead us to a creek.

At nightfall, we climbed a tree and made a nest. We heard less of the frightening noises of the forest than before, perhaps because we were close to the road.

Around midday the next day, we reached the end of the woods, and in the distance, we could see Mernor, its walls charred, its city gate broken. Like a giant carcass, it lay surrounded by barren fields and a village destroyed to the ground. More men hung from the parapets now than I had seen in my vision, and my heart lurched. Leena grabbed my hand and squeezed tight as we prayed none of the blackening corpses was Batumar's.

We waited until nightfall before we moved closer, then climbed in through the cisterns that had once carried water for the palace but now stood in ruin. We crept into the enemy stronghold with care. Our path sloped up, and the trickle on the water channel's moss-covered bottom made the stones slippery.

Soon we reached an opening that led into a strange chamber below us. I saw little beyond a few rough-hewn tables and rows of water-filled buckets. I eased myself through the opening and jumped down as quietly as I could, then helped Leena.

"We must disappear among the servants and find Batumar," I whispered, having no more than that for a plan.

"I pray we are not too late," Leena whispered back.

But no sooner did her feet touch the floor than we heard voices outside. We could not climb back up, had no time to move tables so we could reach the opening. And we had nowhere to hide in the chamber.

Except... A metal grate covered a hole in the floor beneath my feet.

I gulped a few handfuls of water from the nearest bucket, then grabbed the heavy grate. It gave way, opening for us the shaft carved into the rocks below. "Hurry."

Leena drank too, before she slid in. I followed her, replacing the cover just as the chamber door opened. We slid farther down into the sloping curve, until we were out of sight of anyone who might peer down.

The stones were so foul smelling, I had to cover my face with the hem of my dress.

"Hold on tight," I whispered and had no time to say more than that.

Warriors filled the room above us, bragging about the number of lives they had taken and the loot they had gained.

Swords clinked against the stone as they lay their weapons down. Boots thudded as they were dropped. Then buckets clanged, and soon water poured all over us. We dared not to move or make any sound. I tried not to choke and splutter from all the filthy water running down on top of me and could feel Leena squirming below, probably doing the same.

As soon as the men left, we climbed up to leave the strange bathing chamber before others came.

I gasped as I came up into the light. My dress, much reduced and soiled during our arduous journey, had turned red. The warriors had washed blood off their bodies onto us.

I helped Leena up and watched the horror in her eyes as she discovered the same. But then she strengthened her will. "Let us find Batumar."

I gathered my own spirit and opened the door bit by bit, then peered out into a dingy hallway. Torches stood in their brackets at uneven intervals, half of them either missing or burned out. I saw no one, so we emerged from the chamber and hurried down the corridor but hardly took a few steps when we heard men talking ahead.

Before we could turn and run back to the chamber to hide, warriors came around the corner. I froze, but Leena shuffled forward and yanked on my arm until I bent over and followed after her.

The warriors passed us without giving us any notice. My once splendid gown was torn and soiled beyond recognition; my short hair hung in filthy gnarled locks. We probably looked like those unfortunate souls forced to serve the Kerghi. The men did not seem to think it strange that we were both wet and bloody.

Once the warriors passed, we hurried forward and descended the first stairs that led down, eager to reach the dungeons at last. We met with warriors time and time again, most covered with the grime of battle and too tired to pay us much mind. But then another group strode through a thick wooden door to the side, carrying heavy bundles.

"You," one of the men called to us. "Come over here."

We had no other choice but to obey. They piled bundles on our backs until we were bent halfway to the floor, and ordered us to follow after them. Up the stairs we went, Leena groaning with every step. My own knees trembled by the time we reached a large hall.

The floor was covered with moldy old rushes upon which we were finally allowed to set down our burdens. Thinking our task finished, we tried to slink away.

"Stay," one of the soldiers ordered.

Carved wood panels covered the walls; tables littered the room, some broken, some turned over. The room was smaller than Batumar's Great Hall, but it looked as if at one time it had been richly appointed.

At the head table sat the most fearsome of men, surrounded by a handful of others on their feet. His red hair shone with grease as it streamed past his shoulders, his wide chest clad in black leather armor that belonged to no animal I had ever seen, covered with spiking ridges. The man's nose was flat and wide, his eyes sharp and cruel, his stare deadly. I looked down at once, not wanting to draw his attention.

One of the men who stood in front of the table bowed deeply as he talked. "Great Khan Woldrom, I shall carry your message to the Emperor Drakhar with all haste."

"See that you do." The khan spat at the man's feet. "Neither less nor more if you value your life."

The man bowed even deeper.

"Know on whose side you stand. The Emperor might push the Kerghi in front of his troops to use like a whip, but in every kingdom we take, women breed large with Kerghi sons. Before I die, I will see the Kerghi outnumber the Empire's warriors. And who will be Emperor then?"

The man fell on his knees to kiss the khan's boots. The khan dismissed him, then turned his attention to us.

The warriors shoved us forward and told us to spread upon the floor the contents of the bundles we had carried. We did so with distaste, for the loot still had the victims' blood on it: golden chalices, swords, fine cloth. My stomach rolled as I saw a large-stoned ring still on the finger.

I looked away for I could not bear the sight, and my gaze fluttered to the man next to the khan. He looked familiar, and after a moment, I realized why. He was the spy I had healed at the House of Joreb. He caught me looking, so I cast my eyes down once more. Too late. With unhurried steps, he strode toward me.

He stuck his fingers under my chin and lifted my head none too gently. "I have not seen you here before." With his other hand, he fingered my clothes. "You are wet."

"My work is in the kitchen, my lord," I answered, and at once, I knew my mistake, for I spoke in the man's own language. A local servant would not have known it.

His eyes narrowed then. "I know you," he said. "But not from this place." He let me go and turned to the warriors. "Throw her into the dungeons until I remember."

The men grabbed me and dragged me from the room. I did not fight them, for they carried me to the very place I sought to reach. Down many stairs we went and long narrow corridors, my heart beating faster with every step.

Then a door fashioned of iron bars opened in front of us, and at last I found the dungeons, in a large underground cavern. Leena was not far behind. Shortly after I was thrust into an alcove of rough stone guarded with more rusty bars, the men threw her in after me.

I helped her to the pile of filthy hay in the back, and she lay down, bruised and exhausted. I made her as comfortable as I could, even as I gagged at the horrid stench of the place. Human waste soiled the floors, the disgusting odor mixing in the air with the smell of unwashed bodies.

Mostly men filled the dungeon, locked in small nooks carved from the rock on which the palace had been built. Some hang from chains in the wall. A few I suspected were no longer living. I did not see Batumar but could not bear thinking that he had already been killed.

All night, I thought of nothing but a way to escape, talking in low whispers with Leena, but we could not construct a worthy plan. Nor could we sleep. The cries of others sounded without stop. They begged for death.

Toward morning, we were given water but no food. We gulped what we had, both weak with hunger and exhausted from lack of sleep. The man chained to the wall opposite from us, whom I had thought dead before, looked up, his body covered in wounds and dry blood, his face beaten beyond recognition, his nose and cheekbones broken, his jaw shattered. He blinked, his eyelids moving slowly as if even that hurt.

"I had the strangest dream." The weak whisper came out garbled and barely audible, but in the voice of Batumar.

My heart leaped, and I rushed to the bars as close as I could to be able to hear him.

"I dreamt that you were here with Leena, only she was my mother," he told me and lost consciousness again.

And at that, Leena and I wept, for he had called Leena his mother, and we knew on that day he would die.

We talked to Batumar throughout the day as he passed in and out of consciousness. Leena told him about the time he was born and asked for his forgiveness, but he had not the strength to give it. I told him I loved him, and watched his chest rise slower and slower as his breathing grew shallow.

His shackles cut into his bloody wrists—he could no longer stand; only his chains held him in place. When his head fell forward, I could no longer see his face but could still hear him now and then gasping for air.

And then he gasped no more.

Leena keened next to me, her hands extended toward her son through the bars. The pain in my heart nearly tore me apart. I understood now why my mother had been willing to give her life for my father, no matter how much it was forbidden, I knew what I had to do.

I closed my eyes and sent my spirit forth. Batumar's life force was so weak, I barely found it in those last weak pulses of the blood. I drew all his pain into my own body; then I surrounded his life force with my own and pushed against it until they merged.

I saw him lift his head slowly and look at me. A lifetime of understanding passed in that look, forgiveness, love, need. But as he realized what I had done, his gaze flickered.

"No!" Like a wounded beast he roared.

And then the eyes of my body could no longer see, and the ears of my body could no longer hear, for I had sent into him the last of my spirit, and the darkness came to claim me.

I was not sad to die. How could I be, when Batumar would live? If anyone could defeat the Kerghi, it was him. And by saving him, I might have saved all our people. I would die having fulfilled my destiny.

CHAPTER TWENTY-THREE

(Returning Home)

Leena wailed, cradling my body while Batumar raged against his chains, fresh blood running down his arms where he ripped his skin. He roared with grief and fury, lurching forward in his restraints, shaking the wall with his great power. I wished I could give them peace, but I could no longer touch them in any way. I had given all I had to give.

I watched from above with my spirit eyes as four guards rushed in at the commotion. They dared not step close enough to Batumar to use their swords, but their lances fell upon him mercilessly until he hung limp from the chains. He did not move again.

"Is he dead?" One poked him.

Another opened the bars and eased inside, then kicked Batumar viciously. Batumar did not groan, shift or flinch.

Yet I could sense his spirit, still strong within him.

"Hang him from the castle wall." The third guard pushed forward and released the chains.

Batumar surged up and used that very chain to strangle the man. He grabbed the fallen lance and threw it hard, instantly killing the guard farthest from him, who had turned to run for the door.

The High Lord's mighty fist brought down the third man. Then Batumar leaped after his last foe. He showed no mercy but nearly cut the soldier in half with the man's own sword.

The other prisoners watched this in stunned, scared silence.

In a moment, Batumar had the keys in his hand and the door of our cell open. Then he stilled for a breath before taking my body from Leena and cradling it with great gentleness.

Leena moved to him at last and embraced him, tears streaming down her face. "You must leave at once. More men will come."

"You go," he told her without looking away from me. "Hurry."

He kissed me softly and laid my body down, then stood and walked out of the cell. Outside, he ripped a torch from its sconce. Black fires burned in his eyes, his bloodied face fierce. And I knew he meant to take on the castle and die here.

Leena rose like an ancient goddess. "If you fight, I fight. I am the mother of the High Lord of the Kadar." She put her chin in the air and blinked away her tears. "But know this. When you die here a hero's death, there will be none to defend Dahru when the hordes reach our island. The warlords need their leader. Have I birthed a son who would abandon his people?"

Batumar scowled at her. Then he looked her battered body over. He probably saw what my spirit eyes saw, that she could not walk out of the dungeons unaided. "Fight, you would?"

Leena stood her ground and held his gaze without blinking.

His lips flattened for a moment, but then he kicked the keys to the men in the nearest cell, threw the torch on a pile of soiled hay in the far corner, and tied to his waist the sword he had taken from the last guard he'd killed.

"Get out before the fire spreads," he told the prisoners who now clamored for release.

He stepped forward and lifted Leena with one arm while he lifted me with the other, each of us hefted over a shoulder. He burst through the dungeon's door with us.

"To the cisterns," Leena said. "Up, then to the left."

He thundered up the stairs.

When he reached the strange bathing room, he shoved through the door and had enough time to set us down and reach for his sword, while the men inside conquered their momentary surprise. They outnumbered him six to one. I wanted to close my spirit eyes against the great butchery, but I could not.

Leena picked up a fallen sword and fought beside her son. I wondered if I might have done the same to save the people I loved. Maybe I would have.

In the end, Batumar piled the bodies of his enemies under the old cistern hole in the ceiling and helped Leena climb up, then carried me after her, the space a tight fit for his wide shoulders. But they did escape the castle that way, and I was happy for that.

Outside, at the foot of the walls, Batumar found a charred cart and laid my body on it, then lifted Leena and settled her down next to me. She had used up the last of her strength in the fight.

Night had arrived once again. Few walked the road to the castle, and those gave wide berth to the battle-crazed warrior who was dragging two bloodied women off for some dark purpose, one obviously dead, the other still moaning.

None pursued us from the stronghold. They were busy fighting the fire. Flames licked the timber of the southern tower.

Batumar knew which way the Gate lay and walked that road all night, reaching the river by morning. Leena and I had floated far downriver from the island, then had taken a lengthy detour through the endless forest, it seemed.

A great battle raged on the island. Swords clashed, men called out, tigers roared. I saw Lord Karnagh and his tiger with my spirit eyes before Batumar did.

My spirit floated higher now, over the treetops. I tried to return to Batumar and Leena, but I could not. An invisible force pulled me away. One moment I could see, then the next all turned black, as if my spirit eyes were closing too, at last.

———

The next time I opened my eyes, my spirit resided inside my body once again. I was lying upon the bed in Batumar's chamber at Karamur. Leena sat by me, holding my hand.

The window to the courtyard stood open a crack to allow in fresh air. Swords clanged outside, not in desperate battle frenzy, but in the steady rhythm of soldiers practicing.

"What happened?" I could barely push out the words, my mouth as dry as if I had eaten all the dust of the great desert.

Leena's face split into a smile. Her eyes filled with relief, and even a few tears. She wore a blue lady's gown instead of a servant's dress. But she pressed my hand to her cheek, and made as much fuss over adjusting my blankets as if she was still my servant and not the High Lord's mother, a lady of power in the palace.

"Lord Karnagh and his warriors were at the Gate, my lady," she said. "Their fearsome tigers caused much destruction among the Kerghi. False news had reached Lord Karnagh that our High Lord has been captured and killed. Lord Karnagh sought to take the Gate and destroy it even at the cost of his own life and the lives of his men, meaning to cut off Woldrom from the rest of his vast armies. None can sail the ocean around those lands, not through the hardstorms."

"Did he destroy the Gate?"

"He tried." Leena patted my hand. "And Batumar joined Lord Karnagh in the fight. Many good men fell, but more Kerghi troops arrived. We barely escaped."

She helped me drink.

"Shartor is gone. Banished," she said. "When I told Batumar what the soothsayer tried to do to you... The High Lord nearly cut the old leech in half. But then he said you would not wish a life taken on your behalf. He was afraid such an act might yet weaken your barely lingering spirit."

I wanted to ask for Batumar, but before I could, I fell asleep. The next time I woke, the Guardians were with me, standing around me at the points of a perfect triangle. They must have been working some healing, but I still struggled to sit.

"Welcome back," said the Guardian of the Cave. He appeared drawn, as if he had lost weight.

The Guardian of the Gate squeezed my hand with a relieved sigh, his great carved staff in his other hand. He had shadows under his eyes, the line of his thin mouth strained. Even the young Guardian of the Scrolls had worry lines marring his forehead as he looked at me. Frowning like that, he looked so very much like his father, the sight tugged my lips into a weak smile.

"How long have I been ill?"

They exchanged somber glances, then the young Guardian of the Scrolls spoke at last. "Three full days. Had my father not given you what spirit he had left before he died, you would not have left the dungeons of Mernor alive, my lady."

I was relieved to hear no accusation in his voice over his father's death. "The war?"

"The enemy stands ready. They are but waiting for the Emperor's orders," Batumar said, entering.

The Guardians withdrew silently as he strode to me. Tall and strong, a warrior from an ancient myth, he came, his face a map of new scars gained at Mernor. Fierce was his countenance, but he was precious in my sight.

He kicked off his boots, lay upon the bed, and drew me to him. I went willingly into his strong arms that had carried me back from death. I soaked up his love, my body pressed tightly against his. A hardstorm could not have torn us apart.

"You shall not heal anyone. Ever again," he said into my hair in his strictest voice. "You shall not even think of it."

I held on to his solid strength as I looked up. "I have passed into death and returned. Do not think, my lord, that I shall grow frightened at the words of a Kadar."

A smile twitched at the corner of his lips, his dark gaze softening, filling with so much tenderness that my throat constricted. I lay my head back on his shoulder and closed my eyes, thanking the spirits that we were both yet alive.

"I have a mother," he said, his voice carrying surprise and some soft emotion.

"Have you thought, my lord, that your god of war, Rorin himself, had forged you from sword metal?"

He let out a bark of a laugh, then brushed my hair back from my temple. "My mother loves you most fiercely."

"Not half as fiercely as she loves you. The odes I had to listen to in Pleasure Hall about your great strength and handsomeness…"

He chuckled. "Did you not agree with the odes?"

"I agreed with every word," I admitted.

He looked very pleased as he moved to kiss me. When he finally pulled back, he caressed my face, and just watched me for the longest time before his eyes turned somber. "I could scarce believe my eyes when I saw you two in Mernor's dungeon."

I preferred not to think about the dungeon, but I asked, "How came you to be captured by Woldrom?"

A low growl escaped his throat, and I did not think he would answer, but he did.

"I found Woldrom's First Captain as soon as I came through the Gate, for he had been charged with guarding the island. I questioned him at once about who had killed my brother. He admitted to the deed, even bragging." The muscles in Batumar's shoulder stiffened under my head.

"My own guard came through the Gate then." Regret laced his voice. "We outnumbered the men on the island, for some had gone off to patrol the woods on the riverbank shortly before. I ordered my men to lower their weapons."

"But you could have overtaken them," I whispered.

"Honor demanded I fight the captain man-to-man."

"You won," I said. I had seen him with a sword.

"The captain turned the fight so I stood amidst his men. Then he gave a signal. They fell on me, but I fought them, ordering my own guard still to stand back. I cut them down, and I cut down their captain, but his larger force heard the clashing of swords and rushed back from their patrol." Batumar's chest rose as he drew a slow breath. "Ten of my most faithful guards were killed."

We lay in silence.

"I upheld the honor of my House," he said after a while. "And now I find I would rather lose even that than lose you again." He brushed his lips over my hair.

I raised my head to look into his battle-scarred face. He needed no further invitation to claim my lips.

————

In the morning, Lord Karnagh arrived through the Gate with many more men than he'd taken to Mernor, and many more tigers. By the next morning, my strength returned, and Batumar walked with me to the Forgotten City so I could once again examine the scrolls. Having seen the evil and destruction at Mernor, I knew at last that he had been right. There could be no peace with such an enemy. We must fight the Kerghi, or our people would perish.

We went the long way up the side of the mountain. I could just barely talk Batumar out of carrying me the whole way. But I did feel recovered. What healing the Guardians had begun in me, my own body was now rapidly finishing.

This high up, the chill of fall was already in the air. I did not mind. The walk and fresh air did me much good, a welcome change after spending so much time in bed of late.

We found the Guardians in low spirits. The Guardian of the Scrolls sat in the same place his father used to sit, in the back, the same unhappy expression on his face. He had a solemn quality rarely possessed by a man so young. *Maybe too young to shoulder the responsibility thrust upon him*, I thought as I considered the Guardians' strange customs.

"Greetings, Lady Tera." He stood, his face a careful mask. "Have you come to look at the scrolls?"

"I have. With your kind help." I smiled at him.

Batumar sat by the fire with the Guardian of the Gate while the Guardian of the Cave opened the rock, and I followed the Guardian of the Scrolls into the tunnel. I waited when he hesitated at a crossroad. Then he strode forth and led me through the countless passages, until at last we reached the scrolls. As he would not enter the chamber, I walked in alone.

This time, I carried a small blade, for whether the remaining scrolls would readily open or not, I needed their wisdom. I did not open the first scroll, as I knew the prophecy by heart. I reached for the second. As I tugged, the strip of hide holding it together detached easily.

I held my breath as I unrolled the scroll. Oh, but when I read the words, I could have cried. Nothing but old stories, from the history of the First People all the way back to the creation of the world. What a cruel joke the spirits played, crushing the hopes of my heart.

I lifted the third scroll, praying that this one at last would be useful to us. The binding held tight and would not give, so I pulled my blade, cut off the binding and unrolled the scroll.

No words. No even a single picture. Not a mark.

The coldness of the cave seeped inside me and squeezed my heart. We had been left to our fate by the spirits. As I followed the young Guardian back, frustration clenched my teeth.

"I miss your father," I said, the words coming to my lips unbidden.

The young Guardian's shoulders sagged, his father's robe hanging on his lanky frame as he stopped and turned to me. He watched me for a moment, then gave a shuddering sigh. "Everybody does. The other Guardians use whatever excuse they can to stay away from me. I think looking at me reminds them of the friend they lost." His lips twisted into a sour smile. "I am the only one who did not know my father well enough to miss him."

I could feel the pain in his heart as if it was my own. "He always spoke fondly of you."

His face lightened a small measure. "I wish I were more like him."

I nodded. "I never knew my true father, but all my life I wished I were more like my mother."

He looked at me with surprise, so I added, "My powers came to me late. I used to fear I did not inherit any at all."

"I feared the same." He caught himself and fell silent.

"You are not as fast yet as your father, but you found the scrolls."

"I do not feel them," he said miserably. "They call to me not. My father followed their voice. He could have found them with his eyes closed. I follow the carvings on the walls."

"Maybe it is so," I said after some thought. "Maybe now that the scrolls have been opened, they do not need such a Guardian as your father was."

His face twisted into an expression of anguish. "But do you not see? That is even worse. The scrolls are the sole purpose of my life, as they were the sole purpose of the life of every man in my family before me."

"Some traditions are so old they seem to be as inevitable as the sunrise. But they are just traditions. Not unchangeable."

He shook his head.

I said, "Maybe the scrolls call you not. Maybe something else does. The blood of the First People flows in the veins of the Guardians. I am certain you have some gift." When a quick shift came into his eyes, I pushed. "What is it?"

His answer took a long time coming. "I can see things."

"Are you a Seer, then?"

He shook his head. "Not like a Seer. I see people not from the outside but within."

"Their innards?" I often saw that as I healed, blood vessels and bones, the source of the injury.

"The things that are in their hearts." He hesitated before he went on. "The first time I saw you, in your heart you thought I looked like my father, and you felt sad because your heart was so full of love for him and he was gone. And you thought I was angry." He fell silent for moment. "I was. Because nobody ever had so much love in his heart for me."

"I am sure your father—"

"He only met me when I came for my training. He felt fond of me, as you said. Impatient for me to take the weight from his shoulders."

"Your mother, then."

He looked away. "She did not want to be chosen. She loved another man and, after I was born, married him. They had other children, ones born out of love, not duty."

I watched his sad face, my mind filled with thoughts of callings and destinies and whether we had any power to direct our own lives or if we were like little sticks in a creek, carried by the current that was the will of the spirits.

I put my hand on the Guardian's arm. "I called your father 'grandfather'. May I call you brother?"

My heart filled with love for him, and he must have seen it, for he nodded. And then he turned to lead me out of the Sacred Cave, his shoulders no longer sagging.

When Batumar saw me, he stood from the fire where he had been talking to the Guardian of the Gate who sat with his carved staff in hand, looking as drawn as he had when I had seen him the day before. I hoped that by healing me, the Guardians had not weakened their own spirits.

I thanked them for all their help before I said my farewells. And then Batumar and I left for the fortress city.

"I worry about the Guardian of the Gate. He seems unwell," I said when we were a little farther on the path.

Batumar matched his stride to mine. "He is holding the Gate."

"Is that why he will not let his staff out of his hand?"

"I am not certain I understand what he does or how he does it. He can hold the Gate, he said, but the hold can be broken from the other side, although, not easily. He might be able to seal the Gate. But sealing a Gate is a dangerous endeavor. A sealed Gate may stay that way, never to be unsealed. And the sealing requires..." He shook his head. "In their legends, there is only one tale like that. The Guardian who sealed the Gate of Rabutin did not survived it. Their Gate has never been reopened."

I held the horror of that thought as we walked.

"Have the scrolls revealed a way?" Batumar asked after a long stretch of silence.

"Not today." I sighed. "I fear we will have to fight the war."

He took my hand. "Then we will."

My heart clenched. "The scrolls...if they hold help for us, I cannot see it."

And then the rest of it tumbled forth, my disappointment in the vague prophecy of the first scroll and the old legends of the second, my frustration with the empty third.

"I fear we cannot vanquish this enemy," I confessed. "I fear what will become of our people. In my dreams, I see us like tiny grains of sand washed away by the high tide as the dark waves crash into the shore."

We were by then in the forest. He stopped to pull me into his arms.

He held me for a long moment before cupping my face and tilting my head up so I would look into his eyes. "The Kerghi hordes are a powerful army," he said. "Perhaps the most powerful in the world. For many years, they have conquered undefeated. And now they believe they cannot be defeated, and their enemies believe them unbeatable."

I nodded, understanding better than most the power of belief. I had seen many gravely injured men who lived because they believed with every drop of blood in their bodies that they would live, while others with lesser injuries readily relinquished their spirits.

Batumar continued. "If someone stood against the dark hordes and won a single battle, it would show the rest of the world that the Kerghi are not invincible."

I stilled. "And the defeat would show the Kerghi warriors that their army is not as strong as they believe."

He smiled at me. "One such battle could turn the tide. If our warriors believe they can win, they might. And they do believe because we have you. So you truly do have the power to end the war."

I was humbled as I held his dark gaze, for I knew that he believed in me with all his warrior's heart.

As we walked on, we talked about the upcoming battle, and about the Guardians, and the coming siege.

When we returned to the palace, I only went to Pleasure Hall for my bath, then at Batumar's request, I hurried to him. As soon as I walked into his antechamber, he gathered me into his arms. He had bathed too, but had put his leggings back on. I lay my cheek against his warm skin. He carried me to his bed and lay down beside me.

Then he shifted and placed his head on my chest, his ear directly over my heart. He found the exact spot so swiftly, I had the feeling he had listened to my heartbeat many a time while I had been fighting my way back to him from the darkness. When I ran my fingers over the thick locks of his hair, he sighed in contentment.

"This war will be over someday," he said. "Soon, if the spirits will it. And then we will know peace again." He looked up with a playful glint in his eyes. "You and I are going to spend a lot of that peace between the furs."

I felt heat creep up my face, but I could not help smiling. As he stretched out next to me, I burrowed against his warmth, seeking something I could not name. I tilted my face to his, and my breath caught at the hunger in his gaze. I placed my palm over his heart, finding his steady heartbeat as reassuring as he must have found mine.

Even relaxed, he looked so fierce, every inch the warrior. But I knew his heart held much kindness. Did he love me as I loved him? I pressed my mouth against his. How warm his lips were under mine, how gentle the strong arms that encircled me.

I soaked up his strength, letting the steady beating of his heart soothe me. His warmth and his scent enveloped me, and like a small animal in a nest, I burrowed into the safety of his embrace.

He kissed me back softly in return, then said, "I was raised for war. I was taught from childhood that death in battle is glory. I have never been scared on the battlefield." He brushed his lips over mine, lingered. "I have not known true fear until you came to Mernor."

Maybe that was as close as a warlord could come to admitting love, I thought, and smiled. I moved my hand across his chest, my fingers gliding over hills of muscles.

He held still, allowing me to explore him without hindrance. Then, as my hand slid down his chest and across his hard stomach, he captured my wrist with a groan and placed my palm back over his heart, trapping my hand there with his own.

"If the Kerghi will not be the death of me, you surely will be," he said against my lips before he took them, with an urgency this time.

My body heated. When he reined in his passion and pulled back, I moaned in protest.

"You should rest," he said in a rough whisper. "You should have spent the day in bed instead of walking to the Forgotten City. You are still recovering."

I held his hungry gaze. "And if I do not wish to rest?"

He reclaimed my lips before the last word was out. And then he claimed the rest of me.

———

The following day, we lost the Gate.

The Guardian's hold had been broken. The five hundred Kadar warriors guarding the Gate—all the small plateau would hold—had been slain. It happened in the night, suddenly, without time to send word to Karamur for reinforcements.

The first of the Kerghi were on our island, waiting for the rest of their troops to arrive. Our enemies had gathered, and like the night, their darkness spread over the land.

Instead of attacking the seat of the Kadar high lord immediately, Woldrom sent three units of soldiers across the island to scout any possible points of resistance. Some of these Kerghi soldiers were slain by Kadar warriors, others reached far south. Grim accounts of their deeds found their way to Karamur with the first wave of refugees. That first wave was mostly Kadar, but the Shahala followed right on their heels. The Kerghi wrought unspeakable destruction in some Shahala towns.

To protect the Seela, the Guardians sealed the Forgotten City with the strongest wards they had, making it nearly impossible for any stranger to enter or even see the city, but that also meant that the Guardians could not leave to visit me.

In Karamur, the villagers who lived outside the walls now moved inside, into a city that was already filled to the brink with Kadar and Shahala refugees.

Our soldiers were preparing for the battle, while everyone else made sure the harvest was gathered in and safely stored for a prolonged siege. Everyone had chores, even the children. They patrolled the streets and reported any piles of hay and dry wood or waste that might catch on fire from fire arrows. Anything that might easily burn was carried to the cellars. Water pumps were going all day, and every available pail and tub filled up.

Under heavy guard, I led to the forest all the Shahala healers who'd run to Karamur to seek protection. We stayed within sight of Fortress City, not daring to risk the deep woods, and gathered as much medicine as we could carry. Spending time with my people and other healers bolstered my spirit. As all their healing energy surrounded me, I felt stronger than ever. My heart lightened from hearing the language of my childhood spoken around me.

That lightness did not last long. The following morning, the Kerghi horde appeared at the edge of the forest. Many in Karamur rushed to the roofs and the top of the walls to see the endless barbarian force that thirsted for our blood like a ravening beast. Our battle for survival was about to begin.

CHAPTER TWENTY-FOUR

(The Siege)

The blood-thirsty horde waited for Woldrom's orders at the edge of the forest. Outside Karamur spread our army with Batumar at its helm. Lord Karnagh and his men made up the right flank, along with their restless tigers. Thus the defenders of good faced their enemy.

For a moment, silence as deep as a grave covered all living creatures. No birds took flight; no leaves rustled in the wind, for the wind had stopped in shock to watch such evil as was about to take place.

A cloud of enemy arrows pierced the air, so thick it covered the sun.

The Kadar archers responded in kind, and so it went, back and forth, until a wall of bodies lay before each army. And then a deafening roar rose from the Kerghi warriors as they climbed over the bodies and charged. When weapons finally clashed against weapons, the sound was that of thunder, only instead of rain, blood soaked the ground.

I rushed from the roof, for I knew soon I would be needed to treat the wounded. But night fell before the first of the injured was brought in, for none would leave the battle until the fighting ceased for the day.

The wounds gaped deep, from weapons that must have been the work of the darkest spirits. One man had his arm nearly torn off by but a single blow; another had the bone of his thigh smashed to pieces.

Through the night I healed, the Shahala working by my side. And there were many healers among them, so we were able to save a great number of warriors. Those we fully healed returned to their captains, but some had suffered injuries more grievous and needed the power of time to complete what the healers had begun.

At first light, the battle resumed, and from the palace roof I saw that the enemy had lost more men than we. But so great were their numbers, I did not think it would make a difference. Our army stood vastly outnumbered, even hopelessly so, although I refused that thought each time it tried to enter my mind.

The warriors fought on for seven days, and I healed for seven nights. Each day we lost fewer than the enemy, as many of our wounded were able to rejoin the fight, but still the Kerghi advanced toward the city.

By the morning of the eighth day, we could no longer see the battle from the palace roof, for it raged directly under the city walls. I climbed the parapet, many women with me, to watch our loved ones and pray to the spirits and the goddesses for their safety.

We prayed in vain. The enemy fought their way through the Kadar defenses and reached the city gate, cutting off Batumar and his guards from the rest of his warriors. I held my breath as I watched him fight with true Kadar fury.

The Kerghi tried to break through the thick oak planks of the gate. Leena and I hugged each other with relief when we saw that they could not. But relief faded into fear when they carried armloads of dry branches from the forest and piled them high against the gate. They set the pile on fire.

"Water!" I ran and shouted to all in the streets over and over.

Everybody helped, the Shahala working alongside the Kadar. We soaked the gate on the inside. Then women and the stronger children made a human chain. Buckets and pails and tubs of water were handed from person to person up to the wall above the gate. Those at the top threw the water on the fire that burned below them outside.

Many were hit by enemy arrows and fell to their death, but their valor defeated the fire and saved Karamur.

As I leaned over the wall, tipping a large jar to make sure the last of the smoldering embers were out, I saw Batumar fighting with the most fearsome of men, the leader of the enemy horde.

I recognized the red hair that spilled from his battle helmet and spread upon his shoulders. Woldrom.

He had come, then, I thought, to kill with his own hands the man who had set Mernor castle ablaze around him. I saw another Kerghi circle behind Batumar. I shouted but could not be heard over the clamor of battle.

As I watched, the Kerghi swine thrust his sword into Batumar's back and twisted it before pulling it free. Batumar fell onto one knee, and Woldrom swung his double-edged sword. Its blood-soaked blade, like the dark bird of death, flew through the air.

The Shahala have a saying: A lifetime can pass but in a moment, and some moments last for a lifetime. Time stopped as I watched the sword fly toward Batumar's neck.

A great power rose within me, dizzying me, power great enough to corrupt a person's spirit. I thought of my great-grandmother. So this was what had turned her heart. Even as I fought against it, the power surged through me, filled me, until I felt more, bigger, brighter than I had ever felt before.

Then in a moment all the Guardians' lessons came together in my head like the separate colorful threads of a tapestry come together to paint a story. And I understood that the power was neither good nor evil, but would follow the path of the person who wielded it.

I found a fear under all my resistance, a nagging voice that asked what if I claimed my full power and still failed? And the next moment, I knew that the only true failure would be to run from my destiny.

Spirit, be strong. Heart, be brave. My mother's last message came to me.

With a cry, I sent my spirit into Batumar across the distance and drew his pain, and as I sank to the stones with agony, I watched him rise and defend himself. Blood poured down his back, for he was still injured. But he did not feel his injuries. I closed my eyes and began to repair the hideous wound.

If Batumar was defeated, Karamur would fall, all the men, women, and children killed or enslaved. And with Karamur would fall Dahru, our legacy erased from memory forever. We would become like the First People, carvings on cold cave walls hidden in the dark for future nations to look at with wonder and not understand.

No!

I healed the man I loved and opened my eyes just as he ran Woldrom through. The great savage fell at Batumar's feet, blood trickling from his mouth. He stared at me, hate boiling in his gaze.

But the khan's fall did not halt the battle nor did it slow down the fighting, for the fight was so fierce, few of his men noticed his demise.

I expanded my power until I could almost see it, a shimmering cloud above me. And then I shared it, connecting all the Shahala healers on the parapet together with invisible strands. They drew in my bright power, their eyes on the battle, some clutching their shoulders, some their legs, pain on their faces as they healed. On the battlefield, I saw a young Kadar warrior with a lance piercing his side. As soon as the lance was withdrawn, he seemed to regain his strength and fought on to vanquish his enemy.

The fight went on all day and into the darkness. The enemy battled through the night, for they felt victory was close. The Kadar fought back with their swords, and the Shahala fought back with their healing spirits. We even healed the wounded tigers.

Every time a Kadar warrior suffered injury, he sprang back again. And every time it happened, his Kerghi opponent was either slain or lost heart upon witnessing such magic. Soon the cry spread through the enemy that the Kadar were not human, that they were able to rise up from the dead. Woldrom was not there to rally them. That too was at long last noticed.

Slowly the tide turned, the enemy army pushed back by the fear in their hearts as much as by the Kadar. And it seemed there might yet be a chance for our victory. But a small group, perhaps knowing that the miraculous powers of the Kadar had something to do with the Shahala men and women who stood on the parapet, began to scale the walls with ladders crudely made from the tall trees of the forest behind them.

We poured water on them, the only weapon we had, but that did not stop the Kerghi. Then some town people brought boiling water and even boiling oil from the kitchens. That did have some effect.

Dizzy with exhaustion, by chance I turned toward an abandoned section of the wall. The top of a new ladder appeared in that instant, angled cleverly so that it would be difficult to see by the defending force.

Any soldiers who came up that ladder would quickly disappear behind a guardhouse, in cover.

I rushed forward.

Shartor climbed at the top, leading Kerghi warriors. If they secured a portion of the wall, more could climb after them and overpower the people within the city, for the men and women inside were not trained to fight. The walls would be lost then for certain, and the city with them.

I charged as Shartor straddled the wall. I tried to push him back. He laughed at me—his eyes dancing to a mad rhythm—and bent me back as if I were a willow sprig.

I scratched at his face. Not something my mother would have ever done. All my life, all I wanted was to become like her, but I had Kadar spirit too, from my father.

Spirit, be strong. Heart, be brave.

"Sorceress." The soothsayer hissed the single word.

"Traitor." I leaned into him, with but one thought—his feet must not find purchase on the wall.

Yet my strength was no match for his. So I did the only thing I could—I threw my entire weight against him. This at last upset his balance, and as he reeled backward, he took the ladder with him. The ladder and me, for our arms were entwined.

We fell from the dizzying height, the ladder somehow falling sideways, and I could see the corpses below us. But I did not land on the dead. I landed in the last of the hot embers that still glowed in front of the city gate.

I heard the sound of Shartor's neck breaking as we landed, he but a moment before I. All my bones felt broken as I fought to pull in air.

I rolled out of the fire, my clothes alight, and rolled and rolled until the blood-soaked ground doused the flames. Then finally I lay there, panting, seeing little but the shadowy outlines of the corpses next to me, among whom I now belonged. The pain of my flesh paled in comparison to the pain of my heart as I lay on the ground among our dead and the fallen enemy I had helped to kill.

Then one of the dark shapes rose a few steps to my right, staggering—a Kerghi warrior as large as a bear, nearly gutted. Somehow, miraculously, he still hung on to his sword. Blindly, he lurched toward me in the last rallying of his spirit. In but another moment his spirit would leave him, and he would collapse dead. Likely on top of my broken body. I could not move. I held my breath waiting for him to fall and skewer me.

He tilted forward slowly, his sword extended, blood running from his lips, his eyes rolling back in his head. As he crashed onto me, barely missing me with his sword, the air left my lungs in a painful whoosh.

I lay under him, covered in his blood and spilled innards, the foul stench of death all around, his great weight crushing me as I struggled to breathe. I fought to budge his heavy bulk. I could not. I wheezed, fighting for air.

I heard the city gate open and felt the ground shake as the manyinga entered the battle. Since Batumar had few of them, I knew he had decided to hold them back until the end, hoping the very sight of the fearsome beasts would strike terror into the hearts of the enemy. They had to fight on the opposite side of the battlefield from Lord Karnagh's men and their tigers, as the beasts were not used to waging battle together.

I passed in and out of awareness, the noise of the battle rising and receding in my ears like the tide. But after a long while, as the night wore on, the battle clamor quieted. Far out of my reach, wounded men moaned. One who could still talk begged for help, another prayed for death.

I waited. Above me, a wispy, insubstantial cloud—like a decayed funeral shroud—floated over the moon.

Then a roar rent the night, as loud as any manyinga or any tiger. "Tera!"

I drew a ragged breath. Batumar had discovered I was missing. *He lives.*

I could not call back.

Other voices rose, warriors shouting, "Lady Tera!"

Armor rattled as men scoured the battle field for me. The flickering light of torches moved through the darkness.

He lives.

He will come.

He will find me.

I repeated those words silently, held them like a shield against the pain, against the cold, against death that stalked around me.

He lives.

He will come.

He will find me.

"Tera!" Batumar's enraged roar—closer now—swept through the battlefield, demanding, frightful enough to scare death itself away.

He lives.

He will come.

He will find me.

The heavy weight on my chest pressed me into the blood-soaked ground. I fought for each breath. My ears were ringing. When the stars began swirling in the sky, I closed my eyes.

The night wore on, men calling frantically, Batumar bellowing, urging them on, demanding more torches.

"Tera!"

Heavy footsteps neared at last, then the earth shook and armor rattled as Batumar fell onto his knees next to me.

The weight lifted from my chest. I tried to open my eyes, but found the Khergi soldier's blood had crusted my eyelashes together.

"Tera!" Batumar howled like a wounded beast, brushing my matted hair out of my face, wiping blood from my skin. "No!"

He held me to his chest with one arm while he searched me for injury with his free hand, his movements urgent, feverishly so, but so gentle. His great body shook as he kissed my forehead, my eyes, my lips, his kiss tasting of blood and sweat and tears.

"You will not leave me," he whispered hoarsely against my mouth.

Hot tears flooded my eyes, and I could open them at last. I could see little in the dark, but I could see Batumar's eyes, squeezed shut in grief. I drew my first full breath, but I did not think he could feel the rising of my chest through his armor. So I moved my lips against his.

He drew back with a ragged gasp, searching my face. "Tera," he whispered with wonder. "I thought--" He swallowed. "There is so much blood."

"Not all of it mine," I rasped the words weakly.

He gathered me back tighter against his chest and covered my face with kisses. "You live."

I wanted him to never let me go. "We live."

He gathered me into his arms and stood up, calling out to his soldiers to let them know he found me. Then he strode with me toward the city gate. "I thought you were safe in the city." His chest heaved. "And then someone said—"

"You found me," I whispered into his neck that was covered in dried blood and sweat. I did not care. We lived.

His arms around me were as strong and unmovable as a fortress, yet as gentle as a cradle.

"I will always find you," he promised.

———

The Shahala healers gathered around me, but I forbade them to take my pain—they were much weakened already—so they treated my wounds with salves, but they did not use their powers. The Guardians arrived in the morning, but I would not let them further weaken their own spirits to help me. They had been much worn out by holding their protective wards over the Forgotten City for so many days. I did not think they could have held a day longer.

If we had not triumphed over the enemy when we did, all would have been lost.

But we did win.

Batumar scarce left my side as I convalesced in his bed. I asked him to give Pleasure Hall to the Shahala healers in my absence. The many chambers and the heated water of the pool could serve the injured. He agreed, and whenever he did leave for a short while, upon returning he always brought me news of the healings, and of the city.

"The refugees are returning to their villages. Our warriors tracked the last of the enemy who escaped the battle. They were put to the sword. The island is safe. The Gate is secured," he said one night as he held me.

Yet I heard something in his tone that made me look up at him. "There is something else."

"Lord Karnagh returned home with his men and tigers. He does not dare leave his own lands undefended long. Emperor Drakhart has other armies." Batumar drew me closer. "I questioned some of the enemy soldiers we captured. Emperor Drakhar has bound to his service a sorcerer from the east. The Emperor will send more men against us. He cannot allow us to remain free. Word of our victory cannot spread over the world, and give hope to the conquered."

Batumar was right. With everything I was, I sensed an even greater battle ahead. The journey that had brought us to this point had not been easy. And a long and dangerous road stood before us still. But as long as we were together, I could face anything.

"Do you think we will be attacked soon?" I asked.

Batumar thought for a moment. "No. The Kerghi lost their khan and a great number of men on our island. They will need time to build up their forces." He paused. "But they *will* come again."

At least, I was recovering. I *would* leave the bed and visit Pleasure Hall and the other healers tomorrow, I decided. However, like any wise woman, I would postpone the argument with Batumar over it until morning. For tonight... I pressed my lips to the corner of his mouth, then ran my palm up the warm skin of his chest until my hand rested over his strong, steady heartbeat.

So Emperor Drakhar's armies are still coming. Let them come and try to take what is mine. Let them perish.

Spirit, be strong. Heart, be brave.

CHAPTER ONE

(Accidental Sorceress, sneak peek!)

(Concubine Rebellion)

"We may lose the ones we love, but we do not leave them behind, Lady Tera," the Guardian of the Sacred Cave said.

"They are a thread woven irremovably into the fabric of our lives. Because they were, we are." He patted my hand as the two of us walked the parapets in the dusk, the Kadar fortress city of Karamur spread out below us. "If you miss their voices, listen deep inside your heart."

My heart hurt. We had lost too many good men and women in the siege.

The smell of wood fires filled the air; locked-up hunting hounds bayed in the night. The hem of my cape swept the worn stones with a soft whoosh as we walked. I drew the cape tighter around me. Fall had barely ended, but halfway up the mountain as we were, the chill of winter was already in the air.

A small shadow on our path caught my gaze and brought me to a halt. A shudder ran through me. I stared down at the dead bird, and said without meaning to, "A journey through darkness."

The Guardian stopped next to me. He had lost much weight. He might have counseled me in my grief, but he too suffered greatly from our losses. He had aged. His shoulders sloped, the set of his mouth grim, his face drawn, but his eyes radiated endless wisdom and kindness. In the voluminous folds of his robe, he looked like an ancient figure out of myth.

He peered at me. "What did you say, my lady?"

I expelled a small sigh, wishing I had not spoken. I could not tear my eyes away from the slight, broken shadow at my feet. "The Kadar believe a dead blackbird means a journey through darkness for the one who finds it."

The Kadar had many superstitions. My people the Shahala, who lived on the southern half of the island, believed not in omens. Neither did the Guardians, so the Guardian of the Sacred Cave stepped over the bird without giving it much notice, and continued forward.

I drew a deep breath and pushed away the sense of foreboding that tried to settle on me. No sense in becoming as superstitious as a Kadar kitchen maid. I tore my gaze from the bird and hurried after the Guardian, the city around us preparing for sleep behind the safety of the walls.

Karamur clung to inhospitable cliffs that protected it from the back, while the city wall guarded the front, the damage from the siege fully repaired at last. Everything about the fortress city spoke of the warrior nation that had built it: sturdy, stark, battle-ready. The top of the walls we walked were wide enough to drive an oxcart on, no adornments, only sheer, intimidating strength.

But no fortress was impregnable.

"How holds the Gate on the other side of the mountain?" I asked.

"The Gate holds." The Guardian of the Cave folded his gnarled fingers together over his brown robe that hung on him. He sounded confident, perhaps for my sake.

"Any news of the new Guardian of the Gate?" I held my breath for the answer.

The old man shook his head, looking out over the city as we

walked, at the lamplights that blinked to life behind windows. "He has not returned."

We had repelled the fall siege and triumphed over the Kerghi horde. But sooner than we had expected, new troops broke through the island's Gate, and the old Guardian of the Gate had bespelled the Gate to seal it, cutting off the larger enemy force from reaching us.

Our island of Dahru was the largest one of the Middle Islands that dotted Mirror Sea where all could safely sail. The Outer Islands edged the sea, also within reach by ship. But surrounding our small corner of the world spread the wild ocean, ruled by hardstorms that allowed no passage.

Island groups like ours dotted the wild ocean, with a bigger stretch of land here and there, one even large enough to be called the mainland. We could reach those kingdoms only through Gates, the portals of an ancient people whose lost knowledge we could not recover. We could use their Gates, but if a Gate was destroyed or damaged, we could not repair it.

Of all the islands of the Mirror Sea, only Dahru had a working Gate —and it was a special one. But that Gate was now sealed, and we were thoroughly cut off from the rest of the world.

"At least we are saved from immediate occupation," I said, only too aware that we had paid a most high price for the protection. The strong binding spell had required the life of the old Guardian of the Gate.

The three old Guardians—the Guardian of the Gate, the Guardian of the Scrolls, and the Guardian of the Cave—had been like grandfathers to me. Of the three, only the Guardian of the Cave still lived.

When a Guardian dies, his son takes over his duties. But the son of our Guardian of the Gate had been traveling to other Gates, still learning, when his father had died. And with our Gate now sealed, we feared he would not be able to return to us.

I drew my cloak tighter around me against the wind. "Do you think the enemy troops that squeezed through might steal down the mountain and attack when the weather worsens, thinking it is what we would least expect?"

The Guardian considered my question for a long moment before answering. "For now, the strength of our forces is equal. As long as the

Kadar warriors remain in the fortress city, the enemy cannot over-power the defenses. The attackers would be disadvantaged out in the open, standing before the city walls."

And our army could not march to attack them at the Gate on the other side of the mountain. We could not overtake them as they sat behind their makeshift stone and wood-spike fortifications. Our warriors would be disadvantaged there. Several skirmishes had proved this, and now the two forces sat at a stalemate.

The Guardian said, "Likely they are settled in where they are for the winter."

"Can the enemy reopen our Gate from afar and send more troops through?" Emperor Drakhar, who sought to conquer the world, had a sorcerer in his service, the knowledge of which had me steeped in worry.

"It would be best if our young Guardian of the Gate could return," the Guardian of the Cave admitted, then stopped. "I should be leaving. I still have a long walk ahead of me tonight."

He lived even higher up the mountain, in the Forgotten City. For centuries, people believed that the Forgotten City had been lost, their Guardians and their people, the Seela, relegated to myth. Until I had found them...or rather, they had found me.

Our island of Dahru was inhabited by three nations. In the south lived the nine tribes of my people the Shahala, a peaceful nation of healers ruled by their elders. In the north lived the warrior nation of the Kadar, ruled by their warlords and their High Lord. Up the moun-tain above Karamur hid the Forgotten City, the small enclave of the Seela—the descendants of the First People—protected by their three Guardians.

And around us, the world at war.

"Will you talk with Batumar before you leave?" I asked as we turned around and walked back toward the palace.

The High Lord had spent the evening meal discussing something with Lord Samtis, another powerful warlord whose lands lay to the west of Karamur. The Guardian of the Cave and Batumar had only had the briefest of exchanges.

But the Guardian said, "I have come only to see how the city fares."

I had the odd sense that his sentence was unfinished, as if he had meant to say more. And that more I could almost hear as: *one last time.*

Did he feel his own end? Did he wish to follow his friends to the realm of the spirits? Of course, I could not ask such question. But my heart worried.

We reached the spot where the dead blackbird had lain earlier, and I searched the stones in the falling darkness. I could see no trace of the small, broken body.

"A hungry cat," the Guardian suggested.

A shudder ran through me once again.

We walked on in silence, then took the stairs that led to the bottom of the wall where the Palace Guard waited to escort me back to the High Lord's palace—four sturdy men dressed in red and gold, the High Lord's colors.

The premonitions that had assailed me on top of the wall would not leave me, so I asked the Guardian, "Has the Seer seen something?"

But the Guardian only said, "Remember your mother's words. And hold on to your light."

Spirit, be strong. Heart, be brave had been my mother's last message.

The Guardian looked at me with great kindness and the warmest affection, his gnarled hand reaching out to touch my arm in farewell. Then he turned and shuffled away from me, down the cobblestone street.

I watched his progress for some time in the light of the flickering torches before I turned in the opposite direction and hurried off toward the palace.

The Palace Guard escorted me straight to the High Lord's Pleasure Hall, the concubines' quarters, a nest of luxury—in the middle of military order and simplicity—as could scarcely be imagined by outsiders.

Had anyone told me of such a place, back when I'd been a sunborn Shahala girl impatiently waiting for her healing powers to manifest, I would have thought the descriptions a tall tale. Never would I have thought that one day I would end up among the Kadar as their High Lord's favorite concubine.

Only concubine, until recently. My heart gave a painful squeeze as I pushed the door open, hoping against hope that the others would be back in their chambers, settling in for sleep.

Instead, they all waited, gathered in the round center hall, every displeased, suspicious eye on me as I entered.

"You poisoned the High Lord against us." Lalandra spat the words instead of a greeting.

The slender beauty of amber eyes and full lips stepped forward from among the rest of the concubines, the silk of her emerald gown rustling as she moved. Her golden hair towered in an elaborate design of looped and folded braids, making her look like a carved temple statue of some ancient goddess. Even the look she shot me was as cold and hard as marble.

I winced at hearing the word *poison* from her lips. In that regard, the High Lord Batumar's Pleasure Hall had a most unfortunate history.

I squared my shoulders as I stood my ground, between us the sunken pool in the middle of the center hall, its heated water filling the air with the scent of lavender oil that floated in glistening drops on the surface. Fur-covered benches lined the walls; silk wall hangings adding color, depicting couples in loving embraces. Low, octagonal tables offered fruit and drink: mosan berry juice, grapes, apples, pears.

In her lord's Pleasure Hall, a concubine could find anything she ever desired. Anything but peace. The Kadar saying had it right—a warrior *was* safer in battle than a concubine on her pillows.

Since merely holding my ground would not do, I took a few steps forward. I had meant to go to my sleeping chamber, and I would do so.

I faced the women head on. "This is nothing but a misunderstanding."

They had disliked me from the moment of their arrival, but this was the first time they openly challenged me. I had to find a way to turn us back from this road of becoming enemies.

An unhappy concubine dries out a man's bones like the desert wind; but two unhappy concubines are twisting storms that can blow down a whole castle, according to a Kadar proverb. I did not wish to find out what havoc more than two dozen unhappy concubines could wreak.

"You do not want us here," Lalandra accused, the light of the oil lamps glinting off the scented morcan oil she used to soften her hair.

Her emerald gown had been made to accentuate her perfect, curvaceous body, the silk high sheen. She practically shimmered as she said, "You used every excuse to keep us from our rightful place. Lord Gilrem died *before* the siege. Yet mooncrossing after mooncrossing, you found an excuse to keep us away from his brother, the High Lord, to keep *him* away from his lawfully inherited concubines."

Even in her anger she was regal, as graceful in posture and movement as a queen. She had ruled Lord Gilrem's Pleasure Hall, and the other women, for all her adult life. They owed their allegiance to her.

Out of all of them, I had only Arnsha on my side, whose life I once had saved when she'd nearly died in childbirth. But even she was too afraid of Lalandra to support me openly. At least, she stood aside and did not nod at Lalandra's every word like the others.

I filled my lungs. "I could not have you come sooner. After Lord Gilrem died, the High Lord left to avenge his brother's death." And I had gone after him. Shortly after our return, the enemy lay siege to the city, most certainly not the right time for moving the women and children here.

Lalandra scoffed. "The High Lord's Pleasure Hall stood empty with only you here, and you wished it that way."

I would not lie by denying her words. I *had* been the High Lord's only concubine, and I had foolishly convinced myself that life could remain so forever. Unlike the Kadar, my people, the Shahala bonded for life to a single mate.

I offered Lalandra a firm but friendly smile. As the favorite concubine, I was responsible for keeping Pleasure Hall's peace, and I *would* find a way. "After the siege, the High Lord gave these chambers to Shahala healers to heal our wounded."

Room was plentiful here, heat and water readily available, which made healing work much easier.

Of course, Lalandra knew that. Even while concubines did not move outside the palace walls, they tended to know as much about the comings and goings in the city as if they sat all day at the city gate, every bit of news rushed to them by their servant women.

A concubine's days were long, little to do beyond the endless purification and beautification rituals. In any Pleasure Hall, gossip had more value than jewels.

Lalandra's voice dripped with venom as she said, "You kept us away as long as you could. And even now… The High Lord has not called for any of us but you."

I blinked. Batumar had summoned Lady Lalandra just the day before, the knowledge of which was a dagger in my heart. But I could not refute her words. This was not the best time to call her a liar.

Most of the children played in the back, watched by the older girls, but Lalandra's two were stuck to her side. When she took another step closer to me, so did they. She was reminding me that she *had* children while I had none.

Her beautiful eyes narrowed to slits. "You deny us even servants."

The rest of the concubines murmured in agreement, a wall of support behind her. They were mostly daughters of warlords, wrapped in silk and satin, used to the finer things in their fathers' houses and then in Lord Gilrem's, used to servants fulfilling their every wish.

I did not like the bustle of servants around me all day, nor did I need assistance to bathe and dress. Lalandra and the others considered my reluctance to order an army of maids to take care of us an insult most grave.

"You were brought to our lands as a lowly slave," she taunted. "And now you sit beside the High Lord at the nightly feast. He prefers you above all others." Her gaze grew frostier and hardened even more as she leveled her final accusation. "What else can this be but sorcery?"

The women gasped, reaching for their charm belts.

Lalandra's words, like ice-tipped fingers, crawled up my spine. I wished Leena, the High Lord's mother and my friend, was in the palace, but she was on a pilgrimage to the Sacred Pool of the Goddesses. She had gone under heavy guard to thank the goddesses for reuniting her with her son. She would not be back until tomorrow evening.

Of course, that Lalandra would confront me when the High Lord's mother was absent was no coincidence.

"I am a healer," I repeated firmly. "All of Karamur knows it."

Lalandra snapped back with, "All of Karamur knows that you enslaved the High Lord's attention. Because of you, he has forsaken his duty."

Those words I could not rebut. Spending time with his concubines was indeed a warlord's responsibility. The making of sons was required of him. A lord's sons became warriors, and the realm needed warriors to replace the great many men we had lost during the siege. All men who survived the attack—lords, warriors, and servants alike —had the sacred duty to fill their women's bellies.

"You are not Kadar." Lalandra pronounced the words like a judgment. "You wish for Karamur to fall in the next fight."

"I served the city during the siege with my healing," I reminded her.

Lalandra lifted her chin, and her cold gaze turned scolding. "Kadar warriors are the best fighters in the world. I do not think they needed help from anybody. I did not see this great deed of healing that you claim."

Of course, she hadn't. During the siege, Lalandra and the others had been barricaded in Lord Gilrem's palace with their children.

"You wish to rule us all," she accused.

I wished for nothing but peace. *A child's wish*, I thought with heavy heart, when the whole world was at war.

She kept her chin up as she demanded, "Where are the High Lord's other concubines?"

"You well know where they are, Lady Lalandra." *Dead.* The most dreadful story I'd ever heard, jealousy leading to the murder of innocents. None of that had anything to do with me.

"Some say you killed them." Menace hissed in Lalandra's words.

By *some*, I was certain she meant herself. I prayed to the spirits for patience.

"Strange how you always manage to live," Lalandra went on. "During the siege, did you not fall into fire? You protect yourself with an ill-gained power," she said the words as if she was the High Lord himself, pronouncing judgment.

Clutching their charm belts, the other concubines nodded in agreement, their elaborately arranged braids bobbing up and down like a flock of chiri birds pecking for worms.

Lalandra stepped closer to me yet—we stood but a few steps apart—and pronounced her final judgment loudly enough for her voice to fill the hall. "Sorceress."

Even as I moved forward too—I would *not* yield—the small hairs rose at my nape. To be charged with sorcery was the greatest sin among the Kadar.

But before I could defend myself against Lalandra's charge, the carved doors guarding Pleasure Hall rattled. One of the servant girls, Natta, entered and hurried to me, her twin braids flopping behind her. Her wood-bottom shoes clop-clopped on the stones, then fell silent when she reached the thick carpet.

She nearly tripped on her long linen dress, but caught herself and curtsied smartly. She looked straight into my eyes and smiled, a familiarity for which most other concubines would have slapped her. I smiled back.

Her words echoed off the walls in the sudden silence as she said, "The High Lord requests your presence, my lady."

Hate filled the room like smoke—rising, twisting, reaching every crevice.

For a moment, as Lalandra's gaze flared with fury, I thought she might reach out to claw my face. I *would* have to address her burning hatred when I returned. And I *would* address this budding concubine rebellion with the High Lord in but a moment.

I stood my ground long enough to make sure they understood I was *not* fleeing, then followed Natta, knowing I was leaving smoldering embers behind me, embers that could at any moment burst into dangerous flames.

We hurried down narrow hallways lit by flickering torches. Shadows danced on the wool tapestries that depicted great Kadar battles.

Natta left me at the High Lord's quarters with a small bow and a big smile, hurrying on to finish her evening chores. She was a happy girl through and through, quick and smart, proud to be serving in the High Lord's palace.

Batumar kept no slaves, unlike some of the other warlords. All who served the High Lord served him of their free will. I had seen little discord within the palace walls until the concubines had arrived.

On that thought, I pushed the door open and stepped inside.

***

The rest of ACCIDENTAL SORCERESS, book 2 in the Hardstorm Saga series is waiting for you. Happy reading!

"A diamond of a book. Wow! Just finished reading Accidental Sorceress and I really enjoyed it, so much so that I'm going to re-read it again now." Amazon Review

"Truly MAGICAL. I'm at a loss for words!! Tera is one of my most favorite character of all the books I've ever read!!" Amazon Review

***

Could I ask for your kind assistance with helping other readers discover Tera and Batumar? Pretty please? A quick review would make all the difference. And, of course, reviews count toward special placement at the online stores. Because of this, if you could write even just a sentence, I would appreciate your kindness beyond words. Just click here to be taken to the review page. Thank you so much!

***

AUTHOR'S NOTE

Honestly, I still can't believe this series ever got published.

I started writing Tera's story over a decade ago as a project for college. I sent it out to a few publishers. Amazingly, some even responded. This does not happen to a lot of unpublished writers without an agent, so I was twirling in my office while visions of a contract, actual readers, and rave reviews danced before my eyes. Although, seriously, I would have been happy with someone printing a few hundred copies of the book. I just wanted to hold my book in my hands. If any people at all, beyond my friends and family, ended up reading it, that would have been gravy.

The editor-in-chief at a major NY publishing house told me my story wasn't exactly what they published, but referred me to other publishers and even let me use her as reference. Another editor at a big publisher read the first three chapters and requested the full manuscript. By the time I sent it, she moved on and the editor who replaced her wasn't interested. Yet another editor at another major house told me she wasn't sure how to sell this book to her marketing department, but she loved it too much to reject it. To this day, I still haven't received a rejection letter from her. Did you pick up on the pattern here? Lots of love—no contract.

In the meanwhile, I wrote other projects and became successfully published in another genre (romantic suspense). But I never forgot Tera and Batumar, and neither did my college friends who read the story. From time to time, I would receive an email, friends telling me they were still thinking about the characters, asking when the book was going to be published.

Then came the self-publishing revolution, and did I jump on that bandwagon! I published Tera's story, with the original title: THE THIRD SCROLL. And readers flocked to it! ... Yeah, NO. Nada. Nope. Nobody cared. Crickets. Tumbleweeds of no interest rolled through the barren landscape of my writerly hopes.

Luckily, a smart person told me that three things sell a book: cover, title, blurb. So, I changed all three. I even rewrote the original ending and took out a scene that was a sidetrack from the main story. I republished the book in its spanking new glory as RELUCTANT CONCUBINE. And readers flocked to it! Yes! For real! Tera's story spent six weeks as the #1 romantic fantasy at the largest online bookseller's bestseller list. I'm so not kidding this time.

All of this is my very long way of saying: Hang on to your dreams and don't give up!

Spirit, be strong. Heart, be brave. Reader, leave a review. Please.

--Dana

P.S.: Do you know what the most common feedback is that I get from readers on this book? It goes along the lines of "I love the book, but hate the title. So cheesy! Why didn't you give the story a proper fantasy title?" Sometimes I say, "Like what? The Third Scroll?" And I get, "Yes! That would be perfect!"

Hardstorm Saga Trilogy
RELUCTANT CONCUBINE
ACCIDENTAL SORCERESS
GUARDIAN QUEEN

Made in United States
Orlando, FL
04 January 2024

42121422R00186